TAKING MY CHANCES

TAKING MY CHANCES

A CAROLINE SPENCER NOVEL

LESLYN AMTHOR SPINELLI

To Mary
best
with
wishes!

Leslyn Spinelli

DOOR CREEK PRESS

Door Creek Press

P.O. Box 241072

Apple Valley, MN 55124

Publisher's Note: This is a work of fiction. Names, characters, places, and
incidents are a product of the author's imagination. Locales and public
names are sometimes used for atmospheric purposes. Any resemblance to
actual people, living or dead, or to businesses, companies, events,
institutions, or locales is completely coincidental.

Author Photograph © Claire Ogunsola

Taking My Chances/Leslyn Amthor Spinelli - 1st ed.

Library of Congress Control Number: 2018913230

ISBN 978-0-9981124-3-5 (Paperback)

ISBN-13: 978-0-9981124-3-5

ISBN 978-0-9981124-4-2 (ebook)

For my parents,
the late Margy and Fred Amthor,
with love and gratitude

1

My fingers trembled as I stared at the dead victim's picture.

George Cooper sat facing me, watching warily. "I know this is gonna be an emotionally tough case, Caroline," he said, "but you're my clear choice to handle it."

I tapped the photograph, perhaps in a subconscious attempt to rouse the girl it depicted. Shoulder-length blond hair splayed around her face, skin as white as the pillow she hugged to her chest. Dressed in torn jeans and a faded T-shirt, curled in a fetal position on a 1970s-era green print bedspread that screamed cheap motel. I could almost smell the stale air in the dingy room. "She looks to be about Lily's age," I whispered.

George nodded. "The medical examiner guesses mid-teens. We won't know till we ID her and, as I told you, the other girl's not helping."

I gently placed the photograph into the manila file on my desk. "What makes him think this is a criminal matter? And—even if it is—what would make it a federal case?"

My boss got to his feet. "Matt Witte and Jimmy McGee are waiting for us in the conference room. They'll explain."

Matt, a detective with the Janesville Police Department, frequently brought cases to the US Attorney's Office, and I'd prosecuted three of them. FBI Special Agent Jimmy McGee had partnered with him on all three occasions, contributing a different perspective and the resources of his nationwide agency. As different as a Prius and a Hummer and prone to squabbling like my two octogenarian aunts, Matt and Jimmy nevertheless worked well together.

Matt stood at the conference room window and turned to greet us when we walked in. I never knew what to expect when I saw him, since he routinely changed up his look. Today his thick blond hair was shaggy and he sported a scruffy beard and mustache, though he wore a crisp pink button-down shirt and pressed jeans. "Helluva way to start a week, huh?" he said and gave me a quick hug before taking his seat next to his partner.

One could always count on Jimmy—possessing not an ounce of fashion sense and lacking in social skills—to look and act pretty much the same. His rumpled plaid shirt and baggy brown corduroy pants probably came straight from his closet floor. And though I'm sure he showered regularly, his disheveled hair suggested he couldn't afford a barber and might not own a hairbrush. But I noticed the summer sun had lightened his carrot-red hair and connected the myriad freckles on his face and arms, turning his usually pale skin tan. "Hey," he said, glancing up for a nanosecond from the file on the mahogany table in front of him.

"Start us off, please, Matt," George said when we'd gotten settled.

Matt took a sip from his cup of Dunkin' Donuts iced coffee and nodded. "At three fifteen yesterday afternoon, the owner of the Valley View Motel on Highway 11 called 911 to say she heard screaming in room two. She'd tried to open the door with her master key but the security chain was on and she couldn't see what was happening inside. Patrol officers responded and kicked in the door. They found one teenage girl unresponsive on one bed and another sitting on the other bed screaming. No pulse or respiration from the first girl, and since she was cold to the touch, they didn't even attempt resuscitation."

He paused for another sip of coffee, then continued. "The detectives' supervisor and I got there around three thirty and summoned the troops—ME, crime scene techs, more patrol officers—and secured the scene. We had to consider the screamer a suspect, but one look at her told me she'd need to be evaluated, so we called an ambulance."

George gave him an inquisitive look.

Matt nodded. "Pupils dilated, runny nose, clearly agitated—I'm guessing opiate withdrawal. Possibly some psych issues: she was rocking back and forth, clutching a stuffed animal and a book, and put up quite a fuss when the officers took 'em away to cuff her."

Maybe just a kid in shock 'cause she found a dead body, I thought. "Any idea who these girls are?" I asked.

Matt shook his head. "No ID in the room for either of

them. Also, no cell phones, which is weird. They look like sisters, pretty close in age. No adult in sight, and no car parked in front of the unit.

"The motel owner, Gladys Burnside, showed us the registration info. A Caucasian guy giving the name Anthony J. Collingsworth came in around eight o'clock Saturday night and rented two adjoining rooms. Mrs. Burnside made a black-and-white photocopy of his driver's license, which lists him as forty-two years old and from Elgin, Illinois. It's a shitty copy, though. The picture's useless to us, and it turns out the DL is phony. Mrs. Burnside described 'Collingsworth' as of average height and weight. Since he was wearing a baseball cap—Cubs, by the way—she couldn't tell us his hair color and didn't get a good look at his eyes. He paid cash for the rooms. Listed a white 2013 Honda Accord with an Illinois plate number on the check-in card. We ran the plate and found out it'd been reported stolen from another 2013 Accord in Chicago two weeks ago. The motel's got a surveillance cam aimed at the registration desk, but the video quality's on par with the copy machine's."

"In other words, a bunch of dead ends," I muttered, immediately regretting my choice of words.

"Yeah, from *Mrs.* Burnside," Jimmy McGee interjected. "But I interviewed her husband, Harold, and luckily he's a nosy Parker. He engaged this Collingsworth guy in conversation during the check-in and gave us a pretty good physical description—dark-haired, nice-looking, a bit taller than average. The guy told Harold he was driving from Illinois to Wisconsin Dells when one of his two daughters developed a migraine. Her medication was packed in a suitcase in the trunk and they needed to stop to get it. So, he got off the interstate at the Highway 11 Janesville exit, pulled in to the first motel they came to, and decided it'd be wise to stay the night. He figured they'd still have time for a full day at the Dells waterpark—assuming the migraine resolved itself overnight and they got on the road early the next morning."

Jimmy reached for his file and extracted several eight-by-ten-inch photographs, fanning them out on the table in front of George and me. "Harold told me this Collingsworth seemed really suspicious so he took these pics with his cell phone from the motel office when the guy went back out to his car. They're not bad considering he shot 'em through a gap in the blinds. The first one shows the guy getting something out of his trunk—it looks like a man's toiletry bag. Then the two girls get out of the sedan's back seat, both from the driver's-side door, and one seems to be helping the other toward the motel."

"That fits with the migraine story," George said, scratching his head with the tip of his pen.

"Maybe," Jimmy replied. "But, if they're going to spend the night, why don't they take any luggage into the room? The girl who seems to have the headache isn't carrying anything, and the other girl's got only the stuffed bunny and the book. Harold's convinced something's up, so he watches some more. He says that shortly after eleven, a muddy black Jeep Cherokee pulls up next to the Accord and a white male, maybe thirty years old, gets out and heads for room two. It was too dark to take pics, but Harold wrote down what he could see of the license number. He was sure it was a Wisconsin plate, but a couple numbers were obscured. Says this second guy left the room, got back in his Jeep at eleven twenty-five, and drove away."

I swallowed back the bile that rose into my throat. "Do you think Collingsworth was pimping out those girls?"

Jimmy nodded and went on with the story. "A little after seven yesterday morning, Collingsworth went into the motel office and asked Harold for directions to the closest McDonald's. He told Harold his daughter still wasn't feeling well so they'd need the rooms for an extra night." He fanned out several more photographs. "Harold took these shots when he came back with McDonald's carryout bags. He was pissed that Collingsworth threw a cigarette butt on the ground next to his car and stomped it out, and made sure he took a couple pictures of that—which of course is great for us if we can get DNA off the butt. Collingsworth was in the rooms only a few minutes and then drove away. According to Harold, he hasn't come back."

"If he came back toward the motel and saw the cops and EMTs, he probably kept driving," I said.

"Seems likely," George said, then turned to Matt. "What's the reputation of this motel? Is it known for prostitution?"

The detective shook his head. "Nah. The Burnsides are on the up-and-up. They cater to blue-collar workers who are in the area for short periods of time. The occasional hunter or fisherman. I suspect this Collingsworth's engaged in sex slavery and simply stumbled on a mom-and-pop motel he thought would be a safe place to carry on for the night."

"Thank you," I said.

George raised an eyebrow.

"I mean thanks for saying what it really is, namely sex slavery," I said. "People keep calling it *human trafficking,* which sounds almost euphemistic to me. I hate that there's a ton of press about the topic but very little understanding. That most of the victims—even if we *could* manage to rescue 'em—will never be able to have a normal life."

"Easy, Caroline. You're preaching to the choir," George replied. He turned to Matt and Jimmy. "So Collingsworth's gone and we have no idea who he is. We don't know the identity of the dead girl or her sister. And it may take some time to ID the nighttime visitor." The men nodded. "What's the status of the postmortem?"

Matt picked up his notebook and glanced at it. "I just came from the autopsy. No heart defects or brain bleeds, no signs of suffocation. Signs of past and recent sexual trauma but no semen. Abrasions on her wrists, possibly from restraints, but no life-threatening physical injuries. The ME will study tissue samples from her organs to rule out disease. But the cause of death was probably something she ingested, and a couple of partially dissolved pills were found in the stomach contents. As you know, it'll be a while before toxicology results come back."

"Where's the sister, and is she talking?" I asked.

"The EMTs took her to Mercy Hospital, where a blood draw confirmed high levels of oxycodone in her system. We got a warrant from a Rock County circuit judge to seize her clothes and possessions and to do a thorough medical exam. He appointed a guardian ad litem to authorize and oversee treatment, in the likely event she goes from suspect to victim. The ER folks said she'd been sexually abused, too. They did a rape kit but apparently she'd taken a shower, so they probably won't find any DNA. She's in detox for opiate withdrawal now, and a psychiatrist will evaluate her. Last night a nurse asked her what her name is and she mumbled, 'Jennifer,' but that's all she's said."

"Anything of evidentiary value found at the crime scene?" I asked.

"Not so far," Jimmy said. "The techs say the bad guys wiped down the rooms pretty well. The only latent prints they've found belong to the girls. None left over from housekeeping or maintenance staff. By the way, we ran both the girls' prints and came up with zilch."

No one spoke for several moments. The ticking of the wall clock behind my chair sounded cacophonous in my head. *Where do we start?* I thought.

I picked up my purple Flair pen and began making notes. "I want the case," I said to my boss. "I'd say we've got evidence against Collingsworth for interstate sex trafficking of children."

"Agreed," he replied. "The case is yours, Caroline, with Matt as the primary agent."

I knew George wasn't a huge fan of Jimmy McGee and wasn't surprised he didn't put him in charge of the investigation, but I wondered if Jimmy'd be miffed. With one glance at him, though, I realized he couldn't care less about the politics of the case.

George stood to go. "I need you all to catch this guy and lock his ass up. The sooner the better."

2

I'D JUST UNLOCKED the front door that evening when my best friend's son, Trey Foster, pulled up to the curb in my mommy-van. I'd hired him to taxi my four kids to and from this week's summer activities: soccer camp for thirteen-year-old Lily, a Madison School and Community Recreation day camp for five-year-old twins Amy and Luke, and daycare for my youngest, three-year-old Lucy, a.k.a. Red.

"Hey, Mrs. Spencer," Trey yelled to me. "I thought we'd beat you home. Your bus must've been slow tonight."

Lily, who'd been riding shotgun, got out of the van and went around to unbuckle Red from her car seat. Luke bolted from his booster seat, rushed past Amy, and ran up the front steps. "I gotta go potty," he yelled as he tore into the house, holding the back of his pants with one hand.

"Give me a shout if you need help," I said. I hung my vintage Coach briefcase on the coat-tree, tossed my keys and cell phone onto the foyer table, and turned to greet the other kids.

"I made it!" Luke yelled from the upstairs bathroom.

Thank God. I'm not sure I could handle cleaning up poop right now.

Amy, wearing a big grin and a paint-spattered T-shirt, burst through the screen door carrying a finger painting of a beach scene—the theme for this week's camp. "Look at my picture, Mommy! The counselor said it was the best. Luke crumpled up his painting and threw it away, plus he got in trouble for throwing paint at Jason."

I bent down and kissed her head. "I love the cheerful colors you chose, kiddo. No more tattling, though."

"Sorry…" she said, shuffling toward the kitchen. "Can I have a snack?"

"Hang on a minute till I see what's for dinner." Grace, our housekeeper and part-time nanny, came on Mondays to grocery shop and cook meals for the week.

Lily, with Red astride her hip, and Trey, carrying a plastic crate full of lunch boxes and water bottles, followed me to the kitchen. They set down their loads while I perused the menu Grace had left on the table. "'Burgers ready to toss on the grill, potato salad in the fridge, and corn on the cob in the pan on the stove.' I think we can handle that, don't you, Lily?" I gave her shoulder a squeeze, once again conscious that she'd outgrown my five-foot-four stature.

She nodded and turned to her eighteen-year-old chauffeur. "Why don't you stay for dinner, Trey?" she asked. I cringed at her plaintive tone of voice and couldn't bring myself to look either of them in the eye.

He shifted his weight from one foot to the other and

focused on the floor. "Thanks, but I'm going out for dinner with my parents and another Air Force Academy family."

"Oh. Okay… well, have fun," Lily said and stalked downstairs to her room.

I opened the fridge to find juice boxes for the littles. "Want a Coke before you go, Trey?"

"That sounds great." He lifted Red into her booster chair and sat down next to her at the table. "Y'know, I'm kinda worried about my mom," he said as he pulled the tab on his soda can. "She keeps getting, like, all emotional and saying stuff like, 'The house is gonna be so empty when you're gone.' I mean, what's that about? Sarah's got two more years of high school and Jake's only eleven."

I'd known Glenda Foster for almost twenty years: a whirling dervish of a woman with an endless stream of projects, opinions on every conceivable subject, and a heart of gold. I smiled. "Your mom'll miss you for sure, but I predict she'll have adjusted to the new normal before you find your way to the parade ground."

"I hope so." He finished his Coke in silence, stood, and wiped his mouth with the back of his hand. "See you guys tomorrow. And tell Luke I said bye.'"

"Speaking of Luke, I'd better go see what he's doing…"

My phone rang when I was halfway up the stairs. Though tempted to ignore it, I didn't want to miss it if the call was from Matt Witte or Jimmy McGee. I hurried back to the foyer, glanced at the screen, and answered. "Hey, Dominic. What's up? I thought you'd be here by now."

"I'm on the interstate headed back to Madison. I just passed Rockford."

"Were you in Chicago?" I asked, glancing at my watch. Five thirty. *Shit! The kids'll be starved and really cranky by the time he gets here.*

"Yes. Didn't you get the message I left on your work phone?"

"Uh-uh. Sorry. I got wrapped up in a new case today —a real tough one—and didn't bother to check my voice-mail before I left."

I heard him sigh. "Mom's in the middle of another major depressive episode. When my sister called me late last night, I drove right down. She's with Mom at the hospital now, and I'll go back tomorrow to relieve her."

Just what we need—more Alejandra drama, I thought, then chastised myself for being less than empathetic. Dominic's widowed mother, Alejandra Marquez, suffered from bipolar disorder. She and I had been at odds throughout my first, brief romantic relationship with her son. Since he and I'd begun seeing one another for the second time, Alejandra had been cordial though stand-offish to me. I'd never mentioned her chilly demeanor to Dominic, and I tended not to ask about her. "I'm sorry to hear about your mother," I said. "I'd understand if you felt like canceling dinner. Three noisy little kids and one moody teenager can be trying under the best of circum-stances."

"No. I want to see you."

"Okay. We're having burgers. We'll plan to eat at seven."

I found Luke in his room, sending Matchbox cars and trucks flying across the hardwood floor and smashing into the baseboard. I noticed three or four new nicks in the paint. "Hey! What's all this about?"

"Huh?" he asked, looking up at me with fire in his eyes.

"You seem pretty mad about something."

He put down a race car with a broken windshield and shook his head. "Amy's such a pain in the ass."

I sat beside him pretzel-legged on the area rug. "You know language like that's not allowed—"

"But Lily calls me that all the time. It's not fair!"

I pulled him into a hug. "Wanna tell me what Amy did that upset you?"

"She and her stupid friends call me names. And she always tells the counselor on me."

Not for the first time, I felt sorry for Luke, being the only one in our household with a Y chromosome. "Let's all have a little chat about this after dinner. Dominic's coming. Maybe that'll cheer you up."

He shrugged his shoulders and picked up the race car —ramming it into a dump truck on the rug. *Pick your battles. At least he's not defacing the woodwork.*

I struggled to uncross my legs and get to my feet. "C'mon down and have a snack. Dinner'll be a little later than usual tonight."

DOMINIC FOUND me in the kitchen at seven ten, staring into the pot of cold water on the stove. I'd forgotten to cook the sweet corn, and my kids, already seated at the dining room table, were waiting to dig into their meals.

"Sorry I'm late, Caroline," he said, leaning down to kiss me lightly on the cheek. "Anything I can do to help?"

"Yeah," I said with a smile. "Explain to Luke why he'll have to wait to eat his 'favorite food in the world'— corn on the cob—until after his burger. That is, because his mom had her head up her ass and forgot to light the stove." I turned the knob and listened to the swoosh as the gas ignited.

He didn't laugh. "Luke will simply have to live with a little disappointment. It won't kill him."

The hair on the back of my neck immediately rose. "I *know* it won't kill him. But like me, Luke had a difficult day, and I wanted him to really enjoy the meal he's been waiting for."

Dominic trailed behind me as I hurried to the dining room. I sat beside Luke and took his hand in mine. "'Fraid you're gonna have to wait a few more minutes for that corn, kiddo, but I promise you can have the biggest piece. Okay?"

Luke nodded and gave his sisters a gloating grin. He squirted about a quarter cup of ketchup onto his burger and took a bite.

"Eew!" Amy cried. "It'll drip all over."

"Mind your own business," Luke replied with his mouth full.

Red spit out a bite of potato salad. "Ick!"

"It sucks, doesn't it?" Lily asked. "Grandma Abby's is better."

I didn't disagree. Grace's cooking couldn't hold a candle to that of my widowed mother-in-law, Abby, who'd lived with us for the first couple years after my husband David's accidental death. A year ago, Abby had remarried and moved with her husband, Bert, to a condo several miles away, and they often traveled. My kids and I were still reeling from her departure.

"We don't spit out food, Red. And watch your language, Lily." I glanced over at Dominic, whose black eyes were fixed on his plate. "Let's try eating in silence for a while, huh?"

I almost regretted my words. The tension around the table might have been eased by some banter. When the kitchen timer buzzed to signal the corn's readiness, I bounded from my chair to get it.

Luke managed to eat two and a half ears, dribbling with melted butter, before letting out a loud belch. Everyone but Dominic giggled.

LATER, while Lily put the littles to bed, I grabbed two cold Spotted Cows from the refrigerator and joined Dominic on the screened back porch. "I think we could both use a beer."

He accepted the bottle but didn't comment, then took a long pull. I collapsed into the canvas chair next to his.

His cell phone sat on the arm of the chair. I nodded toward it. "Any news about your mother?"

"Yes," he replied quietly. "Dani texted that Mom's being combative with staff. They just gave her a shot of some sedative in hopes they can avoid using restraints."

I reached over and rested my hand on his knee. "I'm sorry. This has to be so hard for you guys."

He hung his head. "It is what it is."

Good God, I hate that saying.

We drank our beers in not-altogether-comfortable silence. When a lock of my sandy-blond hair fell into my eyes, I hesitated only a moment before removing my hand from Dominic's knee to brush it aside.

About five minutes later and completely without preamble, Dominic asked, "Have you considered seeing a family counselor with Luke?"

I choked on a sip of beer. "What?" I asked between coughs. "Where's *that* coming from?"

"You said yourself that he had a difficult day. It seems to me that's becoming more and more common with him. Perhaps it would be helpful to have some guidance in handling his issues, specifically the anger. If you keep coddling him, it'll only get harder to rein him in. And as I become more involved in your life, he'll need to respect me as a father figure."

"What the f—"

"Don't get defensive with me, Caroline. We agreed to be more honest with each other this time around, and I can't sit back and watch you let your son head down the wrong path."

I bolted from my chair and stood directly in front of him, glaring in disbelief. "For God's sake, Luke's not some juvenile delinquent. He's five years old, and it's no wonder he's angry: he lost his father when he was two and lives in a house full of females who don't understand what it's like to be male. I think he's doing damn well under the circumstances."

He opened his mouth as if to respond, but I held up my hand in a *stop* gesture. "I mentioned to you twice that I've had a trying day. Instead of doing what a normal boyfriend would do—namely asking me about it—you've chosen this moment to suggest that my son and I get counseling. I can't even begin to tell you how pissed I am right now. So I suggest you leave, and we'll talk about this another day."

I grabbed his beer bottle and stormed into the kitchen, letting the screen door bang behind me. "Since you're so frickin' wise, I'm sure you can find your way out."

3

THE NEXT MORNING, I sat at my desk with the cup of dirty chai tea and rosemary breakfast scone I'd picked up from Barriques, the market across the street. I knew I should eat, but my anxious stomach threatened to retch up anything solid I might ingest. I pushed the scone aside, warily sipped the espresso-laced drink, and waited for it to kick in. By eight thirty, when I headed to court for three hours' worth of tedious motion hearings, I had some confidence I could face the day.

"HEY, GIRL!" our receptionist chirped at me when I walked into the office around noon. "Someone must be *really* sweet on you!"

"What?"

"Wait'll you get a load of the flowers that hot guy brought by for you. They'll knock more than your socks off. Who is he, by the way?"

I felt my face flush. The "hot guy" had to be Dominic

—it described him to a T. But he'd never been to my office before. "No comment," I said with a forced smile as I hurried past her. *She's probably wondering how a pleasant-looking but not gorgeous woman like me managed to snag someone so classically tall, dark, and handsome.*

The vibrant arrangement of fresh flowers, topped with a bird of paradise in full bloom, took up half my desk. The notecard, written in Dominic's calligraphy-like hand, brought me to tears. "I am profoundly sorry for the way I behaved last evening. There is no excuse for my lack of sensitivity. Love, D." He'd added a little arrow telling me to look at the back of the card. "I hoped to apologize in person before I left for Chicago, but your receptionist said you would be in court all morning. Please call me when you get back."

Sinking into my desk chair, I closed my eyes and drank in the divine scent of the flowers, imagining myself back in Butchart Gardens, where my parents and I had taken the kids during our recent trip to Canada.

A tentative knock on my doorframe cut short my reverie. "Got a few minutes?" Matt Witte asked when I looked up.

I sighed, I hoped inaudibly. *Back to reality—but at least last night's kerfuffle with Dominic took my mind off our awful new case for a few hours.*

"Sure. C'mon in."

The detective, clean-shaven today and sporting a new haircut and a navy gabardine suit, situated himself in one of my visitors' chairs and set his briefcase on the floor.

"Changin' up your look again, I see. I like it," I said with a smile. "What brings you by?"

"Thanks. I hadda look respectable to testify at your

colleague Lauren's bank robbery trial. I just got off the stand and thought I'd come by and bring you up to date on our case."

"Good. What's up?"

"We caught a break and found the owner of the Jeep that showed up at the motel late Saturday night."

"You don't sound as excited as I would expect you'd be."

"You got that right. The owner is Tyrone Harrison, a twenty-year-old black kid who lives in Beloit…"

My heart sank. "But the motel owner said the guy was white."

"Yep. Tyrone works as a nighttime stocker at the Walmart in Roscoe. He says he lent the car to a white coworker named Danny, who'd gotten a call about some sort of family emergency. Tyrone was hesitant to turn over the keys 'cause he'd only worked with Danny for a week or so but said the guy seemed really distraught. Danny brought the car back about an hour and a half later with a full tank of gas and finished out his shift. But he didn't show up for work Sunday night and got canned."

"What'd Walmart have to say about Danny?"

He reached for his briefcase and took out a manila folder. "Here's your copy of the personnel file. Daniel Wallace Thompsen. Thirty-two years old. Multiple DUIs and no current driver's license. Did a stint in Joliet, Illinois, for sale of meth, and another in Missouri for assaulting his kid's mama—he's still on paper for that one. But Walmart hired him anyway 'cause he had a decent reference from another big-box store in Rockford. He worked a total of eight shifts, so the supervisor didn't know much about him. Nobody seems to be living at the address his parole officer has for him. And the number he gave for his emergency contact, a sister in Rockford, is no longer in service."

"Can Tyrone help us find him?"

"Nah. Tyrone's a good kid who got snookered into loaning his car to a lowlife. And I suspect Danny got tipped off to vamoose by his buddy Collingsworth. I'd bet money he's gone."

I wanted to let loose with a string of expletives but had to laugh. "*Snookered* and *vamoose*! Are those some newfangled law enforcement terms?"

"Ya think I watch too many old cop show reruns?" Matt asked with a smile.

"Probably not. So what's the next move?"

"I issued a BOLO for Danny in Wisconsin and Illinois. I'm going down to interview his coworkers and supervisor tonight to see if they can give us any leads. And the good news is his DNA's on file from the assault conviction, so we'll see if it matches any trace evidence found on the dead girl. The ME found skin cells under her fingernails—maybe she scratched one of the perps. Hopefully something'll turn up."

"What's the status of the sister? Is she talking?"

"Last I heard—about ten this morning—she was still being sedated. They tried to bring her out but she got too agitated and her vitals started going wonky."

I shook my head. "We sure don't want her dying on us."

"I hear ya. Jimmy's searching through missing-person databases to see if he can ID the girls that way. So far nothing."

He must've seen the defeated look on my face. "Hey, we've been at this less than forty-eight hours," Matt said as he stood to leave. "Jimmy's boss got the crime lab to put a rush on analyzing the DNA we've got so far: from both girls, from the cigarette butt Collingsworth dropped in the motel parking lot, and on the trace evidence found under the dead vic's fingernails. Maybe we'll get some answers on that before the end of the week."

"I sure hope so."

He turned around in the doorway. "By the way, that's one impressive display of flowers. Someone thinks a lot of you."

Right. And he asked me to call him when I got back here. I grabbed my cell phone and dialed. "You've reached the voice mailbox of Dominic Marquez…"

I left a message and went back to work.

AN HOUR LATER, halfheartedly flipping through the documents in Danny Thompsen's personnel file, I noticed something that grabbed my attention: the Walmart was in Roscoe, *Illinois.* Google maps prominently displayed its location, about five miles south of the Wisconsin/Illinois border.

I dialed Matt Witte and didn't wait to exchange pleasantries when he picked up. "You didn't tell me Tyrone and Danny worked in Illinois," I said.

He laughed. "I thought everyone knew where Roscoe is."

"I'm just glad I know now. Assuming Danny had sex with one of the girls at the motel, he crossed a state line to do so."

"Yeah…"

"Which means—like his buddy Collingsworth—he's violated a federal law with a very hefty penalty, including a mandatory minimum. If we catch him, he'll have way more incentive to roll over on Collingsworth than if he were simply facing state time."

"When."

"Huh?" I asked.

"*When* we catch him. Not *if.* Danny is nowhere near as careful as Collingsworth. I predict we'll find him within the week."

"I like your attitude!"

"What do we need to get an arrest warrant? It'd get a lot more attention than the BOLO we've got out there now."

I paused a moment to think. "If the scrapings from under the dead girl's fingernails match his DNA, we'd have enough for probable cause. I could get a warrant within hours."

"Then let's hope the lab gets back to us quickly."

4

GEORGE COOPER BUZZED me at three o'clock on Friday afternoon. "Oh, good, you're still here. Can you c'mon down?"

"Sure, what's—" He rang off before I could finish my question, immediately raising my anxiety level.

I finger-combed my hair and took several calming breaths as I hurried to his office. With one ear to his telephone receiver, my boss motioned me to sit. "Okay. Send 'em back as soon as they get here," he said and hung up.

I shifted in my chair. "What's up?"

"I just got off the phone with the director of the state crime lab. She wants some positive PR about their cooperation on the Collingsworth investigation. And, given how quickly they did the DNA analysis, I told her I'd issue a press release this afternoon. I'll need your help pulling it together."

"Of course. But what'd the analysis show?"

"I have no idea, but Matt and Jimmy should be here any minute to fill us in." He handed me a yellow legal pad and a pen. "Jot down some initial thoughts, please, while I go to the men's room."

By the time George returned with the two investigators in tow, I'd managed to write "horrific case—teenage victims."

"Let's be comfortable," George said as he lowered himself into the worn leather armchair in his sitting area. Jimmy and Matt took the couch, and I moved to the wingback chair. "Okay, one of you tell us the news in layman's terms."

Jimmy turned to his cohort. "It's gotta be me, or we'll be here until midnight."

Matt flushed and waved his hand. "Go ahead."

"The girls were half sisters; they have the same mother but different fathers," Jimmy said. "Their DNA doesn't match anyone in the FBI's relatives-of-missing-persons database, but that's still a hit-or-miss system. Two pieces of big news: Collingsworth is apparently Jennifer's father, and Danny Thompsen's DNA was found under the dead girl's fingernails. The analyst showed us all kinds of illustrations and charts and explained his conclusions. He'll have his written report done by Tuesday."

The four of us sat in silence for more than a few moments. "Wow," I finally said. "None of this is particularly surprising, but it's still awesome to hear the forensic conclusions."

"Yeah," Matt said. "And now we can move forward on the warrant for Thompsen's arrest. Is it too late today, Caroline?"

I glanced over at George and pointed apologetically to the virtually blank legal pad. "'Fraid I didn't get too far."

"Aw…I was just being a wuss asking you to help," he said. "I can conjure up a press release in my sleep. You guys go draft the complaint and warrant request. Henry's usually in till five." Henry Rees, the clerk of court, served as a part-time magistrate and could sign an arrest warrant once a criminal complaint was committed to paper. "I'll call and let him know you're working on something. Buzz me when you're done and I'll come sign off on it."

"Thanks, George," I said as Matt, Jimmy, and I left his office.

Halfway down the hall, Matt looked at me with concern. "Why are you limping?"

I laughed. "Stupidity. I let my son ride his bike alongside me when I went on my run last evening and I fell prey to his pleas to go 'just a little farther.' I'm not as young as I used to be, and his stamina's increased way more than I'd imagined."

I SAT AT MY COMPUTER, pulled up the complaint template, and hammered at the keyboard while Jimmy and Matt pored through notes and documents reading me details to include. I consulted my well-worn copy of federal criminal code for the correct wording of our charge, interstate travel to engage in a commercial sex act with a child. We had to make sure any reference to the deceased victim or to Jennifer LNU—last name unknown—whom we had taken to calling "Jennifer Lennoo" for short, was not identifiable in the document. George wandered in before we were done and read over my shoulder. "Slow down, Caroline," he said with a grin. "You waste more time deleting your mistakes than you'd use if you took your time."

"Yes, Dad." But of course he was right. *I could sure use a Xanax to counteract this adrenaline.*

We finished at four forty-five. Matt, Jimmy, and I jogged the block and a half to the US Courthouse and took the stairs up to the third-floor clerk's office. "I'll go corral a marshal to enter the warrant into NCIC," Jimmy said, "while you guys get the documents filed."

I nodded as I knelt down to catch my breath. Our efforts to get the complaint done today would've been useless if the warrant sat on someone's desk all weekend. NCIC would transmit the order to arrest Danny to every law enforcement agency in the country.

"Thirsty?" I asked when we left the courthouse half an hour later. "I'll buy, though I'll have to head home after one round." Matt and Jimmy nodded in unison, and we walked toward State Street in search of three empty barstools and some cold beer.

"Date with the flower guy?" Matt asked.

"Nope. He's dealing with a sick mother in Chicago," I said, then realized I'd spoken a somewhat crude double entendre. "I mean his mother in Chicago is literally sick. I've got a date for a movie with Lily."

5

I'D JUST finished bathing and getting the littles to bed on Sunday evening and was pouring myself a glass of Cabernet when I got a text from Matt Witte. *Rockford PD arrested Danny. Call when you can.*

Wine and cell phone in hand, I went to the front porch, lit a citronella candle to fend off mosquitos, and settled into my favorite Adirondack chair. The warm, humid air felt soothing to my bare legs as I stretched them forward to rest my feet on the porch rail.

I savored a few sips of wine, checked my email, then dialed Matt. "Tell me."

He laughed. "I told you we weren't searching for an Einstein. Danny got himself into a fistfight over a game of pool at a bar downtown. An off-duty cop ID'd himself and stepped in to break it up and, instead of walking away, Danny went after him with a pool cue. So, now he's sitting in jail waiting arraignment for attempted assault on a police officer."

"Is the cop okay?"

"Yeah. I'm told he's about a foot taller and a hundred pounds heavier than Danny. He deflected the swing without raising his pulse rate."

"Good. Given the charge and Danny's record, I'm guessing he won't be released on bail, but I'll call the prosecutor's office in the morning to be sure. Our warrant's on file as a detainer just in case, though, isn't it?"

"Yep. I called the jail to confirm."

"Great work, Matt. Thanks."

"Jimmy and I will go sit in on his initial court appearance tomorrow morning and then try to interview him. With any luck, he won't lawyer up."

"It'd be great if you could take the lead on it. Sometimes Jimmy comes on too strong, and we don't want to scare this guy away from cooperating. And I'll tell Jimmy that myself if you want me to."

Matt chuckled. "No need. He and I've had this conversation before, and he prefers to hang back and play the bad cop if it seems called for."

"I'm sorry…I was being a buttinsky. But I'd like more evidence before I take this case to the grand jury. So far we know the dead girl was sexually assaulted shortly before her death, *probably* by Danny Thompsen, given the fact that his skin cells were found under her fingernails. Otherwise all we've got is conjecture."

"I hear ya. When does the grand jury meet next?"

"Two weeks from tomorrow. I'll need you or Jimmy to testify."

"Can do. By the way, Jennifer Lennoo's guardian ad litem, Brad Tollefson, and I are going to visit tomorrow afternoon. Her social worker hasn't been able to make any headway with her; in fact, she says the girl sobbed during their whole meeting and refused to say a word. Brad wants to see if he can get her to open up at all and thought it'd be helpful for me to come along and explain that we view her as a victim, not a criminal."

"Good luck with that. She's still in the hospital, right?"

"Uh-huh, for now. But the social worker wants to move her to a treatment center for adolescent substance abusers as soon as she can. Figures she'll make more progress there than in the psych ward at the hospital."

"She may be right."

"Maybe. Anyway, I'll let you know how things go on both fronts."

6

MATT FINALLY CALLED me around noon on Monday. I'd spoken with the prosecuting attorney in Rockford and knew the judge had denied bail for Danny Thompsen, but I had no idea whether Danny'd agreed to cooperate with my agents.

"What a cluster," Matt said, his voice laden with disappointment. "This guy's a Class A jerk and his lawyer's worse. Bottom line, he's not gonna roll over on Collingsworth."

"I'm surprised he got a lawyer so quick. Public defender?"

"Nah. Some asshole named Oliver Pooley from Chicago. I'm guessing Collingsworth might've had something to do with it."

"What makes you say that? How would Collingsworth even know about his arrest?"

"I talked to the jailers. When Danny got booked in last night, he was mouthing off about how the Rockford case was bogus and he'd be out before noon today. I'm guessing the deputy tried to put him in his place and said, 'You're probably never getting out.' And he told him about the federal arrest warrant and the charge."

I groaned. "And maybe Danny used his one phone call to tip off Collingsworth, who sent a lawyer to shut him up."

"Uh-huh, that's a reasonable explanation. Wouldn't you know Danny was last up on the intake docket this morning so we didn't get out of court until around ten thirty. Pooley was waiting for us when Jimmy and I got to the jail to interview Danny. We read him his rights and showed him the complaint. Told him he'd fare a lot better if he cooperated, but Pooley wouldn't let him say a word. He told his client our evidence is sketchy and he'd be better off rolling the dice at a trial than throwing in with us."

"At this point, our evidence *is* sketchy. Where are you now?"

"Sitting in the parking lot at the jail. Why?"

"We need to get a warrant to search Danny's personal property and cell phone and a subpoena for the phone records. I'll need whatever particulars you can get from his personal property inventory at the jail in order to draft them."

"I gotta run to make it to my meeting with Jennifer and Brad Tollefson. But I'll have Jimmy get the info and call you."

"Thanks. Good luck with the interview—we *really* need Jennifer to tell us what happened in that motel room."

"I hear ya," he replied, and I couldn't miss the apprehension in his voice. *His main fear is probably the same as mine: What if Jennifer never gets well enough to work with us?*

Jimmy called me back twenty minutes later. "Danny had *two* cell phones with him when he got arrested. One's an LG flip phone, most likely a burner, and the other one's a banged-up iPhone with a cracked screen—looks like a 6 or 6S."

"Two phones—can you spell incriminating?" I said with a chuckle.

"I can and will," he said. "I'll be there within the hour with the details."

I hadn't even put down the phone when Matt called. *I feel like an air traffic controller.*

"Jennifer wouldn't say boo," he said. "She sat slumped over in her chair and refused to make eye contact. When I explained how important it was that she talk with us, she started crying and rocking back and forth—just like when we found her at the motel. I think I told you that Brad Tollefson can talk to anyone? I excused myself from the room and let him try alone, but she started moaning and we had to get a nurse to come in and calm her down."

"Poor kid. How does she look?" I asked.

"Lost and confused. The nurses said she's been eating a little better the past couple days but still won't answer their questions with anything other than a nod."

"Shit," I said, shaking my head. "I guess all we can do is wait."

"Hear anything from Jimmy?" Matt asked.

"Yeah, he's on his way here with info on Danny's *two* cell phones. We'll have a search warrant this afternoon."

～

WITHIN THREE HOURS, Jimmy and Matt were back at the Winnebago County Jail in Rockford. The warrant allowed them to compel Danny Thompsen to use his fingerprint to unlock the iPhone. We could only hope he had touch ID enabled, because he couldn't be forced to give us a passcode.

I startled when my phone rang at four thirty. Jimmy didn't bother with a hello. "The fingerprints didn't work, and believe me, I made the son of a bitch try every finger on each hand twice."

I groaned. "Nothing's coming easy on this case."

He ignored my lamentation. "I called our IT guy and asked him to stay late and see if he can find a way into the iPhone. The throwaway's got four contacts programmed into it but no names associated with the numbers. There's a bunch of recent calls we can follow up on."

"Okay, let me know when we're ready to subpoena records. One more thing, Jimmy: Could you and Matt come by tomorrow sometime and meet with George and me? I'll feel better if we can formulate some contingency plans."

"Hang on, I'll ask him." I heard their muffled exchange and Jimmy said, "How's ten o'clock?"

"Sounds good. I'll text you if George has a conflict, but he told me earlier he has a pretty free week."

7

NANCY OFFERED to drive to the treatment center Thursday afternoon. The gray skies let loose a downpour as we pulled out of the parking garage, and I watched apprehensively as the wipers *thwapped* back and forth across the windshield. "I'm glad you're at the wheel," I said. "I hate driving in the rain."

I'd never ridden with Nancy, and by the time we reached the highway, I wished I'd declined her offer. She drove as aggressively as my late husband, David, though I wasn't sure she was as skilled as he'd been. "Oh, sorry," she said when she noticed me applying an imaginary brake pedal and clutching my seat belt. "I'll put it on cruise control."

I decided the risks of hydroplaning were less than those of excessive speed and murmured, "Thanks." And to distract myself, I reached behind my seat for the plastic bag containing the items Jennifer had been clutching when the police found her at the motel.

I pulled out the dingy stuffed bunny, which had probably been pink at one time. It was missing an eye and its tail. "I get the attachment to this stuffed animal," I said to Nancy. "My thirteen-year-old daughter sleeps with her favorite one now and then, especially when she's stressed. But I'd sure like to know what draws Jennifer to this book."

The weathered hardback copy of Charles Portis' *True Grit* looked like it had been found in a "free" bin at a rummage sale. Sans dust jacket and with many of its yellowed pages dog-eared, the 1968 edition was no collector's item. The crime lab had been through it for prints and trace evidence and found nothing of note. I flipped through the pages, recalling the wonderful acting in the Coen brothers' remake of the old John Wayne movie. "Maybe she's drawn to the character of Mattie Ross—they're both about the same age," I said.

"Mattie Ross was no victim," Nancy replied.

"True. Maybe Jennifer was looking for tips to steel herself against the men who victimized her?"

I looked at the book's inscription, the ink now faded and almost illegible, and read it to Nancy. "'Christmas 1988. Dear Cassandralynn, Mom gave this book to me when I was twelve. I hope you enjoy it as much as I did. Always, Your Loving Sister.' Do you suppose Jennifer is somehow related to this Cassandralynn?"

"It's an odd name. Did anybody look into it?"

"I dunno." I pulled out my phone, typed the name into the Google search window, and waited. "Nothing, though there are some hits on Cassandra Lynn—two words." I sent myself a text message reminding me to ask Matt about it and to set up a Google alert when I got back to the office.

I STRUGGLED to hide my shock when Nancy and I saw Jennifer in the rehab facility's visiting room, slouched among a pile of mismatched throw pillows on an ancient gold couch. Her vacant eyes and expression looked every bit as dead as the photos of our motel room victim. And I had no doubt they were indeed sisters. They shared the same blond hair, porcelain-doll features, and too-thin bodies.

Her counselor, Lydia Davis, a twenty-something black woman with much older eyes, sat beside her and gently brushed an errant strand of hair from Jennifer's face. "Honey, these are the women I told you about." She nodded toward me, "Caroline Spencer is the prosecuting attorney," then toward my colleague, "and Nancy Drummond is the victim/witness coordinator in her office. Are you still willing to talk with them?"

Jennifer picked at the frayed edge of her cutoff shorts and mumbled, "I guess…"

When Nancy had called Lydia to set up the meeting, she told her not to expect much. She said Jennifer never spoke voluntarily and would only answer questions with shrugs or a few syllables.

Nancy and I took chairs facing the couch, across a coffee table with chipped veneer and multiple water stains.

"Thanks for seeing us," I began. "I'm told your name is Jennifer but you prefer to be called Jen?"

She looked at her lap but replied quietly, "Yes, ma'am."

"Please call me Caroline."

No response.

"How old are you?" I asked.

A puzzled look crossed her face, as if she were trying to remember. "Fourteen."

"Will you tell me your last name, Jen?" I asked.

She shook her head.

"Why not?" Lydia asked.

"It doesn't matter anymore," she replied. She raised her head slowly and gazed out the window. "I don't have any family."

"Jen," I said, "we know the girl found in the motel room with you was your sister. And we're very sorry she died. How old was she?"

"Sixteen," Jen replied, almost inaudibly.

"What was her name?"

"Jo—" She stopped, shook her head, and covered her eyes with her forearms. "No. You don't need to know."

Nancy glanced at me and held up her hand in a *stop* gesture. We watched as Jen took a few deep breaths and lowered her arms. She kept her eyes closed.

"You remember Mr. Tollefson?" Nancy asked. "The man who's been appointed by the court to protect your interests?"

"Uh-huh."

"Well, he suggested we give you back your belongings, since they're not needed for evidence anymore. Would you like them?" She gently placed the stuffed animal and the book on the coffee table. We waited.

After what felt like an eternity but was probably only a minute of silence, Lydia spoke. "Honey, I don't know for sure, but I think these things might mean a lot to you."

Jen warily opened one eye and looked. She lurched

for the objects and hugged them to her chest. She buried her face in the rabbit's matted fur and drew a deep breath. "Thank you."

"You're welcome," Nancy and I said, almost in unison.

Lydia stroked Jen's back, then stood up. "May I suggest we continue our conversation another day?" she asked us. "Perhaps early next week?"

Nancy and I nodded. Jen—lost in her own world—didn't respond when we said our good-byes. But when I glanced back at her from the hallway, I saw the hint of a smile in her eyes.

8

THAT EVENING, after I'd settled the littles in bed, I texted Glenda. *You free?*

Her response came a nanosecond later. *Be right over.* And within minutes my best friend was sitting next to me, the bottle of Corona she'd brought along resting on the arm of her chair.

"I'm glad you texted," she said, then paused for a long pull on the beer. "I'm a basket case and Hank is too engrossed in the Brewers game to talk to me."

"What's up?"

She sniffled and dabbed at the end of her nose with her T-shirt sleeve. "Missing Trey like crazy. Wondering how he's doing. Second- and third-guessing whether we should've nixed the whole military thing. I mean, it's so frickin' serious."

I wanted to laugh. Glenda and Hank had been proud as peacocks when Trey received his appointment to the Air Force Academy. He'd been talking about going *far* away to college as long as I'd known him, and this was an all-expenses-paid opportunity of a lifetime. I reached over and held her hand. "Relax. He's a great kid and he's up to this challenge. When will you get to see him?"

"Acceptance day is August ninth, but we'll only be able to spend a couple hours with him. Parents' weekend is over Labor Day. It seems so far away."

"I'm sure it does," I said, pushing myself up from the chair. "I'm gonna get some more wine. You want another beer?"

She shook her head. "Too much and I get maudlin, and something tells me I'm already there."

By the time I got back to the porch, Glenda'd lit a cigarette. She looked up at me and exhaled with enthusiasm. "Don't judge me, okay? I'm grieving."

This time I did laugh.

We didn't speak for a while, the silence broken by the persistent high-pitched buzzing of a mosquito. Glenda finally swatted it on my forearm. "Take that, you little bastard!" she said and flicked the corpse off with her thumb and forefinger. "So what'd you want to talk to me about?"

"Huh?"

"When you asked me to come over? I assumed something was on your mind."

I swirled the wine in my glass a time or two, then took another sip. "Did you hear about the teenage girl who was found dead in the Janesville motel?"

Glenda nodded. "Yeah. Wasn't there another girl, too? I read they might have been sex trafficking victims with their dad being the pimp. And that drugs could've been involved."

Why the hell did that nosy motel owner have to go and talk to the press?

"Uh-huh. My boss assigned the case to me and I can't get the pictures of the victims out of my head."

"Oh, kiddo, I'm sorry. From what I read in the paper, they haven't found the dad?"

"Nope. We've located one of the Johns but he's not talking. And the girl we rescued is so messed up it might be better if she were dead, too. I get so pissed that vulnerable human beings are treated like commodities. That perpetrators can think of countless ways to use and abuse people."

I finished my wine and set the glass on the floor next to my chair. "I'm sorry I mentioned the case. I've already said more than I should've, and you don't need to think about any more sad stuff."

"Yeah, well, it sure puts my troubles in perspective."

"There is that."

Glenda lit another cigarette. "What's new with you and Dominic? I haven't seen his car here lately—not that I'm trying to be nosy or anything."

"I haven't actually seen him for about ten days. His mom had another major depressive episode and was hospitalized for a week. I guess she's not responding very well to the meds and they're keeping a pretty close eye on her. We talk every day, but he seems kinda hesitant to tell me much about it."

"How can he afford to spend all this time in Chicago? Private investigators can't make that much money, and I'm sure they don't get paid if they're not working."

"He's got another investigator—apparently someone

from his old agency in Chicago—helping out temporarily."

"It's not that blond bimbo, is it?"

I let out a mirthless laugh, flashing back to Dominic's short-lived affair with Emma, his very attractive former associate. "I hope not. I'm pretty sure he called him Tommy."

"He's not stupid enough to let his mother come between you two, is he?"

"I dunno, Glen. Before we got back together, he went to see a counselor to help him learn how to deal with his mother. You know, detaching, setting boundaries, stuff like that. I haven't heard him talk about the counselor lately, and I haven't asked if he's still seeing him. Sometimes I say to myself, 'Not my circus—not my monkeys.' But I guess if Dominic and I are gonna commit to each other, it'd be my circus, too."

"Just like your circus would be his."

"Ouch!"

9

WINCING and limping my way from my car to the parking garage elevator on Monday morning, I decided the first order of business for the day would be to make an appointment with my GP. "Can you make it at eleven this morning?" the receptionist asked me.

I'd be presenting the Danny Thompsen case to the grand jury at nine thirty and was confident it wouldn't take long. "Yes. I'll be there."

In fact, the Thompsen case went smoothly, but the one on the calendar ahead of it took longer than anticipated. Luckily my doctor was running as far behind schedule as me, and I had time to catch my breath before he walked into the examining room.

"Hey, Caroline," Dr. Woorley said, his eyes crinkling into a smile. "Good to see you."

"Wish I could say the same," I said with a wry grin. "But I'm in pain, I'm swamped at work, and I don't have time to be hobbled."

He settled his bulk onto the small computer chair and

turned to log in. "My self-esteem is quickly diminishing—no one's happy to see me, and this damn computer keeps rejecting my input." Swiveling back to me, he looked over his reading glasses. "What hurts?"

I pulled up my left pant leg. "My knee, and look how it's swollen. It's bothered me when running for a couple weeks, but in the last day or so it's been sore almost all the time."

"Wait'll you get to be my age." He rose slowly and reached out his hand to help me onto the exam table. "Have you fallen or run afoul of any large stationary objects recently?"

I shook my head.

"Twisted it?"

"Nope."

With practiced efficiency, he donned a pair of purple gloves and examined me. I scowled as he gently poked and prodded and moved my lower leg in various directions.

"Nothing to indicate it's broken," he said, heading back to his computer. "The ligaments and tendons seem sound. It's probably a torn meniscus—you know, the cartilage that cushions your knee. That can happen with even minor trauma. It wouldn't show up on an X-ray, and I'm thinking it's premature to order an MRI."

"So…what next?"

"I'll wrap it and have Kimberly take you over to physical therapy. They'll fit you with some crutches to keep your weight off it until it settles down. Ice it every few hours and keep it elevated whenever you can. Make an appointment next week for PT to evaluate it further and give you some exercises to strengthen your leg. Ibuprofen or naproxen should help the pain, but if not, call me and I'll write you a script for Vicodin."

I shook my head. "I don't think that'll be necessary."

Shit, shit, shit! I thought, fighting back tears as Kimberly, Dr. Woorley's assistant, pushed me in a wheelchair toward the elevator. *Why now?*

"Lucky it's your left knee," she said.

"Huh?"

"For driving. Unless you have a stick shift?"

I laughed ruefully. "No, I haven't had one of those for years. So, yeah, I guess I am lucky."

But I didn't feel lucky when I left the clinic. My purse kept clunking the crutch and halting my progress during the ten-minute walk to my car. An elderly man with a cane limped over to open the door and hold my crutches while I deposited myself onto the driver's seat. "Thank you, sir," I managed to croak through tears I simply couldn't control, "you're an angel."

He patted me on the shoulder before closing the door. "It'll all work out, honey. You're stronger than you think."

I sat in the car and typed out a few text messages: one to George Cooper saying I wouldn't be in the rest of the day, one to Nancy Drummond asking her to contact Jen Lennoo's counselor to schedule another meeting, and one to my mother-in-law, Abby, accepting her offer to cook dinner for us tonight. I left a voice message for Dominic, who'd called while I was in the doctor's office, explaining the diagnosis.

DURING HIGH SCHOOL I'd been on crutches for six weeks after a volleyball injury and had easily mastered the mode of locomotion. Like riding a bike, my ability to maneuver on them came back quickly. Using Lily's old messenger bag that had been hanging on our coatrack for months, I transported a sandwich and bottle of beer from the kitchen to the living room couch. Half an hour later, my stomach full, my nerves relaxed, and my leg elevated, I took the nap of a lifetime.

ABBY AND HER HUSBAND, Bert, were bustling around my kitchen conjuring up a feast when I woke up and wandered in for a bottle of water. "Hey, sleepyhead," she said to me, "hope we weren't making too much noise."

"I didn't even hear you," I said. "And thanks for helping out tonight."

"Happy to do it, dear," Bert replied. Seconds later, our new summertime nanny, Amanda, called from the front door to say the kids were home, and chaos ensued.

I made my way out to meet them, leaning against the hallway wall to avoid being bowled over by my rambunctious son. "Hey, guys! How was everyone's day?"

"What happened, Mommy?" Amy asked, her wide eyes filled with concern.

"Cool! Crutches! Did you break your leg?" Luke yelled as he dropped his backpack on the floor.

I leaned down to kiss their heads and looked up, surprised to see Dominic walking in a step behind Lily, carrying Red on his shoulders. "Luke!" he said. "It's not acceptable to tell your mother it's cool that she's on crutches." He set Red on her feet and moved to hug me but hesitated after observing my stony expression.

"I can speak for myself, thank you," I said to him,

sotto voce. "And I've asked you before not to correct my son." Then, turning to the kids, "C'mon in the kitchen. Grandma's got some snacks laid out and I'll explain why I'm walking with these things."

I couldn't miss his crestfallen look and felt a momentary tinge of guilt for hurting his feelings. *Stop it!* I told myself. *He hurts your feelings every time he patronizes you and chastises Luke.*

After satisfying the kids' curiosity and settling them around the table for veggies and cheese dip, I put two beers into my shoulder bag and headed back to the living room. Dominic sat on the couch with the remote control in his hand, clicking through the channel guide at a furious pace, and made a move to stand when he saw me in the doorway. "Don't get up," I said a tad too harshly. "I've got this."

I handed him a beer, sat down next to him, and opened the other one for myself. "When did you get back from Chicago?"

"Just now. I left when I got your message."

"I hope you didn't come back early on my account."

"No," he said, looking down at his lap, "I have a meeting here first thing tomorrow morning."

I didn't believe him for a minute and didn't know what to say.

Dominic reached over and covered my hand in his. "I've missed you."

The warmth of his touch and his loving tone diffused some of my anger. "I've missed you, too."

We sat in silence for a while before I got up the energy to ask the obligatory question, "How are things with your mom?"

"Better, I think. She swears she's not suicidal, though her mood still changes from day to day."

"I know it's difficult for you and Dani."

He nodded. "It is. We're not sure she's ready to be alone, so Dani's covering tonight and tomorrow."

I did a double take. "You mean to tell me you're still babysitting her round the clock?"

"Caroline, bipolar disorder is a serious, sometimes life-threatening illness. We can't take it lightly."

"Of course not," I said with exasperation, "but I'm sure her psychiatrists wouldn't have released her from the hospital if they thought she couldn't take some personal responsibility for her own mental health."

"Perhaps, but none of them knows her as well as we do."

"Dominic, it's their *profession* to make judgments like that."

"I guess we'll simply have to agree to disagree on this one," he said, stroking my hand with his thumb. Rather than calming me, the gesture irritated me and I wriggled my hand free. "Just as we'll need to agree to disagree about Luke," he added.

I felt the blood rush to my face, and if my leg hadn't been ensconced in a pillow on the coffee table, I would have stormed from the room. A major blowup was averted by the sound of Lily's disembodied voice, speaking through the intercom on the wall behind us, "Mom, Grandma says it's time for dinner and we've set a place for Dominic."

Why in God's name did I ever think an intercom system was a good idea? I thought. *And please, please, Dominic, decline the invitation!*

"I'll have to take a rain check," he said to me. "I've got lots of work to catch up on tonight. I should be back in Madison this weekend. May we get together then?"

I nodded, pushing aside his proffered arm and getting to my feet. "Sure, give me a call when you know your schedule."

In the foyer, he leaned in to kiss my cheek. "We'll work it all out, Caroline. I promise."

10

"I'M PERFECTLY CAPABLE OF DRIVING," I told Nancy Drummond the next afternoon, grabbing the keys to the G-car we'd use to travel to Janesville. "I didn't want to say anything the other day, but your driving scares me to death. I've got four kids who depend on me making it home in one piece!"

Nancy laughed. "Have at it. I need to catch up on Pinterest anyway."

We spent half the forty-five-minute drive in compatible silence, though Nancy periodically urged me to look at a Pinterest pic on her iPhone. "Show me later," I said each time.

As we neared Janesville, Nancy muttered, "For chrissakes, stop tapping the damn steering wheel and fiddling with the seat belt, will you? You're distracting me!"

"I will if you put down your phone and talk with me about how we plan to get Jen to open up. We really need her testimony against her father and Danny Thompsen."

Nancy sighed. "Frustrating as it might be, we need to

take it slow, and my advice is not to mention her testifying against her dad."

"What? If the scenario we believe is true—namely that he held her and her half sister hostage with opiates and forced them to have sex with who knows who—she's gotta hate his guts. Why wouldn't she want to see him in jail?"

"Most of these victims have very mixed emotions about their captors. They depend on them for everything: food, shelter, and what passes for love and attention. Even if given the opportunity, many of them don't try to escape. In this case, the captor was Jen's *father.* I'm guessing she loves him as much as she hates him. And who knows what horrors he's threatened her with if she snitches on him."

I glanced over at her. "So what do we do?"

"We start by just talking with her. You mentioned you were going to reread *True Grit* over the weekend. Did you?"

"Uh-huh. Finished it last night."

"I'm about halfway through it. We can ask her about the book and see what develops. The main thing right now is to get her talking. We can follow up on things she says by asking non-threatening questions—nothing too personal and definitely not related to sex trafficking. If you sense she's getting hinky, back off. You've got good instincts."

I signaled to pull into the parking lot next to the treatment facility and found a spot at the edge of the cracked blacktop pavement. "I see what you're saying. You take the lead, though, okay?"

Nancy nodded. "Sure. And though it'd be tempting to

jot down what she's saying, don't do it. Keep that damn yellow pad of yours in the car, and we'll make notes on the way home."

WE MET Lydia in her office, a cinderblock, closet-sized room that would have been depressing but for the glass-block window that magnified the outdoor light, the glossy yellow walls, and the brightly colored paintings adorning the walls. "Have a seat," she said, directing us to a worn but surprisingly comfortable camelback couch.

"How is Jen doing this week?" I asked.

"She seems less distressed," Lydia replied. "The medical director prescribed her a low dose of Suboxone, which helps with both opiate withdrawal symptoms and cravings. She's still not talking in group sessions, but at least she's making eye contact and paying attention. I worry a little that this group might not be right for her, though. Jen seems much less streetwise than the other kids. As I told her guardian, a foster home and individual treatment might be more appropriate. But I'd like to give it another week or so before we consider a change."

JEN'S FACE seemed fuller today and her eyes less sunken. Sitting on the couch beside Lydia and still clutching her stuffy, she mumbled hello and watched us warily as we got situated in the chairs facing them.

"Do you want me to stay while you talk to Nancy and Caroline?" Lydia asked.

Jen nodded.

"That's fine," Nancy said. "We don't have any secrets

and we want you to feel comfortable. Is there anything you want to tell us or ask us about?"

Jen gave an almost imperceptible nod in my direction. "How did you hurt your leg?"

Wow! Six syllables, I thought while I pondered her unexpected question. "Uh, I'm not sure. The doctor thinks I have a torn cartilage that caused some inflammation. I'm supposed to start physical therapy when it calms down."

"Does it hurt much?"

I shook my head. "Not too much now that I'm staying off it. Thanks for asking."

Jen looked down at her lap.

Nancy finally broke the arduous silence that followed the oh-too-brief conversation. "Caroline and I were talking about *True Grit* after we left here the other day. We were both assigned to read it when we were in middle school. I started rereading it over the weekend and I'm so glad 'cause it's one of my favorites. Yours, too?"

Jen's eyes lit up as she nodded but she remained quiet.

"Did you read the book in school?" Nancy asked.

Jen shook her head. "No."

Nancy tried again, "I really admire Mattie's spunk, don't you?"

Another nod.

You can't keep asking yes or no questions, I wanted to yell at Nancy. *She'll never talk if you give her the option to answer nonverbally.*

After a prolonged pause, Jen spoke. "Mattie Ross is the bravest character I know." And it was as though a dam had burst, because she proceeded to describe to us several of her favorite scenes.

"Did you ever see the movies that were made from the book?" I asked. "There was one from the 1960s with John Wayne and a newer one that came out a few years ago."

"No, but I'd like to."

"If it's okay with Lydia," Nancy said, "we'll bring it down and watch it together sometime."

Lydia smiled. "Of course it's okay, as long as I can sit in!"

"There's one thing I wanted to ask about your book, Jen," I said quietly. "The inscription in it is to someone named Cassandralynn. Is that somebody you know?"

Tears welled up in Jen's eyes. "Uh-huh."

"Who is she, honey?" Lydia asked.

"Was," Jen replied, crying now. "She was my mom."

Lydia put her arm around the girl's shoulder and drew her closer. "What happened to her?"

"She died."

"I'm sorry," Lydia said. "When did she die?"

Jen paused as if to think. "A couple years ago, I guess."

We waited while Jen blew her nose on the tissue Nancy proffered.

"It looks like the book was a present to your mom from her older sister—your aunt," I said. "Is she still alive?"

Jen shrugged. "I never knew her. Can I go back to my room now?"

"Certainly," Lydia said. "I'll come and get you for group."

"Shit," I said to Nancy when we got back to the car. "I'm sorry I made her clam up."

"Forget it. We know a few more things about Jen than we knew yesterday: Her mom is dead, and her dad probably kept the mom and kids isolated from family, which is typical for a controlling abuser. Based on the passages she liked in the book and from her concern about you and your leg, we know she's a compassionate kid who's still in touch with her emotions. That's encouraging for her future—if we can get her the help she needs."

"I hope you're right," I said. "Did you notice her Southern accent?"

"Uh-huh. But I couldn't say where in the South. And it only came out once in a while. Like maybe she was trying to hide it."

"Maybe."

"What do you make of Lydia's comment that Jen might be better off in a foster home?"

"I dunno. I guess it would depend on the foster home. But I'm worried that being in a group setting with some pretty streetwise kids might do her more harm than good. You saw her almost childlike innocence when she was talking about *True Grit*—it's so incongruent with the life we believe she's been forced to live."

"Could you reach out to DCF and see if they have any prospective foster placements that might be a good fit?" I asked.

"Sure, I'll make some calls tomorrow morning. I've got a few names written down back at the office."

The kids and I walked over to Glenda and Hank Foster's

for dinner that evening to help celebrate their son Jake's birthday. When she'd called a week earlier to invite us, Glenda had warned me about the menu: hot dogs and bratwurst cooked on the grill and Jake's favorite side dishes—marshmallow fluff Jell-O salad, barbecue potato chips, and coleslaw. I'd volunteered to bring a watermelon, which we now transported—along with Red—in the wagon Luke proudly pulled. My upper-body strength was sorely tested by walking with crutches, but I was determined to give my knee the rest Dr. Woorley had recommended.

When we arrived, Jake and his two best buddies were running around the front yard, shrieking and shooting one another with gigantic squirt guns. They made Luke's day by inviting him to join them, and he quickly suffered several soakings with a huge grin on his face.

The girls and I made our way to the front door virtually unscathed. Glenda greeted us, mopping her brow with the dish towel she always wore on her shoulder, and relieved Lily of the watermelon. "C'mon in to some peace and quiet. Hank fogged the backyard so we can sit on the deck without getting molested by mosquitoes."

The get-together felt incredibly relaxing to me. After dinner, Glenda's fifteen-year-old daughter, Sarah, and my Lily kept track of the littles so we adults could sip white sangria and chat, and Hank excused himself to go watch the Brewers when he'd had enough "girl talk."

"This evening is great," I said as I reached over to pour more wine into my glass. "How's Hank doing without Trey?"

Glenda paused and blotted the end of her nose with the dish towel. "Sorry. I tear up at the mere mention of

Trey's name. Hank's doing a damn sight better than me, I'm afraid."

"I know it'll get easier as time goes on, but that doesn't help much right now, does it?"

"Nope. I'm sorry I didn't take the counseling gig at that summer camp in the Dells. All those at-risk kids would've tested my patience, but at least I'd've been busy till school starts."

"Hey, speaking of at-risk kids, I could use your opinion about the Janesville victim. Our victim/witness coordinator and I visited her today at the treatment facility where she's staying. Her counselor is concerned that the more streetwise kids might be bad influences on her. Even though she's been through a lot, she doesn't really fit in with the other residents who've been abused and/or addicted. It's almost as though she's been sheltered from the world."

"More like deliberately isolated so she'd remain powerless."

I shrugged. "Maybe. The counselor thinks she might be better off in a family foster home with one-on-one treatment. What d'you think?"

Glenda's eyes brightened and she leaned forward in her chair. "I agree with her. And I know the perfect placement for her—with us."

"What?"

"I told you when Trey got accepted to the academy that Hank and I decided to get certified to be foster parents, remember? Well, we're all set except for the home visit and that's scheduled for this coming Monday. You know we'll pass." Glen stood up and began talking more rapidly. "We'd be a perfect family for her: Sarah'd be a great sister to her, and you couldn't find a more mild-mannered, honorable father figure than Hank. Plus I could put my social work skills to good use helping her with post-traumatic stress. And I learned a ton about sexual predators when Sarah was being tormented by that perv."

"True, but…"

"But what? We could get Jen settled in for several weeks before school starts, and she could go to Edgewood, where the classes are small."

I shook my head, marveling at the leaps my friend had taken in a few short seconds. "I doubt social services has a budget to send foster kids to private schools."

"I can get her a scholarship easy peasy."

"I dunno, Glen. It might be a conflict of interest to have a victim—and one who I hope will be one of my primary witnesses—living with my best friend."

She pointed toward my cell phone sitting on the picnic table. "Well, call your boss and ask."

"I can't call him now. We're both off the clock and this certainly isn't an emergency. Plus you're not even official foster parents yet."

She slumped onto her chair. "All right. I get it. But talk to him tomorrow, okay? I'll see if I can get our home visit moved up."

I laughed. "I'll talk with him, but I've gotta do what's best for the girl."

"This is what's best. I just know it."

11

As Glenda'd predicted, she and Hank passed the home visit test with flying colors and were officially approved to become the Foster foster parents. "It's kismet!" she said when she called to tell me the news on Friday morning.

"Oh, please…"

"Did you talk to your boss about the girl living with us?"

"Uh-huh. Late yesterday afternoon, but things were too crazy at our house last night for me to call and tell you about it. He doesn't think it's a great idea."

Even through the ether, I could feel her ebullience instantly deflate. "Why the hell not?"

"He says my close relationship with your family could compromise her ability to make an independent decision about whether to testify against her abusers—when doing so might not be in her best interest."

"That's horse shit! You would never ask her to do something that wasn't in her best interest. For God's sake, doesn't he know you well enough to know that?"

"Unfortunately, I can think of a few victims I convinced to testify who later regretted their decisions."

"Were they under-aged girls who were pimped out by someone who supposedly loved them?"

"Easy, Glen. You didn't let me finish. George said he didn't *think* it was a great idea, but he agreed it should be presented to the Rock County circuit judge who's still overseeing the girl's case. Nancy Drummond, our victim/witness coordinator, and the guardian ad litem will get input from the counselor and psychologist at the treatment facility and then let the judge decide."

"Can I make a pitch to him, too?"

"No! This is a confidential matter that you shouldn't even know about—the only reason I even mentioned her to you was to get your opinion, not to get you involved. The DCF social worker'll let the judge know she's got qualified foster parents and a treatment plan ready in Madison if he agrees it's a good move."

"Okay. We'll sit tight. Any idea when the proposal will go to the judge?"

"Nope. And if I knew I couldn't tell you. Let's just say it won't happen overnight."

"I get it. I'll put on my big-girl panties and try to be patient."

"Good idea. You can come over and smoke cigarettes on my front porch if it'll help."

"Might hafta take you up on that."

Nancy Drummond called me the following Monday afternoon. "Hey, what's up?" I asked.

"Why do you sound like you've run a marathon?" she replied.

"Because I just finished my first physical therapy session with a sadistic prick who says I need to work hard to build the muscles supporting my knee. He put me through the ringer. I'm thinking of quitting."

Nancy laughed. "I never took you for a slacker. Just do what he says and drown your sorrows in beer."

"Thanks for the advice. Now, back to *my* question: why'd you call?"

"Oh, yeah. To let you know that the Rock County judge decided to hold a hearing on Jen's living situation. Brad Tollefson let him know, off the record, that friends of yours were *coincidentally*—wink, wink—being considered by DCF as potential foster parents. He wants to meet with them and you to get some assurances that Jen won't be under any undue pressure to cooperate with the government."

"Fine. Glenda'll be happy to meet with him, and so will I."

"The husband, too. Especially since she's been victimized by so many men."

"I get it. When does he want to hold the hearing?"

"Nine o'clock tomorrow. Can you be there and also arrange it with the Fosters?"

"Geez, Hank's a veterinarian with a booming practice. A little more notice woulda been good."

"I know, but Lydia Davis wants Jen out of the treatment center ASAP. Says she's getting tight with an older girl who's likely to start hitting on her for sex."

"Oh, good God! I'll call Glenda right now and get back to you."

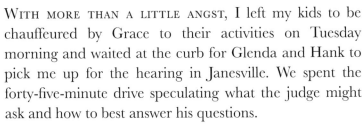

WITH MORE THAN A LITTLE ANGST, I left my kids to be chauffeured by Grace to their activities on Tuesday morning and waited at the curb for Glenda and Hank to pick me up for the hearing in Janesville. We spent the forty-five-minute drive speculating what the judge might ask and how to best answer his questions.

Still sore from my exercises, but pleased that the fiendish physical therapist had urged me to throw off my crutches, I walked gingerly from the car to the courthouse on my own two feet.

The light and airy second-floor courtroom felt too large for our little proceeding. Jen and Lydia walked in a few moments after the Fosters and me and took seats in the second row, directly behind us. I turned and greeted them. "It's good to see you both." I didn't know if it was appropriate for me to introduce Hank and Glenda, so I skipped it. "How're you doing, Jen?"

She shrugged. "Okay, I guess."

Jen had to know the hearing would directly impact her living situation in the weeks to come, and I found it surprising she didn't look nervous—especially without her stuffed bunny. "I finished rereading *True Grit*—"

The entrance of the court clerk interrupted my attempt at small talk. "Sorry we didn't make it clear," he said, "but we're meeting in Judge Baker's chambers. Follow me, please."

Like lemmings, we proceeded single file through the door behind the judge's bench and into his office. A small man with thick white hair and mustache, dressed in a blue button-down shirt with the sleeves rolled to his elbows,

Hugo Baker came out from behind his desk to shake our hands. Jen first, then Lydia, Hank and Glenda, and me. Jen's guardian, social worker, and Nancy Drummond appeared moments later. Judge Baker welcomed them before taking one of the chairs that had been arranged in the circle in front of his desk.

"Thanks for coming on such short notice," he said, motioning for us to join him. "This'll be somewhat informal, but I want to wait until my court reporter arrives to make a record of our meeting."

We all sat in silence, broken only by the melodious ticking of a mahogany grandfather clock in the far corner of the office. The judge nodded toward it and smiled. "Sometimes the darned thing lulls me to sleep."

Well, it's making me *frickin' nervous!* I wanted to tell him.

After what felt like forever—and in reality was probably two minutes—the court reporter rushed in with her transcription machine. "Sorry, Your Honor. The elevator's acting up again and I got stuck between floors."

"Good to know, Deirdre. Let's all remember to take the steps when we leave." He paused until Deirdre took her seat and nodded her readiness.

"I understand your name is Jennifer, but you prefer to be called Jen. Is that correct?"

Jen nodded.

The judge leaned toward her. "I'm afraid I'm going to have to ask you to speak your answers so my reporter can hear them."

"Yes, sir. I like Jen."

"Good job. Jen, it is. Now, I'm going to ask each of these people to state his or her name and role here." He nodded toward Nancy to begin.

"I'm Nancy Drummond, the victim/witness coordinator for the US Attorney's office. My role is to make sure Jen has the support services she needs during the apprehension and prosecution of her... er, the people who abused her."

Judge Baker looked directly at Jen and smiled. "Did you understand all that?"

She nodded, then smiled back. "Yes, sir."

"Alrighty, then. Next..."

We went around the room, until it was Hank and Glenda's turn, when the judge took over. "As I understand it, sir, you are Dr. Henry Foster, a doctor of veterinary medicine."

"Yes, but I go by Hank."

"And you are Mrs. Glenda Foster, a part-time school social worker."

"Yes, Your Honor," my friend said with a tremulous voice.

The judge nodded. "Now, Jen, I'm gonna explain why the Fosters are here 'cause it's more than a little unusual. They've been approved by the state Department of Children and Families, DCF for short, to take in foster kids— kids such as yourself who need temporary homes. They don't have criminal records, they've been interviewed at length to make sure they're good people, and their home and neighborhood have been found to be safe."

Judge Baker paused, I suspected to consider his words. "What's unusual here is that the Fosters happen to be close friends with Mrs. Spencer, who's pressing charges against your father and any other folks who might've been involved in abusing you. You with me so far?"

"Uh-huh."

"And there might come a time when Mrs. Spencer wants you to testify in court against those people. Do you understand that?"

Jen fidgeted in her chair and mumbled, "Yes, sir. She might want me to be, like, a snitch."

The judge nodded. "Yes. And if you go to live with the Fosters, I don't want you to feel you have to agree to be a snitch. So now I'm gonna ask Hank and Glenda here to tell me how they'll make sure you don't feel any pressure—one way or another."

Though we'd practiced our responses to such a question during the ride to Janesville, Glenda launched into a stream-of-consciousness soliloquy about their oldest son, Trey. How she'd been supportive of his desire to attend the military academy, even though it wasn't what was easiest for her. How it's important for kids to find their own paths. How she checked herself regularly to make sure Trey didn't know her true feelings about his departure…

Finally Hank reached over and put his hand on her knee. "Glenda, I'd like a chance to say a few words." Judge Baker nodded—gratefully, I thought.

"Jen," Hank said, "my wife just gave you an *example* of our philosophy of raising kids: Simply put, the family needs to do what's in each child's best interest. We have two children living at home now, Sarah, who's fifteen, and Jake, who just turned twelve. Something that might be right for Sarah—like going away to sleepover camp—might be completely wrong for Jake 'cause they have different personalities, interests, and abilities. We always encourage them to express their opinions, even if we disagree. And unless health or safety is a concern, we try to let them make their own decisions. We'd treat you the same way if you lived with us. And we'd do everything in our power to make sure you weren't pressured into doing *anything* you weren't comfortable with."

I'd watched Jen's face while she listened intently—as though transfixed—to every word of Hank's recitation. It surprised me when she spoke. "I've always been home-schooled. What if I'm not comfortable going to a, like, real school?"

Hank glanced at Glenda, as though imploring her to reply. She inhaled deeply before she began. "School doesn't start for more than a month, so we'll have plenty of time to find an educational setting that *will* be comfortable to you. I promise."

Apparently satisfied with the answer, Jen nodded.

The judge turned to me. "Mrs. Spencer, describe your relationship with the Fosters and how you'd be likely to interact with Jen if she lived with them."

Whoa! Talk about an open-ended question!

"Sure," I said, feeling slightly light-headed at the enormity of the situation. I willed myself to focus and began, "I have four children. My oldest daughter, Lily, is thirteen, twins Amy and Luke are five, and Lucy—who goes by Red—is three. We live around the corner from the Fosters and see them once or twice a week, sometimes for meals. Their daughter, Sarah, and my Lily are a year apart in school, so they don't hang out much but get along well when the families are together. Jen, if you and Lily happened to become close, you'd be welcome in our home even without the rest of the family."

"Would you tell the other kids about my past? You know, what my dad made me and my sister do?"

My eyelids stung as I shook my head. "No way."

"Honey, we wouldn't tell them, either," Glenda added. "There was an article in the paper about your sister's death that included some rumors, but I'm pretty sure none of our kids would have heard about it."

"Do you have any more questions for anyone here?" the judge asked Jen.

"Not that I can think of."

"Well, Ms. Davis is worried that if you stay at the treatment center you'll be pressured by some of the older residents into doing things you might *not* be comfortable with. Do you agree with her opinion?"

Jen brushed a tear from the corner of her eye. "I guess so."

"Given that, I'm inclined to follow the DCF recommendation that you move in with the Fosters. But I'll certainly listen if you want to tell me reasons why that shouldn't happen."

Jen didn't speak, but her eyes glistened with more tears. Lydia put her arm around her. "Please say what's on your mind, Jen. As we've discussed in group, your feelings are important and people need to know them."

Jen wiped her eyes with the back of her hand, swallowed a couple of times, and took a long breath. "Well...I don't really *like* most of the kids at the center and I'm kinda afraid of some of them, but at least I know 'em. And I, like, know what to expect. And I'd miss you, Lydia—"

"I'd miss you, too, honey. But we'll keep in touch no matter where you go. We can message each other and

Skype and even write real letters. You're in my heart and always will be. And my heart tells me living with these great people would be best for you right now."

Jen nodded.

Judge Baker glanced down at his feet and sniffled, then continued. "I agree with your counselor, Jen. And I approve the proposed foster placement, effective immediately. Young lady, you are strong and bright. I know you'll make the most of your circumstances and do positive things with your life." He stood up, went to his desk, jotted something on a Post-it Note, and handed it to her. "Here is my address. Please feel free to write to me if you'd like—about anything you want me to know. Okay?"

"Thank you, sir."

We all walked solemnly to the parking lot, Jen arm-in-arm with her counselor, and the rest of us looked away during their tearful farewell. The girl's shoulders heaved when she got into the back seat of Hank and Glenda's car.

I'd texted Nancy before the hearing about riding back to Madison with her, and now I followed her to the G-car. "It's been a pretty emotional morning," she said. "Would you be more at ease driving?"

I laughed despite the tears that remained on my own cheeks. "As a matter of fact, I would. Thanks."

"Full disclosure: I've got some emails I need to catch up on, and you're a pokey enough driver for me to get 'em all done."

I slid in behind the wheel, blotted the end of my nose

with a crumpled Kleenex, and adjusted the seat forward.
"Frickin' tall people."

12

THE FOLLOWING WEDNESDAY, I booted up my computer, headed to the break room to grab a cup of coffee, and came back to clear the cobwebs and begin my workday.

I almost missed the email from Google, halfway down the list of inbox messages. The alert I'd set weeks ago for any news of Cassandralynn—whom we now knew was Jen's mother—had turned something up: an obituary in that day's *Birmingham Times*. I held my breath and read.

> *Birmingham, AL – Prominent cardiac surgeon, Dr. James C. Whitaker, age 89, passed away on Sunday, after a lengthy illness.*
>
> *Dr. Whitaker is survived by his daughters, Barbaralynn (Taylor) Edwards and Cassandralynn Pickett Corbell; grandchildren, Cody and Taralynn Edwards, and Josielynn and Jennifer Corbell; and great-grandson, Trevor Edwards. He was preceded in death by his parents, his beloved wife, Annalynn, and his son-in-law, Christopher Pickford.*
>
> *Funeral arrangements are pending.*

Wow! Finally some names! I thought.

I forwarded the article to Jimmy and Matt and sat back to make sense of what I'd read: Jennifer's aunt Barbaralynn was still alive, but the family was unaware of Cassandralynn's death. Jen's father wasn't mentioned in the obit, so he must be *persona non grata* with the Whitaker family. And his last name was obviously Corbell.

And sometimes people pick aliases with the same initials as their true names. Is Anthony John Collingsworth really someone with the initials AJ Corbell?

I noodled around further on the computer and found a phone number in Birmingham for Jen's aunt and uncle, Barbaralynn and Taylor Edwards. But, not wanting to usurp my investigators' roles, I resisted the temptation to dial it.

Jimmy called ten minutes later. "The obit's a great lead," he said. "We'll get right on it."

"Since I emailed you, I found a home number for Jen's aunt and uncle. How 'bout you call it and ring me in on three-way? My curiosity is killing me and I'd love to hear the contact firsthand."

"Sure, but let me get to my office. The sound quality will be better and I'll be able to take notes as we go. I'll be there in a few."

WHILE I WAITED, I Googled some more. I found an Ambrose Josiah "AJ" Corbell, listed in a 1990 newspaper article from Pensacola, Florida, as one of twenty kids who were confirmed in a Methodist church. A grainy black-and-white photo accompanied the article. AJ stood in the back row—among the tallest of his adolescent peers. All I could tell was that he had dark hair. *He's about the right age. Could this be Jen's father?*

A lengthier 1996 newspaper piece reported AJ's appearance in a Pensacola high school musical, playing the lead male role of Emile in *South Pacific*. The article's color photo depicted a handsome young man with thick, wavy hair and alluring brown eyes. *That figures—he's probably irresistible.*

I could find nothing more. No Facebook page. No LinkedIn account. No addresses or phone numbers. *Looks like Ambrose Josiah Corbell went under the radar after high school, which would fit our bad guy's profile.*

As I typed "Cassandralynn Corbell" into the Social Security Death Index, the shrill ring of my desk phone startled me.

"You ready?" Jimmy asked.

"Hang on one sec." I scanned through the list on my computer screen. "I'm just looking at the SS Death Index. There's a Cassandralynn Corbell who died at the age of thirty-eight in Arkansas two and a half years ago."

"That's probably her. Okay, let's do this interview. I need to take the lead, though," he said, and I heard him dialing.

I held my breath and counted as the call rang ten times. A woman answered, "Edwards' residence, Marcy speaking."

"Hello. My name is Jim McGee and I'm calling for Barbaralynn Edwards. Is she available?"

"I'm afraid Mrs. Edwards is unable to come to the phone. May I ask what this is about?"

"Certainly. I'm with the FBI in Madison, Wisconsin,

and I'm calling with information that may pertain to Mrs. Edwards' nieces, Josielynn and Jennifer."

We could clearly hear Marcy's intake of breath. "Oh…my…Mr. Edwards will want to talk with you. Let me get him." She put the receiver down, and we heard muffled voices in the background.

"Hello, this is Taylor Edwards. What's this about? Are the girls okay?"

Jimmy handled the call masterfully, calmly explaining who we were and that we were attempting to locate the family of two teenage half sisters, possibly Josielynn and Jennifer Corbell, who'd been found in Wisconsin.

"My wife waited for news of those poor girls and their mom for years—" he said, then paused to choke back a sob. "Unfortunately…she's now suffering from early-onset Alzheimer's disease. She can't speak or understand what's said to her."

"I'm sorry, sir," Jimmy replied. "Perhaps you can answer some questions for us."

"I'll certainly try. I met Barb eight years ago, well after AJ left with Cassie and the kids, so I never knew them. But I *feel* as though I did after all I've been told. You said you were calling about the girls. What about Cassie?"

"It appears she may have died in Arkansas a couple of years ago, but we'll need to check into it further to be sure."

"My God. And to think that son of a bitch never even told the family. My father-in-law was right to hate him."

The half-hour conversation was heartbreaking. We learned that Cassie's mother had died shortly after her birth, and her sixteen-year-old sister, Barbaralynn, had practically raised her. After Cassie graduated from college, she'd married her high school sweetheart, Christopher Pickford. A year and a half later, while Cassie was three months pregnant with Josielynn, Pickford died in a car accident.

The child had been six months old when her mother began dating Ambrose Josiah Corbell, newly arrived in Birmingham for a sales manager's position with a Cadillac dealership. Though he went by "AJ," Cassie had been enamored of his full name and often called him by it. The family had approved of AJ, since he doted on Cassie and baby Josie.

After a headlong courtship, the couple married and AJ adopted Josie. Cassie's father, Dr. James Whitaker, purchased a home for the family and also hired AJ to run a charitable foundation that had been established by his late wife, Annalynn. A year into the marriage, Jennifer was born. "My wife told me that the first hint of discord between AJ and the Whitaker family was when he forbade Cassie from carrying on the 'lynn' suffix tradition," Edwards related. "You know—Annalynn, Barbaralynn, Cassandralynn. He said he'd never saddle a child with another 'god-awful' long name."

When the girls were about four and six years old, AJ abruptly left the job with the Whitaker Foundation, sold the house, and moved his wife and kids to Pensacola, supposedly for a better employment opportunity. Within a year, they'd moved again, severing all contact with Cassie's family. "Barb told me she and her father were devastated, mostly because they missed Cassie and the girls. But an audit had also revealed a considerable sum of money was missing from the foundation—most likely stolen by AJ. Dr. Whitaker hired someone to try to find the family, but it was as though they'd fallen off the face of the earth."

Toward the conclusion of the interview, Jimmy told Edwards he would be asking an agent from the Birmingham field office to come interview him. "I'm not sure how soon someone will get out there," he said, "but it would be helpful if you could pull together whatever documents the family might have about Cassie, AJ, and the girls."

"My wife's got several boxes of her sister's records and memorabilia—stuff that she left at their folks' in Birmingham when they moved. Do you want me to FedEx them to you to look through?"

"That would be very helpful, Mr. Edwards," I said hurriedly, afraid Jimmy would leave it to the Birmingham agent to secure the information. "We'll reimburse you for the shipping costs."

"I'll have it done today."

"Before we hang up—" I said nervously, "although we're not yet sure that the girls we're calling about are your wife's nieces, it certainly sounds likely. And there's something you need to know: the older of the two was deceased when they were located."

Edwards gasped, then paused to collect himself. "How did she die?"

"An overdose of pain medication. The younger girl, who says her name is Jen but hasn't been willing to tell us her last name, is in foster care here. She's been badly traumatized but is receiving great treatment. I think she'll come out of this okay."

Edwards sighed. "I certainly hope so. Their grandfather left a trust fund for the girls—one that can't be touched by AJ. If this girl is in fact Jennifer, she'll have any resources she needs."

I swallowed the lump in my throat. "Would any family member be able to take her in? Perhaps one of Barb's children?"

"How I wish. Barb's son is a drug addict, and her daughter is a single mother of a special needs child," he said, his voice cracking with emotion. "But I can promise you Jennifer won't be abandoned again."

When the call ended, I closed my eyes and cried. For Cassie and Barb and Dr. Whitaker. For Josie and Jen. And for Taylor Edwards, who cared enough to try to pick up the pieces of a shattered family.

13

ON FRIDAY MORNING, I waited in the conference room for the meeting with my investigators. Jimmy appeared first, wheeling a dolly bearing the three Bankers Boxes that had been FedEx'd from Taylor Edwards in Alabama. Matt walked in five minutes later with his usual offering: a half-dozen Dunkin' Donuts and a Box o' Joe. He poured three cups, affixed the lids, and cautioned us, "Careful with this. We don't want to spill on anything important."

"Way to ratchet up my nerves." I took a sip, then set my cup on the credenza behind me. "My hands were jittery already."

Jimmy stood up, sliced through the boxes' packing tape, and slid one in front of each of us. "Let's get to this. Make three piles—one for stuff with evidentiary value, one for stuff that's not, and one for stuff you're not sure about. We'll tag the useful items and do chain of custody when we're done."

We immediately became absorbed in the task. My box contained Josie's and Jen's baby books. Cassie had religiously recorded their milestones with photographs, memorabilia, and perfectly penned captions. *I wish I'd had the time or inclination to do this for my kids,* I thought with a tinge of guilt. Each book contained a snipping from the child's first haircut. "Hey, would locks of hair help us confirm the girls' identities?" I asked.

"Not without the follicles," Jimmy said.

I closely examined the family photos of Cassie, AJ, and Josie—and later those including Jen—searching for hints of the horrors that lay ahead. I couldn't find any. AJ gazed lovingly at his wife and daughters, Cassie looked radiant, and the girls were obviously happy and content.

About a half hour later, Matt spoke up. "Cassie had a million-dollar life insurance policy that her dad bought for her when her first husband died. Doesn't look like the policy itself is in here, but here's confirmation that it's paid in full. You think AJ offed her for it?"

"Wouldn't put it past him, though he might not have known she had it," Jimmy said. "We should call the company and see if the payout was ever made."

Matt jotted something in his notebook. "On my list."

I flipped through stacks of kids' artwork and home-made greeting cards. I found Josie's kindergarten and first grade report cards, both with glowing comments from her teachers.

Near the bottom of my box, I came upon a manila envelope with an unsigned note scrawled across it: "These are the kits that Tom ordered for your kids and mine. I think he's overreacting, but we're sending ours in." I opened the envelope and found two cards, dated in 2005, providing identification data and Josie's and Jen's fingerprints. Apparently their mother had completed the cards but never mailed them to the child-find organization.

"Guys," I said springing from my chair. "Guess what! Cassie took the girls' fingerprints."

Jimmy took the cards from me and looked closely at them. "Some of 'em are smudged, but there are enough good ones to get a positive ID. Lemme fax 'em in."

An hour later we had our confirmations: our dead victim was sixteen-year-old Josielynn (nee Pickford) Corbell, and "Jennifer Lennoo" was fourteen-year-old Jennifer Louise Corbell. Jimmy called Taylor Edwards to inform the family.

Unfortunately, we were no closer to finding their father.

WE'D JUST FINISHED SORTING our evidence and completing chain of custody forms that afternoon when Jimmy received a phone message from his office. "A woman named Magnolia Barr, who says she was Cassandralynn Corbell's best friend, just called and wants to talk with me," he told us, gesturing toward the speakerphone on the conference room table. "Wanna listen in?"

Matt and I nodded and watched as he dialed.

"Mrs. Barr, this is Agent Jim McGee, returning your call. Detective Matt Witte and AUSA Caroline Spencer are on with us, too. What can we do for you?"

"I just spoke with my friend Marcy, who's Barbaralynn Edwards' caregiver, and she told me about Cassie and the girls. I just can't believe it. I want to help and I need to see Jenny."

"Tell us how you knew Cassandralynn," Jimmy said.

"Sure." She paused for a moment—as though she hadn't expected to be questioned. "We grew up together in the same neighborhood. We were best friends all through high school and were roommates at Auburn. I was her maid of honor when she married Chris, and she was in my wedding a month later. I helped her through Chris's death and Josie's birth. Josie and Jenny were like siblings to my two kids—Sam and Nicole... I'm sorry I'm rambling. I just want you to understand we were *close.*"

Jimmy cleared his throat. "When and how did you lose touch with them?"

"That effing Ambrose Josiah Corbell drove a wedge between us. When Cassie first met him, we all thought he was a gift from God; he was sweet and kind and treated her like a queen. But I noticed things changing when Jenny was a couple years old. AJ gradually became more controlling, and we saw less and less of Cassie and the girls.

"Sometimes I'd overhear him saying demeaning things to her, and if she took offense, he'd say she was being overly sensitive. He told Cassie I was a bad influence on her and criticized how my kids treated hers. Finally, when his subtle manipulations to break up our friendship failed, he told her that I'd come on to him. And she refused to listen when I told her it was a flat-out lie. Before I knew it, they'd sold the house and moved away." Magnolia sobbed and stopped to compose herself. "I'm just sorry I didn't try harder to stay in her life. She didn't deserve to end up estranged from the people who really loved her. And those poor girls didn't deserve whatever hell he put them through."

Amen to that! I wanted to shout.

"My husband, Tom, and I've talked, and we'd like to become Jennifer's legal guardians."

Matt, Jimmy, and I looked at one another, each of us hoping someone else would respond.

"Mrs. Barr," I said, "it's great to find out that Jen has family and friends who love her. Right now, though, she's been entrusted to the care of a court-appointed guardian ad litem, a DCF social worker, and two highly qualified foster parents. They'll sort out how to proceed—"

"Ms. Spencer, is it?" she asked.

"Yes."

"I don't mean to be pushy, but I'm Jenny's godmother. Her mother gave me that responsibility fourteen years ago, and for a decade I've been unable to fulfill it. I need to bring her home as soon as possible."

I took a deep, cleansing breath and tried to collect my thoughts. "I'll talk with Jen's guardian—Bradley Tollefson—and have him call you."

"Today?"

"I'll do what I can."

"Thank you."

Jimmy disconnected the call and we all sat back in our chairs. I noticed my hands were clenched in fists and Jimmy's face was flushed. Only Matt looked composed. "This could be just what the doctor ordered," he said.

"What do you mean by that?" I asked, surprised at the vehemence in my voice.

"We've got no idea where AJ's at, and it could be months before we arrest him. In the meantime, Jennifer could be back among family and friends, settling into some stability."

"We don't know anything about this Barr woman,"

Jimmy said. "For all we know, she's cut from the same cloth as AJ."

"I believed her," Matt said quietly. "And neither Brad Tollefson nor the court will release her to someone's guardianship without a shitload of assurances that it's the right thing to do."

"I suppose," I said. *This would be a whole lot easier if Jen weren't living with my best friend, who's growing more and more attached to her by the day.*

"Do you wanna call Brad or should I?" Matt asked me. "I'd prefer you do it, since you're up to date on her situation."

"I'll do it. I need to go back to my office to look at her file, though."

"We'll pack up here and talk to you Monday," Jimmy said.

THE KNOT in my stomach grew as I limped down the hallway. Like Glenda, I would sorely miss Jen if she moved back to Birmingham. Though she remained quiet and reserved, she was kind and generous to everyone around her. My kids gravitated toward her whenever she was around.

Tollefson picked up after two rings. *Shit!* I thought. *Why couldn't you be out till Monday?*

I explained the reason for my call. "Now that we've located Jennifer's family—and a purported godmother who wants to be her guardian—how do you suggest we proceed?"

"Give me a minute to think."

During the silence, I gripped the receiver with white knuckles and bit at a hangnail on my free hand.

"Let me make sure I understand. No one in Jen's extended family is in a position to take her in, and Jen hasn't had any contact with her godmother since she was around four years old?"

"Uh-huh."

"Given all she's been through, I doubt the court or DCF would agree to uproot the girl at this point in her recovery. But down the road, it sounds promising. I'd suggest we start by having someone in Alabama vet the woman and perhaps arrange for her to visit here."

"Who'd do the vetting?"

"I'll contact social services in Birmingham and see if they can help. Could you have the FBI interview her and do some background work?"

"Yeah, I think so. Jen might be a primary witness in a pretty big federal case, and we'd want to guarantee her safety. Thanks, Brad."

I hung up and emailed Jimmy to start the ball rolling but hoped it'd roll at a snail's pace. And I decided *not* to tell Glenda just yet.

14

"LET's meet in the conference room," George said when I buzzed him on Tuesday morning to say that Matt and Jimmy had arrived. "I want Nancy to join us."

Nancy Drummond, our office's victim/witness coordinator, had what I considered a dreadfully difficult job. Charged with providing all manner of assistance to victims and witnesses of serious federal crimes, she served as a helping hand to the most vulnerable people we encountered.

Almost six feet tall, model thin, and dressed as though she'd just stepped off a page in *Vogue*, at first glance Nancy looked like she belonged in a high-power law firm in Manhattan rather than in a government office in Middle America. But she never failed to listen intently, speak compassionately, and give sound, valuable advice. And when she took off her helper hat, Nancy could be incredibly funny and often irreverent.

I didn't need to ask who had brought the treats spread out across the conference room table: a Dunkin' Donuts

Box o' Joe, coffee cups, a four-inch stack of napkins, a mound of little half-and-half containers and sugar packets, and a box with an assortment of donuts. "Thanks, Matt," I said with a smile as I poured myself a coffee with two creams. "You've managed to derail day one of my latest diet."

"Good," he replied, passing me a napkin and pushing the donut box toward my chair. "There are a couple of chocolate ones with sprinkles—as I recall, your favorite."

I felt my cheeks flush but didn't decline the offer.

We exchanged a few pleasantries as we settled in and indulged our taste buds. Then Nancy licked some frosting off her fingers, wiped her lips with a napkin, and sighed. "I've only got half an hour so we'd better get down to it. I understand this girl in Janesville has been unable or unwilling to talk," she said. "How can I help?"

"I want you and Caroline to meet with her and get her to open up to you," George said. "Matt, Jimmy, and her GAL have all tried but struck out. Given that Jennifer has clearly been victimized and probably held captive by men, it doesn't take a rocket scientist to realize that she might be more likely to trust women."

"I don't disagree," Jimmy said, "but her social worker's a female, as are many of the staff at the hospital, and she hasn't spoken with them."

"Nevertheless," said George with a touch of irritation in his voice, "I want our experts handling this and seeing it through. Nancy has years of experience dealing with sexual assault victims, and Caroline—who will prosecute the girl's father if we can ever find him—will need to be able to guide her through some tough testimony. Matt, how long is Jennifer expected to be in the hospital?"

"They're moving her to the drug treatment center today."

Nancy consulted the calendar app on her phone. "I'd recommend we give her a day or two to get settled before we go see her," she said. "I'll coordinate our access with the guardian ad litem and her counselor. Caroline, will Thursday afternoon work for you?"

"Uh-huh."

"Great. I'll text you with the appointment time," she said, pushing back from the table. "You can fill me in on the case on our drive down."

After Nancy left, George poured himself another cup of coffee and passed the cardboard carafe around. He turned to Jimmy. "Any luck on Danny Thomspen's phones? Caroline told me your IT guy was optimistic he could crack the iPhone."

Jimmy fidgeted in his chair. "I'm not sure I said optimistic. Maybe hopeful. We went through Danny's wallet first and did find a scrap of paper with a four-digit number written on it. The IT guy—Hector—tried to use it to open the phone. No luck, either frontward or backwards. He tried a couple other common numbers, like his DOB and birth year, and still struck out. We don't want to strike out ten times or it'll erase all the phone's data. So we need to try to find a computer that Danny might've used to set up the phone. If so, we can go into his iTunes and unlock the phone."

George tapped the table several times with the end of his pen. "Sounds like a long shot to me."

"Maybe," Jimmy replied. "But believe it or not, he did have two emergency contacts listed on his phone's home screen. Maybe they can help us find his computer. We've also got the contact numbers and photos on the burner to track."

"Photos? What kind of photos?" I asked.

"Not sure. I didn't look at 'em." Jimmy said. "Hector was gonna run them through a facial recognition database first thing this morning to see if he'd get any hits."

Matt rolled his eyes. "Why don't you call and ask what he found?"

Jimmy grabbed the phone that had been sitting facedown on the table in front of him and glanced at the screen. "Speakin' of the devil—there's a text from Hector: *Many images of kiddie porn.*" He clicked to the full message and grinned. "He says more than a hundred."

"Well, well, well," I said. "It might be easier to indict Danny for possession of child pornography than for interstate travel to patronize a child sex slave. We could still use the kiddie porn charge as leverage to get him to roll over on Collingsworth."

"Are any of the pics of Jennifer or her sister?" Matt asked Jimmy.

"He didn't say, and I'm not sure he knows what our victims look like. I'll head back to the office, though, and get right on it."

George stood up to leave. "Good work, guys. And Jimmy, I don't usually abide folks using their phones in my office. But when there's fast-breaking stuff going on— like in this case—feel free to keep an eye open for incoming messages."

MY OFFICE PHONE rang a few minutes before five o'clock. Jimmy McGee.

"Glad I caught you before you headed out," he said. "I spent the afternoon looking at the images from Danny Thompsen's burner phone. There's one of him having intercourse with our dead vic in the Janesville motel. She must've scratched him before the photo was taken, though, 'cause it shows her tied up. And gagged."

"Wait—he's *in* one of the porno pics on his own phone?"

"Yeah."

"You're sure it's him?"

"Uh-huh. You can't see his face very clearly. But the tattoos match those in his jail booking photos."

"Why—"

"Why would a guy keep such incriminating evidence of his own criminal activity? Who the hell knows? I'll bring copies over tomorrow if you want."

"Okay. Thanks, Jimmy."

I hung up and leaned heavily against the back of my chair. The photo would make it simple for me to get an indictment against Danny Thompsen the following Monday, but I dreaded having to see the victim bound and gagged. I knew I would never be able to un-see it.

15

Eight days later, on a Saturday afternoon, Brad Tollefson met Magnolia Barr at the airport and drove her to meet her goddaughter. The vetting had happened quicker than Glenda and I'd selfishly hoped. As Matt Witte had predicted, Magnolia was "squeaky clean." And, though wary, Jen had agreed to meet with her—if Glenda was present.

I so wanted to be there, too. Instead I took the littles to the children's museum and reminded myself every few minutes to savor their excitement at the new exhibits. After hearing, "Mommy! Look!" for the hundredth time, I suggested we head home so Red could nap. The promise of an interim stop at Michael's Frozen Custard sealed the deal.

Glenda finally texted me when I was unwrapping frozen pizzas for dinner. *You free?*

Yes, I typed back.

See you in ten.

I put the pizzas in the oven and buzzed Lily's room on the intercom. "Honey, c'mon up, please."

A few minutes later, she stalked into the kitchen with her everyday thirteen-year-old demeanor—not exactly sullen but certainly not enthusiastic. "What d'ya want?"

What happened to the sweet, anxious-to-please girl I remember? "Would you mind feeding the kiddos in the family room? They're already engrossed in a movie down there."

"Okay—but why can't you do it?"

I stifled a sigh. "Glenda's coming over in a few minutes and I really need to talk with her privately."

Lily's eyes widened. "Is it about Jen's godmother visiting?"

"How did you hear about that?"

"Sarah told me when I was over there yesterday. She just texted to say the lady left and Jen was in her room crying."

I sank onto a chair at the table and took a sip from my mug of cold tea.

"What d'ya think that means?" Lily asked, echoing one of the thoughts swimming in my head.

I shook my head. "I guess we'll see." I stood up and reached into the fridge for a bottle of apple juice. "Grab some paper plates and cups from the pantry. I'll let you know when the pizza's done."

A HALF HOUR LATER, Glenda appeared at the kitchen door and I took her—a proverbial hot mess—into my arms. "Sorry. I wanted to stop crying before I came…but I can't seem to pull it off."

"No worries." I hugged her until her breathing eased. "Let's go sit. D'ya want something to drink?"

She shook her head and followed me into the living room, collapsing onto one end of the sofa. Her face, puffy and blotchy from tears and streaked with melting makeup and mascara, looked like something out of a pirated horror movie.

"It was *so* hard," she said.

"Tell me."

After a few deep breaths, she began. "Jen waited in her room while Magnolia and I talked for a bit. I told her Dr. Peters and I'd been preparing Jen for the meeting. That Jen said she didn't remember her but was willing to get to know her again. That Dr. Peters recommended she not initiate physical contact with her until Jen gave an explicit okay. Magnolia nodded like she understood, but she seemed kinda overwhelmed. And really, really nervous."

Glenda stared out the window for a few moments, and I knew she was reliving the scene in her mind. "When Jen walked into the room, Magnolia was sitting on the couch but she got up like she was in a trance. She hugged Jen and said something like, 'My lord, it really *is* you. Oh, my little Jenny Lou, I've missed you so much. Thank God you're safe.'"

"Did Jen freak?"

"Not at all. I kinda did, though. It felt like I was seeing everything in slow motion. And when Magnolia said 'Jenny Lou,' Jen just got this dreamy look on her face and hugged her back."

"So she *did* remember her?"

"It was obvious she *knew* her but didn't really

remember her. They spent the afternoon going through old photo albums, and Jen didn't recognize anyone but her mom, dad, and sister. Not even her grandfather—and from what Magnolia said, it seems like they were pretty close. It was heartbreaking how she squinted at the pictures and tried to recall. But maybe we were hoping for too much. What do you remember from when you were two or three years old?"

"Just snippets, I guess. And I wouldn't remember people from back then if I'd lost all contact with 'em. How did she react to seeing pictures of her dad?"

"Her eyes never lingered on them long, and sometimes she turned the pages pretty quickly. Magnolia didn't talk about AJ—just about the rest of the family and Magnolia's kids. The whole time she was there, Jen hung on Magnolia's every word, as though her voice was mesmerizing. And I gotta admit it is. That sugary-soft Southern drawl."

"Do you like her?"

Glenda sniffled and blotted her eyes. "Yeah. She seems great."

"Did you talk about her maybe going back to Alabama?"

"No. Brad and Dr. Peters said it's too soon for that. Magnolia's gonna go to church and breakfast with us tomorrow before she heads back. She wants to come to visit again soon."

"Sarah texted Lily to say Jen was crying when her godmother left."

"Uh-huh. Magnolia gave Jen a picture from one of the albums. It'd been taken on Easter, shortly before they left Birmingham. Cassie and the girls were standing under a lush, green tree in the sunshine, wearing fancy dresses and hats and laughing as they posed. Jen's eyes welled up when she saw it. She mumbled thanks and good-bye, then ran to her room.

"I gave her a few minutes before I went to see how she was doing. She'd put the picture on her pillow and was all curled up on the bed crying quietly."

"What'd you do?"

"I sat with her and stroked her back. Asked if she wanted to talk. She nodded and said she was just so *sad*. Sad because she couldn't remember all the people who'd loved her. Sad because she'd forgotten how much she missed her mom and Josie. And sad because she was afraid she'd never be as happy as she looked in the picture. That's when *I* lost it…"

"Because you know she might be right."

"Uh-huh."

16

ON THIS RAINY "SCREEN-FREE SATURDAY," I sat at the kitchen table enjoying a cup of tea and the challenge of the six-star Sudoku puzzle in the morning paper. Abby and Bert had taken the littles to see a matinee. Lily, Sarah, and Jen convened in the dining room to play Sorry! Having just gotten underway, the game was in the mindless phase and I heard them chatting.

I looked up from the puzzle when Jen's voice caught my ear. "So, Lily, were you adopted when you were a baby like Amy and Luke?"

"Uh-huh."

"Did you ever meet your real parents?"

Real parents—one of my most hated phrases.

Lily paused a moment before responding. "My bio mom—Kate—was a friend of my mom's, but I didn't know that until after she died."

"She died? How?"

I held my breath. I'd been proud that during the several years since Kate's death, Lily had learned to speak of her matter-of-factly and without shame, but this situation felt weird to me.

Lily didn't miss a beat. "She was addicted to drugs and died of an overdose. We don't know if she did it on purpose or on accident."

Jen didn't miss a beat, either. "My sister died of an OD, but she did it on purpose."

Sarah, who'd been silent during this conversation, chimed in, "How d'ya know? Did she leave a note?"

"Yeah."

"What'd the note say?" Sarah asked.

"It said 'Sorry,' and she signed it with *x*'s and *o*'s. I was the one who found her. I'd been in the bathroom a really long time, and when I came out, she was dead."

"What did you do?" Lily asked, her voice quivering.

"I freaked and started screaming. I just wish I'd found her in time, so I could've called 911."

"Yeah," Sarah said. "I'm so lucky my brother found me when I cut my wrists. Things would've gotten better for your sister, just like they did for me."

"I'm not so sure," Jen said—sadly, I thought—then rolled the dice and proceeded with the game.

I listened as the conversation changed quickly to the topic of last year's contestants on *The Voice*. *WTF is this world coming to? Suicide is such a common topic that you can talk about it while playing a board game? And then just move on?*

My fingers trembled as I reached in my pocket for my cell phone. *Screen-free Saturday be damned,* I thought as I typed out a text to Matt: *Just overhead Jen say her sister OD'd on purpose and left a note.*

His reply came five minutes later. *Who did she tell?*
Lily and Sarah.

I'd say it's good news. If she told them, maybe she'll agree to tell a jury.

We can hope.

I WENT out onto my screened porch, closing the door behind me. I called Glenda and told her about the girls' conversation. "What should I do, Glen? Should I tell the girls I heard them?"

"That'd be my first inclination, but maybe you should ask Nancy or Dr. Peters first. I know you want her to testify and you don't want to spook her."

"Spook her?"

"Yeah. I mean, she needs to trust you, and eavesdropping on a private conversation isn't exactly a sign of trust."

"Shit, shit, shit! This situation is harder than I thought it'd be."

"I know, kiddo. But Jen's adjusting pretty well and that's my main goal with her. If you can put her dad away, I'd consider that icing on the cake."

IN THE END, I didn't tell Jen about overhearing the suicide conversation. I wish I could say it was a conscious decision not to rock the boat or undermine her trust in me, but in truth I just never got around to deciding.

17

WHILE SITTING AT PANERA, sopping up the last of my broccoli cheddar soup with a piece of baguette, I got a text from Nancy Drummond: *Doc Peters says Jen will talk.*

I popped the gooey morsel into my mouth and typed while I chewed: *Back in the office in ten. Let's discuss then.*

"FOR GOD'S SAKE, CAROLINE," George Cooper said as I followed Nancy into his office half an hour later, "when are you gonna get that leg looked at? The PT's obviously not working."

"As a matter of fact, I'm having an MRI at four thirty today—so you can quit harping at me."

He laughed. "Have a seat and feel free to use the coffee table for a footstool. What'd you guys want to see me about?"

"Jennifer Corbell's shrink called to tell me she's willing to give a formal statement against her father," Nancy replied.

"That's great."

She nodded. "Yeah, but there are a couple of caveats: Jen doesn't want any men around while she's giving her statement—including her GAL. She wants Dr. Peters, Glenda Foster, and Caroline to sit in. And she wants me to do the interview."

George scowled. "I don't have an issue with the 'no men' thing, but Caroline can't sit in and prosecute the case as well. And I'm not crazy about you doing the interview—it kinda blurs your helper role. Would those be deal breakers?"

"I'm not sure," Nancy said, "but let me call and see. Glenda and Jen were still in Dr. Peters' office as of a few minutes ago." She placed the call while George and I looked on and turned on the speaker when the psychologist finally got on the line. "Caroline Spencer and I are here with our boss, George Cooper, and we're talking about the arrangements to debrief Jen. Are she and Mrs. Foster still there?"

"Yes."

"Caroline won't be able to participate in the interview, and it's really not advisable for me to do the questioning. I'd be happy to sit in with you and Glenda so Jen will feel truly supported. But we really need someone from law enforcement to handle it."

"Hang on a minute while I discuss it with them," Dr. Peters said. We sat listening to her classical "hold" music, staring at Nancy's phone, during what seemed like an interminable wait.

Dr. Peters chuckled as she resumed the call. "Jen says it's okay. She'll talk with a cop, as long as it's 'the blond guy.' I assume you know who she means?"

I laughed. "Detective Witte from Janesville PD. He's a great choice. What do your schedules look like in the next several days?"

"I hate to throw a monkey wrench into things," Dr. Peters said, "but I'm heading out of town at noon tomorrow and won't be back for a week. I'm willing to meet tomorrow morning at nine if you can get it together that quickly. Mrs. Foster says she and Jen can make it work."

Nancy and I exchanged quick glances and nods. "Let's plan on it," I said. "I'm sure Detective Witte will rearrange his schedule to be there if he has to. Where would you like to meet?"

Dr. Peters must've covered the phone with her hand because we could hear muffled voices in the background. "Jen would be most comfortable doing this at the Fosters' house," she finally told us.

"All right," Nancy said. "We'll see you there tomorrow morning. And thanks for working this out."

I texted Matt, who responded immediately. *Nine tomorrow is fine. I'll call you in a bit to put together a list of questions.*

"Matt's in," I told my colleagues.

"Thank heaven," George said with a sardonic smile. "I felt like we were brokering some Middle East peace deal or something."

"Shame on you, boss," Nancy said. "This is sensitive stuff."

He nodded. "I know. Which is why I didn't bring up videotaping the interview. But try to persuade Jen and her foster mom to allow it. It'll give us the best record and maybe preclude her having to be interviewed again."

"Will do."

NANCY and I'd spent a grueling afternoon on the phone with Matt and Jimmy, trying to decide what questions needed to be asked of Jen and how to phrase them in the least upsetting manner. We'd come up with a good list, but I worried Jen would clam up midway through it. And I wouldn't blame her if she did.

Now, sitting at the imaging center and waiting for my injection of contrasting dye to reach its destination before my MRI, I practiced a few breathing exercises to clear my mind. I hadn't taken the time to worry about the scan or what the results might dictate. *If I need surgery, so be it. At least I'll know what's wrong and can get on with recovery.* I played several games of Words with Friends. I caught up on my Facebook feed and *liked* a few posts.

Finally, the radiology tech—a kind-eyed woman smelling of lavender—came to lead me to the changing room. "I'm Jane," she said, "and I'll be doing your scan. Have you ever had an MRI before?"

"Uh-uh."

"You'll need to lie still for about forty-five minutes. Your head won't be in the tube, so claustrophobia shouldn't be a problem. The machine's obnoxiously noisy, but you'll have sound-blocking headphones. What kind of music would you like to listen to?"

Her question—prompting the most innocuous decision I'd had to make in a month—flummoxed me. "Uh… I dunno. Classical, I guess."

She smiled and put her arm around me, guiding me to the bench in front of the lockers. "Long day, huh?"

I felt my eyelids burning and couldn't speak.

"Try to relax. This'll be a piece of cake."

Though uncomfortable, the test *was* a piece of cake. Jane's reassuring voice came through the headphones every now and then, asking if I was okay. Each time, I answered yes. I grinned and gave her a thumbs-up when the machine stopped its thumping and clanging and the table slid me out of the tube.

"Good job," she said, helping me to my feet, but she seemed reluctant to make eye contact.

A jolt of panic shot through me. *What's wrong? Did she see something bad on the scan?* I collapsed back onto the exam table, too woozy to trust my legs. "Sorry. I'm a little dizzy."

"Take your time," she said, looking directly at me with no hint of alarm. "Probably low blood sugar. I'll get you some juice."

When she returned, I took a deep breath and asked, "Did you notice anything on the scan?"

"Oh, honey," she said, fitting the tiny straw into the box of apple juice, "I have no idea what I'm seeing in there. As soon as the radiologist looks at the images, he'll let your doctor know. Probably by tomorrow afternoon. The next day at the latest."

Seems like she's telling the truth. After a few sips of juice, I warily got to my feet. "I'm good," I said. "Thank you."

MY MOTHER-IN-LAW GREETED me at the door when I got home ten minutes later. "Hope you don't mind that we let Amanda go early," Abby said. "Bert and I were bored and decided to bring pizza for the kiddos."

I had to laugh. "And what else?"

"Oh," she said with a sheepish grin, "just a batch of cookies I made this afternoon and stuff for ice cream sundaes. How was your test?"

"Way to change the subject," I said, kissing her cheek. "The scan went okay. The tech couldn't tell me anything today, but hopefully I'll get the results tomorrow."

"We've been praying about it."

"Thanks, Abby." *I'm glad you have, 'cause I haven't found time.*

18

THE NEXT MORNING'S guilty plea and motion hearings were godsends for me—distracting me from worrying about Jen's interview and the results of my MRI. Matt Witte texted me just as I was leaving the courthouse after the last hearing. *We're done. I'll bring the tape over after lunch.*

Eating at my desk, I typed back. *Come when you want.*

MATT AND JIMMY knocked at my doorjamb shortly after one o'clock. "Sorry it took so long," Matt said, holding up a flash drive. "We went to have Hector copy it first."

"Makes sense," I said. "How'd it go?"

They sat in my visitors' chairs and Matt paused to consider his response. "Hardest interview I've ever done. But I think we got what we need. Let's watch and see what you think."

He handed me the drive and I plugged it into my computer, turning the twenty-seven-inch monitor to face them. I wheeled my desk chair around next to them and used my upside-down wastebasket as a footstool.

After several seconds of blue screen, the video began. Jen faced the camera, sitting on a couch flanked by Glenda and Dr. Peters. Nancy Drummond sat in a wing-back chair off to one side but angled toward the camera. Matt wasn't visible but gave the date, time, and location, then greeted the participants by name.

I found myself scratching a raw spot on my scalp as the interview commenced:

"Thanks for agreeing to talk with us, Jennifer," Matt said. "It's really important and very brave of you."

Jen nodded shyly.

"I know some of this will be hard. You've got three fine women here for support, but you're the one who has to answer the questions. If you need to take a break, or if a particular question is too difficult to deal with, you let me know. Okay?"

Another nod.

"Great. Let's start by having you tell me your full name and how old you are."

"Jennifer Louise Corbell but I prefer Jen. I'm fourteen."

"And your father is Ambrose Josiah Corbell, sometimes called AJ. Is that correct?"

"Yes."

"You understand that a federal warrant has been issued to arrest your father and one other man for alleged crimes against you and your sister?"

"Yes."

"What was your sister's name, and how old was she when she passed away?"

"Josielynn Pickford Corbell. Her real dad—Mr. Pickford—died before she was born, and AJ adopted her when he married my mom. She didn't have a middle name before, but my mom wanted to keep Pickford... What was the next question? Oh, wait—she was sixteen when she died. When she killed herself, that is."

"We'll come to that in a bit. I'd like to start at the beginning, though. We know you were born in Birmingham, Alabama, and that you moved to Pensacola, Florida, when you were about four years old. Do you remember that?"

"Sort of. Mostly I remember living in Arkansas. First in Little Rock and later near Hot Springs."

"Where did you and your sister go to school?"

She shook her head. "We didn't. I mean we wanted to go but my dad wouldn't let us. He said the Arkansas schools were full of trouble. My mom was a teacher before we were born and she homeschooled us."

"How long did she homeschool you?"

Jen paused to consider the question. "I guess till about a year before she died. When she got too weak, Josie and I just studied on our own."

"Your mother died two years ago. Were you still living near Hot Springs then?"

"Uh-huh."

"It sounds like she was sick for a while. Do you know what was wrong with her?"

"Not for sure, and she never went to the doctor. But I think she had anorexia—after she died, Josie and

I saw a documentary on TV about it. And I think my dad caused it."

"How do you think he caused it?"

"Well, he was constantly telling us to watch what we ate and would say mean stuff to us if we gained weight. Sometimes he called Mom names, like Porky or Hungry Heifer. Eventually Mom hardly ate at all, and all she wanted to do was take pills and sleep." Jen's voice trailed off and she leaned against Glenda on the sofa.

"Take your time and tell us when you're ready," Matt said.

After a big intake of breath, Jen continued. "One morning Josie and I woke up and Mom wasn't in bed. We found her on the floor of the shower with blood on her head, and it didn't seem like she was breathing. Dad wasn't home and we didn't know what to do. We didn't have a phone, so Josie ran to the closest house— like maybe a half a mile away—and they called an ambulance. But it was too late."

"I'm sorry." Matt paused to let Jen gather herself, then asked, "What happened next?"

"My dad drove up when the ambulance was there and followed it to the hospital. They knew she was already dead, but he hadda fill out forms and stuff. The autopsy said she had a heart attack."

"Did you stay in Arkansas after your mom died?"

"Just for a couple months. Josie and I were, like, crying all the time, and my dad was worried it was too painful there. He got some money from our mom's life insurance and said we'd use it for"—she stifled a sob —"for a new start."

Dr. Peters spoke up. "Could we take a short break? I need to check in with Jen to see if she's prepared to go on."

"Of course," Matt replied, and the recording stopped.

She's not the only one who needs a break, I thought, rubbing my throbbing temples. I got up, pushed the pause button, and looked at the guys. "Until that last question, she was so dispassionate—almost like she was drugged," I said.

"Yeah," Matt said. "I noticed that, too. After the interview, I asked Dr. Peters whether Jen was sedated. She said no, but they'd practiced talking about this stuff before so Jen could remain pretty detached when she spoke with us. Kind of a protective device."

"Ready?" I asked. They nodded and I resumed the playback.

"For the record, Dr. Peters," Matt said, "do you believe Jen is ready to proceed?"

"Yes. We completed a brief desensitization exercise, and she's prepared for your questions."

"All right. Jen, tell us about this 'new start.'"

"My dad sold all the stuff in the house we were renting and we packed up and left. He told us we could each take only one suitcase because we'd be traveling light. We got in the car and drove to Kansas City. I remember we stayed in a beautiful hotel that, like, looked out over this fancy shopping area. He bought us some new clothes and we had room service and got to watch movies on TV. It was really nice, and Josie and I tried to have fun but we still couldn't stop crying. Then he started giving us pills so we wouldn't be so sad."

"Did the pills help?"

Jen looked puzzled. "Well...at first they just made us sleepy, but after we got used to them, they made us feel kinda peaceful and happy. Later, when I was in the hospital and in treatment, I learned that the pills were for pain, not for depression. That makes sense now."

"Do you remember what else happened while you were in Kansas City?"

Jen closed her eyes and nodded. "That was where the first man came to have sex with Josie." She paused, but Matt waited for her to go on. "We'd moved to a different hotel by then. Not as fancy. We had two rooms with a connecting door. One night there was a knock on the outside door and my dad answered. He brought this man into the room that Josie and I shared and said I should go into the other room and close the door. I did, and I heard Josie saying something like, 'Don't make me do it. Please!' Then my dad came in and waited with me till the man left. Josie was crying when we went back in, but Dad hugged her and said she was a good girl. I remember he gave her another pill and she calmed down."

"You said the man had sex with Josie. How do you know that?"

"She told me the next day. She said Dad told her she had to because we needed money."

"Did there ever come a time when your dad asked you to have sex with someone?"

"Uh-huh." She waited a beat, as if gathering the courage to continue her account. "The first time was at a hotel in Chicago. A man and his son came to our rooms. The man said he wanted to give his son a present for his fifteenth birthday because he'd never had sex before. My dad smiled at me and said that was good—that it would be my first time, too. He'd given me a pill just before they got there, and the whole thing was almost like a dream. It was over pretty quick, but I remember bleeding and it hurt."

"When you say 'it,' what do you mean?" Matt asked quietly.

"I laid on my back and he put his penis in my vagina and kept moving until he came."

"Did he use a condom?"

"Uh-huh. My dad watched to be sure before he and the other man left the room. After it was over, I just laid there and cried, and my dad came in and snuggled with me. Then I heard the boy go into the other room. Josie told me later the man and his son both had sex with her."

Before Matt could ask another question, Jen spoke again. "It kept happening. I didn't want to do it, but Dad would cry and say he was afraid we'd have to go to foster homes because he couldn't support us. He'd go out looking for work every day but said no one would hire him because someone he used to work for in Alabama lied and, like, gave him a bad recommendation."

"When he went out to look for work, did he leave you and Josie alone in the hotels?"

"Uh-huh. He told us not to use the phone or answer the door, but we got to watch anything on TV we wanted."

"Did you ever think of running away?"

Jen shook her head. "We'd talk about it once in a while, but where else were we gonna go? Dad was nice to us a lot of the time. When we went out to eat, we got to pick whatever we wanted off the menu. He took us to an amusement park in Wisconsin once…"

We all startled when my phone rang. I stood up quickly, hanging on to my desk for balance, and hobbled over to pause the video and answer it. "Caroline Spencer."

"Hello, it's Dr. Woorley calling. I'm sorry to disturb you at work, but I wanted to let you know about the radiology report."

I leaned against the edge of the desk. "Thanks for getting back to me," I said, my voice quivering. "What'd they say?"

"They found a mass on the facet of your femur or thighbone, where the posterior cruciate ligament attaches it to your shin."

"What do you mean by a mass?" I could feel my heart racing and see my peripheral vision narrowing. I felt Matt easing me into the desk chair he'd wheeled over beside me.

"A tumor," Dr. Woorley said. "But I don't want you jumping to conclusions. More often than not, bone tumors are benign rather than cancerous."

"You can't tell from the scan?" I asked, hearing hysteria in my voice.

"No—we won't know until it's biopsied."

He knows more than he's saying, I thought but didn't have the courage to dig deeper. "When can I have the biopsy?"

"First you'll need to make a choice about who you want to do it, and I recommend an orthopedic surgeon. I had Kimberly email you a list of folks in the area. You can schedule something yourself or give us a buzz and she'll coordinate it. We can usually arrange to have it done pretty quickly—perhaps within a couple of weeks."

A couple of weeks? I can't imagine being in suspense that long.

"I've got another patient waiting," he said, "but feel free to call me at home tonight if you want to talk further. My number's in the book."

"Okay, Doc. Thanks." I sat speechless in my chair for what probably felt to Matt and Jimmy like an eternity.

Matt cleared his throat and I looked up. "What can we do to help?" he asked.

I closed my eyes and raked my fingers through my hair. "I just assumed it'd be a torn ligament or cartilage or something. I never expected they'd find a tumor." I glanced at the agents, touched by the concern I saw in their eyes. "He says it's most likely benign, but I need to find an orthopedic surgeon to do the biopsy. And it could take two weeks to arrange. Shit, shit, shit!"

"My ex-wife works at Froedtert Hospital in Milwaukee but knows docs all over the state," Matt said. "I'll ask if she's got any recommendations."

"Good. And my doctor said his assistant sent me a list." I logged into my email and clicked on the message, printing the attachment. "Here it is. Maybe see if she knows any of these people?"

He took a picture of the list with his phone and typed out a text. "She's usually pretty quick to answer messages. I'll let you know what she says."

I sighed. "Guys, I'm not up to watching a minute more of this video right now. Can we do it another day?"

Jimmy popped up from his chair, as though he couldn't escape fast enough. "Sure. You can keep the flash drive here—we have more copies."

"Thanks, Jimmy," I said as he walked out the door.

Matt rose slowly from his chair. "You oughta head home. I can give you a lift and find somebody to shuttle your car to you later if you want."

"That's a lot of trouble..."

"What are friends for?"

I nodded. "That'd be good, Matt. I'm not thinking too clearly right now."

We made the ten-minute drive to my house in silence. "Your van's here," Matt said with bewilderment, nodding to my driveway.

"Yeah, our nanny needs it to pick up the kids. I've been renting a car since I hurt my leg so I don't have to take the bus to work. The rental's at the office."

"Ohhh. Then why don't I just pick you up tomorrow morning and take you back to the office?"

"You're gonna come all the way from Janesville to drive me to work?"

He laughed. "No, I gotta be at the FBI office in the a.m. anyway. Jimmy and I are meeting with Hector to sort through more electronic records, looking for clues as to AJ's whereabouts."

"Okay, then," I said, opening the passenger door. "It's a deal."

19

No one heard me when I walked in. The littles were all at the dining room table with sour looks on their faces, the twins playing rudimentary math games on their LeapPads and Red squirming in her booster seat trying to grab a fat red crayon just beyond her reach. Grace sat in the corner flipping through a *Better Homes and Gardens* magazine.

I put on a smile and knocked on the doorframe. "Greetings, dear ones. How's everybody doing?"

"Mommy!" the kids yelled in unison as I leaned down to kiss Red. The twins slid down from their chairs and ran to hug me.

"I didn't expect you home so early," Grace said with a stony expression. "Amy and Luke have just begun those math games you wanted them to practice, and I haven't even started supper."

Why in God's name don't I find a replacement for this sour-puss? And math games are supposed to be fun, *not a chore.*

"Y'know what, Grace, I think they deserve a little

fresh air right now—and maybe some Chinese food for dinner. You're welcome to head out."

She gave me a tight-lipped smile. "If you're sure."

"I'm sure."

THE LITTLES and I had just finished a hotly contested game of croquet in the front yard when Glenda pulled to the curb. Lily and Jen got out of the car and ran up the sidewalk. "Can Jen stay for dinner?" Lily asked as she breezed past me.

"If it's okay with Glen." I motioned for my friend to roll down her window. "Okay if Jen stays here to eat?"

"If I can stay, too. Hank took Jake and Sarah to pick up another rescue dog that we're gonna foster, and I don't want to eat alone."

I grinned. *This is just what the doctor ordered—a house full of people to take my mind off my "mass."* "Of course. We're ordering Chinese—come look at the menu."

Once Red and the twins were settled in the family room to watch *Shaun the Sheep*, I joined Glenda in the kitchen, where she'd already drawn red stars next to several menu items. "Dominic just texted to say he's running behind and to eat without him," I told her, "but I'll get him an order of moo shoo pork."

She put the pen down on the table. "Geez, I wouldn't have invited myself if I'd known he was coming."

"Why not?" I asked, reaching for two wineglasses on the top shelf of a cupboard. "It's not like you'd be interrupting a romantic tryst or anything—I've got four kids, remember?"

"Point taken. When's the last time you were alone together anyway?"

"Last Saturday. Abby and Bert took the kids up to Great Wolf for an overnight."

Glenda grinned. "You're blushing! I guess that means you two remembered what goes where!"

I threw a dishtowel at her. "Do you want Pinot Grigio or Cab?"

"Whatever you're having."

I poured two glasses of Cabernet and sat down at the table to look at the menu. I called in our order and leaned back to enjoy my first sip. "I wanted to start drinking at three thirty but I guess waiting made me appreciate it even more."

My friend nodded. "I dropped Jen off at tennis camp after yesterday's interview, and I was sorely tempted to hit the Laurel Tavern for a Bloody Mary. Instead I went home and took a Xanax and a nap."

"I can imagine you needed it. I watched part of the video today and that was hard enough. How'd Jen react after it was over?"

A lone tear wandered down Glenda's cheek, and she brushed it away impatiently. "She actually did better than me. She didn't say much, but her mood seemed lighter. I told her she could stay home from camp, but she said she didn't want to miss it. Sarah tells me she's got a crush on her doubles partner, who's supposedly a very sweet guy."

I spun my wine around in my glass a few times, then took another sip. "I gotta say that's pretty amazing. After all the shit she's been through—which must've completely distorted her view of sexual relationships—she's still able to get a crush on somebody?"

"I know. Caroline, it broke my heart to watch Jen answering questions about what her dad and all those men did to her and Josie. I'm glad she found the courage to do it, 'cause I think it'll make her stronger in the end. But I couldn't help picturing some of the things she described, and I got so pissed off I almost came out of my skin. I mean, how can there be so much evil in the world?"

"I wish I knew. And I wish I knew where her shit-bird of a father was right now. I'd send the meanest of the mean cops to arrest him and hope like hell he'd resist."

WE SPREAD the carryout containers and a stack of paper plates on the dining room table and had our feast there. I said a silent prayer of thanks as sounds of laughter and childish chatter echoed from the walls.

Jen showed the kids how to eat with chopsticks. "Where'd ya learn that?" Luke asked in amazement.

"My dad taught me," she replied without missing a beat.

Glenda and I exchanged wary glances, but the conversation moved on and our moment of discomfort passed as quickly as it'd come on.

Amy, Luke, and Red went downstairs to finish their movie. Lily and Jen cleared the table and went to Lily's room to watch a different video on her computer. Dominic walked in as Glenda and I were heading to the living room with what was left of the wine.

He hugged me and said hi to Glenda. "Sorry I missed dinner."

"No biggie," I said. "There's a container of moo shoo

in the fridge if you want it. You can eat in the living room."

"Thanks. I'll just go grab a beer for now."

Glenda curled up in my favorite overstuffed chair and I took one end of the couch, resting my feet on the coffee table. "He gets more and more handsome every time I see him," she said to me, none too quietly.

"Shush," I said, as I heard his footsteps approaching.

"What am I missing?" he said, settling in next to me.

"Nothing," I said with a nervous laugh. "Glen's just giving me a hard time."

Dominic took a long pull on his beer, then turned to me. "Did you hear from the doctor today?"

His abrupt question took me by surprise though I knew, of course, that he'd ask it at some point. "Yeah. He called around three."

"And?"

"And it seems I have a tumor on my femur."

Glenda sat forward in her chair. "Oh, shit, kiddo. I completely forgot to ask… even after you told me you wanted to start drinking at three thirty. Do they think it's cancerous?"

"Dr. Woorley says benign bone tumors are more common than malignant ones, but we won't know until I have a biopsy." I paused for a moment to recall my phone conversation with him. "I've got a sneaking suspicion that they believe it's cancer but just don't want me to freak out till we know for sure."

Dominic reached for my hand and squeezed it. "You haven't told your children, have you?"

"No. I told Lily that I'd asked Dr. Woorley to order a scan to diagnose the problem but nothing more specific."

"Good," he said, easing his grip on my hand. "The less they know right now the better."

Glenda raised an eyebrow but didn't comment.

"When will they do the biopsy?" Dominic asked.

"I don't even know who 'they' are yet. I've got a list of orthopedic surgeons to call tomorrow—the doc says it should be someone who specializes in oncology. I have no idea how long it'll take to get in."

"I'll make the calls for you," he said. "I can probably be more objective about what they have to say."

"No, thanks. This is something I need to do myself."

Dominic didn't reply, and the ensuing silence felt charged with emotion.

Glenda put her empty wineglass on the end table, pushed herself out of the chair, and came to kiss me on the head. "Jen and I'd better get home to see our new foster dog. Call me tomorrow, okay, kiddo?"

I nodded and watched her go. I couldn't help feeling like she'd abandoned me with a stranger.

Dominic volunteered to help me put the littles to bed—something he'd never done before. "Thanks, but I've got it," I replied. I avoided his gaze as he left my house to go rest up for an early-morning surveillance.

I let Luke play in the tub with his baking-powder-powered submarine for an extra ten minutes and painted the girls' toenails after their bath. Three bedtime stories later, we called it a night.

My cell phone rang at ten o'clock—Glenda. "I can see by the little green dot that you're playing Words with Friends, so I know I didn't wake you."

I sat up in bed and fluffed the pillows against the headboard. "Guess I'll just have to start calling you Nancy Drew."

"How you doin'?"

"Pretty good."

"You're not worrying?"

"I'm trying not to…. Remember the Russian agent in the Tom Hanks movie *Bridge of Spies?* Tom Hanks asks him if he's worried about what'll happen when he gets back to Russia, and the guy just looks at him and says, 'Would it help?'"

She chuckled softly. "Yeah."

"That's what I keep asking myself—will worrying help?"

"I'm impressed. Keep it up."

I waited a beat, unable to think up any small talk.

"So…" she finally said, "you seemed kinda disturbed about Dominic's reaction to your news."

"I guess I was."

"How come?"

"I can't quite put my finger on it, but I felt like he was trying to take over. I mean, saying not to tell the kids. And that he could be more objective than me about who should do my biopsy. It just rubbed me the wrong way."

"He loves you. People can get weird when someone they love has a health scare."

"Yeah. I guess we'll see. How's the Fosters' new foster dog?"

"Ah—time to change the subject, huh?"

"Uh-huh."

"He's a cute little mutt—kinda needy but in a sweet way."

"Thanks for the call, Glen. Love you."

"You, too, kiddo."

20

I'D PARKED my mommy-van in the driveway after taking the kids to their activities just as Matt pulled up to the curb. "I need to go grab my briefcase and another cup of coffee," I said to him. "Want one, too?"

He nodded and followed me into the kitchen. "Have a seat," I said. "Do you have time to wait while I brew another pot?"

"Uh-huh," he said, sinking into a chair at the table. "I'm not due at Jimmy's office until ten."

I divided the remaining coffee into two to-go mugs and set about making more.

"I talked with Hannah—my ex—last night."

I sat down across from him and stirred milk into my cup. "Did she know any of the docs on that list?"

"Not personally, but she Googled 'em and made some calls. She recommends you skip the Madison guys. They're all great orthopedic surgeons, but none specializes in orthopedic oncology. There's a woman at Froedtert who does—Gianna Giacomino is her name. Hannah knows her and says she's the best around."

"She's in Milwaukee."

"I know it's not as convenient as here, but Hannah says it's advisable to have an ace do the biopsy. They get better snippets of the tumor and make sure not to bollix up vital areas around it."

I laughed. "Were those the technical terms she used?"

"Glad to see you can find some humor in this," he said with a smile. "Anyway, it's completely your decision. But Hannah gave me a direct number for Giacomino's nurse and said you can mention her name if you decide to call."

I got up to pour us more coffee and felt a sudden sense of clarity. "If you don't mind, I'll call right now."

"Sure," he said, reaching into his breast pocket for a piece of paper. "I wrote it all down—the nurse's name is Susan. D'you want some privacy?"

"Nah," I said, placing a pad of paper and pen on the table. I texted my office to say I'd be in late. I dialed the nurse's number and, to my surprise, she answered in person on the third ring. "Hi, Ms. Spencer. Hannah told me you might be in touch."

"I don't really know the protocol here," I said, "but my GP called me yesterday to say they found a tumor on my femur and I need a biopsy. I'm wondering if Dr. Giacomino is taking new patients."

"As a matter of fact, she is," Susan said. And with calm efficiency, she explained the process: they'd request records from my doctor and physical therapist, including a copy of the MRI scan. Dr. G, as she called her, would review the records before the initial consult and then schedule the procedure. "She's got an opening next Friday at ten o'clock. Would that work?"

I glanced at the calendar on my phone. "Uh, yeah. How long would it be before she could do the actual biopsy?"

"It's usually within a few weeks." She must've heard my intake of breath because she added, "I know it sounds like a long wait, but bone tumors are usually benign or slow growing even if malignant. I'll email you a consent form so we can gather the records—if you sign it electronically, we'll get right on it."

I hung up and called Glenda. "Are you doing anything next Friday morning?"

"Yeah. Meeting with the superintendent for that confab I told you about. You know—staffing for next year. Why?"

"I'm meeting with a doctor in Milwaukee and thought I should have an extra set of ears with me. Not to worry, though, I'll find someone."

"You should really ask Dominic to go. You don't want him to feel shut out, do you?"

"You're probably right." *I'll ask him when hell freezes over.* "Talk to you later."

I looked up from the phone, lost in thought and puzzling over my next move, halfway surprised to find Matt still there.

"I'd be happy to take you if you want," he said. "I've got vacation time up the wazoo."

"Thanks, but I suspect my mother-in-law would be hurt if I didn't ask her." *Maybe, but you* know *you'd never ask her—she can't hear for beans, and she'd worry herself to death.*

"Okay. Just keep it in mind."

I stood up abruptly. "What say we top off our mugs and head to work?"

GEORGE COOPER STOPPED me in the hallway near my office. "Nancy told me the interview with Jennifer was productive. Any thoughts on filing a superseding indictment based on what she said?"

"I haven't finished watching the video yet. That's my plan for today."

"My mistake. I saw Agent McGee yesterday and I thought he said he was coming to look at it with you."

"He did, but something came up and I had to leave early."

"There's no rush. Just thought I'd ask." He took a few steps, then turned back to see me leaning against the wall. "I meant to ask, did you get the results from your scan?"

I nodded but couldn't trust my voice to speak without breaking.

"Ah…geez," he said as he put his arm around my shoulder. "Bad news?"

"Uh-huh. A tumor. Good chance it's benign, but I'm still scared shitless."

He walked me to my office and ushered me into my chair, then sat on the desk facing me. "Tell me about it."

George listened without comment until I finished. "I like the idea about the Milwaukee doc," he said with a smile, "and someone with a cool name like Gianna Giacomino's gotta be good. Now quit crying and tell me what I can do to help."

I sniffled a few times and wiped my cheeks with my fingers. "Please keep this under your hat for now. Matt and Jimmy were here when I got the call yesterday so they know, but I'd rather the whole office didn't. At least not till I get the biopsy results."

He twisted an imaginary key in front of his mouth. "My lips are sealed. Now why don't you go home and relax?"

"If I go home, I'll just worry. I need the distraction."

George stood up to leave and made a sweeping gesture toward my desk. "Have at it then."

I CHECKED both my email and snail mail: the only thing that caught my eye was an FD-302 that Jimmy'd sent me —the report of a Pensacola FBI agent's interview with AJ Corbell's parents. *Wow! I didn't know they'd been located.* I started reading.

> *Arthur and Margaret (nee Robinson) Corbell were interviewed in their apartment at the Buena Vista Senior Center in Pensacola, FL. They confirmed that Ambrose Josiah Corbell (DOB: 6/17/78) is their only child. They reported his childhood was unremarkable, he was healthy, and had no known problems with substance abuse or delinquent behavior. He received average grades in school and was confirmed in the Methodist church. However, Arthur Corbell stated he asked Ambrose to move out when he was eighteen because he quit going to church and refused to follow their house rules.*
>
> *The couple had no contact whatsoever with Ambrose until about ten years ago when he, his wife, and two daughters came to their house uninvited. The Corbells had previously been unaware that their son was married and that he had children. Margaret located a photograph taken during the visit, depicting*

Ambrose, Cassie, Josie, and Jenny Corbell. Ambrose told his parents the family had relocated to Pensacola and promised to visit soon. However, they later learned the phone number he gave them was not in service, and they never heard from him again.

Margaret Corbell was tearful during the interview. She said she regretted sending their son out on his own at such a young, impressionable age and was sorry she had missed the opportunity to know her only grandchildren.

Arthur Corbell caught up with this agent outside the building after the interview concluded. He stated he and his wife had not been completely forthright about their son's childhood behavior. He stated Ambrose had been arrested at the age of fifteen for setting fire to a neighbor's shed, and several months later for assaulting a classmate. Arthur stated Ambrose had spent about ninety days in a juvenile facility as a result.

Hmmm—from arson, assault, and juvie to the lead in a high school play. *Sociopath?* I made a note on my legal pad, *AJ's juvie file still available?* It was a long shot but worth checking.

LATER, when I could find nothing more on my desk to sidetrack me, I inserted the flash drive into my computer and settled in to watch more of Jen's interview. A few seconds after Jen had mentioned her father taking them to an amusement park—as evidence of his goodness—I noticed Nancy Drummond tugging on her ear almost imperceptibly. Neither Glenda, Dr. Peters, nor Jen had appeared to see it, but Matt obviously had.

"Ladies, I'm sorry to interrupt," he said, "but I just got a message and need to answer it. Five-minute break?"

Jen and the women nodded, and the screen turned blue.

When the picture returned, Matt asked—in a very soothing voice, "Jen, you told us a few minutes ago that your dad came in to snuggle with you after you had sex for the first time. Did he ever have sex with you or touch you inappropriately?"

Jen waited a beat, then hung her head. "Not with me, he didn't. Just Josie."

"Did he have sexual intercourse with her?"

"Uh-huh. Almost every day."

"Do you remember when it started?"

"Not exactly. But it was before Mom died. He would come into our room at night and try to be quiet, but I could hear them and I watched one time. Like, I couldn't believe it was happening."

"Did your mother know?"

"We told her, but she didn't believe us. I remember she was pretty out of it from the pills, and she said something like, 'Don't ever say such a thing. Your daddy loves you and would never hurt you.' Josie hated it and hated him. Sometimes she'd say, 'Why me? Why not Jen?' and he'd say that I was his flesh and blood and that'd be just wrong."

I pushed the *pause* button and took a deep breath, trying to get the image of Jen's face out of my mind. She'd answered Matt's questions—and the ones Nancy'd obviously suggested he ask—without making eye contact and with a wooden expression. *How in God's name do you recover from trauma like this? Seeing your mother waste away. Seeing your father repeatedly rape your sister. Being forced to have sex with strangers.* My stomach lurched and I had to swallow the bile it produced.

I texted Matt and Jimmy, *This vid is making me physically ill. Tell me you've found a way to catch this MF'er.*

Matt replied, *I wish.*

I simply couldn't watch more. I buzzed George. "I'm leaving for the day after all. Maybe catch a matinee."

"Good. Whatever's on your desk'll keep. Have a good weekend."

21

I SAT at my desk Monday morning, contemplating the busy week ahead. School would start for the twins on Wednesday and for Lily the following day. I'd meet Dr. Giacomino on Friday morning.

I tried to silence the niggling voice in the back of my mind that kept saying, "Tumor, tumor, tumor." *So what if it's a tumor—it's probably benign. And even if it is malignant, a diagnosis of cancer isn't a death sentence. They've made great strides in treatment. You'll be around to raise your kids.*

Stop it! Focus on work.

First and foremost, I needed to finish watching the video of Jen's debriefing. Armed with a sticky caramel roll —and a package of baby wipes to clean my gooey hands —and a cup of Barriques coffee, I leaned back in my chair and pushed *play*.

"Did you or Josie ever try again to tell your mother— or another adult—about your father abusing her?"

Jen shook her head. "There weren't any other

adults in our lives. Mom kept getting sicker and sicker and we didn't want to upset her. There wasn't anything she could do about it anyway."

"Do you know how your father advertised the prostitution business? And whether he had anyone else helping him run the business—a partner perhaps?"

"I'm not sure. Lemme think." After a moment, she began speaking again. "If he had a partner, Josie and I never knew about it. I think he got business on the Internet. He was always looking at his laptop or his smart phone, and he took them with him wherever he went—even in the bathroom. Maybe he met customers when he was out looking for work… Come to think of it, he probably never really looked for work."

"Did you ever get a look at the laptop or phone? Or see his email address or cell phone number?"

"No way," Jen said. "I remember one time Josie glanced over his shoulder for a second to see what he was doing on the computer. He slammed the lid shut and yelled that if either of us tried that again, he'd stop giving us our pills."

"Were you afraid of what would happen if you didn't have the pills?"

"Yeah. Sometimes he didn't give them to us at the usual time, like if he was out longer than usual or something, and we'd start to sweat and get headaches. It didn't feel good, that's for sure."

I stopped the video and stood up to stretch. Matt had told me he'd ask Jen about her sister's death. It would be important to see if her recorded statement matched the one I'd overheard her telling Lily and Sarah. I suspected those questions would be next. *Please be consistent, kiddo.*

I resumed the replay.

Matt took an audible breath before he began. "Jen, the toxicology reports done by the medical examiners indicate Josie's cause of death was a lethal amount of oxycodone. Do you know how so much of the drug came to be in her system?"

Jen lowered her gaze. "Uh-huh."

"How?"

"She saved up pieces of the pills that Dad gave her —she'd, like, bite 'em in half and only swallow enough to keep the withdrawal away—and took them all at one time. To commit suicide."

"Did you know she was going to do it?"

Jen brushed a tear from her cheek with the back of her hand. "Not until after. But we'd talked about it lots of times. You know, like, how we'd do it. I always said I'd fill up the bathtub really full and drown myself, but she said my reflexes would kick in and make me come up for air. She said she'd start hoarding the pills AJ gave her and take an overdose one day. And she did."

"Did you see her take the pills?"

"No," Jen said quietly. "I was taking a bath when she did it—using the motel shampoo to make as many bubbles as I could and pretending I was at a fancy spa or something. I guess time, like, got away from me. When I came out, I found a note and she was dead."

"She left a note?" Matt asked.

"Yeah. It said 'Sorry' and she signed it with *x*'s and *o*'s."

"What happened to the note?"

"I tore it up into little pieces and flushed it down the toilet. I don't know why. I guess I just freaked out."

Who wouldn't have? I thought.

With Matt's gentle questioning, Jen went on to describe how she could see Josie wasn't breathing and had tried to take her pulse. At that point, Jen said, she just started screaming and eventually the police came.

"Thanks for telling us, Jen," Matt said. "I know this isn't easy. And we're almost done."

Jen took a deep breath. "Okay."

"Another thing they found during your sister's autopsy was marks around her wrists and ankles, suggesting she'd been tied up. Can you tell us anything about that?"

"Uh-huh. Sometimes our dad let customers tie Josie up, like, to the corners of the bed. Or sometimes just her hands tied behind her back. But they'd have to put a scarf in her mouth to keep her from yelling 'cause she hated it so much."

"Did your dad help the customers do this?"

"Sometimes, or once in a while he'd just give her extra pills so she wouldn't fight it. I guess some customers liked it when she fought them, though."

"Jen, were you ever tied up by a customer or your dad?"

"No, 'cause he said I was too young. One time Josie told him that was bullshit. You know, like, if she was old enough, I was, too. But he didn't give her a pill that afternoon and she never said that again."

"Did he ever allow customers to hit or kick you or Josie?"

Jen shook her head. "No. He said he wouldn't tolerate violence toward us."

Matt paused. "You mentioned your dad took you to Kansas City, Chicago, and Wisconsin Dells. Can you remember other places you went? And did you always go by car?"

"Uh-huh—always by car, but Dad would trade the cars in pretty often. Maybe once a month. We always stayed pretty much in the Midwest. Though I guess we were in Texas one winter 'cause my dad doesn't like the cold."

"Mostly big cities?"

Jen shrugged. "I guess. Josie and I slept in the car a lot, and we'd usually get places at night. So it's hard for me to remember."

"I understand," Matt said. "One final question: do you know where your dad is now?"

"No."

When the recording ended, I dialed Matt, who picked up on the first ring. "I just finished watching Jen's interview and I'm so pissed I want to scream. Corbell has the audacity to tell his daughters he won't tolerate violence against them, but he forces them to be raped by strangers. And allows one of 'em to be bound and gagged in the process. If that's not violence, I don't know what is."

"Yeah. I almost lost it during the interview. I hadda choke back tears and try to sound calm, when in fact I wanted nothing more than to get out of that room and *do* something to punish that son of a bitch."

"You did do something: you got Jen—who'd vowed never to be interviewed by a man, by the way—to tell you all kinds of stuff that'll contribute to AJ's punishment when we find him."

"If we find him."

"We will find him." My phone beeped with an incoming call. "Hey, Matt, Jimmy's on the other line. I'm gonna ring him in."

"Tell us some good news, Jimmy," I said.

"I've got news—not sure it'll do us much good, though. First of all, AJ Corbell received the proceeds from Cassandralynn's life insurance policy five weeks after she died. A million dollars deposited into a bank in Kansas City. Within a week, he made two cash withdrawals—one for $5,000 and the other for $8,500—three days apart."

"Good chunks of change but not large enough to trigger CTRs," Matt said. I knew he referred to the IRS's requirement for banks to file currency transaction reports on any cash transactions of more than $10,000.

"Yep," Jimmy said. "And the balance was transferred to a numbered account in the Caymans a week later. I don't hold out a whole lot of hope for getting access to those offshore bank records."

"Was the Kansas City bank account in AJ's true name?" I asked.

"Yep."

"What'd he use for ID?"

"He opened the savings account five years ago using a valid US passport—which has since expired—and his social security card. Right around that same time, Corbell got a Missouri driver's license, using those same documents and the address of an apartment he rented for a month. Since he was signed up for online statements, no mail ever got returned to the bank. And the DL isn't up for renewal for another two years, so DMV hasn't sent him any notices."

"Did he ever use the passport?" Matt asked.

"Uh-huh. A cruise to the Caribbean in January 2002, which just happened to stop in Grand Cayman. Maybe he opened the bank account then. Who knows?"

"If memory serves," I said, "that was during the time AJ was working for Cassie's mom's charitable foundation —and probably embezzling funds. Good place to put his ill-gotten gains."

"You're right," Matt said. "But even if he didn't stash money there in the early 2000s, he's got close to a million there now. If I were him, that's where I'd head."

"We could extradite him to stand trial here," I said.

"True, but we'd have to find him there first," Jimmy said. "No—we gotta hope he's still in the US of A, where we've got the resources to look for him."

"Since we've got his SSN, what about work records?" I asked.

"IRS says he hasn't filed a tax return since he left Birmingham ten years ago. Likewise, there's no record he earned any money—no W-2s, 1099s, or other reportable income. That Kansas City savings account was opened with a hundred bucks and never earned enough annual interest for the bank to issue a 1099-INT. And he withdrew the million bucks before any interest accrued on it. This guy has been smart enough to stay under the radar."

"So he's got a real driver's license but doesn't use it," I said. "Instead he gets fake ones to check into motels."

"And most likely fake credit cards. The credit bureaus

don't show any activity with AJ's true SSN for the past decade," Matt added.

"Do you think he'd be able to get a fake passport to flee the country?" I asked.

"Why wouldn't he?" Jimmy asked. "He's clearly familiar with the dark web and all its offerings."

22

WEDNESDAY ROLLED in hot and muggy, the sky filled with ominous storm clouds. Though I'd kept the air conditioning set at seventy degrees overnight, my bed sheets felt clammy and rumpled. Clearly I hadn't slept well.

Amy bounded into my room at six thirty, just as I'd pushed *snooze* on my iPhone alarm. "Can we have a special back-to-school breakfast today, please? Like pancakes and bacon and strawberries?"

I stifled a groan. *Stop It! This is a moment worth cherishing.* "Absolutely. But I need two minutes of snuggling before I get up to cook."

She climbed into bed and curled up beside me. I drank in the scents of little girl sweat and Johnson's Baby Shampoo.

"I'm so excited I don't know if I can be still for two minutes," she said, squirming a bit. "It's gonna be so cool to be in *real* kindergarten." I found it interesting that she viewed her previous year in 4-K as some lesser form of school.

"Y' know what? I think we'd better get up and get going—we want to have time to enjoy our pancakes."

"Thanks, Mommy!" she said and ran down the hallway toward her room.

After a quick shower, I went to rouse Luke and Red. "I don't wanna go to school," my son grumbled. "It's still summer. The public school kids don't hafta go yet, so why do we?"

"I guess we Edgewood parents are just mean," I said with a laugh. "But I'm making pancakes to make up for it. Hurry up and get ready if you want to eat before we leave."

Red was already awake. She stood in front of her dresser concentrating on pulling clothes from the bottom drawer. "Good morning, sweetheart. Whatcha doin'?"

She looked up at me as though I'd materialized from a parallel universe. "Amy said get dressed."

I knelt down and picked two sleeveless shirts from the pile on the floor. "Which one?" I asked. Red pointed at the blue flowered one. I selected a matching pair of shorts. "Do you think these would be good with it?" She nodded. I breathed a sigh of relief—my youngest child was often the most contrary, and blowups over wardrobe choices were commonplace.

I repacked her drawer and watched while she dressed and brushed her teeth. No sense bothering with a hairbrush—that mass of red curls would look the same no matter what we did with it. "Okay, I gotta get cooking."

The eighth-grade class didn't start till tomorrow, but I buzzed Lily on the intercom and asked her to join us for breakfast. "It's a big day for the twins—starting 'real' kindergarten." To my surprise, she didn't argue and, in fact, appeared in the kitchen a few minutes later bearing a colorful hand-made sign reading FIRST DAY OF 5-K to use in our obligatory photos.

ON THURSDAY, Lily and Jen joined the ranks at Edgewood School. Glenda worried incessantly about Jen. Though she was old enough to start high school, everyone thought eighth grade would be a better fit. Jen had never attended *any* school, much less one filled with angst-ridden, hormone-driven teenagers. Glenda had had her tested academically, and Dr. Peters had administered a battery of intelligence and personality tests. The results were compelling: Jen was bright, resilient, and academically ready for most of the eighth-grade course work. We marveled at how well Cassandralynn had homeschooled her, and at how well Jen had retained what she'd learned, even after her mother's sickness and death.

It made sense, too, that Jen should be in the same class as Lily. It was Lily's fifth year at Edgewood and she had an established tribe of good friends, many of whom had already met Jen.

I wanted Jen to adjust well in school, but I had some misgivings about what her enrollment might cost my daughter. I truly liked Jen—and God knows I felt sorry for her—but the mother bear in me was wary. *What if she's a bad influence on Lily? What if Jen drives a wedge between Lily and her friends? If Jen acts out, will the teachers brand Lily as guilty by association?*

I made a mental note to keep the lines of communication between Lily's guidance counselor and me open.

Don't let this health scare put parenting on the back burner. There's nothing more important than your kids.

23

As it turned out, I never got around to asking Dominic or Abby or anyone else to go with me to meet Dr. G on Friday morning. I asked Grace to take the kids to school, citing an early meeting with a colleague in Milwaukee, climbed into my rental car with a mug of strong coffee, and hit the road.

I'd managed to make *Worry—would it help?* into a mantra, repeating it in my head a hundred times a day. And George Cooper had given me a puzzling new bank fraud case, which proved as distracting as he'd promised. I doubted, though, that I could keep my fears at bay during the hour-and-a-half drive on the interstate to Milwaukee.

As I got closer and closer to the Froedtert Clinic, my anxiety rose. A former victim of panic attacks, I pulled out age-old weapons to fend off another: pouring the remains of my coffee out the window, singing to oldies on the radio at full volume, thumping on the steering wheel till my palms hurt. I made it without passing out or freaking out. With weak knees and trembling hands, I pushed the elevator button and emerged in the second-floor lobby. Moments later, I was greeted by a smiling male receptionist, who directed me to a comfortable seating area with a few other waiting patients. "Dr. G is running a bit behind, but her nurse will be out to get you in a few minutes."

I closed my eyes and silently started in on my mantra. I was befuddled when I heard someone sit next to me—I knew there were several empty seats—and say, "Caroline?"

I looked up to see a thirty-something woman with auburn hair and lustrous green eyes, gently touching my arm. "I'm Hannah Witte—Matt's ex. He told me you had an appointment this morning and I thought I'd pop by and say hi."

"Thanks. I appreciate everything you've done. How'd you know it was me?"

Tiny wrinkles formed around her eyes as she laughed. "Matt and I were living together—trying to reconcile—during the time you guys were working on that bank robbery trial, and he couldn't stop talking about you. Then I saw your picture in the paper after you convicted the guy."

I felt my cheeks flush and didn't know how to reply.

She looked around. "Did you come by yourself?"

"Uh-huh. I figured I could record the consultation on my phone and listen to it later if I missed something."

A door to the waiting area opened, and a nurse appeared carrying a folder. "Caroline," she said.

I popped up from my chair and turned to thank Hannah.

"Want me to come in with you?" she asked, glancing at her Apple watch. "I've got a free hour."

"Uh, yeah," I said, surprising myself. "I'd like that."

She waited outside until I changed into a gown, then sat wordlessly beside me in the examining room while I answered the nurse's questions.

Though I'd Googled her and had seen her picture, Gianna Giacomino was nothing like I'd expected. Small and lithe—about five feet, two inches tall and weighing perhaps a hundred pounds—she floated into the room on red wedged sandals. She wore a red silk button-down shirt under her white coat, and diamond earrings sparkled through her shoulder-length black hair. She took both my hands in hers and said in a throaty voice, "Hello, Ms. Spencer, I'm Dr. G. What would you like me to call you?"

"Caroline is fine."

She turned to Hannah. "Hey, Hannah. Are you here for moral support?"

Hannah nodded. "I didn't think you'd mind."

"Of course not. It's always good to see you."

Dr. G booted up the computer and motioned me toward the exam table. "I need you on your tummy please. Susan had you keep your undies on, didn't she?"

"Yep," I said, squirming facedown onto the table.

She examined the back of my knee, gently moving my leg through various positions. "You said your pain is about a level five today?"

"Uh-huh. Except when you move it."

"And you first started noticing the pain about two months ago?"

"Yes."

"Sit up please." She reached out a hand, helped me

reposition myself, and prodded some more. A few pokes on the left side of my knee caused me to jump. "I'm sorry. Almost done."

She stepped back and removed her exam gloves. "Okay, you can hop down now."

I resumed my seat next to her workstation while she typed on the computer keyboard, then turned the monitor toward me. With the tip of her pen, she pointed to a picture on the screen. "As you can see from this shot, you have a good-sized tumor on the back of your knee. I'm surprised you've only experienced pain so recently. You must have a fairly high pain tolerance."

I shrugged. "It's probably just that I'm too busy to focus on it."

She smiled. "Maybe you're related to Wonder Woman. We'll need to take a couple samples of the mass to determine what kind of cancer we're dealing with—"

My heart lurched into my throat. "Wait, I thought you couldn't tell from the MRI whether it was cancer or not."

Dr. G paused. "Is that what your doctor told you?"

"Uh-huh. He said you wouldn't know till the biopsy."

"He's technically correct. But I've seen countless scans, and benign tumors virtually never look like this. I'd be lying to you if I told you otherwise."

"But—"

"Why did they tell you it might be benign?"

I nodded.

"Maybe the radiologist didn't have much experience with osteosarcoma and wrote his or her report with an abundance of caution. In any event, the biopsies will give us much better information."

"Is this life-threatening?" I croaked, then held my breath.

"We'll need to know more about the specific cancer to know the prognosis. But the good news is that your tumor appears fairly localized—there's no evidence that it's spread to other parts of your leg. With localized osteosarcomas, we've got good success rates."

I exhaled slowly. "What kind of treatment will I need?"

"Surgery to remove the tumor and surrounding tissue. Chemotherapy before and after surgery if it's an aggressive type of cancer. Most often we can spare the limb."

I couldn't formulate another question. Hannah reached over and squeezed my hand.

"Susan tells me I've got time to do the biopsy on Monday afternoon," Dr. G said. "Would that work for you?"

"I'll make it work."

Dr. G put orders into the computer for blood work, an EKG, and a chest X-ray, which I'd have done before heading home. "I'd recommend you have someone drive you to the appointment on Monday. We use only local anesthesia, but I'd like to give you a Valium to keep you calm during the procedure and you'll probably need some pain meds afterward."

"Okay."

Thankfully, Hannah escorted me back to the lobby, where I felt at least less claustrophobic. "I've gotta get to work," she said, "but if you want, I can find someone to hang with you while you wait for your tests."

"Thanks. I can handle it."

She gave me a quick hug and pressed a business card

into my hand. "My cell number's on the back. Call if there's anything I can do to help."

I teared up when she walked away.

THE EKG WAS DONE in fifteen minutes and the blood draw in five, but the receptionist in radiology told me it'd be an hour before anyone could do my X-ray. "You could head downstairs and have lunch first," she suggested.

I made three passes around the cafeteria, incapacitated by indecision. *Just pick something.* Finally, a piece of banana cream pie caught my eye and I grabbed it before I had time to change my mind. I filled a large carryout cup with ice and unsweetened tea, paid the tab, and found a table where I could be alone. The first bite of pie tasted heavenly. *Not exactly health food, but WTF?*

After another bite, I picked up my phone and dialed the number I'd learned in kindergarten: the number to my parents' home in St. Cloud, Minnesota. My dad answered. "Louise," I heard him yell, "it's our favorite daughter. Pick up the extension."

I cringed. "Dad, it's okay if she's busy." *Please, please, let her be busy.* "You can fill her in after we hang up."

"Well, okay. I guess she must be out in the backyard having a smoke. To what do we owe the pleasure?"

"It's not exactly great news," I began, and I filled him in on what Dr. G had said.

I cringed again when I heard the hitch in his voice. "Everything's gonna be okay, honey. We'll pack up and drive down tonight. Or tomorrow or Sunday. Your choice. Whatever'll work best for you and the kids. Your mom can mind the home front and I'll take you to

Milwaukee on Monday. Or, if you'd rather have Dominic be with you—"

"Dad. You're babbling," I said, smiling despite myself.

"Right. I just want to be helpful—and not be in the way."

The biggest way you could help is to come by yourself, I wanted to say. But I knew my difficulties with Mom weren't easy on him. "You're never in the way. But why don't you wait till tomorrow to come."

"You got it."

"And, Dad…"

"What honey?"

"The kids don't know about this yet. I gotta figure out what and when to tell them."

"Easy peasy: Sit 'em down tonight, tell 'em you're gonna need an operation on your leg, and that you'll find out more about it after some tests on Monday. They already know something's wrong. When we last Face-Timed, Amy sighed and told me you were icing your knee—*again.*"

"It sounds so simple when you say it that way. And I guess there's no need to say the C word right now."

"No, there isn't. I'll go find your mom and see what time she'll be ready to head out. I'll text you when I know."

"Thanks, Dad. I love you."

"Love you, too."

I finished my pie and read through the printed materials I'd gotten from Dr. G's nurse. I dutifully signed up for an online account so I could track test results, appointments, and the like. And I texted Matt to tell him how much I'd appreciated his ex-wife's help.

Heading back up to radiology, I felt empowered. The X-ray tech was all business and came back from checking the films with no trace of alarm on his face. *Whew!* I thought, heading to my car.

I MET ONLY light traffic on the way home. With the radio set at half volume, I tuned in to a classical music station—conducive to prayer. *Dear God, give me strength to cope with whatever the coming days may bring. Please keep my children safe and happy and healthy. And, please, give us many more years—*

My plea to the higher power was interrupted by my phone.

"Hi, honey. It's your dad again. Are you driving?"

"Yes, but Lily set up the hands-free feature so I can talk."

"Good for her. I wanted to let you know I'll be coming by myself tomorrow."

One prayer answered! "How come?" I managed to ask with nary a trace of glee in my voice.

"Your mom's hosting bridge club on Monday and didn't think it'd be fair to cancel at this late date. Plus, she figured you'd have enough help—you know, with Abby and all."

My high-maintenance mother had always been jealous of the easy relationship I had with my down-to-earth mother-in-law. Of the way we were able to talk and laugh and kid each other.

"She says she'll come down when you have the surgery, though."

"That's fine, Dad."

"Alrighty then. I should be there around four thirty."

"See you then. And drive safely."

TEN MILES LATER, I got another call. "Hey, Matt."

"I spoke with Hannah and she told me she sat in on your consultation. I hope you didn't think she was over-stepping."

"Heavens no! She was a godsend. I should've realized it'd be too hard to handle alone. She's a really sweet person."

"She is that… So, the real reason I called was to fill you in on a new development in the case."

"What is it?"

"Jimmy followed through on your request to get ahold of AJ's juvenile court record. But when the agent in Pensacola went to request it, they told him it wouldn't be accessible without a court order."

"That's absurd. There's always a law enforcement exception."

"Be that as it may, Jimmy's SAC called George Cooper this morning to discuss how to proceed. And Cooper went ahead and got an order from Magistrate Judge Brillstein."

My breath caught in my throat. *Is this how it's gonna go? Other people doing different parts of my job when I have an appoint-ment or a test or surgery? Until eventually it's not my case anymore?*

"Oh," I said. "That's good."

"The Pensacola agent went back with the order this afternoon. Turns out his juvenile file's been destroyed, but the woman who actually had AJ on post-release supervi-sion in Escambia County is *still there*. She said she'll never forget him because he scared the shit out of her."

"Did she say why?"

"I'm not sure, but we should have the 302 by early next week."

"That's great, Matt. Thanks."

"You're welcome. And good luck Monday."

I switched the radio to oldies, cranked it up, and resumed banging on the steering wheel.

24

Dominic called as I pulled into my driveway, and I decided to answer in the peace and quiet of my car.

"How did the appointment with the oncologist go today?" he asked.

Don't you dare cry! I told myself. I inhaled deeply then forged ahead. "I liked Dr. G a lot. Unfortunately my GP —or the radiologist here, I'm not sure which—wasn't exactly forthright about the MRI results. She says my tumor is almost certainly cancerous. The next step is to find out what type. If it's aggressive, I'll need chemo before they do surgery."

"You need to get another opinion."

"What?"

"I don't understand why this surgeon would badmouth your general practitioner or the radiologist. It's unprofessional."

"Dominic, this woman is an expert in bone cancers. I think she knows it when she sees it. And you generally wait to get a second opinion until after you've got a diagnosis and possible treatment plan."

"Perhaps. We can discuss that later. When are they doing the biopsy?"

"Monday at three o'clock."

"Monday?" he asked, disappointment evident in his voice.

"Uh-huh. What's wrong?"

"It's just that my mother's having her first electroconvulsive therapy session on Monday afternoon, and I promised her I'd be there."

"Electroshock? Like in *One Flew Over the Cuckoo's Nest?* I didn't know they did that anymore."

"Yes, they do. It's a much more controlled procedure than it was in the past, and the success rate is quite remarkable."

"Huh. Well, in any event, my dad's coming tomorrow and he's gonna take me to my procedure on Monday."

"May I come over to see you tonight?"

"I don't think that's such a good idea. I plan to talk with the kids tonight and I think it'd be best if it were just family."

"I don't think it's wise to tell them now. They're likely to blow it all out of proportion."

"Dominic, they're smart kids. They know something's wrong with my leg—I've been limping for months. And they're sure to pick up on my heightened anxiety and preoccupation. I don't intend to spell out worst-case scenarios, but they need to know that I'll be having some kind of treatments sometime soon."

"I think it's a mistake."

"Well, Dr. T. Berry Brazelton, I disagree. And they're my kids, not yours." I hung up.

I STORMED INTO THE HOUSE, and the loud "clump" when I threw my keys on the foyer table brought me to my senses. *Calm it down, kiddo. And remember there's good news: Amanda did after-school duty today instead of Grace.*

"We're on the back porch," Amanda called. "But beware, we've got finger paints!"

I laughed. "I'll be in as soon as I change."

Stiff and sore from a day of sitting and driving, my leg rebelled the moment I began walking up the stairs. A sharp pain radiated down my calf—a symptom I hadn't felt before. I shifted my weight to my right leg and leaned heavily on the bannister, proceeding slowly to the landing. I hobbled to my room, collapsed onto the bed, and stretched out to seek relief. The pain subsided as quickly as it'd come, but I felt shaken to the core. *What if the kids had seen me struggling up the steps? It's definitely time to tell them.*

I changed into yoga pants and a T-shirt, threw some water on my face, and went down to join my family.

My four children—Red sitting on Amanda's lap— were gathered around the picnic table, which had been covered with a camping tarp. Plastic bowls full of paint and a stack of finger-paint paper littered the table, and each kid wore a faded oversized T-shirt. They were all grinning, Luke most of all, and painting away.

"My goodness," I said, "have I stumbled upon an artists' colony?"

"I don't know what that means, Mommy," Amy said, "but we *are* doing art. It's way more fun than at school."

"Look at my dinosaur," Luke said.

"It's amazing," I said. "All your pictures are amazing."

"Hope you don't mind, Mrs. S," Amanda said. "I found all this stuff in a bin in our basement and thought the kids would get a kick out of it. I'll get the littles bathed before I leave."

"I don't mind a bit. What'd Grace leave us for dinner? I must say it smells pretty good."

"Crock-Pot beef stew. And there's French bread all wrapped up and ready to heat in the oven."

"Hallelujah!" Lily said. "Grace's beef stew isn't half bad."

I pulled a canvas chair up to the end of the picnic table and watched the creative process unfold. And, when Luke lost interest after five minutes, I took him and Sparky, our ever-genial golden retriever, into the backyard for a hose-down. Luke squealed with delight and yelled dares to his sisters to join him. They wisely chose the bathtub.

AFTER WE'D all finished eating, Lily got up from the kitchen table to clear the dishes. "Our chores can wait, kiddo," I said. "There's something I want to talk with you all about."

Lily's brow furrowed as she sat back down. Luke and Red continued to finger-paint in the leftover gravy on their plates. Amy looked at me with mild curiosity. "I know what it is," she said. "You're getting married to Dominic!"

"Yuck!" Luke cried.

"No, I'm not getting married. It's about my leg. It

didn't get any better when I used the crutches, and it hasn't gotten any better since I've been going to the physical therapist."

"Does that mean it'll *never* get better?" Amy asked.

"No. But I need some more tests to help them decide how to make it better. I saw a doctor in Milwaukee today—"

"By the children's museum?" Luke asked.

"Stop interrupting," Lily said.

"Pretty close to the children's museum, yes. Anyway, the doctor told me I'll need to have an operation to fix what's wrong with my knee. She's gonna do another test on Monday before she decides when and how to do the surgery."

"Are they gonna cut your leg off?" Luke asked.

I sure as hell hope not…but how do I answer this one? I think Dr. G's words were "most often we can spare the limb."

"No, stupid," Amy said, "That only happens in wars and car accidents."

"Amy," I said sharply, "I've asked you not to call your brother names, and you know he's not stupid. Now, I have more to say." *And please let me bypass the amputation question.* "Your grandpa's coming tomorrow and he'll take me to the test on Monday."

"How come you can't go by yourself?" Amy asked.

"Because they'll give me medications during the test that will make me too sleepy to drive home."

"Oh."

"One more thing: it takes a few days to get the results of the test back, so I won't know anything more on Monday than I know now. But I'll tell you when I do, okay?"

The twins nodded, Red licked the gravy off her finger, and Lily looked faint.

I stood up and reached into the freezer. "Okay, anyone who's five years old or three years old, go to the back porch with one of these ice cream bars." I helped Red down from her booster chair and unwrapped her treat, then watched with gratitude as my three youngest followed instructions. "And anyone who's thirteen years old can stay and help their mom."

I resumed my seat at the table and grabbed Lily's trembling hand. "I'm guessing you have more questions."

She nodded. "Do you have cancer?"

"I have a tumor on the back of my knee that looks cancerous, but they won't know for sure until the biopsy results come back. And even if it *is* cancer, Dr. G says the success rate with treatment is very good. She's a bone cancer specialist who's really smart and super nice. She gave me a lot of confidence when I talked with her today."

"Will you have to have chemo? Becka Jorgensen's mother is having it now and is awfully sick from it."

"It depends on what the test results say. Patients with some cancers don't need it."

Lily didn't speak for a moment but anxiously twirled a strand of hair around her index finger.

"Lily?"

"What?"

"I get the sense there's more you want to ask or say."

"You can't die…"

I scooted my chair closer and hugged her tightly. "I'm not planning on it. And that's why Matt helped me find the best doctor around—to make sure I don't."

25

My FATHER's arrival did wonders for my spirits—and the kids', too. He'd stopped at a Costco on the way and had a trunk full of treasures to bestow upon us.

"What do you want for dinner, Dad?" I asked when he'd finished passing them out. "I've got a pan of Abby's lasagna, or we could eat half of this package of steaks! Dominic's coming over, but he doesn't have a preference."

"Why don't I take the kids to Chuck E. Cheese's and you and he can have an evening alone?" he asked.

Amy and Luke hugged his legs, and Red yelled, "Yay!"

"Clearly the littles will love it, but Lily? Not so much."

Dad looked at Lily. "Would it be more fun if you brought a friend?"

She nodded. "I think Jen would get a kick out of it, don't you, Mom?"

"Yeah. I do."

"Great, I'll go call her," she said and trotted off to her room.

"I don't remember having met Jen," my dad said. "Is she someone new?"

"Uh-huh. Glenda and Hank have been her foster parents for a little over a month now. She's been through a lot in her short life but seems to be handling things pretty well. Don't expect her to be chatty, though, and I'd recommend not asking her too many questions."

He raised an eyebrow.

I TEXTED Dominic to tell him the news. *Wonderful. Why don't you come to my place?* he wrote back.

Good. I'll bring steaks for you to grill and wine.

Six o'clock?

OK. No talk about my kids or your mom?

He sent a smiling emoji and another blowing a kiss.

I should've added another caveat: no talk about cancer or doctors.

I FELT UNACCOUNTABLY nervous as I dressed for the evening. Dominic and I'd had infrequent sex since we'd started seeing one another for the second time, but each time had been great. I found him breathtakingly attractive, and when naked he reminded me of a Greek god. In turn, he treated me like a goddess—caressing me tenderly and slowly savoring every touch, every movement. Quite frankly, he made me wild with desire. *You're not nervous, you're excited! Why have you waited so long to find time alone with him?*

Dad and the kids left for their dinner outing at five

thirty, and I followed them out the door. *Dominic won't mind if I'm twenty minutes early.*

His front door was locked when I arrived. I rang the bell, entered the combination into the keypad, and let myself in. "Hello!" I called as I kicked off my shoes and walked into the living room. The kitchen lights were on and classical guitar music emanated from a Bluetooth speaker on the counter. "Anybody home?"

He must be in the shower. And I hope he won't mind if I join him.

I padded down the hallway toward his bedroom and stopped in my tracks. Dominic was on the phone, and I couldn't not listen. "No, I can't drive down tonight, Mom. I have plans… Yes, with Caroline…" He waited for her response, then continued with a tremor in his voice, "You keep saying you want me to have a happy life, but then you make me feel guilty when I'm not at your beck and call…"

Talk about feeling guilty. Eavesdropping is about as low as you can go. And obviously the conversation is emotionally charged—he didn't even hear the doorbell or you calling to him. I turned around and snuck back to the kitchen, well out of earshot of his bedroom.

While pondering my next move, I found a corkscrew, opened the bottle of Cabernet rosé that I'd wanted to try, and took a sip. I grabbed my phone and sent him a text: *Don't want to scare you. Got here early and let myself in.*

I didn't expect him to interrupt his call but knew he'd see the message before he emerged. He responded, though. *I'm sorry I didn't hear you come in. I'm on the phone and will be out soon. Please make yourself comfortable.* Not for the first time, I marveled at his complete and grammatically correct text. And this time he'd done so during a conversation with his mother.

I'd finished the first glass of wine and poured myself another before he finally appeared—God help me—wearing nothing but a towel. He strode into the living room wordlessly, extended a hand to help me from the couch, and led me back to the bedroom.

He stood before me and slowly removed every stitch of my clothing. Though tempted to scream *hurry up,* I found his methodical movements both tantalizing and mesmerizing. I deliberately slowed my breathing. When I was finally naked, he lifted me gently to the bed.

"It's been way too long. And you're too beautiful for words," he said. A long, slow kiss led to long, slow lovemaking.

Afterward I burrowed under his arm, resting my head on his chest, basking in his warmth and strength. "It *has* been too long," I said.

"Give me a minute and we'll make up for lost time," he said with a smile.

I leaned up on my elbow and looked him in the eye. "Only a minute? Who are you? Superman?"

"You're right. I could probably use some dinner first. Would you like to rest here while I cook those steaks?"

I thought for a moment. "Yeah. That'd be heavenly."

I watched in awe as—without a hint of self-consciousness—he walked naked across the room. *Oh, for that kind of confidence.* He went to the living room and retrieved my glass of wine. "I took the liberty of taking a sip—this is a winner."

"I think so, too. The rest of the bottle is yours, though. This is my limit."

He sat heavily on the edge of the bed. "Are you saying that because you plan to drive home tonight?"

"Uh-huh. I'd love to stay, but with everything going on, it wouldn't feel right."

He sighed and gently brushed a strand of hair away from my eyes. "Well then, I think we should skip the steaks and make the most of our limited time."

"I think you're right."

It was nine thirty and the house was quiet by the time I got home. My dad sat in the living room with a can of his favorite beer—Pabst Blue Ribbon—and looked up lazily when I walked in. "Nice evening?" he asked.

I felt my cheeks flush and hoped he didn't notice. "Very nice, thanks. How was your outing?"

He shook his head and gave me a sardonic smile. "I'm sure glad Lily and Jen came along. No way could I have kept track of those three little ones without their help. That place is chaos!"

"I take it they had fun."

"Uh-huh. The little munchkins were still wired when we got home. Took me an hour to get 'em to sleep."

"You're my hero, Dad. Can I get you another beer?"

"If you'll join me."

"Sure. Gimme a few minutes."

I changed into my pj's and robe, popped a bag of microwave corn, and returned to the living room bearing it and two cans of PBR. I handed one to my dad along with a wad of paper towels. "Want some corn?"

"I'm good, but thanks."

"All the more for me," I said, settling into my favorite chair and propping my feet onto the ottoman.

"No time for dinner?" he asked with a wink.

"Mind your own business," I said lightly, and put a handful of popcorn into my mouth.

He took a long pull on his beer. "So...how you holding up?"

"All in all, not too bad. My conversation with the kids last night got a little dicey, but I managed to sidestep Luke's question about whether I'd have my leg amputated."

Dad did a double take. "Holy cow! I never would've predicted one of 'em would ask that."

"Me, neither. Amy told him he was stupid—that people only lost their legs in wars and car accidents. I corrected her characterization of her brother's intelligence but let her premise about amputations stand."

"Probably a good thing. *Is* that a possibility?"

"Dr. G said most often they're able to spare the limb. I haven't researched any of this on the Internet—given my history of anxiety, I think it's best I remain in the dark."

Dad smiled. "That's bullshit! You're one of the strongest, most resilient people I know, and fully capable of handling facts. You've never given yourself enough credit."

"Yeah? Well, I'm sure I'll get my fill of facts next week, and we'll just have to see whether you're right."

"How scared are you—on a scale of one to ten?"

I took a sip of beer, stalling while I considered my response. "Right now, about a four. The level fluctuates, but in all honesty it hasn't gone higher than about a seven."

He didn't reply.

"How 'bout you, Dad? How scared are you?"

He, too, paused before answering. "Two or three."

I couldn't help laughing. "Liar," I said. "I'm your first-born child, you've just learned I have bone cancer, and you're only a little scared? Nice try."

He lowered his eyes. "It's way harder when it's your kid."

"I can imagine," I said, rising from my chair. "Want to go to church with us tomorrow?"

"Can't hurt."

I laughed again.

26

MONDAY DAWNED with spitting gray skies and cooler-than-normal temps. I'd left the window near my bed open and awoke to a fine mist blowing onto my arm. My knee had stiffened up during the night and walking to the bathroom felt anything but comfortable. Gazing at my reflection in the mirror while I brushed my teeth gave me pause—I looked like I hadn't slept in days, when in fact the Bailey's Irish Cream I drank before bed had knocked me out cold. *I'm glad we're finally gonna get to the bottom of this. The suspense isn't doing me any favors.*

The alluring aromas of coffee and bacon wafted up from the kitchen as I made my way downstairs, and I found Dad in the kitchen pouring blueberry pancake batter onto the griddle. *Damn it, Dr. G! Why'd you have to tell me not to eat or drink anything for eight hours before the procedure?*

"You're up early, kiddo. I thought I'd have breakfast on the table before everyone woke up."

I kissed him on the cheek. "I've gotta throw the twins' soccer uniforms in the dryer—they have a game scheduled after school, though it looks like it might be a rain-out."

"You shoulda told me. I could've done that."

"I didn't remember till I saw it on my calendar this morning. Guess I've been a little preoccupied. Anyway, Amanda's got it covered."

The littles, mollified by their favorite breakfast, managed to make it to their seats in the minivan by seven thirty with minimal complaint, and Dad chauffeured them to school and daycare.

I'd briefly considered going to the office that morning, but the notion of sitting at my desk without caffeine dissuaded me. Instead, I'd gone to my office on Sunday afternoon and picked up a few files for distraction.

MY DAD APPEARED in the living room doorway at noon. "Ready to go?"

"It doesn't take three hours to get to Milwaukee," I said, forcing a smile.

"You never know about traffic. And you're s'posed to be there at two thirty, right?"

"Uh-huh, but still—"

"Humor me, okay?"

I sighed and struggled to my feet. "Okay."

DAD TALKED nonstop for the first half hour of our trip, filling me in on the whereabouts of my former classmates, the deaths of folks I might know from St. Cloud, and which of his neighbors had the best garden.

"And remember Gerry O'Sullivan?" He didn't wait

for my response. "You know, the bank president. He's sitting in jail for embezzling two million bucks. They're saying the case might go federal. D'ya think he'd get much prison time for that?"

"I'd guess a couple years, at least."

"Really?"

"I don't *know*, Dad. I can't think straight—this no-caffeine headache is killing me. And all your chatter isn't helping."

He didn't reply, and the hurt look on his face cut me to the quick.

I reached over and touched his shoulder. "I'm sorry. I didn't mean to bark at you. God knows I appreciate everything you're doing for me and I hope you know it, too."

He turned toward me and said quietly, "I do, pumpkin."

We rode for a while in silence. As we crested a hill, we could see traffic becoming more congested in the distance. "That doesn't look good," Dad said, nodding ahead. "Probably an accident. There's an exit coming up —I think I should take it."

"Lemme check Waze," I said, pulling out my phone. I clicked on the app. "One guy says it's a little slow, but there's nothing else reported yet. I'd just stay on the interstate."

He nodded and we passed the exit, still traveling at fifty miles per hour in the left lane. But after rounding another curve, he was forced to brake as traffic ground to a halt.

"Shit!" I said. "We should've listened to your instincts."

It took twenty minutes to drive a mile—inching forward for a car length or two, then sitting still for five minutes—and my dad's knuckles were white from gripping the steering wheel with impatience. Three police cars and a fire truck sped past us on the shoulder. I checked Waze again. "A tanker truck overturned near Waukesha—they've shut down I-94 in both directions."

Dad checked his rearview mirror and pulled onto the shoulder. "Hang on."

I grabbed the passenger assist handle—what Dad had always called the "oh shit" handle—as he drove across the grassy median toward the westbound lane. "You know this is illegal, don't you?"

"We're *not* missing your appointment. Now get on your fancy phone and find us an alternate route."

We arrived at Dr. G's office at two thirty-five.

I LAY SHIVERING in the procedure room, wishing I were wearing flannel pj's instead of the scratchy hospital gown, fixated on the IV port they'd inserted into my hand. The Valium hadn't kicked in yet and I couldn't tell whether I shivered from nerves or cold air.

"I found one," my dad said, beaming as he walked into the room carrying a blanket. "It just came out of the oven, too."

He covered me with the blessedly warm blanket, tucking it around my neck. "The doc says they'll be ready to start in a few minutes."

Dr. G came in a moment later. "Hello, Caroline. I wanted to catch you before you get too groggy. Your father and I met in the hallway." We listened as she explained the procedure. "The back of your leg will be sore for a few days, but probably not much worse than it is now. I'll have the results back from pathology and I'd like to meet with you Friday morning to explain them and make plans to move forward. Does that sound okay?"

I tried to picture my Friday schedule in my mind but nothing came clear. "Guess so."

She smiled. "I see you're groggy now—which is good." She turned to my dad. "Gene, I'll have Susan call to set up a specific appointment time. And if Caroline needs to reschedule, we'll fit her in early next week."

I remembered only bits and pieces of the procedure: being strapped face down with my leg in restraints, a needle poke for local anesthetic, the whirring sound of a drill, and aching pressure when the biopsy needles were inserted. I recalled being reassured by the melodious voice of Gianna Giacomino throughout it all.

I woke up in a recovery area, cocooned in more warm blankets, my dad seated by my side. "Doc G said you did well and she got three good samples. We can leave in an hour or so."

27

I FOUND a copy of Special Agent Otto J. Reingold's FBI-302, reporting his interview with AJ Corbell's juvenile probation officer, displayed prominently on my desk Tuesday morning along with a hastily scrawled note from Jimmy McGee. *Caroline, S/A Reingold says to call him w/ ?s. The PO wants to talk w/ you too. —JMcG* He'd jotted the phone numbers for the agent and probation officer on the back of the note.

I burned my tongue on my first sip of coffee and silently cursed the McDonald's drive-thru for making it so hot. I took the lid off to let it cool and began to read while I waited.

Juvenile Probation Officer Jeannette Williamson was interviewed at the Escambia County Juvenile Justice Center. She provided a data card, which showed that she had been assigned to supervise Ambrose Josiah (a.k.a. AJ) Corbell following his discharge from his court-ordered term in a residential treatment center. Supervision extended from November 20, 1994, through

Corbell's eighteenth birthday on June 17, 1996. The court and supervision files were destroyed five years after the latter date.

Ms. Williamson recalled that AJ Corbell was a handsome, intelligent young man, the only child born to married parents. To the best of her recollection, neither AJ nor either of his parents had a substance abuse problem. Ms. Williamson stated she believed AJ was disingenuous but could not cite specific reasons for this opinion. She said he was a gifted actor, having been cast as the male lead in his high school's musical during his junior year. The data card showed that no violation reports were filed during the term of supervision.

Reading between the lines: AJ's PO couldn't trust him as far as she could throw him but hadn't been able to gather ammunition to revoke his supervision. I couldn't wait to call her.

"Ms. Williamson," I said when she answered, "this is Caroline Spencer from Madison, Wisconsin. I'm prosecuting a federal criminal case against—"

"Ambrose Josiah Corbell! Agent Reingold told me you've indicted the SOB. I've been waiting more than two decades for news like that."

I laughed. "That's a long time—and a long time to work in the juvenile justice system. Most people get burned out after a few years."

"Yeah. My husband says I have a messiah complex— you know, the irrational belief that I can actually save some of these kids—but he says it with love." I could hear the self-deprecating twinkle in her voice, and I liked her immediately.

"Sounds as though you never believed you could save AJ."

"Nope. He was one of my first cases. I was fresh out of graduate school and still idealistic as hell. But the moment I met him, the hair on the back of my neck stood up. He could be very charming. In fact, I believe he charmed the judge into giving him far less time than he deserved. When he tried to schmooze me, though, I wanted to puke."

"So how'd you handle him?"

"I watched him like a hawk and enlisted cops and teachers and the high school principal to watch him, too. Though nothing ever came to light, I'm sure he didn't stop manipulating and victimizing people during that time. I'm guessing he had his way with lots of pretty high school girls—especially after he got the lead in *South Pacific*. He was simply too smart to get caught."

"You say he was smart. Do you mean book smart?"

"I mean innate intelligence. By the way, my husband, Richard, is the psychologist who evaluated AJ before sentencing. Richard is anal as hell—and I say that as lovingly as he does when he calls me messianic—and after Agent Reingold was here the other day, I asked him if he still had a copy of his report. Of *course* he did. He'd given AJ an IQ test and he scored 130. Not quite Mensa material, but close."

"What else did his report say?"

"Nothing too specific. It wasn't considered kosher to label a fifteen-year-old kid. But AJ's lack of empathy was one thing that struck Richard. And the MMPI—a personality inventory—showed he tended to lie to make himself look better."

"Can we get a copy of that report?"

"I called Agent Reingold when Richard found it. He already came and got it yesterday."

"Great, thanks for your diligence."

"When I heard about the horrific things he did to his daughters, I vowed I'd do anything to help put him away. I've been racking my brain trying to recall details that might be important."

"Did he have any close friends? Anyone he might have kept in contact with over the years?"

"Good question. Let me think."

I could almost picture her leaning back in her chair, eyes closed, trying to remember.

"Now that you mention it, there was a kid he met in juvenile detention. Came from a wealthy family who got fed up with him stealing from them to buy coke. The dad had him locked up temporarily to scare him straight. I heard that AJ moved in with the family after his own parents kicked him out. I never confirmed it though, 'cause he was off supervision by then. I don't recall the kid's name, but I'll ask around."

"I'd appreciate it. It may be a long shot, but we're desperately trying to find AJ before he victimizes any other young girls."

My phone rang ten minutes later. "It's Jeannette Williamson again," my caller said quickly. "I remembered the kid's name—AJ's friend, I mean. It's Zachary Thomas Prescott III."

"That's great! Especially since it's not a common name. We may actually have a chance to find him."

"I checked for any recent criminal arrest record. He had a possession charge—marijuana—in 1999, and a DWI in 2000, but wasn't convicted for either. Nothing more recent. I also Googled him. His dad died about five years ago and mom last year. Like AJ Corbell, Prescott was an only child. The parents' obits said Zach lived in Little Rock, Arkansas."

"Jeannette, you're amazing. I can't thank you enough."

"One more thing: our data card on Prescott lists a number you might find useful. Got a pencil?"

"Uh, sure." I listened while she read me a series of digits and wrote them carefully on my legal pad.

"Keep me posted, please," she said and hung up before I had time to reply.

WTF? What kinda number is this and why would I find it useful? Why'd she hang up? I counted nine digits and stared at them. It finally hit me. *Holy shit—it's Zachary Prescott's social security number! She broke the rules to give us a key to tracking his whereabouts. Let's hope he can lead us to AJ.*

I called Matt and Jimmy to tell them the news.

28

Jimmy and Matt came to my office on Wednesday afternoon, clearly excited. "We located Zachary Prescott," Jimmy said. "He's been living in Little Rock, Arkansas, for the past fifteen years. Currently in a four-hundred-thousand-dollar McMansion—and believe me, that kinda money buys a *very* nice house in Arkansas. He works as an investment advisor for a local bank with a salary of one hundred K. Trophy wife twenty years younger than him. No kids. We've got numbers for his landline and his AT&T cell phone."

"Great!" I said. "Probably no coincidence that AJ and his family relocated to Arkansas. When can someone from the Little Rock office get out to interview him?"

"We've been thinking that might not be the best course of action," Matt said. "If, as we suspect, he and AJ are tight, he might get hinky and alert him. We'd rather get a look at his phone records first."

"No way could we get a warrant for the phone records on our sketchy probable cause," I said. "What would I write: 'AJ and Zach were friends from juvie and lived in Arkansas at the same time. Ergo Zach's probably involved in AJ's crimes'? We need more."

"What if we ask Jen if she knows him?" Jimmy asked.

I cringed. "I don't really want to ask for another debriefing—one was traumatic enough."

"We wouldn't need a full interview unless she says she knows him," Jimmy persisted. "She and your daughter are friends now—couldn't you just casually ask her some-time when she's over at your house?"

"Who knows when that opportunity will arise?" Matt asked. "I'd rather be up-front about it. I could call Glenda and say I want to come by to find out if Jen knows someone we think might be a lead."

"And if she does?" I asked.

"Then I call Brad Tollefson and request permission to take an 'official' statement, recording it on my phone with Glenda present to protect Jen's interests. He'd be fine with it. If Glenda thinks we need to do it later—with the shrink and Nancy present—we can still set it up pretty quickly."

"Lemme text Glenda and see what she and Jen have on the calendar after school today."

I typed the text, and we all sat looking at my phone in anticipation. "Does she usually answer right away?" Jimmy asked.

My phone pinged in response. "Yeah," I said with a smile, reading her response. "She says she's picking up Jen at four o'clock and heading to the grocery store, then home. Matt's welcome to come over around five. Will that work for you, Matt?"

"You bet."

"How 'bout we call Brad now and get his okay—just in case Jen does know this guy?" Jimmy asked.

"Will do," Matt said and made the call, giving us a thumbs-up midway through the conversation.

"I sure hope she knows him," I said. "We need more leads, even if they're long shots."

GLENDA TEXTED me on Wednesday evening when Matt Witte left her house. *Your friend just left. It went well. Jen knew this Zach guy. Not traumatic. Going to Jake's game. TTYL.*

Matt texted the news as well. *I'll bring the vid tomorrow a.m. Nine okay?*

HE AND JIMMY arrived at eight forty-five, before I'd even gotten through my emails. "A little anxious, are we?" I asked. "And no Dunkin' Donuts?"

Matt laughed and handed me a flash drive. "Sorry, I was in a hurry this morning. And we really want to get the search warrants."

"Okay, then," I said, "let's roll it." He and Jimmy took their usual seats; I wheeled my desk chair over and plugged in the drive.

The preliminaries went quickly—date, time, location, and the fact that Jen's guardian ad litem and foster mother had given consent for the interview. The quality of the cell phone video surprised me. "Did you use a tripod?" I asked Matt.

"Uh-huh. One of those little three-legged rubber thingies. Now be quiet and listen."

"Okay, okay…"

"Jen, the reason for this interview is for you to tell us what you know about a man named Zachary Thomas Prescott III," Matt said. "The person we're asking about is a white male, with a date of birth of August 11, 1978. This is a copy of his driver's license photo."

Jen picked it up and studied it. "This is Uncle Zach. He's, like, not really my uncle, but we called him that. He's my father's best friend."

"Do you remember when you first met him?"

Jen shook her head. "I don't remember *not* knowing him. As we got older, though, my mom seemed to like him less and less. So he didn't come around all that often when she was still alive."

"Do you know why your mom didn't like him?" Matt asked.

"Not really."

"Did Zach ever touch you or Josielynn inappropriately?"

"Uh-uh. He was actually pretty nice to us. After our mom died, he brought us some presents to try to cheer us up."

"What kind of presents?"

"Bottles of nice-smelling lotion and some T-shirts. He said he'd gotten them on a trip to some island in the Caribbean."

Jimmy paused the video. "Maybe Zach set up the account in the Caymans for AJ? As far as we can tell, AJ hasn't left the country for more than a decade, but he might trust his best friend enough to do it for him."

"I don't know much about off-shore banking, but I guess it's possible," I said.

Jimmy pushed *play*.

"Did you see Zach after you moved away from Arkansas?" Matt asked.

Jen paused before answering. "Maybe three or four times, I guess. I remember he visited in Kansas City after we left the fancy hotel. That was when he gave us the presents from his trip. And he came once when we were someplace in Tennessee. But he and my dad talked on the phone more often."

"Do you remember how often?"

Jen shrugged. "Maybe once a week? Dad'd get done with a call and say something like 'Uncle Zach says hi.'"

"Did you get the sense Zach and your father were doing business together?"

"What d'ya mean?"

"For example, did Zach ever bring men over to have sex with you or Josie?"

"No, never."

"Did you ever overhear your dad talking with Zach about the men having sex with you?"

"No."

"Did Zach ever bring pills or drugs of any kind to your dad?"

"If he did, I never saw it."

"Do you know how Zach was employed?"

"He worked in a bank, like as a vice president or something."

"Has Zach been in touch with you since Josie died?"

Jen looked surprised. "No—how would he know how to reach me?"

"I didn't think he would know how," Matt said calmly. "I just wanted to be sure. Would you know how to reach *him*?"

She shook her head. "I've never had his number."

"Did you ever visit him at his house?"

"We went to his old house a few times, but he, like, built a different one after he got married, and we moved away before it was done."

"Did you ever meet his wife?"

"Uh-uh. My dad said she was really pretty, though."

"Did you ever meet any other friends of your dad or Zach? Or hear them talk about any other friends?"

Another pause. "No. Now—living with the Fosters, I mean—I realize that's kinda weird. Like, most people have more than one friend. But my mom and Josie and I didn't have *any* friends...so I guess we never thought it was weird that Dad just had Zach."

Matt leaned forward and pushed the *pause* button. "That part was so effing sad," he said, shaking his head. "I wanted to ask why they didn't have any friends, but it wasn't really relevant to the interview. We all know that a-hole isolated his wife and daughters on purpose... Sorry for the rant." He resumed the playback.

"Is there anything else you can remember about Zach that might help us locate your father?"

"Not that I can think of," Jen said, then took a deep breath. "Do you have any leads?"

"Let's just say it's coming along slowly. That's why we really appreciate your talking with us about Zach—any little clue might help."

The video ended.

"Was it my imagination," I asked, "or did she seem a little relieved when you told her the investigation was slow going?"

"I noticed that, too," Matt said.

"Well, we can get warrants for the phone records this afternoon," I said. "Let's hope the companies are quick to provide them."

29

I'M NOT sure what jolted me out of my deep, dreamless sleep Wednesday night, but I awoke disoriented and terrified, my heart pounding so rapidly I couldn't breathe. I knocked over the bedside lamp fumbling for the switch. I grabbed my cell phone and struggled to turn on its flashlight, convinced I'd be calmer without darkness. It didn't help.

Questions began running amok in my head like flashing neon lights, buzzing with electricity: *What if this isn't some slow-growing cancer? What if it kills me? How could my kids possibly survive the loss of another parent? Who'll be able to raise them like I'd want? My parents don't have the physical stamina to deal with four kids permanently—and they'll be in nursing homes before Red's done with college. Glenda and Hank said they'd be the kids' guardians, but they've got three kids of their own...*

Before I could derail the runaway train, I'd ridden it into a full-blown panic attack. Racking my brain for ways to stop it did nothing but exacerbate my terror. I tripped over a tangle of sheets as I tried to get out of bed and fell to my knees in tears.

I'm not sure how long I sat sobbing on the floor but, like all panic attacks, this one eventually dissipated. I hobbled to the bathroom and splashed cool water on my face and looked in the mirror. *You're okay*, I told myself. *Just breathe.*

My cell phone clock read three thirty when I rearranged my sheets and climbed back into bed. I remember reciting the names of all fifty states—counting them carefully on my fingers—at least four times before I fell back asleep.

EMOTIONALLY DRAINED, I made it through my Thursday schedule on autopilot.

I'd just finished reading the littles their bedtime stories and was tucking Red in Thursday night when the home phone rang. *Probably a telemarketer—no one else calls the land-line. It can go to voicemail.*

"Caroline," my dad yelled from downstairs. "It's Dr. G."

My heart began beating wildly and I couldn't feel my feet as I hobbled to my bedroom to pick up the extension. "Hi, Dr. G," I said, "and... uh, Dad, stay on the line, okay?"

"I hope you don't mind my calling so late, but I wanted to share the good news with you before tomorrow's appointment. I just reviewed the pathology report. You have what's called parosteal osteosarcoma—a low-grade tumor that rarely turns into the highly malignant form of osteosarcoma. It's slower to metastasize, and the survival rate is greater."

"So it's a good kind of cancer?" my dad asked.

Dr. G laughed. "Exactly. And even better, I took samples in three different portions of the tumor and none of them evidenced progression beyond the parosteal stage. So...you won't need chemo before surgery, Caroline."

I flopped back on the bed. "Thank heaven. I've been reading about the chemo they use for higher-grade osteosarcoma and it sounds just brutal."

"I thought you were staying off the Internet," my dad chided.

"Yeah. Well..."

"Don't feel bad, Caroline," Dr. G said. "Almost no one can resist the temptation. What this all means is that we're ready to discuss the surgical procedure. After we talk tomorrow, we can go ahead and schedule it if you want. Or, if you'd like to get another opinion, you're welcome to do that."

"If I decide to go ahead, how soon would you be able to operate?" I asked.

"I can't say for certain, but one patient I have scheduled for next week may decide to go a different route. Otherwise, we'd be looking at the following week."

"That soon?" I asked. I'd been hoping to get things resolved quickly but hadn't expected it to happen *that* quickly.

"Uh-huh. When we're dealing with cancer, time is often of the essence. Since you have a slow-moving type, you have the freedom to put off your decision."

"Or maybe to agonize over it," I said.

Dr. G laughed. "At the very least, I recommend you savor your good news and get a good night's sleep tonight."

I HUNG UP, peeked in at my sleeping kids, and went downstairs. My dad almost bowled me over in the foyer as he rounded the corner from the kitchen, carrying two beers and a can of 7-Up. "I buzzed Lily to come up," he said. "This calls for a celebration!"

"What does?" Lily asked, shuffling up behind us in her fuzzy pink slippers.

"C'mon into the living room," he said.

Lily sat beside me on the couch and Dad perched on the edge of the coffee table facing us. He ceremoniously popped the tab on the soda can and handed it to her, then opened the beers. "Cheers to good news from the oncologist," he said, clinking his can with ours. "Dr. G just called to say your mom has a good kind of cancer and won't need chemo!"

Lily took a sip and leaned into me. "Oh, Mom, I'm so glad. Everything I was reading on the Internet scared me shitless!"

"Language!" Dad said with a laugh.

"So what happens next?" Lily asked.

"We meet with her tomorrow and discuss surgery. She says she can probably do it next week or the week after."

"That's great, Mom. I'll be glad when you're not limping anymore. And so will the littles—Amy's really got her undies in a bunch about it."

30

Our appointment Friday morning was set for eight thirty—meaning we'd contend with rush-hour traffic on the way to Milwaukee. Dad and I met Grace at the front door at six o'clock and headed to the car with travel mugs of coffee. We swung by the Greenbush Bakery for a half-dozen fresh-from-the-oven donuts and made our way east.

"How'd you sleep last night?" he asked me once we were on the interstate.

"Pretty good—when I wasn't tossing and turning. It was hard for me to hear that the kids are worried about me, so I pretty much decided I'd take Dr. G's first surgery opening. But then I started wondering if I owed it to the kids to get a second opinion. You know, to make sure I have the best chance to live long enough to raise 'em. What do you think?"

"I think you should make a list of every question on your mind and ask her. Listen to her answers and your gut, then decide if you want another opinion."

"You're right." I reached into my purse for the Moleskin notepad on which I'd already jotted down a few questions. "Help me brainstorm, please."

By the time we'd gotten to the Highway 41 exit, I had two pages full of things to ask. We arrived at Dr. G's office thirty minutes early. Hopped up on coffee and sugar, Dad paced the hallway outside the waiting room. I played fourteen games of Words with Friends while squirming in my chair.

TODAY SUSAN LED us down the hallway, past the examination rooms, and into Dr. G's office—a windowless room painted nondescript beige. The doctor was seated behind the desk, on the phone, her back to the door. She swiveled to greet us, covering the phone's mouthpiece with her free hand. "I'm sorry, this'll just be a minute. Sit, please."

We settled into two visitors' chairs facing the desk, and while we waited, I stared unabashedly around the room. Large, serene watercolors adorned the walls. Every inch of the desk was covered: two computer monitors and two keyboards, stacks of files, a stack of medical journals, a brick-red Yeti thermos and matching coffee mug, and two pinch pots—one containing pens and pencils and the other paperclips. A framed family photograph was prominently displayed on her credenza: Dr. G and her husband with two brown-eyed girls about the age of Luke and Amy. *A working mom with twins.*

"I certainly understand," Dr. G told her caller. "Let me know if you change your mind." She hung up and turned to us. "Again, my apologies."

She stood up and shook our hands, then moved her

chair from around the desk to sit beside me. She turned one of the monitors to face us, and we saw four images on the screen.

"I've been studying your MRI and these ultrasound images, which I took during your biopsy, to plan how best to excise the tumor and surrounding tissue. Our number one goal is to remove all the cancer, which means taking wide margins around it. Our number two goal is to ensure you have pain-free mobility for what we believe will be a long life."

My stomach knotted. "Why do I sense bad news coming?" I asked.

"Because achieving goal number two is going to be tricky here," she said. "Patients in your shoes almost always choose limb-sparing surgery—and justifiably so. But the outcome isn't always rosy. Some patients end up contending with considerable pain. Last week I had a patient come in in tears, saying she wished she'd opted for amputation during her original surgery two years ago."

My dad sat forward in his chair. "What are you saying, Doc? Are you recommending *amputation?*"

"Not necessarily. My concern is that we'll need to remove a fair amount of muscle and cut into some major nerves in this area to do the wide-margin excision"—she pointed to an area on one of the pictures—"and I won't know the extent of the damage that will cause until I get in there. And I'm saying amputation *might* be the option that would result in the best quality of life post-op."

"How much of my leg would you have to take?" I asked in a hoarse whisper.

She ran her finger across my thigh, several inches above the knee, then rested her hand on my arm. "I want you to think about how it's been for you living with the pain and limited mobility you've had for the past few months. If we do limb-sparing surgery, you'll have less mobility and a lot more pain for a while—possibly for life."

She waited a beat. "If we do amputation, you'll have significant short-term pain and you'll be dependent on crutches or a prosthesis for life. But...you'd be likely to get on with your life a lot more quickly."

"What would you do if you were me?" I looked over at her and saw tears in her eyes.

"I can't say because I'm not you," she said gently. "What I recommend is that you think it over and tell me what's most important to you: having a leg or living pain-free. Hopefully, it won't turn out to be an either/or situation. But I'd need to know the limits of your consent before we go into surgery."

"Do you need to know today?"

She smiled. "No, but the day before the surgery would be helpful. Now, I'm not saying this to put pressure on you, but the person I was talking to when you came in canceled his Tuesday surgery. That slot is open, and it's yours if you want it. Or Susan can give you some other potential dates if you need more time to think about it. Or if you want another opinion, she'll arrange to forward your records. That's perfectly okay with me."

"I don't need more time. I'll take Tuesday and call you on Monday about the amputation option."

My dad's jaw dropped and I was sure he was going to start sputtering. I patted his hand. "I'll tell you my reasoning in the car."

"Okay, then," Dr. G said, somewhat taken aback, I

thought. "Hang on a minute while I go get Susan. She's got some pre-op stuff to go over with you, and she'll tell you how to let me know your decision about consent."

DAD FOLLOWED Susan and me to an exam room, but I stopped him at the door. "Why don't you head to the cafeteria and get us some coffee and sandwiches to go? I'll meet you in the lobby."

"Uh…okay."

Dr. G's nurse gave me a list of things to do and not to do before surgery and explained what to expect four days later. "You'll be in great hands," she said. "All her patients give her glowing recommendations."

"Uh-huh. I've seen them on the Internet. One thing I forgot to ask her, though, is how many surgeries has she done that are similar to mine?"

"I'd say at least fifty since she's been here at Froedtert and probably at least that many during her residency at Sloan Kettering."

"Wow."

Susan smiled. "She's an ace."

MY DAD OPENED the car door for me and waited until I'd situated our coffee in the cup holders and buckled up before getting into the driver's seat. He placed his hands on the wheel, but made no move to start the car. He looked straight ahead, his eyes glistening.

I leaned over and nudged his shoulder with mine. "Hey, let's not lose sight of the big picture: my cancer's unlikely to be life-threatening, especially if she removes wide margins around the tumor. The sooner she operates, the sooner I can get on with healing."

"And you don't think this is important enough to get a second opinion?"

"Not when I'm already seeing the best doctor around. She's had lots of experience. More important, I trusted her the minute I met her. She's smart and compassionate. And even if I decide to allow amputation, I have confidence she'll only go that route if she thinks it's gonna result in the best outcome."

"Don't you want to talk it over with Dominic?"

I scratched my head. "Why?"

"I dunno…"

"Seriously, Dad. If he'd have a problem with having a one-legged girlfriend, would you really want me to be with him?"

"No, I wouldn't. Forget I asked."

"Okay then. Let's get moving. I need to get my ducks in a row at the office since I'm bound to be out for at least a few weeks." I said it cavalierly, but truth be told, I worried about whether George would let me keep my caseload—and especially the Corbell case.

I texted George to ask him to make time for me that afternoon. His response came quickly, *Leaving at noon for long weekend. Can you meet at 11:30?*

"Shit," I told my dad. "My boss is taking off at noon today and I really need to talk with him. Do we have enough gas to get there without stopping?"

"Uh-huh."

I leaned over and peered at the gas gauge, just to make sure.

"Geez, Louise! You think I'd lie about something like that?"

"No, not really. I'm just nervous, I guess."

"Who wouldn't be?"

GEORGE KNOCKED on the doorframe to my office at eleven thirty on the dot. *Lucky I got my dad to drive more like a bat out of hell than a little old lady from Pasadena.* "Does this meeting have anything to do with your biopsy results?" he asked, his brow furrowed with concern. "Do you have cancer?"

I hadn't shared Dr. G's earlier assessment that the tumor was most certainly malignant, so my boss hadn't had a heads-up. "Uh-huh. But the good news is that it's a non-aggressive cancer with a pretty great survival rate. I'm going in for surgery to have it removed next Tuesday."

His face relaxed and he lowered himself into a chair across the desk from me. "I'm glad they're jumping right on it. How long'll you need to be off work?"

"I'm not sure yet, but probably at least a few weeks."

He raised an eyebrow.

"Even though the cancer's not particularly aggressive, it's been there awhile and has gotten pretty large. The surgery's gonna involve lots of muscle and nerves and stuff. Bottom line: I might be better off—pain-wise, that is —to have them amputate my leg."

"Oh, man," he said, shaking his head. "I'm so sorry. When will they know?"

"Not until the operation's underway. If I don't give consent to amputate, the surgeon will remove the tumor and surrounding tissues, patch me up, and hope for the best."

"And if you do consent?"

"She'll use her best judgment when she sees the extent of the damage. This weekend I need to decide which is more important to me: having two legs or having pain-free mobility. I'm hoping it won't be an either/or proposition."

George looked shaken. "I can't imagine having to make that kind of decision."

"Maybe I'll flip a coin," I said, and was surprised to hear the near hysteria in my voice. I took two deep breaths and continued. "Right now I need to concentrate on work. You know I hate to ask someone to pick up my slack…"

"I do know, which is why no one here will have any problem covering for you." I couldn't make eye contact with him, afraid I'd let loose with tears of gratitude. Until he continued, "I'll go over your cases and reassign 'em."

"No, George," I said, a tad too sharply for diplomacy. "I want to *keep* my cases. I don't have any trials scheduled in the next month. I just need someone to cover hearings and deal with any emergencies that arise while I'm gone."

"I understand, but from a management perspective, that's not a good way to handle things," he said, lowering his head. "If I actually *assign* the cases to other people, they'd be the ones responsible for knowing when there are hearings or emergencies. If I let you keep your caseload, somebody's gotta monitor 'em all—and that somebody would be me. Sorry, Caroline. Much as I'd like to do what you ask, I've got too much on my plate already."

My mood instantly deflated. *I've invested so much of myself…it's not fair!*

George tilted his chair onto the back two legs and looked me straight in the eye. "I'd like you to hold on to the AJ Corbell/Danny Thompsen case, though—"

"Thank you," I said, wanting to leap across the desk to hug him.

He chuckled. "As I was going to say, it's in kind of a holding pattern anyway, what with Thompsen's attorney using delay tactics and Corbell still on the loose. Matt and Jimmy can call me if they need any more subpoenas or search warrants, and I'll deal with any motions the shyster files on Thompsen's behalf."

"And I'll have the guys keep me up to date on the investigation—I can review records and reports as well from home as I can from here."

He tipped his chair onto terra firma and stood to leave. "For the immediate future, how 'bout you just concentrate on recovery? And don't worry, Matt would never let us keep you out of the loop."

He walked around the desk and gave my shoulder a squeeze. "I'll be thinking of you this weekend and on Tuesday. Have someone call afterward and let us know how the surgery went."

I nodded.

"Be well, kiddo." On his way out, he pulled the door shut behind him.

That simple gesture—knowing I needed privacy to collect myself—caused the dam to burst. I cried huge, fat tears filled with a flood of emotions: gratitude, fear, sadness, anger. And, I realized, loneliness. I had lots of people supporting me, but the one person who'd truly understand my dilemma—Glenda—was out of town. I couldn't ruin her parents' weekend visit at the Air Force Academy by calling to ask advice about my Hobson's choice.

IT TOOK me several hours to review my cases and make notes for the attorneys who would inherit them from me. I did several Lexis searches for case law on pending motions and double-checked all my due dates. By the time I left the office at six thirty, I felt confident that the transitions would go smoothly.

31

I ARRIVED at home to find my dad, Abby, Bert, and Dominic sitting around the dining room table, eating salad and Italian bread dipped in olive oil. "I hope you don't mind," Abby said nervously, holding a forkful of greens in midair. "The lasagna is 'resting' and it'll be ready to cut in about five minutes."

"Of course not," I said. "Didn't you get my text saying to start without me?"

"Well, yes," she said.

I couldn't help laughing. "Why would I be upset that you did what I suggested?"

She blushed.

"Where are the kiddos?"

"Lily's got 'em downstairs having a pizza party," my dad said. "I thought you'd appreciate some, uh…conversation with the adults around this table."

"You told 'em?" I asked, giving him the stink eye.

Dad nodded sheepishly.

Dominic got up and came to hug me. "Don't be

angry, please. This is an emotional situation for Gene. We're the ones who asked him about what happened today, because you didn't answer my texts."

I halfheartedly returned the hug, sat down, and poured Cabernet into my waiting wineglass. "I'm sorry— I didn't even look at my texts till I sent the one to Abby. I had lots of work to finish this afternoon since who knows how long I'll be off. I knew you were coming to dinner and I could explain in person." *And why do I feel like I have to defend myself?*

The tension in the room felt ominous but I couldn't bring myself to feel responsible. Abby, on the other hand, had to try to fix it. "Honey, I can put the lasagna in the oven on *warm* for a while so you two can talk privately."

"No, thanks. I'm starving. You can *all* ask your questions after we eat."

Abby and Bert hustled into the kitchen to plate up the main course, clearly relieved to leave the dining room. My dad finished his beer and got up to get another one. Dominic reached over to take my hand. "I'm sorry," he said, "it's just that I'm worried, and I feel as though you're keeping me in the dark."

"I guess we're all on edge," I said. "It'll pass when the surgery's done."

"I hope you're right, but since it's a non-aggressive cancer, you don't need to rush into it."

Returning with his beer, my dad cleared his throat. Bert and Abby proceeded behind him, each bearing plates full of steaming lasagna and marinara sauce.

"This smells wonderful, Abby," I said with relief. "Thanks so much for making it."

"You're welcome, dear," she said, and I noticed a hitch in her voice. "Anything to help."

My own appetite surprised me—until I paused to consider I hadn't eaten anything since the Greenbush Bakery donuts that morning. I hadn't been able to stomach the sandwich my dad had gotten me at the Froedtert cafeteria before our drive back to Madison.

I finished my salad, lasagna, and two pieces of bread while my dining companions picked at their entrees. Of course, all but Dominic periodically stopped eating to tell me bits of news: my mom would be taking the train from St. Cloud on Monday, Luke scraped his leg falling off his scooter, Red had a meltdown at McDonald's, and Bert and Abby were taking the kids to see the Labor Day parade. I smiled at the appropriate times and managed to avoid non sequiturs in response.

"There's tiramisu," Abby said when everyone had pushed aside their plates. She began to rise.

"Please sit, Abby," I said. "Let's wait on dessert until after we've talked." I refilled her wineglass and mine and leaned back in my chair. "First of all, I'm completely confident in my selection of Dr. Giacomino and don't believe I need an opinion from another doctor."

I paused to read their reactions. My dad, Abby, and Bert remained calm. I could see the vein throbbing in Dominic's temple. "What, specifically, makes you so confident?" he asked. "You just met her."

"I looked into her background and got a recommendation from a doctor I know. She's got the best credentials of anyone in the area for dealing with bone cancer. Plus, *she's* confident. And honest. And caring. It's my body that's gonna get operated on and I'm listening to it—my gut says she's the one to do it."

"Listening to your gut…" he muttered.

I ignored him. "Since I've selected my surgeon, it makes sense to take her first available opening. Even though this cancer's 'non-aggressive,' I want it removed as soon as possible. I realize it's inconvenient, what with school having just started and all, but I can't imagine *any* time when it would be convenient for me to be disabled for weeks."

My dad nodded. "Your mom and I can stay indefinitely to help out."

"And we're not scheduled to travel anywhere until December," Bert chimed in. "You know we love spending time with the kids."

"I appreciate that more than I can say," I said, blinking back a few tears. "Now, for the elephant in the room: I'm sure Dad told you I need to decide whether to authorize amputation should Dr. G determine that's the best option?"

Dominic, Abby, and Bert all nodded—Dominic without looking up from his lap.

"I intend to do some research this weekend. Dr. G's nurse gave me a list of articles to read and I ordered a couple books from Amazon about living with the loss of a limb. I'll probably ask you for your input, but this isn't a decision I'm gonna put to a vote. Agreed?"

Dad, Abby, and Bert nodded. Dominic pushed back his chair, threw his napkin on the table, and stalked out. We heard the front door open and close and saw him through the front window—storming to his car.

"What the f—" my dad started to ask.

I gave him a *stop* gesture. "Dominic appears to have a different view of how our relationship should work."

"Seems like he's a control freak," Abby said, then put her hand over her mouth. "I'm sorry. I shouldn't make judgments like that. And you know my mouth gets ahead of my brain when I have a second glass of wine."

I patted her hand. "Not to worry, Abby. Families need to say what's on their minds, filters be damned."

"And they can be free to disregard someone else's opinion," Bert added with a smile.

AFTER WE'D GOTTEN the littles to bed and Lily had gone to her room, my dad and I sat on the front porch enjoying the quiet and the smell of freshly cut grass. Occasionally a car would drive past, and we heard the faint hum of traffic on Monroe Street. By and large, though, the sound of birds chirping and neighborhood dogs barking was all that disturbed the silence. I knew my dad was as lost in thought as I was.

Finally, he cleared his throat and voiced his concern. "Abby might be right. Do you think Dominic *is* a control freak?"

"Wow, Dad. Those are virtually the same words I've been mulling in my mind."

"Have you figured out an answer?"

I scooted my Adirondack chair closer to the porch railing and rested my feet on it. "Maybe not a control freak but definitely an obsessive caretaker. Dominic's dad died when he was ten years old. Apparently on his deathbed he made Dominic promise to be the 'man' of the family. And I think he relished that role with his mom, especially with her mental health problems. Now he's so intent on making sure she doesn't kill herself, he's taken away any responsibility she had for her own life."

"Hmmm."

"And remember how he worked so tirelessly to find the guy who caused David's accident so we could win the insurance settlement?"

"Of course."

"He was obsessed with rescuing me and the kids. Then he watched over them—and my niece and nephew —like a hawk when that pedophile lived in the neighborhood."

"Yeah, and I was grateful for everything he did. But now do you think he's frustrated because you won't let him be the *man* of your house?"

"Uh-huh. That's my best guess."

"And how do you plan to deal with it?"

"I'm not sure," I said, shaking my head. "After all, I'm indebted to him for the help he's given us. But I've worked hard since David died to take responsibility for my own well-being and that of my kids. I've surrounded myself with people who *partner* with me, not people who believe I'm incapable of managing my life. I ask for help when I need it, not when I don't."

"I know, and I can't tell you how proud I am of you. You've got four amazing kids who are all doing well. You've got a great career. You're smart and attractive and loving. Any man would be lucky to be your partner."

I tried without success to swallow the lump in my throat and couldn't even murmur a *thank you*.

"Do you love him?"

"I thought I did. Now all I feel is irritated because I

think he's patronizing me. Am I being too judgmental of him?"

Dad uncrossed his legs and rested his elbows on his knees. "I don't know. But if I were you, I wouldn't worry about that at this point. You gotta do what feels right for the moment. You can sort out your feelings about him later—after you're back on your feet again."

"Or *foot*," I said, "as the case may be."

He laughed out loud.

32

TRUE TO THEIR WORD, Amazon delivered my living-with-limb-loss books on Saturday morning—not by drone but in the hands of a thirty-something UPS driver in brown shorts. I took a moment to appreciate his tan, muscular legs. *Even if I get to keep them both, mine will never look that good!*

While the littles and Sparky played in the backyard, I sat on the screened porch with a glass of iced tea and began to page through the book with the most upbeat title.

WHEN I WOKE the littles for church on Sunday morning, I silenced their grumbles with a promise to take them out for breakfast and mini-golf afterward. Lily required more persuasion. Though tempted to play the guilt card—*I'm going in for surgery next week and we need God on our side*—I refrained and used bribery: I told her if she got ready without complaint and helped with the kiddos on our outing, I'd buy her the sweater she'd been wanting at Gap.

The agreed-upon rewards were worth every penny. We dropped Red off in the church nursery and I led the kids toward seats in the second-to-the-last pew. "Let's go up closer," Luke said. "I wanna see better." My dad and I exchanged surprised looks and followed my son to the front row. Luke listened with rapt attention while the pastor used a Jesus hand puppet to tell the children's sermon, and he even raised his hand to answer one of the questions the pastor posed to the group. Then the twins dropped their offering envelopes into the collection plate and trotted off happily to the children's activity.

Lily sat between her grandfather and me. She turned toward me and stifled a grin at his enthusiastic but off-key singing during the hymn of praise. Dad's unbridled gratitude and faith touched me.

The pastor's sermon, based on verses from the fourth chapter of Philippians, felt as though it was meant just for me: don't worry about anything but pray with thanksgiving about everything.

The kids behaved like angels throughout breakfast at the Copper Top, a restaurant on Madison's west side, featuring endless choices of diner fare. Lily and I split a Mediterranean omelet and a Belgian waffle—joking about our worldly choices. Dad had steak and eggs, and the littles all chose Mickey Mouse pancakes.

Our stomachs full, we putted around the Vitense mini golf course, where Red even managed to win one hole. Dad dropped Red and me off at home and volunteered to take Lily to the mall and the twins to the zoo.

Red begged to snuggle with me before her nap, a

noteworthy event for my squirmy-the-worm youngest child, so I took her into my room to take advantage of the opportunity. *Is it possible she understands how much I need this?* She nestled under my arm as we lay on our backs watching the ceiling fan make its lazy rotations. "Did you have fun playing golf today, pumpkin?"

She nodded, unable to respond verbally with her thumb in her mouth. With her free hand, she rubbed the satin binding of her blanket bunny against her cheek. "I did, too," I said quietly.

Within minutes, her thumb fell aside and her breathing deepened. I knew she'd sleep for an hour or two. I thought briefly of getting up to do my medical research, but chose to take our pastor's advice to pray instead.

Thank you, God, for inspiration, sunshine, and the support of my earthly father and so many more loved ones. Help me make good decisions for my family and me, and to always remember how richly you have blessed us…

I awoke when Red began stirring at four o'clock. I tiptoed from the room, went into the hallway, and called Dr. G's answering service. "This is Caroline Spencer," I said, "Dr. G is doing surgery on my leg on Tuesday and needed to know whether I'd consent to amputation if she deemed it the most viable option. I've made my decision…"

AT DINNER THAT EVENING—BURGERS and corn on the cob —I told the kids.

∾

AFTER DINNER, I took the remains of my glass of wine to the front porch, lowered myself into a chair, and dialed Dominic. We hadn't communicated since he'd bolted from my dining room on Friday evening—no texts, emails, or voice messages.

"Hello, Caroline," he said. I detected coolness in his voice and pictured him looking at me with a creased brow and arms crossed.

"Are you somewhere where you can talk?"

"I'm at my mother's." *Of course you are.* "Why do you ask?"

Duh—d'ya think maybe so we can speak freely? "Because you might want privacy when you hear what I have to say."

"Fine," he replied testily. "I'll step into the kitchen... Okay, what is it?"

"I'd prefer to have this conversation in person, but it's too important to wait till we have that opportunity." I took a breath—not to gather courage but rather to make sure I kept my tone level. "Our relationship isn't working for me anymore, and I've decided to break up with you."

"Is this because I disagree with your hasty and unilateral decision to have surgery on Tuesday? I thought you *wanted* my open and honest communication. Wasn't that what you said when we got back together?"

"Despite what you might think, I do value honest communications. But I'm finding we disagree on too many fundamental points: child-rearing, my health, your relationship with your mother. I don't need or want a caretaker, and you're not happy unless you get to *be* the caretaker."

"After all I've done for you and your kids—"

"That's it exactly," I said. "You *have* done a lot. I appreciate it and always will. But our romantic relationship is over."

"Are you saying you want to be *friends?*"

"No," I said, "I don't think that scenario is possible, which makes me sad. I honestly wish you all the best."

I hung up before he could respond and powered off my phone. I could live without being connected to the outside world till *my* world settled down.

33

I OPENED my eyes from yet another nap—momentarily at a loss for where I was—and glanced at the calendar prominently displayed on the wall of my room. *How can it be Thursday already?*

Situated like a large V with the foot of my bed elevated and my torso propped on a pile of pillows, I resisted the urge to push the morphine button, then vaguely remembered my mother's admonition when I'd spoken to her last night, "Don't be a hero, Caroline. You need to stay *ahead* of the pain." *No! Wait awhile—you need to gather your wits. It's been two days.*

A half hour later, when I'd just finished a round of calming breaths, Glenda burst through the door carrying a bunch of roses, her eyes glistening with tears. "If Jake hadn't gotten hit with a frickin' lacrosse stick in gym class and needed stitches, I would've been here yesterday." She leaned down to plant a kiss on my head.

"I couldn't have visited with you yesterday anyway—I

was practically comatose. My dad sat here all day and said the only words I uttered were gibberish."

"Yeah. I talked with him last night. How ya doing? Does it hurt much?"

I nodded and blinked back my own tears.

"What happened?" she asked, her voice breaking. "Last time we talked you said it was a non-aggressive cancer and it hadn't spread. So why'd they have to… amputate?"

I grabbed a bunch of Kleenex from the box on my bedside table and handed them to her. "Pull that chair over and sit down. Amputation's not a contagious condition."

She groaned at me but did as I asked.

"My dad and I met with the surgical oncologist on Friday, after she'd studied all the scans to plan the operation. She said there was a lot of nerve involvement with the tumor, and the best option for a pain-free outcome might be *not* to try to save the leg. I gave her the okay to use her best judgment."

"You just let *her* decide?"

"I had to give written consent before we went into surgery, but I took a chance and decided to trust her completely."

"Why didn't you call and tell me on Friday?"

"And ruin your trip to Colorado? There wasn't anything you could've done."

Glenda blew her nose and tossed the used tissue toward the wastebasket.

I gave her a playful stink eye. "These nurses have enough to do without picking snotty Kleenexes up off the floor."

"I was gonna do it before I left," she said as she got up, retrieved the litter, and disposed of it. "I'm not a barbarian, you know. Lemme go find a vase for these flowers."

I didn't comment when she left the room, knowing full well she needed time to compose herself. I closed my eyes, trying to visualize the pain floating away. It didn't work.

Glenda returned five minutes later with a vase and a scissors. I watched while she cut off the bottoms of the stems—diagonally, as per the directions on the little preservative packet—and started to place the roses into the vase one by one. "To hell with this," she finally said, putting the remaining bunch in together. "I'm no Martha Stewart and can't pretend to be."

She sat back down and covered my hand with hers. "So what's next?"

"We pray that the pathology reports are good: that the *whole* tumor was, in fact, the non-aggressive type and that the margins around it were all clear. If so, I won't need chemo. I heal a few days while we wait for the results. Then I go to a rehab facility in Madison to learn how to get around. My goal is to be back home and back to work in a couple weeks."

Glenda stifled a sob. "I love your optimism. You know I'll help you any way I can."

I smiled. "I know. Tell me about your trip to parents' weekend. How's Trey?"

She got a faraway look in her eyes. "It was great to see Trey. He seemed about five years older than when he left —all tanned and muscular and confident. He says he loves it and hasn't had any problems with hazing by upperclassmen or anything. You know I was worried about that."

I nodded.

"Jake and Sarah were jealous of all the attention Trey got, though, and acted like a couple of spoiled brats. I wanted to leave 'em there when we left—maybe the discipline might make 'em grow up or something."

"How'd Jen do on her first family trip?"

She didn't respond.

I leaned toward her. "Tell me."

"We probably shouldn't have taken her," Glenda said, almost inaudibly. "But I thought it'd be such a good experience…you know, so she could be a part of a normal family on vacation…"

I gave in to the morphine button and waited for her to tell me at her own speed.

She finally continued, "Jen was fine on the flight to Denver and on the drive to Colorado Springs. She kinda hung on Sarah, but Sarah and Jake were very patient with her. The problems were at the hotel."

My heart sank.

"We got adjoining rooms. Hank, Jake, and I took one, and Sarah and Jen had the other. Sarah came and woke me up in the middle of the first night 'cause Jen was moaning and thrashing in her sleep. I went in to try to comfort her but she pushed me away. She was sitting up, half-awake and mumbling, 'Please, Daddy, please.' I felt so helpless, not knowing how to help her."

"What'd you do?"

She shook her head. "Nothing. Eventually she lay back down, hugging her bunny, and fell asleep again. Everything seemed okay on Saturday and Sunday. But on

Monday morning, though, I was in our room putting on makeup—Jake and Hank were down getting breakfast—and overheard her ask if she could use Sarah's phone. Sarah said sure, 'cause she was gonna take a shower anyway. She called her dad."

"What do you mean she called her dad?" Even through my opiated fog, I could hear the shrill tone in my voice.

"I thought she was probably gonna use the phone to look up something on the Internet, but after a few moments I heard her say, 'Daddy, it's me—Jenny.' Then, 'I miss you so much, too. I'm in Colorado with the foster family. Can you come pick me up?' I didn't know what to do so I just listened. It was clear he said no, because Jen started crying. She said something like, 'Can I call you again?' I assume he said no to that as well because she started crying harder and said, 'I understand...' Finally she said, 'Love you, too,' and hung up."

"Please tell me you got the number."

She lowered her head. "I went into the room and told her I'd heard the call. She was fiddling with the phone and by the time I got to her, she'd deleted it. It was just so sad. I know intellectually that trafficked people often have true affection for their captors, but I'd never witnessed it."

"You *didn't* get the number?" I asked, trying to tamp down my impatience. She had to realize how important this was.

"For chrissakes, Caroline, I was trying to comfort her. She'd just been rejected by her father—the only person she's truly close to. And then it was time to go to Trey's ceremony. I tried calling you Monday afternoon before we left to come home, but your phone went straight to voice mail. I called Matt instead and he got right on it."

"How long after Jen's call did you reach Matt?"

"About five hours."

I closed my eyes. *Five hours. Long enough for him to be miles away from the cell tower that had transmitted the call.*

"I'm sorry," Glenda said, squeezing my hand.

I nodded. *Let it go—Matt can handle it,* I told myself and drifted off to sleep.

I WOKE up around four o'clock, when the nurse walked in. "How are you feeling?"

"Like I ran into a buzz saw," I said, trying to smile.

"An amputation joke! That's a good sign, especially since they removed the spinal block this morning. Don't hesitate to push the morphine button—without the spinal, you'll need the extra relief."

When she rolled me onto my side to check my dressing, I noticed the three-tiered set of fancy boxes from Gail Ambrosius Chocolatier—my favorite guilty pleasure—bound in a gold ribbon, prominently displayed on my bedside table. A cream-colored envelope sat propped up beside it. "Where'd those come from?" I asked.

"Dunno. But I'll hand you the card when I'm done."

While the nurse finished charting her visit, I opened the envelope and read the notecard it contained:

"Dear Caroline, I stopped to see you on my way to Chicago but didn't want to wake you. I called your father yesterday to inquire about the surgery. He told me the surgeon was fairly confident she'd gotten all the cancer and that the margins were clear. That's

good news. I want you to know I'll always care about you, but I'll respect your decision about our relationship. I wish you a smooth recovery and all the best, now and forever. Dominic."

I found myself befuddled that the note moved me so little. "They're truffles from my ex-boyfriend," I told the nurse. "Please, open it and take one—they're to die for. In fact, I'll have one, too."

She grinned. "I was hoping you'd say that."

I reached into the box she proffered, selected a piece, and took a tiny bite. "Caramel," I said, sighing with pleasure.

I thought about texting my thanks, but decided against it. I'd felt relief when Dominic stormed out of my dining room last week, and I didn't trust myself to compose a we're-just-friends thank-you message in my semi-sedated state.

34

ROBERT, my physical therapist, knocked on my door and pushed in a wheelchair at promptly eleven o'clock on Friday. "Your chariot awaits, m'lady," he said in an amateurish British accent.

I groaned. "You need some better lines than that."

"Ya think? Maybe that's why I'm still single."

Robert stood about five ten and carried not one ounce of excess fat—his muscled biceps and broad shoulders strained the seams of his polo shirt. Though not conventionally handsome, his angular face radiated warmth whenever he smiled, which he did often. "Must be," I said, "since an attractive guy like you could probably have your pick of partners."

"Flattery won't win you an easy workout," he said with a smile. "Especially if you want to get out of this place pretty soon." He lowered the side rail on my bed. "Now move yourself into position. I want to see if you're ready to get into the chair by yourself. That's it. I won't let you fall."

I scooted myself to the edge of the bed, established my footing, and lowered myself into the waiting wheel-chair. "Phew! No easy task."

"You did good. Now wheel yourself out to the elevator and I'll grab your crutches."

WHEN I'D BEEN on crutches earlier in the summer, I'd realized the need to increase my upper-body strength and had begun a fairly routine regimen of push-ups and weightlifting exercises—using a set of dumbbells that had belonged to my late husband, David.

"It's good that you've been working out," Robert said after the first fifteen minutes of today's session. "You've got quite a bit of stamina on those sticks."

I beamed with pride.

"You're clearly ready to try a temporary prosthesis."

My heart skipped a beat. "Do I have to?"

Robert seemed mystified. "We talked about this yesterday. How it's a good way to avoid contractures, which keep your joints from moving smoothly."

"Sorry. I must've spaced out that conversation. I was thinking I'd wait till I'm back to my normal life—or my 'new normal' life—before deciding about a fake leg."

"I want you to at least try," he said. "The prosthetic person's set aside time to meet with you."

I gave him a pouty look that probably rivaled any Red had ever thrown at me. "Okay, okay."

Robert walked me over to a room where Jamie, the prosthetist, awaited. A short, stocky woman with twin-kling blue eyes, she exuded competence. "Hey, Caroline," she said. "I'm Jamie. Climb up on the table, please."

"Uh, hello…" I said. "I've only got one leg, so *climbing* is kinda tough for me."

She ignored my snarky tone. "But you have two crutches," she said with an infectious smile, "and there's a step at the end of the exam table."

I wasn't buying into her cheerfulness and pouted some more. But I did follow her instructions.

"I'm going to take some measurements of your good leg and your residual limb," Jamie said, "and then I'll adjust a temporary prosthesis for you to try out." She used her tape measure and jotted down notes, disappeared into an adjacent supply room, and emerged ten minutes later with the mechanical contraption.

As expected, using the prosthesis hurt like hell. Hanging on to a set of parallel bars, I walked gingerly on it while Jamie scooted behind me on a wheeled stool, making sure the leg moved as it was intended. After two laps, she had me try with crutches. I made two more laps with tears streaming down my cheeks.

"Can't I wait to use a fake leg till my stump heals?" I asked her. "I just got the real one cut off three days ago."

Jamie laughed. "That's up to you. You can't get a *permanent* prosthesis until you're completely healed and the swelling's gone down. But we like to give folks the option of using temporary ones until then. What are your goals? Do you want to be walking and running with your kids sooner rather than later?"

"Honestly, I want to get home and back to work as quickly as I can—and I don't care if I have to use crutches."

"Okie doke," she said. "But you'll have to do some pretty serious exercises to keep your remaining joints mobile. And you need to graduate to forearm crutches. It's better for your posture and it'll help your gait if and when you decide you want that 'fake' leg."

I sat in a chair while she removed the prosthesis, and she escorted me—on my underarm crutches—back to Robert.

He raised an eyebrow. "Didn't go so well, huh?"

Jamie shook her head.

"It's not something I want to pursue right now," I said. "It's not worth the frickin' pain. Can I go back to my room, please?"

"Not until you master the forearm crutches," Robert said sternly.

After half an hour, I'd learned the basics. "Good job," he said. "Let's take a little break, get you something to drink, and then I'll show you some exercises for your left hip and side."

Later—completely exhausted—I held my new crutches on my lap as he wheeled me back to my room.

After lunch, the nurse came to disconnect my morphine pump. "You'll do fine with oral meds," she said. "We'll try to get them to you on schedule, but don't hesitate to buzz us if we're late—or if the pain gets too overwhelming."

I nodded, took my first dose, and lay back against the pillows to doze.

"Wake up, sleepyhead," I heard someone saying in a faraway, lilting voice.

I struggled to consciousness to find Dr. G standing by my bedside grinning. "I don't usually like to wake someone from a well-deserved nap, but I didn't want to take one of those truffles without asking your permission."

I groaned. "You woke me up to ask for candy?"

"Just kidding. I woke you up to tell you the good news about your pathology reports: the margins were all clear, and none of the tumor had progressed beyond the parosteal state. You don't need chemo!"

I choked back a sob. "I'm so glad. I'd been trying not to worry about it, but the fear of getting bad results kept niggling at me."

"I can imagine. But you can relax about it now and concentrate on getting on with the long life you have ahead of you."

"I think this calls for chocolate."

"Amen, sister!"

Dr. G selected a piece and nibbled at it delicately, licking her fingers between bites. "This is heavenly."

"Mm-hmm," I said. "My ex-boyfriend brought them yesterday."

"*Ex*-boyfriend?"

I nodded. "I broke up with him last weekend."

"Right before a major operation." It was a statement, but a question lurked between her words.

I shrugged. "Maybe not the best timing, but we disagreed about lots of important things. For one, he thought I rushed into surgery. That I should've gotten a second opinion and—implicitly—one favoring the limb-sparing option. I realized he was always gonna be a heli-copter partner. You know, one who hovers around to rescue me from myself?"

She nodded and took another truffle.

We sat in silence for a moment before I asked her, "When can I be discharged?"

"Probably on Tuesday if the wound's looking good. You should have more of your strength back by then. But you realize you'll be going to a rehab facility, not directly home?"

"Yeah. I remember your saying that. Will you be the one who decides when I'm ready to get out of *there*, too?"

Dr. G shook her head. "No, they've got staff to evaluate when you're ready. Usually it takes at least a few weeks to become adept at everything they set as criteria for discharge."

"Three more days here and a few weeks there…"

"Hey! You don't strike me as a glass-half-empty kind of person. Please don't lose sight of the great news we got today."

She's right. You gotta leave this pity party and count your blessings. "Thanks for reminding me, Doc. Would you mind texting me some wise words every day until I get on the road to gratitude?"

Her laughter brought an instant smile to my face. One I felt in my heart.

35

Turns out walking on crutches *with* only one leg is different than doing so while *using* one leg and holding the other aloft. And forearm crutches were trickier than the under-the-armpit kind. During our Saturday morning PT session, Robert stopped me from toppling no less than three times. "Hey," he said with what seemed to me a truly enthusiastic tone, "you'll get it. Your sense of balance is off 'cause you're missing a ten-pound piece of a major extremity."

I couldn't help laughing. "Well, when you put it that way…"

"Just one more lap across the room and we'll call it a day. How's the pain?"

"About a seven."

"I'll buzz your nurse to have some pain meds delivered ASAP."

When Robert wheeled me off the elevator, Matt Witte

stood at the nurses' station asking for me. "There you are," he said, leaning down to hug me.

"Just getting back from the gym. Meet Robert, my new trainer. Robert, my colleague, Matt."

The men shook hands. "Lemme get her situated, Matt, and you can come in and visit." He turned to me. "Recliner or bed? And don't be a hero."

"Why does everybody feel compelled to say that?" I said with a groan. "Bed, but only so I can elevate my missing appendage. I'm not exhausted at all."

The nurse followed Matt into the room. "I hear you're ready for some meds."

"Maybe just an ice pack for now? I want to actually hear what this guy's got to say."

Matt glanced away while the nurse situated the ice pack around the stump of my leg. "You can look if you want," I said. "I've got shorts on under this robe."

"I'll pass, thanks," he said sheepishly. "My mom wanted me to be a doctor but I faint at the very thought of blood. Even being a cop is challenging in that respect."

I took a long pull from my omnipresent thermal mug of ice water. "Do you have any good news on the cop front? I could use a pick-me-up."

He waggled his hand in a *so-so* gesture. "How 'bout I tell you and you decide?"

"Glenda told me about Jen calling her dad. Were you able to find the number?"

"Yeah. When Glenda and I notified Verizon on Tuesday that her daughter's phone had been used to contact a suspected sex trafficker, they had the printed records for us in a matter of minutes. The number Jen called is for a burner phone with a 501 area code, ostensibly from Arkansas. The day she called her dad, he was somewhere near Kansas City. But the phone's off now, so no way to know his current whereabouts."

"Had she ever called him before?"

"She told us she did—several weeks ago."

"Wait. Jen *talked* with you about this?"

"Yeah, last evening at the Fosters' house. I called Nancy Drummond and asked her to come with me. It actually went better than any of us expected."

I raised the head of my bed to get a better look at Matt's face. "Go on."

"Nancy took the lead. She told Jen it's understandable that she feels love and loyalty to her dad and that she'd want to be in touch with him. Then she reminded her that his actions toward her and her sister were in fact criminal and asked Jen how she would feel if her father found other girls to take her and her sister's places. The look on her face was pitiful—obviously she knew he'd do it in a minute." Matt shook his head. "In fact, later in our conversation, Jen said another girl from Arkansas was with them for a few weeks last year. She said she didn't know what had happened to her. I take it Jen and her sister didn't much care for the girl. Jen called her 'hateful.'"

"That's sad—do you think Jen and Josie resented her for taking some of their father's attention?"

"Yeah. That was my take on it. And I think Jen has at least some guilt for not empathizing with the girl."

"Poor kids—"

Matt nodded. "Back to the phone call—I asked Jen how she knew how to get in touch with her father. She said that when their mom died, he'd made the girls memorize two phone numbers and told them if they needed him anytime—night or day—they should call. Jen admitted she'd called the first number shortly after she moved in with the Fosters, using a cell phone she'd borrowed from a kid at Vilas Beach. During that call, she told her dad that Josielynn was dead and that she'd been 'arrested' by the cops but let go. He asked her not to tell anyone about him and said if she needed to call again, to use the second number. I'm guessing he ditched the first phone right after her call."

"Did she tell you the number so we can follow up, just in case he didn't toss it?"

Matt nodded. "Yeah, it was another throwaway with an Arkansas area code. No longer in service. We'll keep trying both numbers periodically in case AJ activates them again, but my guess is he's too smart for that. Interestingly, Jen confessed that she hadn't asked the kid's permission to use the phone and didn't even know him. Said she was sitting on the beach when he went into the water to have chicken fights with his friends and left the phone on his towel. Jen just reached over, 'borrowed' the phone, and made the call while the kid was distracted."

"It sounds so unlike Jen to just use it without asking. She must've really wanted to talk to her dad."

"Uh-huh. She said that when she called from Colorado Springs on Sarah Foster's phone, she asked him if she could call again, and he told her it would be too dangerous. And that's the only time during the whole interview when she got noticeably emotional. Her eyes teared up but she didn't cry."

I swallowed a lump in my throat. "So...she understands that her father's completely abandoned her."

"Yep. I left the Fosters' shortly after that, but Nancy was gonna stay and chat with her some more. And Glenda said Jen had an appointment with her shrink this morning so they'd address this stuff then."

I leaned into the pillows.

"You're grimacing," Matt said. "Why don't you buzz the nurse and get those meds."

I nodded and pushed the call button.

"By the way," Matt said, standing to leave, "I saw Luke, your dad, and Sparky in the front yard when I left the Fosters' last evening and stopped to say hi. Luke told your dad I used to be your boyfriend but now I just work for you." He chuckled.

I felt my face flush and stared down at my nonexistent foot.

"Anyway, they were getting ready to take Sparky for a walk. Or vice versa, judging by how he was pulling on the leash. I asked if they wanted to go to the dog park instead. They jumped at the chance."

I grinned, picturing the outing in my mind. "How'd Sparky do at the park?"

"We didn't stay long, but he and Luke burned off a lot of energy and avoided tussles with any other boys or beasts. And your dad insisted I stay for pizza when we got home. They're nice people. You're lucky."

I blinked back tears. "Thanks, Matt. That was super sweet of you."

"No problem. And you know I'll keep you posted on the case," he said, walking out as the nurse came in.

"He's a cutie," she said, handing me a small paper cup with my blessed pain relievers.

"He is that."

36

I STARTLED when the dietary aide came in to bring me my breakfast on Sunday morning. Though I'd been awake earlier, I had apparently dozed off again.

"Sorry, Mrs. Spencer," he said, lowering his long eyelashes over his cocoa-brown cheeks. "I didn't mean to scare you."

I glanced at his name tag. "No worries, CJ. I guess I fell asleep after I called in my order."

"Are you ready to eat now? I can take the lids with me and get 'em out of your way."

"Yes, please."

He set the tray on my over-the-bed table and lowered it onto my stump. I felt a jolt of pain and couldn't help but wince and yelp.

"Oh, my God! I'm so sorry," he said, fumbling to raise the table up again. The stainless steel cover from my entree plate teetered toward the edge of the tray, and in the process of catching it, CJ knocked over the cup of coffee. Thank heaven the lip of the tray prevented it from spilling onto my legs—I couldn't have dealt with that. "I don't know what's wrong with me this morning," he said. "I'm not usually this clumsy."

"Relax. I'm gonna take a couple deep breaths and you should, too—we'll both feel better in a second." CJ followed my instructions.

"Okay," I said when we finished, "there are a couple used towels in the bathroom you can use to sop up the coffee. I'll start on my bacon and eggs, and you can bring me another cup whenever you get a chance."

"Yes, ma'am," he said, scurrying to the bathroom for the towels. I hate being addressed as ma'am but held my tongue, afraid to rattle him any further.

"On second thought, I don't need any coffee. I'm nervous enough already."

"How come?" he asked.

"My kids are coming to see me today and I know they're gonna be freaked 'cause I had my leg amputated. I was hoping to be able to move around pretty well on my crutches when they come—you know, to set them at ease —but it's harder than I thought. I'm afraid I'll fall walking down the hall or something."

"How old are your kids?"

"My youngest daughter is three and my oldest daughter is thirteen, and I've got twins—a boy and a girl —who're five."

"Yeah, I can see why they might be a little freaked. But all but the littlest one should be able to help you. That's a good thing." He finished cleaning the tray and took the stained towels to the bathroom to wring them out.

"Would you mind lowering the table yourself?" CJ

asked when he returned. "I can push the release button if you guide it down."

"Great idea." We managed to adjust the table to a comfortable eating height without inflicting any more pain. "Thanks, CJ."

He smiled and headed for the door. "And, Mrs. Spencer?" I nodded at him. "You'll do fine on those crutches if you just remember to breathe!"

"Thanks, I will."

Though not particularly hungry, I ate the bland hospital fare with relish. After all, I needed my strength to make it through the morning's PT routine. I was determined to be proficient on the forearm crutches when my kids arrived.

AFTER PT AND LUNCH, the nurse got me situated in the recliner chair wrapped in a blanket. My stump—or "residual limb," to be medically and politically correct—was enveloped in ice packs, which chilled me to the core. I pulled my hoodie up over my head and waited for my visitors. Though every bone in my body ached and the surgical site throbbed with level-eight pain, I hesitated to ask for pain meds. I dreaded dozing off or slurring my words in front of the kids.

Dad came into the room first. "Are you sure you're ready for the onslaught?" he asked, grabbing my hand and holding it to his lips.

"Absolutely. I can't tell you how much I've missed 'em all."

"They're a little hinky about all this amputation and hospital stuff, so don't take offense if they're standoffish."

I nodded and he went to summon my brood.

Luke ran into the room and halted in front of my chair. "I heard they cut off your leg, Mommy! Can I see it?"

"If you give me a hug first!" He leaned his head into my chest in an awkward embrace. I saw my daughters in the doorway: Lily held Red on one hip, and Amy leaned against the other.

"We miss you," Amy said, moving slowly in my direction.

"Me, too. And I need a big hug and kiss from each of you." I shoved the ice packs and blanket aside and pushed myself to a standing position, quickly realizing I couldn't bend over to greet them without losing my balance. *Shit, shit, shit! Better to sit than fall.* I sat heavily and opened my arms. Amy gave me a tentative hug but planted a huge kiss on my cheek. Lily set Red on the right arm of the recliner so I could hug her without inviting her to my lap, then kissed my cheek as well.

"Does it hurt, Mommy?" Amy asked with tears in her eyes.

"Yes, but they give me medicine that helps a lot."

"Can you walk?" Red asked.

"Remember when I first hurt my leg and I walked with crutches?" She nodded. "Well, you can use crutches to walk when you only have one leg, too. I got some new ones that are more comfortable. In a little while, we'll take a stroll down the hallway and I'll show you how I can use them."

"Let's see your leg!" Luke said.

"Gross," Amy said, turning toward the doorway. "I don't wanna see it."

"You can't see much with the bandages on, but nobody has to look if they don't want to. Lily, why don't you pull that curtain around the bed? Luke and whoever else wants to can stay inside and take a peek. Anybody else can stay outside. Okay?"

All four kids and my dad nodded like bobble-head dolls. Luke, Lily, and Dad stayed on my side of the curtain, while Amy and Red went to stand near the bathroom door. I undid the safety pin and rolled the leg of my yoga pants up over the bandages—slowly—both to ease my pain and to give the scene a little drama. "Ready?" More nods. "Okay… here it is. Or rather, here's where it was!"

Lily groaned. "Mom—that's not funny."

"Wow!" Luke said. "It's really gone!"

Not to be left out of the loop, Red pushed through the curtain opening and stood wordlessly beside the chair. I reached over and tousled her curls. "Not too exciting, is it, kiddo?" She shook her head.

"Can we touch it?" Luke asked.

"Not yet. When the stitches are out and the wound is healed, I'll certainly let you touch it. Amy, I'm rolling down my pants leg now, so you can c'mon back in in a sec."

Once I was re-situated in the chair, Lily pulled the curtain aside. "Sure you don't wanna look, Amy?" Luke asked.

She shuffled her sneakers against the floor and pretended to be intrigued by the squeaking noise. "I *said* no once already. Now leave me alone."

"Okay, *okay*," Luke shot back. "Don't have a cow!"

"Enough already," I said, trying to maintain a level

tone. "I'm told there's juice and cookies in the family lounge down the hall, and I could use some practice with the new crutches. What say we take a walk?"

"Yeah," Amy and Red said in unison, obviously relieved at the thought of leaving the room.

"Hand me those crutches please," I said. Eyes downcast, Lily grabbed the crutches that were leaning against the window ledge and passed them to me. *Is that pity or concern I see on her face? I can't stand to be pitied. And it's not my kids' job to worry about me; their job is to be kids.*

My dad must've read my mind, for he placed a steadying hand under my elbow to help me out of the chair and whispered, "Relax, kiddo. They'll get used to the 'new normal' before you know it."

"I'm growing to hate that phrase," I whispered back.

Red and Luke raced down the hallway, earning a reprimand from a nurse's aide escorting an elderly man hunched over his walker and shuffling in their trajectory. "Hey! Watch where you're going."

Lily and Amy walked ahead of Dad and me, but kept turning to watch my progress. "At least I'm moving faster than that geezer with the walker," I said, sotto voce.

My dad laughed. "Don't get cocky."

He was right, of course. The doorway to the lounge —where Luke and Red awaited us—began to seem farther away with each step. I made it without falling but collapsed, grimacing, into the closest chair.

We visited for perhaps twenty minutes and the littles had each consumed two packages of Lorna Doone cookies and a juice box before the pain in my residual limb had risen to a crescendo. As nonchalantly as possible, I blotted the sweat from my brow with the hem of my oversized T-shirt. *How in God's name am I gonna walk back to my room?*

This time, it was my nurse who must've heard my thoughts. She breezed into the lounge pushing a wheel-chair. "Sorry to break up the party, Caroline, but you're due for some meds and the physical therapist will be by in ten minutes." She winked at me as she helped me into the chair.

I said my farewells to Dad and the kids in the hallway. "I'll be moving to a rehab center in Madison on Tuesday or Wednesday, and you'll be able to come see me after school," I said. "And, don't forget, I expect good behavior reports from Grandma and Grandpa."

Ever the spokesperson, Amy piped up, "We'll be good, Mom. Don't worry."

My dad rolled his eyes.

37

As PROMISED, Dr. G came by at seven thirty on Tuesday morning and signed my discharge orders. "You're healing nicely," she said, "and I think you're ready to go full-tilt into rehab."

I wanted to kiss her. "Thank you! And about rehab: I'm not sure if they told you, but I decided to pass on the temporary fake leg for now. I think I'll be able to get around well enough on crutches. And with a wheelchair or scooter for longer treks."

She nodded. "I certainly respect your choice. Just let prosthetics know when 'well enough' doesn't do it for you anymore."

"Don't you mean 'if'?"

She raised an eyebrow.

"You said 'when' rather than 'if,'" I said. "What if I *never* want to use a prosthesis?"

"Again, your choice. But I'd bet a year's salary that you'll be ready to walk—or run—on two legs before you know it. Those kids of yours won't let you off the hook!"

"We'll see. What time can I leave?"

"Whenever PT and the nursing staff are done going through their checklists with you. I'm guessing nine o'clock. And I'll see you in two weeks for your post-op checkup."

"Thanks for everything, Doc. You've been great."

As she leaned over the bed to give me a hug, I noticed tears in her eyes. "I only wish I could've spared your limb."

"If wishes were horses, then beggars would ride."

Dr. G sniffled, then laughed. "I've never heard that one before."

"My mom must be a generation older than yours. She used to say that to me and my brother *all* the time."

"I just might use it on my kids," she said as she walked out the door.

I TEXTED my dad to let him know my estimated time of release. He called a second later. "I'm leaving now. There's some construction on I-94 so it'll probably be after nine."

"No rush. Just text when you get here and I'll meet you downstairs."

The nursing assistant wheeled me to the curb with my crutches and overnight bag on my lap. Dad jumped out of the car and rushed around to open the passenger door and take my bag. "What can I do?"

"Chill, Dad! I got this."

He and the aide watched but kept their distance as I maneuvered from the wheelchair into the car. "Let's roll!" I said.

"Copy that," Dad said with a smile. "There's a pillow on the floor behind your seat if you wanna take a nap."

"Sounds like a great idea."

I woke up when Dad pulled into my driveway. While he reached into the back to retrieve my bag, I opened the passenger door, got out, and headed toward the front porch. One glance over my shoulder told me he was uneasy not being at my elbow. When I reached the stairs, he called out, "Hold on, Caroline. I'm sure you're fine, but cement steps can be unforgiving."

He's right. I waited until he caught up with me before ascending to the porch, taking each step cautiously. He opened the door and I walked straight to the living room, where I sank into my favorite chair. "It feels *so* good to be home. I only wish I could stay."

"Louise," Dad called out, "we're home." My mom didn't answer.

"My guess is she's out back having a cigarette," I said. "But wherever she is, Sparky's with her—otherwise he'd be clamoring to say hello."

"Do you want me to go upstairs and put together the things you'll need at the rehab facility?"

"No, thanks. That's the kind of thing I need to do myself. I just need a few moments to regroup."

"Would you like something to drink?"

I shook my head.

"I'm gonna go grab a Coke," he said and headed toward the kitchen, while I got up to go pack.

As Robert had taught me, I used the railing to navigate the stairs, holding the spare crutch in my right hand. It was slow going and more awkward than it had been in the hospital PT area, but I breathed a sigh of relief when

I made it to the landing. I turned around and looked down to see my dad standing in the foyer, giving me a thumbs-up. "You don't need to babysit me," I said.

He laughed. "Not babysitting. Just admiring your moves."

"Whatever."

In my room, I grabbed a nylon duffel bag hanging from a hook in the closet and threw it onto the bed along with the clothes and shoes I wanted to pack. I took a makeup bag from the bathroom, hooked it over the handle of one crutch, and filled it with the toiletries I needed. Back at the bed, I sat down and carefully packed the bag, which ended up weighing about ten pounds.

Good job! I told myself. Until I stood up again and tried to carry the bag. First, I slung it over one shoulder and took a few steps. Completely off balance, I fell—thankfully onto the bed. I tried putting the duffel's shorter handles over the crutch handle but realized I would trip over the bag when walking—if not in the hallway, certainly on the steps. Defeated, I sat, head in hands, fighting back tears.

I looked up when my mom knocked on the door-frame. "Can I come in?"

I nodded.

She sat beside me on the bed, put her arm around me, and pulled my head onto her shoulder. "Oh, sweetie. It sucks, doesn't it?"

"Uh-huh," I snuffled, then paused in amazement to realize she'd used a crass colloquialism. And that she was acting motherly.

"You've always been so independent," she said, "even as a little girl—always wanting to do things by yourself.

Teaching yourself how to ride a two-wheeler. Cutting your own hair. Doing your own homework, even if it was too hard for you. It was difficult for me and your dad, watching you struggle when we would've been so happy to help."

"I let you help me. You're helping me now—taking care of the kids while I'm recovering from surgery."

"Sure, you let us help *sometimes*. But your first inclination's always to do it yourself."

"Maybe."

"Well, I can assure you you'll be able to do it yourself again soon. But for now, how about I carry your bag downstairs?"

I hugged her, reveling in the smell of her time-honored *Taboo* body powder as she hugged me back. "That would be super. Thanks, Mom."

"By the way," she said on her way out, "I've got good news: I quit smoking!"

"What? I've heard you say a hundred times that's the *last* thing you'd ever do."

"Amy shamed me into it. She's a persistent little thing, isn't she?"

"To put it mildly."

AFTER I REGAINED MY EQUILIBRIUM, I walked over to stand before the full-length mirror next to my closet. I looked downward and focused on my *residual limb*, clearly swollen beneath the bandages and my empty pant leg. *Did I make a huge mistake when I authorized Dr. G to amputate? What if my pain's just as bad as it would've been if she'd saved my leg?*

That phantom pain they sometimes talk about—that can last a long frickin' time.

My rumination was interrupted by my dad's voice from downstairs, "You ready, kiddo? I thought you were supposed to be there by noon."

I SAID good-bye to Dad when we got to the check-in desk at the University of Wisconsin Rehabilitation Hospital on Madison's east side. An aide welcomed me and wheeled me to where I'd be staying, an inviting room with huge windows and a bed that beckoned me. "Can I nap now?" I asked her.

"Sorry. You're scheduled for a team meeting at one o'clock. Have you eaten?"

"Uh-huh. My dad and I grabbed a sandwich on the way over here. So…who's on the team and where will we meet?"

"They'll come get you. It'll be the hospitalist, your social worker, and your physical therapist for sure. Maybe a few other folks. Why don't you unpack while I go get you some ice water? Hydration's a big focus around here."

She returned with another insulated water mug with a straw to add to my collection and I dutifully sipped.

The social worker, Bobbi Ann, came to my room a few minutes later. "Settled in?" she asked after introducing herself.

"As much as I want to be," I said with a smile. "No offense."

"None taken. It's our job to get you out of here as quickly as possible. Dr. Arya, the hospitalist, will be in in a few minutes to check you over. When he's done, we'll start the staffing."

Dr. Arya, a diminutive dark-skinned man, introduced himself to me with a wide smile and what I detected was an Indian accent. "Sorry to make you move, but I need you to be sitting on the bed so I can examine your residual limb." He paused and turned to the doorway. "Ah, and here is my efficient nursing assistant, Ms. Maryanne. Maryanne, our new patient, Caroline Spencer.

Maryanne, a young woman two inches shorter and several shades darker than the doctor, handed me my crutches and watched intently as I moved myself from wheelchair to bed. "'Fraid I'm gonna hafta take off your pants so we can undo the bandages. Lean back, relax, and I promise I'll be as gentle as possible."

I cringed at the thought—dressing changes at the hospital had been beyond painful.

"Relax," Maryanne said in a soothing tone, laying her warm hand on my shoulder. "Close your eyes and breathe deeply. This won't take long." With uncommon tenderness, she quickly removed my yoga pants and bandages.

"My God, you're good," I said when she patted my hand to signal she'd finished the task. "How'd you do that without hurting me?"

She smiled. "Magic."

"She's a tough act to follow," Dr. Arya said. "Now when I poke and prod, I'm the bad guy! Roll onto your right side, please." I did as he asked. "The incision looks very good. No sign of infection and you seem to be a rapid healer. Now onto your stomach, please."

I turned as instructed and moved the pillow aside so I could continue my calming breaths.

"Now I want you to lift your residual limb up off the bed." I did. "Ah, good. You must've been quite fit before the surgery."

"Not so much. The PT folks in Milwaukee are tough taskmasters."

"Good for them, then. You're clearly ready for what our staff has in store for you. Maryanne will reapply the bandages and bring you to the conference room. I have a few more patients to see before our meeting."

Before putting the dressings back on, however, Maryanne massaged my residual limb with varying degrees of pressure. "What are you doing?" I asked.

"Desensitization. It helps reduce your responsiveness to pain stimuli. Now I'm gonna apply some ointment to your skin. Hopefully it'll feel good. But if it doesn't today, it will eventually. And we'll be doing it regularly throughout your stay with us."

At first I felt pain, but as the session proceeded, I could distinguish between the types of touch. "It doesn't feel bad."

Maryanne grinned. "Yay. Progress."

I'M NOT big on meetings and certainly don't enjoy being the focus of attention. Nevertheless I found the initial staffing conference at the rehab facility uplifting and encouraging. Bobbi Ann led things off. "We've received the reports from the physical therapy folks in Milwaukee and Dr. Arya tells us you're well on your way to recovery. Let's talk about what you need to do to get out of here with the team's blessing. First off, I understand you want to pass on a prosthetic leg at this point?"

I looked down at my lap. "Well…that's what I thought when I left the hospital. But I've changed my mind."

The corners of Bobbi Ann's hazel eyes crinkled into hundreds of minuscule lines as she smiled. "Didn't you just leave the hospital this morning?"

"Uh-huh. But I stopped at home first and went upstairs to pack some things. And I realized I don't want to be tied to crutches or a chair."

"I commend you on your determination," Dr. Arya said. "It will be about six months before you can be fitted for a permanent prosthesis, but you can use a series of temporary ones in the interim."

"There are some benchmarks you need to hit before release," the physical therapist said, "and my team will have you start on them tomorrow: walking up and down hills, falling so you don't hurt yourself, getting up from a fall. You'll learn practical things, like placing your crutches by your bedside so you don't mistakenly try to walk on your missing leg if you wake in the middle of the night."

"You mean to tell me that someday I'll actually forget it's missing?"

"Sooner than you think," Bobbi Ann replied.

38

I GROANED with irritation on Friday evening when, midway through my delectable dessert, my phone signaled an incoming text. *Are your kids still there?* Glenda asked.

No way could I type a response with my sticky fingers, so I called her back. "No, the kids left an hour ago," I said without preamble. "And whatever you're texting about better be important 'cause I'm just finishing a perfectly tart yet sweet lemon bar. The food here is amazing."

I'd expected at least a chuckle but heard my friend sigh. "I just dropped Jen's godmother and aunt off at the airport and thought I'd stop by and tell you about it."

"Oh, shit. I'm sorry, I completely forgot about their visit. Absolutely, c'mon over. I'll be back to my room in five."

"As AN ACT of contrition for my obliviousness about what's happening in your life," I said when Glenda walked in, "I smuggled a lemon bar out of the dining room just for you."

"Geez, gimme some credit," she said, leaning over to kiss my cheek. "I realize you're kinda preoccupied right now. But since you went to all the trouble, I won't turn down your penance."

She sat down, took a bite of the dessert, then said in a deadpan voice, "Wow—I'd give an arm and a leg for this recipe."

I burst out laughing. "That's why I love you. You are so-o-o bad!"

"Guilty."

"Okay, tell me all about the visitors."

"Where do I begin? I told you Magnolia Barr'd called and said she wanted to come visit yesterday and today?"

I nodded.

"I was a little put out that she wanted Jen to miss part of a school day. I mean, why couldn't she come on the weekend? But turns out, she was also bringing Jen's aunt Barbaralynn—the one with Alzheimer's—and needed to make the trip when the aunt's attendant was available to come along."

I sat forward in my chair. "Why on earth?"

"My thought, exactly. But Magnolia thought seeing her aunt might help Jen remember her childhood and, as a matter of fact, it did. And even weirder, Barbara remembered Jen."

Glenda paused to finish the last bite of lemon bar, and—I suspected—to keep me in suspense a few moments longer. "Anyway, I went to the airport at two o'clock yesterday expecting to pick up one person and an overnight bag, and instead I find there's *three* women with luggage up the wazoo. We left the bags with the bellman at the Hotel Red and got to our house just before school let out. Magnolia and Barb were sitting in the living room when Jen walked in. She looked at them and said, 'Auntie Barb?' and ran right over to hug the woman. Barbara got tears in her eyes, started rocking Jen back and forth, and even hummed her a lullaby. Magnolia and I just sat there staring, too stunned to talk."

"Had Jen seen photos of her aunt before the visit?"

Glenda shook her head. "Magnolia says there weren't any in the albums she brought the first time she came, and Barbara's husband hasn't sent any. Caroline, she just *knew*. And she told me that she recognized her aunt's perfume—Chanel—which Magnolia said Barb has worn forever."

"Wow."

"I let Jen stay home from school today to go to Olbrich Gardens and for lunch with them, and I was a little nervous about not going along…"

"Why? Did you think they were gonna kidnap her?"

Glenda stared out the window and waited a beat before answering. "Not exactly. Maybe that they'd put ideas into her head about moving back with them— before I think she's ready."

"I'm sorry to have to remind you, but that's kinda what you signed up for when you became foster parents. The kids leave. And I doubt you'll *ever* think they're ready."

"You're right, I know. But Jen's making such good progress in therapy and school…"

"And you've grown very attached to her."

"There's that."

"How did Jen seem when she came home?"

"Happy." Glenda's voice cracked as she continued, "Said it was nice to know she'd been loved by more than just her mom and sister. She didn't mention wanting to go live with Magnolia and was anxious to get back to school in time for biology class."

"Did Magnolia say anything about wanting custody?"

"Uh-uh. But Auntie Barb was pretty confused and agitated by the time I took them to the airport, and everyone was focused on keeping her calm."

"Well, Judge Baker's not likely to agree to a move at this point. And eventually—after Jen's off the Suboxone and psychologically stable—he'll let *her* make the call. Remember what we all said about respecting kids' opinions?"

Glenda groaned. "You can be so frickin' annoying sometimes, y'know?"

I laughed. "Yeah. I know."

We sat in comfortable silence for a few minutes before she shattered my mood with her question. "So when do you think you'll get sprung from this place?"

"That's a touchy subject," I mumbled, hoping she'd let it slide.

No such luck. "What do you mean?" she persisted. "And don't you dare tell me you don't wanna talk about it."

"But I don't."

"Sorry, kiddo. Not an option. You're my best friend and best friends don't get to keep secrets."

I blinked back my angry tears. "Fine. If you must know, I got some disappointing news at my frickin' team meeting today. They want me to have my pain 'significantly more controlled'"—I made air quotes to highlight my disdain—"before they'll recommend discharge. Which means I've gotta be less dependent on Vicodin than I am now."

She came to sit on the arm of my recliner chair and held my hand. "I'm sorry."

I shook my head and pulled my hand away. "All this physical therapy *hurts*. And it's exhausting. Sometimes I don't have the energy to do the effing meditation and relaxation exercises or to wait for the ice packs to work. When I want and need to sleep, nothing's better than Vicodin."

"You know it'll get easier, don't you?"

"Yeah, but not fast enough. I miss my home and my kids. I miss my job. And this asshole Dr. Arya who's calling the shots is so evasive about his criteria. I mean, how many pain pills a day is too many? He can't or won't say. Just that I'll probably be here at least a couple weeks."

Glenda did a double take. "You're bitching about a couple weeks? I figured it'd take *months* to recover from having your leg amputated. That's *major* surgery, for God's sake."

I didn't reply.

"You get to see your kids, but your parents and in-laws cart 'em around and make sure they bathe and eat and wear clean clothes. You said yourself the food here's amazing. And this room seems pretty damn sweet. I've got two words for you: buck up!"

At first I felt as though she'd slapped me in the face. After a moment, though, I couldn't help laughing. "Point taken."

39

WITH CONSIDERABLE PRIDE and a fair amount of pain, I donned a fake leg to wear home from the rehab center on a Monday, thirteen days after my admission. Glenda practically bounded into the room at four o'clock but came to an abrupt halt when she saw me standing near the window. "Oh. My. God. Will you fall over if I hug you?"

I laughed. "I hope not. But the good news is that they taught me how to get back up again if I do."

She approached more slowly and engulfed me in her arms. "You are amazing," she said, her voice cracking.

"I'm not so sure about that, but thanks for the vote of confidence. Where's my dad?"

"Waiting out front with the car. He wants to make it home before rush hour."

"The 'big city' traffic still flummoxes him," I said with a smile. "Not to worry, though. I'm all signed out and just need to call the CNA to take me downstairs."

The aide arrived five minutes later, pushing my wheel-chair. "Have a seat please, young lady," he said.

I did so gladly. "Seems kinda weird that I worked so hard to learn to walk on this contraption and now you're making me ride outta here!"

"I think so, too. But the suits see it differently!"

MY DAD STOWED THE WHEELCHAIR—WHICH I might still need for long distances—in the trunk. I rode shotgun and Glenda got in the back seat with my crutches and belong-ings. "Hallelujah!" I said. "I can't wait to sleep in my own bed."

"I'm a little surprised to see you wearing the leg," Dad said. "I thought you said it still hurt."

"It does, and I'll probably take it off pretty soon. I just wanted the kids to see that it won't be long till I'm almost back to normal."

"They're gonna be so proud," Glenda said. "But I'm not sure you've ever been *normal!*"

"Thanks for reminding me," I said with a smile.

AS IT TURNED OUT, I didn't have the opportunity to remove my prosthesis for a while. A welcome home party awaited: my mom; all four of my kids; Abby and Bert; Hank Foster with Sarah, Jake, and Jen; and my dear friend Rosalee—just back from a two-month trip to Italy. "Surprise!" they all yelled when Glenda, my dad, and I walked in. The twins ran toward me but stopped short of hugging distance. "Mommy!" Red shrieked as she bounded into me. Were it not for Glenda, standing behind me and propping me up, we would have toppled to the floor.

"C'mon into the living room and take a load off," my dad said, clearing a path toward my chair. I collapsed into it and opened my arms for hugs.

I'd seen the kids most every day during my stay at rehab, but they'd always seemed wary—as though they couldn't count on my return home. And, in fact, the discharge hadn't been scheduled until this morning. "This is what I've been waiting for!" I said as tears streamed down my cheeks.

Bert opened a bottle of champagne for the adults and a bottle of sparkling cider for the kids and me. Amy carefully ferried the glasses to the guests, spilling only a few drops along the way. And when everyone had been served, my dad lifted his glass. "A toast to Caroline's rapid recovery and to the many years of good health she can look forward to!"

"Speech!" Hank called out after we'd clinked glasses and taken our sips.

"Darn it, Hank," I said, wiping my eyes with the back of my hand. "Can't you see I'm too overwhelmed for words?"

"Sorry," he said, looking down at his feet.

"But," I said with a grin, "I'd be remiss if I didn't say a few. You guys mean the world to me, and I can't thank you enough for all the support and encouragement you've given me these past several weeks. I love you!"

When Abby and Bert brought in two huge trays of warm nachos, the focus shifted—thankfully—away from me. I leaned back in the chair with my real and fake legs propped up on the footstool and looked around the room.

Lily sat cross-legged on the floor, fiddling with her empty glass, away from her usual cohorts Sarah and Jen. *That's weird.*

Rosalee zeroed in on Red, who struggled to extricate a tortilla chip from a mound of cheese on her plate. "Want some help?" Red nodded, and my friend picked her and her plate up and plunked them both down onto my ottoman. "This girl needs some Mommy time…and a hand at getting her chips out of the goo."

Red inched herself away from my exposed prosthetic ankle, and I could see her trying to decide whether to flee. "It's okay, kiddo. It's just a hunk of metal and screws—like those transformer cars Luke plays with. Go ahead and touch it." She shook her head. "Okay. Another time, then. But come sit in the chair with me and we'll tackle those nachos."

Red handed me her plate, climbed up beside me—carefully avoiding my left thigh—and snuggled under my arm. As usual, Abby's nachos were delicious.

Ten minutes later, Amy, Luke, and Jake—who'd inhaled their food—left to take Sparky for a walk. Sarah and Jen came over to greet me, then went home "to do homework." Lily disappeared shortly afterward.

My mother handed Red her smartphone with a Netflix movie cued up, and the adults were free to talk. "Now to logistics," my dad said without preamble. "Caroline, we all want to help but don't want to step on your toes."

"That should be easy, since I've only got half as many for you to avoid," I said with a laugh.

"Too soon!" Rosalee said.

"Seriously," Glenda said. "Tell us what we can do to smooth the transition for you."

Truth is, I didn't have to *tell* them anything.

"Your mom has to get back to St. Cloud," my dad said, "but I plan to stay as long as you need me. I can take the kiddos to school and activities."

"I'd be happy to drive you to your PT appointments," Rosalee said.

"Bert and I will cook," Abby said. "And if you need to keep Grace on the payroll, she can grocery shop and clean."

I felt a flood of emotions—most prominently gratitude and sadness. "This is giving me a sense of déjà vu, like when everyone rallied 'round to help me after David died. I mean, I appreciate everything you're all doing, but it's scary-sad again."

Rosalee came and sat on the arm of my chair. "Honey, I know it's scary. But the loss of your leg is nowhere near as sad as losing your husband. You'll bounce back quicker than you think."

Interestingly, it was my often-self-absorbed mother who noticed my physical pain. "You're scowling every time you breathe. Is it time for a Vicodin?"

"Uh-huh. And to take off this leg and get some ice on my wounds."

"I'm guessing it's also time for a nap," Hank said.

I nodded.

The friends departed, Dad and Bert went outside to entertain Red, Abby got ice, and my mom retrieved the pain pills from my overnight bag. I didn't have the energy to tackle the steps, so I maneuvered over to the couch, removed my prosthesis, and settled in. Within minutes, I was asleep.

I AWOKE DISORIENTED and hungry and looked around the deserted living room. Deserted, that is, except for Lily, curled up under a throw on my chair and staring in my direction. "Hi, honey. What time is it?"

"Seven thirty."

"Where's everyone else?"

"Grandma and Grandpa took 'em over to Michael's Frozen Custard for dessert."

"On a school night? What were they thinking? We'll never get 'em to sleep."

Lily didn't respond and I finally noticed the troubled look in her eyes. "You've been waiting for me to wake up to tell me something, haven't you?"

She nodded.

I sat up and patted the spot next to me on the couch. "What is it?"

She came over and settled beside me. "It's about Jen," she said tentatively.

My heart sank. "Just spit it out, kiddo."

"You know she and I walk to school with Benjy most every day?" I nodded, knowing she referred to another eighth grader who lived down the block from us. "Well, Jen's been acting all weird around him lately. Like, flirting or something. She usually wears her hair up in a ponytail or a knot, but the last few days she's been leaving it down and shaking it around like she's a movie star or something."

Lily paused and absently twirled a strand of her own

hair around her fingers, something she'd done since she was little—more often when anxious. "Today she had the top few buttons of her blouse undone, and she kept, like, touching Benjy's arm while we walked. It was so embarrassing, but Benjy didn't seem to notice. He's so clueless about girls sometimes. And Jen wasn't here to get the memo."

I couldn't help laughing. About a year ago, Benjy'd come out as gay and he'd *literally* sent out a memo to his friends announcing it. I'd worried at the time that he'd be subject to ruthless bullying for both his sexual orientation and his method of disclosure, but thankfully I had been wrong.

"Lemme get this straight," I said. "Jen's got a crush on him, but Benjy hasn't noticed. And she doesn't realize that no matter how much she flirts, he's not gonna be attracted to her."

"Exactly. But believe me, Mom, it gets much worse."

My stomach knotted as I watched Lily reach for her phone. She clicked on a text message from Benjy and showed it to me. The message read simply, *WTF?* But attached to it was a photo of a torn scrap of paper with a handwritten note: *Benj, If you want, I can make you come. XOXO, Jen.*

I read it again, then dropped the phone onto my lap. "Oh, my God. How'd she get the note to him?"

"She passed it to him in third-period study hall."

"Who else knows about this?"

Lily shrugged. "I didn't tell *anyone*. Not even Sarah. But Jen knows I know."

"How?"

"She saw me talking to Benjy after school. Then,

when he left to go to football practice, she came up to me and said, 'He told you, didn't he?' I just nodded but didn't say anything."

"Glenda needs to know."

"Oh, Mom. Couldn't we keep her out of it? Y'know, just talk to Jen and, like, tell her it's not appropriate or something."

I rubbed my temples and tried to think. "No. I'll admit it's tempting. I know Glenda can be kinda over-the-top with her reactions sometimes. But she's Jen's foster mother *and* a social worker—we have to tell her."

Before I could second-guess myself, I reached for my own phone and texted Glenda. *Can you come over? Need to talk ASAP.*

There in 5, came her reply.

"She'll be over right away," I told Lily. "Would you mind grabbing me a yogurt from the fridge? I need to take some ibuprofen and shouldn't do it on an empty stomach."

"Sure." As she popped off the couch and headed for the kitchen, I felt a twinge of guilt for not getting my own snack. But I realized it'd take every ounce of energy I possessed to deal with the new issue Jen had presented.

I'D JUST FINISHED HALF a carton of strawberry Greek yogurt and swallowed two pills with a glass of water when Glenda frantically rushed into the living room. "What's wrong? Is there bad news you didn't tell us before?"

I sighed. "There's bad news but I didn't know it when you were here before. You'd better sit down."

She plunked herself onto my ottoman, leaning forward, elbows on knees. "What is it?"

"Lily," I yelled toward the kitchen, "come in here, please."

Lily shuffled into the room as if she were headed to her own execution and didn't sit until I nodded toward a chair.

"Glen," I started, "Lily told me something about Jen that you need to know, and I need you to let her finish before you start asking questions. Go ahead, honey."

Staring down at her lap, my daughter repeated her account of Jen's actions toward their friend Benjy. Glenda looked more and more agitated as the story progressed, and I had to signal to her twice not to interrupt.

When Lily finally handed her the phone to show her the note, Glenda's face fell. "Shit…"

"Uh-huh," I said.

"I was afraid—" Glenda abruptly stopped herself. "Lily, thanks for telling us about this. It couldn't have been easy. I need to talk with your mom alone for a while so we can decide how to handle it, but we'll tell you what you need to know. Okay?"

Lily nodded and bolted from her chair. "I'll be in my room."

My friend got up to make sure Lily was out of earshot, then resumed her spot on the ottoman. "I've been afraid something like this might happen. It's not uncommon for kids who've been sexually abused to act out sexually. Then yesterday Hank told me he'd been getting some weird vibes from Jen—like she's trying to come on to him."

I cringed. "Oh, no…"

"Uh-huh. I'd noticed he'd been keeping his distance from her since our trip to Colorado and I finally asked him why. He said he hadn't wanted to say anything in case he was just imagining it. But you know he's not one to overreact and the things he described were, in fact, unnerving."

"Like what?"

"Like Jen coming out of the bathroom after a shower with her robe undone—at the exact time Hank *always* walks down the hallway to rouse Jake for school. Like asking him to rub a knot out of her neck. Like standing too close to him and touching him when she talks."

I swallowed the lump in my throat. "Are you guys thinking of having her removed from your care?"

"Heavens no. We love Jen and want to help her adjust to her new life. But we've gotta nip this behavior in the bud. I was planning to bring up the thing with Hank at our appointment with Dr. Peters on Wednesday. But now —with the Benjy thing—do you think it'd be better to discuss it with Jen sooner?"

I wanted nothing more than to sleep—and for this brouhaha to have been nothing more than a bad dream. "I think so," I finally said. "Lily says Jen knows that Benjy told her, so she's probably already wondering when somebody's gonna confront her."

"Should I call her over here now to talk?"

"Oh, Glen—I really can't be part of that conversation."

"I know," she said with a sigh. "You're right. I gotta do this."

"It's one of those frickin' 'teachable moments,'" I said with a wry smile. "Lemme know how it goes."

She nodded mutely and left me to doze on the couch.

THE SOUNDS of the front door opening and closing and several little feet trampling into the foyer woke me from another catnap. I heard my mother's voice, "Shhh. Your mommy may be sleeping and she needs her rest."

"It's okay. I'm awake," I said, struggling to a seated position.

Luke bounded into the living room carrying a paper bag. "We got you a cheeseburger with bacon!"

Amy followed close behind, bearing an insulated bag. "And a turtle sundae for dessert!"

"How did you know that's just what I was hungry for?" I opened my arms and they came to give me tentative hugs. My dad lingered in the doorway with Red weaving atop his shoulders, her eyes half-closed. "I think she's down for the count," I told him.

"She's sticky as all get out," Dad said. "I'll give her a quick bath."

"Nah. There's plenty of baby wipes in her middle dresser drawer. Clean off the top layer and put her in bed. I'll be up in a few to tuck her in."

Luke looked heartsick. "What about your dinner?"

"Tell you what, how 'bout you guys bring it upstairs for me and I'll have dinner in bed?"

Amy grinned. "Like breakfast in bed only dinner?"

"Yeah, it'll be a big treat," I said. "Like Mother's Day!"

Twenty minutes later—after my mother had supervised pajama donning and teeth brushing and after I'd changed into a nightgown—the twins and I sat on my bed for my special feast. Leaning back against the headboard with a bath towel spread across my lap, I took a bite of the burger. *Thank you, Mom, for your microwave skills—the temp's just right.* "This is delicious!" I said truthfully. "I didn't realize how hungry I was."

Luke laughed hysterically and managed to scoop up a bite of melted cheese when it dribbled onto my towel. He licked it off his fingers and burped with pride, while Amy looked on in disgust. *And thank you, God, for bringing these precious characters into my life.*

"Are you ready for the sundae?" Amy asked when I swallowed my last bite of burger and wiped my mouth with a soggy napkin.

Stuffed to the gills, I couldn't imagine eating another bite. But I couldn't disappoint her. "I'm pretty full, but I'll eat some now and save the rest for breakfast. Okay?"

Amy nodded and ran downstairs to get it from the freezer. Michael's turtle sundaes are to-die-for. Though the melted caramel and hot fudge had solidified, their flavors melded perfectly with the rich vanilla custard and chunks of pecans. I closed my eyes and sighed after the first bite. "Amazing!"

I managed to take another bite before my mom knocked on the doorframe. "Luke, Amy," she said, "it's *way* past your bedtime. Say good night and scoot on down to your rooms. I'll be there in a minute."

After quick hugs and kisses, they trotted down the hallway. "Thanks, Mom. And would you mind taking this sundae downstairs when you go? I'll explode if I eat any more."

"Sure, honey. Anything else?"

I checked the bedside table: phone plugged into the

charger, full thermal mug of water, pain pills. "Oh, yeah," I said, nodding toward an aluminum walker standing in the corner. "Push that thing over next to the bed, please. They said I might forget I only have one leg if I wake up in the middle of the night and have to pee."

Mom's jaw dropped, and I thought she might drop the sundae. But she quickly recovered and did as I asked. "Sleep well, and yell if you need us," she said, blowing a kiss on her way out.

Exhausted, I turned out the light and tried to sleep. After twenty minutes of restlessness, however, I gave in and reached for my phone. I texted Glenda, *Can't sleep. How did it go with Jen?*

My phone rang in response. "I figured you'd be out cold by now," Glenda said. "I thought I'd wait till tomorrow to call."

"Yeah, I *am* tired but can't sleep. Might have something to do with the bacon cheeseburger and several bites of turtle sundae I ate before bed. Or maybe I just can't get Jen out of my head. Did you talk to her?"

"Yeah. And I must say it went pretty well. She was mortified when I explained how inappropriate it was to proposition Benjy. She started crying and said she just wanted him to like her and that's the only way she could think of to make it happen. I guess she got discouraged when she found out the tennis partner she had a crush on has a girlfriend."

"She had no idea Benjy's gay?"

"Uh-uh. Said something like she didn't think gay guys played football. She's had next to no social interaction with peers, so it's no wonder she doesn't know what to make of things."

"Did you talk to her about Hank?"

I heard her intake of breath. "Yeah. That was harder though 'cause her behavior toward him wasn't as overt. I explained that her relationship with her own father wasn't a healthy one and that Hank is hypervigilant to make sure they have a comfortable—non-sexually-charged—relationship. I told her it wasn't appropriate for her to let her robe fall open around him or to ask him to massage her neck. She kept saying she was so sorry and asking if I could forgive her. I told her of course, that we love her and only want the best for her. And she agreed to talk with Dr. Peters about it in greater detail."

"Sounds like it turned out pretty well. I'm glad."

"Me, too. Now go to sleep!"

"Will do. Love you!"

40

My abrupt awakening from a convoluted dream—about a camping trip on the Boundary Waters during a rainstorm—came not as a result of a lightning strike but from the shrill ring of my cell phone on the bedside table. I rolled onto my side to grab it, resulting in a jolt of pain in my residual limb. "Shit!" I yelled, loud enough to bring my father running to help.

"What's wrong?" he asked, as I pushed the button to accept the call.

"Moved wrong onto my stump reaching for the effing phone," I told him and waved him away. "Hello?"

"She's gone," came Glenda's hysterical voice on the other end of the call.

"What?"

"Jen ran away."

"What d'ya mean ran away? What time is it?"

"Six thirty. I got up to pee and saw her bed hadn't been slept in. We looked all over the house and yard. She's gone."

"Did she leave a note?"

"No. I don't think so. Hank's checking. Should I call the police?"

I heard Hank's voice in the background.

"Glen, lemme talk to Hank."

"Sorry to wake you, but we're pretty worried," he said. "After the talk Glen had with her last night, we're afraid she might've gotten the idea we didn't want her here."

"Okay. Let's think this through. Did Jen leave a note?"

"Not that we could find. I woke Jake and Sarah, and neither of them has a clue where she would've gone."

"Are any of her belongings missing?"

"Her backpack and Air Force Academy hoodie. And I'm guessing she had the hundred bucks in cash that her godmother gave her when she visited. Where could Jen go? The only ID she has is the one from school. She doesn't have a credit card. Or even a cell phone."

"Check to make sure she didn't take one of yours," I said.

Glenda came on the line. "Obviously she didn't take mine 'cause I'm using it. Hank went to look for his and ask the kids."

We waited wordlessly for Hank to return. "Jake's phone is missing," I heard him say in the background.

"She took Jake's," Glenda said to me.

"It's an iPhone on your family plan, right?"

"Uh-huh."

"Click on your Finder app—it's the one with the green circle. Unless Jen turned it off or dumped it, you should be able to see where the phone is now."

"I'll call you back."

While I waited, I swallowed a pain pill, put the phone in the pocket of my pj's, and maneuvered myself to the bathroom with my walker. It felt heavenly to brush my teeth and splash water on my face, still wrinkled from heavy sleep. I went back and sat on the edge of the bed. *How long can it take to run the app?*

The answer, it turned out, was ten minutes. "Sorry," Hank said when he called back, "we didn't realize all our phones are listed under my number, not Glen's. The app shows the phone's near McDonald's on Regent Street. Hopefully Jen is, too. Glenda and Sarah are on their way over there right now."

"Okay. Keep me posted."

Sarah texted me half an hour later. *Found her.*

Thx, I replied and headed downstairs to join my family for breakfast.

As USUAL, my dad had made too much food: pancakes, bacon, scrambled eggs. My mom cringed when the littles hugged and kissed her good-bye with syrupy hands and faces—she'd be flying to Minnesota later that morning—but she wisely held her tongue. They trotted off happily after my father for his school and daycare shuttling.

Mom stood at the sink and used a paper towel to wash her own hands and face, then poured herself another cup of coffee. "Want more?"

"Yeah, thanks. And kudos for not criticizing Dad's breakfast or childcare skills."

"He's so good with them. Better than I'll ever be," she said, resuming her place at the table. "And, you should know, I *am* aware of my tendency to require high maintenance."

I smiled.

"So, how are you *really* coping with all this? I mean, breaking up with Dominic, losing your leg, dealing with pain?"

My eyes welled with tears. "Oh, Mom, so many hard questions. I loved lots of things about Dominic, and maybe I'll wake up one day and regret my decision. But right now, it's a relief not to have him around, hovering and undermining my confidence. And though I thought the kids might miss him, they sure don't seem to. Probably the scariest thing is the reality that I may live my life without another intimate relationship. I mean, a one-legged widow with four kids isn't exactly a great catch."

Mom nodded.

I wiped my nose with a paper napkin and laughed. "This is where you're supposed to jump in and say, 'Nonsense. Any man would be *lucky* to have you!'"

"It's true, but—sadly—a lot of men are too blind to see beyond the surface."

I nodded. "That's probably the biggest issue I have with the amputation. It sets me apart, makes me different. You know I'm not big on being the center of attention, but this is gonna draw attention to me. People are gonna be overly nice and helpful, they're gonna do double takes and look away when I'm at the pool with the kids, they're gonna pity me. And even though I'll be able to do most things for myself, people are gonna assume that I can't. I hate that."

My mom blinked and sniffled several times. "I'm

sorry, honey. I wish it'd been me rather than you. I'm perfectly amenable to accepting attention and help."

I laughed again, spitting out the sip of coffee I was swallowing when she spoke.

"You didn't answer my last question," she said when I'd finished blotting the table. "About the pain."

"It's getting better every day," I said truthfully. "Dr. G said I must have a fairly high pain threshold to have been able to tolerate that big a tumor for so long. So maybe that'll serve me well. Also, the PT folks tell me she did a masterful job of sewing me up. And thankfully, I haven't had any of that phantom pain you hear about. A few bouts of itchiness in my nonexistent toes in the first several days, but none lately."

"You think you'll be able to get off the pain meds soon?"

I patted her hand. "You don't have to worry about me getting addicted to opiates—I hate being constipated and I hate not being able to drink wine. I'm cutting back on the pills and my goal is to be off completely next week so I can get back to work."

"You have to be off pain meds to work?"

"To drive to work. And to have my wits about me to do my job. My boss is bringing some files over later this morning so I can ease back into it."

"Just make sure you don't overdo things," she said, pushing her chair away from the table. "I'd better get moving. Your dad'll be back soon to take me to the airport."

AN HOUR LATER, I stood at my front door watching my

dad wheel my mom's suitcase past George Cooper, who was wheeling a dolly, loaded with two Bankers Boxes, up the sidewalk. "I didn't mean you had to bring *all* the Corbell files," I said with a grin.

"Now you tell me!" George said, parking the dolly at the foot of the stairs. He carried the boxes one by one into the dining room. "Seriously, I didn't have time to sort through them and decide what to bring. Matt or Jimmy can come get the stuff you don't want or need right now."

"Got time for a cup of coffee?"

He looked at his watch. "Half a cup," he said and followed me to the kitchen. Sans prosthesis, I walked quickly with my forearm crutches.

"Sit," I said, grabbed a mug from the cupboard, and placed it on the table in front of him. I turned to the counter, picked up the coffeepot, and balanced it on the crutch handle, and went back to fill his cup.

He raised an eyebrow.

"I'm just showing off," I said with a laugh. "I spilled a lot yesterday so I got up early this morning to practice for your visit. Donut? I saved you an apple cinnamon." I nodded toward the bag on the counter.

My dad had stopped at Greenbush Bakery after dropping the kids off and brought me a half dozen of their freshly baked donuts.

"Greenbush?" George asked, and I could practically see him salivating.

"Uh-huh." I carried the bag to the table. "Help yourself."

He made it a point to dawdle over his choice but—as I knew he would—selected apple cinnamon. He swallowed the donut in three bites and washed it down with two sips of coffee. "Just what the doctor ordered," he said, leaning back in the chair.

"Anything new with Danny Thompsen? I assume you approached his attorney with the plea agreement I drafted before I left?"

George cleared his throat. "Yeah, I talked to Pooley after our motion hearing last week. He says no way will his client take a plea. Which is weird, given we've got his DNA under the fingernails of a dead teenager."

"I've been thinking about it. Thompsen's hang-up with the proposed agreement is probably not the guilty plea itself, but with having to testify against AJ Corbell. So either he thinks his life would be in danger if he did or he's indebted to Corbell for something. If the latter is true, he wasn't just some random John who answered Corbell's Internet ad for kiddie sex. They'd have to have known each other before."

George nodded. "True. And how does Danny Thompsen have the money to retain a Chicago lawyer? I checked into Pooley's background. He's not top tier, but he's not the cheapest shyster around."

"Maybe Corbell's paying the fees?"

"That's what I'm thinking. Anyway, Thompsen's trial is still on for late next month." He stood up from the table, brushed donut crumbs into his hand, and threw them into the sink. "If you come up with anything helpful in those boxes of records, I'd sure appreciate it. We've got a good case against him, but I'd like to slam-dunk him."

"George, I appreciate all you've done to handle this, but I fully intend to be back in time to do the trial."

"Let's talk more next week," he said. "Don't get up—I

can let myself out. And get some rest, kiddo. Healing is
hard work."

*What the hell does that mean? You don't think I'm up to trying
the case? You've gotten into it and want to do it yourself?*

I reached for the donut bag. I'd eaten a chocolate old-
fashioned earlier, but now a cherry one called my name.
After the first bite, I put it down and picked up my phone.
Can you talk? I texted Glenda.

Five minutes and three bites later, she replied. *Nope.
With Jen at home today. Talk to you after Dr. P appointment
tomorrow.*

Dr. P appointment? I wondered. *Oh, yeah. Glenda said they
had a shrink appointment Wednesday morning.*

I CLEARED the table and loaded the mugs into the dishwasher, then headed upstairs to don my fake leg. I'd
promised myself and my physical therapist that I'd try it
at least twice a day. Even when using crutches to carry
some of my weight, it still hurt to wear it.

I'd made several laps around the four upstairs
bedrooms and hallway when I heard my dad come home,
trying to close the front door quietly and to calm Sparky's
excited pitter-patter on the foyer floor. "It's okay. I'm
awake," I yelled. Then, with the added security of
another adult's presence in the home, I trekked up and
down the stairs five times.

Exhausted and sore, I retreated to my bedroom and
the hazy comfort of a Vicodin-induced nap.

41

GLENDA CALLED me around ten thirty Wednesday morning. "I just dropped Jen off at school. Are you up for some company?"

"Sure. Dad's at the grocery store and I'm in the living room, so let yourself in."

I did a few relaxation exercises while I waited for her arrival, hoping to stave off the need for a pain pill. I wanted to be alert enough to really hear what Glenda had to say.

Though the Jen crisis was only a few days old, my friend looked as though she hadn't slept—or showered—in a week. Her perpetually messy blond hair, typically worn in a knot, hung in tangled, greasy strands around her face. Her sunken eyes, shot with red and underscored by eggplant-colored moons, alarmed me. She wore a faded denim jumper that she'd probably bought while pregnant with Jake, stained with what might have been coffee. She shuffled into the living room and collapsed onto the couch.

"Rough few days, huh?" I asked.

When she nodded, tears trickled down her cheeks. She wiped them impatiently with her hand. "I can't stop this frickin' crying."

"Would coffee help? Mineral water? A beer?" I asked, getting up from my chair.

She nodded. "Mineral water, I guess."

I went to the kitchen, put two cans of key lime LaCroix into the messenger bag I used to carry multiple items, and returned to the living room.

Glenda looked up at me sheepishly. "Oh, geez. I can't believe I let you wait on me."

"If I'd been wearing my fake leg, I wouldn't have waited on you. But this is no sweat," I said, handing her her drink. "Plus, how am I gonna get in shape for the Paralympics if I don't challenge myself?"

"Are you serious?" she asked.

"Glen, they amputated my leg, not my sense of humor. And I was pulling yours, mostly to see if you were listening. You seem miles away—but not in a good spot."

"I know. I'm flummoxed. The couple days have been so scary. I completely misjudged Jen's reaction to our conversation on Monday night. I thought she understood—that we were just concerned about her, not angry with her. I guess her embarrassment grew out of proportion. She said she couldn't sleep, what with thinking about having to face Benjy and anyone he might have told about her note. And she couldn't envision living in the same house as Hank anymore."

"She actually planned to run away?"

"Uh-huh."

"To where?"

"Unclear. She admitted she left our house when everyone was asleep, probably around eleven o'clock. She wandered around *all night*, for God's sake. Mostly in the arboretum. Can you imagine how scary that must've been? Anyone could have been lurking behind the trees. Something *worse* than what she's already experienced could have happened to her. Why didn't I realize she couldn't be left alone? I'm a frickin' social worker, for God's sake."

"Stop kicking yourself. This kid has been through stuff we can't even fathom. How could you possibly foresee how she would react?"

Glenda hung her head. "Jen said she thought of contacting her godmother in Birmingham but realized she didn't have the number with her. And she had no idea how to go about finding it. She had Jake's cell phone but no clue that she could use it to get the number off Google. It's like she's been beamed in from some other planet—her only frame of reference has been TV, which is all kind of nebulous to her."

"How did she react when you and Sarah came to get her?"

"Like a deer in the headlights. Not knowing whether to run toward us or away. Sarah approached her first, gave her a gentle hug, and asked if she was okay. Jen just started crying and saying, 'I don't know, I don't know!' It was heartbreaking, and I felt terrible that Sarah had to witness it. Plus it's hard not to be able to let Sarah in on the root causes of Jen's problems."

"Jen came home with you willingly?"

"Yeah. I think maybe because she was so tired and scared she didn't know what else to do. She didn't talk at all yesterday, and I didn't dare leave her alone. So I just sat with her and held her hand when she'd let me. I had her sleep with me last night and we went to the appointment pretty soon after we woke up."

"Did you sit in on it?"

"Yeah. Dr. Peters wanted to see Jen alone first but came out a few minutes later to get me 'cause she wouldn't speak. We discussed everything—the session went way beyond the scheduled time—and Jen seemed better when we left. It was the doc's idea to send her to school."

"Is she okay about staying with you guys?"

"For now. She said she wanted to go back to Alabama, but Dr. Peters got her to think through what that would be like: She doesn't really remember her family there and has come to know our family. She's never been to school in Birmingham, but she's got a month under her belt here and at least a few friends. She's in therapy and drug treatment here and would have to start all over in Birmingham. After thinking about it, Jen agreed to stay, at least through the end of the semester. But she says she wants another visit with her godmother—either in Alabama or here. Of course, I agreed."

Picturing the counseling session made my head hurt. "Makes sense."

"When are you gonna need Jen to testify against that John—what's his name, Thompsen?"

"Yeah, Danny Thompsen. His trial's scheduled to start in about four weeks. But I'm still hoping we'll have a strong enough case without using her as a witness. I doubt that'll be possible when and if we get around to trying her father."

Glenda nodded. "I'm praying she never has to take the stand—against either of those sons of bitches."

"You know I'll do everything possible to make sure she doesn't. Now why don't you go home and take a shower and a long nap?"

"I'm that odiferous, huh?" she said with a grin.

"No comment."

AFTER GLENDA LEFT, I squirmed to get comfortable on the couch, gently lifting Sparky's head off my lap, and reached for the thick folder on the coffee table. *I need distraction—I* don't *need a Vicodin.*

This particular file contained the information about Danny Thompsen: his rap sheet, his booking photos, the report of his arrest, and copies of the pornographic images found on his burner phone. Jimmy's IT guy had been working on a higher-priority assignment and still hadn't gotten around to cracking Danny's iPhone.

I reread the file, shuffling hurriedly through the images, but stopped to look again at the worst of them— one that depicted Thompsen with Jen's sister in the Janesville motel. IT told us it had been taken on another device and sent to Thompsen, so AJ must've been the photographer. *What kind of person takes photos like this? Moreover, what kind of person poses for an incriminating trophy picture of himself raping a kid? One that shows identifying features like the tattoo on his forearm: "Joni" encircled in roses. Would Joni, whoever she is, be supportive of his sick behavior?*

Still, the work couldn't distract me from my pain. I grabbed the pill bottle from the end table and took my first dose of the day, dutifully typing the time into my iPhone notes.

That same phone, set to vibrate, rattled me awake two hours later. I fumbled to answer, "Hullo?"

"Oh, shit—I woke you, didn't I?"

"No. Uh…yeah. But it's okay. What's up, Matt?"

"You're on speaker. Jimmy and I are eating lunch and thought we'd give you a call."

"Are there any developments in the case?"

"No," Matt said. "We spent the morning going through AJ's buddy Zachary Prescott's phone records— comparing numbers with ones we found on Danny Thompsen's burner phone—but didn't come up with any matches. And no record that Prescott ever called the 501 numbers that Jen used to call her dad. How're you feeling?"

I took a sip of water, trying to wash away the taste of defeat. "Thanks for asking. I'm better, but I wasn't able to make it through the day without the frickin' pain meds. And the doc won't let me go back to work till I can."

"It won't be long," Matt said.

"I had George bring over a few files yesterday so I can study up on my cases. I had to call it quits halfway through—" I paused, trying to recall something that'd hit me just before I dozed off.

"Halfway through what?"

"I was reviewing Danny's file this morning and I noticed something I thought might be important. Now, in my dopey state, I can't seem to remember what it was."

"We'll let you go," Matt said. "Let us know if you think of it."

"No—wait. It was that awful pic of Danny raping

Josielynn. I didn't notice it before, but he's got the name Joni, J-O-N-I, tattooed on his arm. D'you think he might use her name as the password for his iPhone?"

"Holy shit," Jimmy said. "It could be."

"Where's the phone now?" I asked.

"At my office," Jimmy replied. "Lemme call Hector and have him try J-O-N-I."

"Okay. Let me know as soon as you know," I said and waited for Matt to disconnect. *Did you have to sound so pathetic?* I asked myself.

I STARED at my phone for an hour, willing it to ring. Finally, I got off the couch and went to do my PT exercises: lifting dumbbells to increase my upper-body strength and walking and stair climbing with my prosthesis. As I stood on the second-floor landing wiping sweat from my brow, the call from Jimmy finally came.

"It worked!" he said, too excited for any pleasantries. "Talk about a treasure trove of stuff. More pics. Two hundred emails, texts to eight or ten people, and calls to six more. Matt and I'll be busy going over 'em for the next day or so, and we'll need subpoenas for phone records."

"That's great. George said he'd get any needed subpoenas until I get back. Just call and let him know the particulars. I'll give him a heads-up."

"Thanks. And, uh…great pickup on the Joni thing."

I sat down on the top step, buoyed by Jimmy's praise and determined to maneuver the flight of stairs five more times. *I need to get back to the office before George decides to try Danny Thompsen's case himself.*

42

OUR LANDLINE RANG about eight thirty on Thursday morning, just as I heard my dad return from taking the kids to school. I yelled down to him, "I'm awake, Dad. I'll be down in a sec if it's for me."

"It's Matt," Dad yelled back. "He says he'll call you on your cell."

"Hey, Matt," I said when he called back. "What's up?"

"I tried the landline so I wouldn't disturb you if you were still asleep. But, come to think of it, the landline probably rang loud enough to wake you anyway. Sorry—"

"Stop beating yourself up for no reason. I was already awake. The reason I didn't answer is 'cause the phone battery's dead and I haven't gotten around to replacing it."

"You probably should, for safety reasons. The 911 call center sometimes has difficulty tracking cell phones, and in an emergency, time could be critical."

I laughed. "Point taken, and I'll get my dad right on it. But I doubt you called to lecture me about safety."

"True that. I called to see if you'd be up to helping Jimmy and me go through the stuff his intern copied off Thompsen's iPhone. So far he's used three reams of paper, and he's only about halfway done. But we should have room to sort it out on your dining room table. And we'd promise to work quietly if you needed to take breaks to nap."

I blinked back tears before I answered. "That's a great idea, Matt. I'd love to help."

"Okay. I'm guessing it'll be about an hour before the copying's done. Would ten or so work for you?"

"Yep. I'll put on a pot of coffee so you don't have to stop at Dunkin' Donuts."

"But do you have *donuts*?"

"With my dad staying here, I'd say the chances are pretty good. And if we don't, I'll send him out for some."

I finished my exercise regimen and took a shower, pleased that my wound had healed enough to allow it— and at my progress in getting in and out of the bathtub. My dad had installed a hand-held showerhead, a stool, and some grab bars, enabling me to enjoy my long, steamy respite without assistance. I felt invigorated and almost normal as I stood to towel off and dry my hair.

I stared at my face in the mirror less critically than I had since my surgery. My skin looked healthier and fresh. I finger-combed and fluffed my hair, which I'd had cut while at the rehab center, and was satisfied with the result. I applied bronzer to my cheeks, swiped mascara onto my lashes, and finished it all off with a subdued LipSense stain and gloss.

Next step: choosing clothes for the day. *Dare I try jeans? Maybe the skinny, stretchy ones that won't be so binding on my stump.* I selected a pair from the closet and sat on the bed to pull them on—happy they still fit and didn't irritate my wounds—and to pin up the left pant leg. I donned an oversized chambray shirt and stood to check my look in the full-length mirror. *Not bad for a forty-year-old amputee!*

I WALKED downstairs moments after my dad had ushered Matt and Jimmy into the dining room. "Hey, guys," I said as Jimmy uncovered the Bankers Box he'd set on the table. "Thanks for bringing the evidence over—I was beginning to feel completely out of the loop."

Jimmy nonchalantly nodded his hello. Matt turned around to greet me. "Wow, you look great!" he said, engulfing me in a quick bear hug. "Like a hundred times better than when I saw you in the hospital."

"Thanks. I'm feeling way better, too. Can I get you some coffee?"

"Your dad's already on it," Matt said with a grin. "And he offered to share the donuts he bought on the way back from dropping off your kids."

"He must think a lot of you if he made that offer."

"To be precise, he was looking at me at the time—I doubt he meant Jimmy could have any."

Jimmy groaned. "Better not quit your day job to take up comedy."

My dad returned with three coffee mugs hooked over one finger, a carafe in his other hand, and a bakery bag wedged under his elbow. "Here you go. Oh, I forgot the cream. Does anyone take sugar?"

"Chill, Dad. I'll go get the cream and some napkins. None of us uses sugar."

As I left the room, I heard him whisper to my colleagues, "It'll do her so much good to get back to work. Y'know, help keep her mind off the pain and all."

Leave it alone, Dad! I wanted to yell. *I don't need their pity.* But I couldn't argue with the substance of what he'd said.

JIMMY'S INTERN had separated the copies into groups: photographs, text messages, phone numbers, contacts, and emails. Reviewing the information was slow going. Matt went through photographs, looking for familiar faces or locations, Jimmy checked the phone numbers and contact info with those he'd found on Zachary Taylor's phone records, and I read text message and email threads.

Determined to stay alert, I'd taken ibuprofen rather than Vicodin after Matt's call. Though my pain nagged at me, the clarity proved worthwhile. "I found something," I said, looking up from a page I'd been studying. "It's a text sent from an anonymous number to Danny at nine fifteen p.m. on June eighteenth, the night AJ and the girls checked into the motel in Janesville. It reads, *Change of plans. Stopping overnight. Call B#3 for location.* Can you check Danny's outgoing calls to see what B#3 might be?"

"Hold on, lemme see," Jimmy said. "I'll bet B#3 means *burner number three.*"

"Makes sense," Matt said. "We already knew he had two. Why not more?"

"Danny didn't call from his iPhone," Jimmy said a moment later, "but I've got the list of calls from his burner phone in my computer." He typed onto his laptop and studied the screen. "Bingo. Danny called this 501 number at ten o'clock that night." He read us the digits.

"That fits," Matt said, jotting down the number. "AJ's two other burners had 501 area codes, so this has gotta be his. Want me to try calling it and see if it's still in service?"

Jimmy shook his head. "I'd rather have Hector do it from the office. He's all set up to record with one-party consent if someone answers, plus he's got software that'll give him the name of the carrier." He picked up his own phone and called Hector. "D'ya have time to do it now? Great, get back to me when you know."

Matt and I looked at Jimmy, who'd already returned to his stack of documents.

"Uh—Jimmy?" I asked.

"Huh?"

"What'd he say?" Matt asked. "Is he trying it now?"

"He's onto something else right now but said he'd do it in about an hour."

Matt and I groaned simultaneously. "I gotta take a break and have something to eat," I said. "The ibuprofen's giving me heartburn."

Matt stood up abruptly, knocking his knee against the table in the process and causing Jimmy's highlighter to go astray on the paper he was marking. "Watch it, will ya?"

Matt ignored him. "I'll run out and pick something up for lunch. What sounds good?"

"I've been hungry for a New Orleans Take-Out roast beef po' boy," I said. "I'm buying, by the way."

"I'll have jambalaya with corn bread," Jimmy said.

"Okie doke," Matt replied. "I'll ask your dad if he

wants anything on my way out, Caroline. He could probably use a break from mowing the lawn."

I stood up and followed him to the foyer to get cash from my purse hanging on the coat-tree. "This should be enough," I said, handing him a hundred-dollar bill, "unless you and my dad are really, really hungry."

He grinned. "Do you want any change, or should I leave a really, really good tip?"

"Ha ha. I'm gonna rest on the couch till you get back with the food. I doubt Jimmy'll notice."

"She said she was super hungry," I heard Matt whisper to Dad, "but I hate to wake her. What d'ya think?"

"Geez, I don't know," my dad whispered back.

I propped myself up on one elbow and called from the couch, "I'm awake and I'm starved. For God's sake, bring me my sandwich!"

The dynamic duo peered from around the living room doorway. "Sorry. We just didn't know if food was more important than sleep," Matt said sheepishly.

"Yeah," Dad said. "And you looked so peaceful there zonked out with drool on your cheek."

I gave an exaggerated shudder. "Do you know how weird it is to find out that you guys have been staring at me while I sleep?"

"It was just for a second," Matt said, laughing, "and I hadn't noticed the drool until Gene just mentioned it." He set the carryout bags on the coffee table. "I'll go get Jimmy."

"And I'll get drinks," Dad said. "What d'ya want, honey?"

"Diet Coke, please, on ice."

Jimmy ambled in a moment later and handed me my Coke.

"Any news from Hector yet?" I asked as I opened the first paper bag to locate my sandwich. The aroma of Cajun spices emanating from the bag made my mouth water, and I smiled when I found the one labeled *roast beef*.

Jimmy nodded. "Yeah, but let's wait for Matt. I don't wanna have to repeat it."

"Fine with me, but I'm *not* waiting to eat." I sat on the edge of the couch, leaned over the paper wrapper, and took a big, drippy bite.

Jimmy grabbed the other bag—which clearly held rigid food containers—settled himself on the opposite end of the couch, and extracted his order of jambalaya. "Did they send any forks?"

I nodded and passed him one, along with a few paper napkins.

Matt and my dad returned, bearing plates, real silverware, and more cold drinks. "Sorry," I mumbled and paused to swallow my most recent bite, "couldn't wait. And I think we're good with throwaway dinnerware and cutlery."

"Speaking of throwaway," Matt asked Jimmy as he unwrapped his sandwich, "did you hear from Hector?"

Jimmy wiped the corner of his mouth with a napkin, took a sip of soda, and nodded. "Yep. Burner number three isn't in service. But it's a Sprint phone, just like the other two."

"As criminals go, AJ's the creepiest I've ever seen, but he's certainly not the stupidest," I said.

"No," Jimmy said, pushing his empty food container

aside, "but he did leave his DNA on a cigarette butt outside a crime scene. Which gives me hope that we'll be able to track his ass sooner rather than later."

I crumpled my po' boy wrapper into a ball and threw it into the empty paper bag. "Come to think of it, maybe AJ didn't *physically* ditch the three burner phones and he still uses them—or plans to use them—sporadically. Why don't I draft a warrant to compel Sprint to ping the three numbers for ninety days just in case?"

"It's certainly worth a try," Matt said. "Do you have your laptop here?"

"Uh-huh. In the dining room."

During the next hour, with Jimmy and Matt standing over my shoulder feeding me the details, I typed up the warrant request and sent it to George Cooper for approval and filing. I closed the laptop lid and stood a bit awkwardly. "I hate to say it, but I really need a pain pill and a nap. Can you muddle through without me for a while?"

Matt and Jimmy nodded.

"Thanks."

I walked into the living room, where my dad sat watching *Deadwood* on HBO. Tempted to join him, I leaned on the edge of the couch for a moment—this was one of my all-time favorite episodes. But the throbbing in my leg made me think better of it. "Dad, I'm heading up for a nap. Please make sure to wake me when you get back with the kids."

"Even if you're drooling?"

"Especially if!"

I MUST'VE JUMPED six inches off the bed when I heard the Wiffle Ball smashing against the window—of course, I didn't know what it was at the time. The bedside clock read five fifteen. *What? Dad was supposed to wake me up. I was s'posed to get in an hour of fake-leg practice before dinner.*

I hobbled on the walker to my window and looked out at the yard. Matt, Dad, and seven or eight kids—including my four—were cheering Jake Foster, who was running around some makeshift bases toward home plate, which happened to be an inverted red snow saucer. Sparky stood barking in what must've been the outfield. I couldn't help laughing.

I peeled off my skinny jeans, put on my prosthesis and a pair of yoga pants, and headed downstairs on my crutches.

I'd just settled into a canvas sling chair outside the downstairs patio doorway when Glenda appeared, carrying a mini-cooler full of Spotted Cows. "Want one?" she asked, pulling out one for herself. She must've noticed my hesitation. "I see you're wearing your faux appendage and I assume you're still taking a Vicodin now and again?"

I nodded.

"And you're worried drinking might make you a little tipsy?"

"Wouldn't you be?"

She shrugged. "I think you can handle one beer. And if not, there'll be four adults to get you up the steps." She opened a bottle and handed it to me.

"*Four* adults?"

"Yep. Your dad invited me and Hank and our three

kids over for dinner, and it appears your friend Matt is staying, too."

I took a small sip of the ice-cold beer and let it sit on my tongue a moment before swallowing. "Wow. I'd almost forgotten how good it tastes. What's Dad got on the menu?"

"Brats and potato salad from Jacobson's Deli. Hot dogs and chips for the littles. And I sent Hank out to buy a watermelon."

"Sounds great, and this game does my heart good," I said, nodding toward the playing field.

We watched as my dad pitched the ball to my son. "You almost had it," Matt said when Luke swung and missed, then gently showed him how to lower his elbows. Luke hit the next pitch into the neighbors' yard, charged around the bases with his arms raised in triumph, and crossed home to high-five Matt.

"Way to go!" I yelled. Matt looked my way and gave a thumbs-up.

Amy batted next, and Dad pitched to her as slowly as humanly possible. She connected on the third try and the ball caromed over to Jen, guarding first base. *Who do I cheer for here? My less-than-athletic five-year-old daughter or a fourteen-year-old girl who's had the worst imaginable life?*

Jen bobbled the ball but managed to pick it up and tag the base just as Amy arrived. "Great plays, guys," Matt called. "It's a tie, but the tie goes to the runner." Both girls beamed.

The game ended when my dad decided it was time to start the grill. The kids regrouped—under Sarah's direction—to play a game of Captain May I? When Matt ambled over, Glenda handed him a beer. "I'm gonna go help with dinner," she said. "You can have my chair as long as you keep an eye on this wild and crazy invalid and make sure she doesn't tip over."

I laughed out loud.

"Good nap?" Matt asked.

"Good but way too long."

"I know for a fact your dad went to get you up when he came home with the kids," Matt said with a grin. "He told me you mumbled something like 'jus' five more minutes.'"

"Ah, well… Any more progress on the case?"

"A bit. AJ used a program to make his emails anonymous so, while some of the messages were interesting, we couldn't find any clues to help track him. Jimmy and I decided to call it a day about an hour ago."

"Didn't my dad invite him to stay and eat?"

"Yeah, but he had a date."

"A date? With who?"

Matt laughed. "He didn't say. Come to think of it, maybe he was just trying to get out of the dinner invite."

"That makes more sense."

"BRATS AND DOGS ARE DONE," my dad yelled a while later. "Let's convene on the screened porch."

Matt tossed the empties into Glenda's cooler and moved toward the wooden staircase leading up to the porch. "Need a hand?" he asked me.

I stood up and assessed my balance. "Nah. I'm good, but walk behind just in case. And stay far enough back so you don't get whacked with my extra crutch."

I proudly climbed the stairs and opened the door by

myself, flashing a big smile to my kids, already situated around the picnic table. "Wow, great idea to set up the extra table and folding chairs so we can all eat together, Dad!"

"That was all Glenda," my dad said. "Have a seat."

I moved to sit on the end of the bench next to Luke. "No!" he said. "I want Matt to sit by me."

"Okay, okay," I said and took a spot between Hank and Glenda at what turned out to be the adults' table.

Seven kids can't be expected to carry on civilized dinner conversations. I heard giggles, burps, and petty squabbles—about who took the last potato chip and whether ketchup or mustard was best on hot dogs. My heart soared when I heard the twins laughing at a corny joke Jen told, and when she laughed in turn at Luke's.

Matt sat wordlessly throughout the fray, but his bemused expression spoke volumes to me. I was glad Luke had an ally at the table.

Suddenly, during a momentary lull, I heard Luke say, "Hey, Matt. Y'know my mom dumped Dominic, so now you can be her boyfriend again."

As I glanced at Matt with embarrassment, I choked on a bite of bratwurst and began coughing uncontrollably. "Can you talk, Caroline?" my dad asked. "Do we need to do the Heimlich?"

"I'm okay," I croaked between coughs. My face felt as hot as Matt's looked.

The moment passed but my mortification didn't. *Why did you feel compelled to tell the kids you broke up with Dominic? Given how infrequently he was around, it might've been months before they noticed his absence. Poor Matt—the last thing he needs is a five-year-old matchmaker. Should I say something to him?*

When Dad, Hank, and Matt went to the front porch to smoke post-dinner cigars—a ritual my dad and Hank had started some years ago—I accepted Glenda's offer to split the last beer. "Kids say the darnedest things, don't they?" she asked as she poured it into my glass.

"Yes, they do. And you can wipe that smirk off your face, my friend. Should I apologize to Matt?"

"For what? Luke just said what we've all been thinking."

"Glen, Matt and I gave it a try two years ago. It didn't go anywhere."

"As I remember, Matt broke it off because he thought his marriage deserved another shot."

"Uh-huh."

"And obviously that shot fizzled—probably because he was enamored with you."

"Oh, good lord."

"I looked it up on the Internet. He's been divorced for a year now."

"Glen!"

"Just sayin'."

43

When Jimmy arrived at my house on Friday morning to resume our records review, his freckled face broke into a wide smile. "I've got AJ's smartphone number!" he told me.

"That's great! How'd you find it?" I said, ushering him into the dining room.

"I texted Matt with the news but he'll want to hear it, too. He's right behind me."

Matt walked in a few minutes later, balancing a donut bag and a to-go cup of coffee on top of a file box.

"I told you I wanted to break my sugar habit," I said with a laugh. "Between you and my dad, I'm gonna get too fat for my prosthesis."

He grinned. "Nobody said you had to eat 'em."

"Could you two quit arguing and sit down?" Jimmy asked.

Matt and I took our places at the table and watched while Jimmy opened a file folder and extracted two stapled stacks of paper, each about a quarter-inch thick.

"These are lists of outgoing calls from Danny Thompsen's and Zach Prescott's smartphones going back two years," he said. "I was looking for any number that might appear on both lists—which logic says would be AJ Corbell's. I started searching for numbers with 501 area codes—you know, 'cause AJ's three burner phones had 501 numbers—but after an hour I realized that was a dead end—"

"You didn't really have a date last night, did you?" Matt asked.

"Huh?" Jimmy replied.

"That's the excuse you gave for not staying for dinner."

"Okay, you caught me," Jimmy said. "Now can we get back to important stuff?"

"Yes, please do," I said.

"So then I started writing down all the area codes on each list. Zach had calls to twenty different ones, and Danny had eleven—and there were three common area codes on both lists. I finally narrowed down one 312 number that they both called—a Verizon number from Chicago! It's unlisted and not registered for a business. Has to be AJ."

"How many times did they call him?" I asked.

"Not as often as I would've expected. Zach did fifteen times and Danny did thirty."

"Great work, Jimmy," I said. "Let's get going on the subpoena for the phone records and the warrant to ping for his location."

AFTER WE FINISHED THE PAPERWORK, Jimmy went to shepherd the warrant through the filing process and make contact with Verizon. Matt and I—highlighters in hand—went back to reviewing stacks of paper records. This time he pored over text message threads and I tackled emails.

"Even criminals get bazillions of advertising emails," I said, raking my fingers through my hair. "I would've thought they'd be immune."

"There're quite a few text ads, too. And the texts Danny actually sent and received suggest he and some of his buddies are dumber than dirt."

"I feel like I'm wading through quicksand trying to find any messages worth reading." *And I badly need a distraction from this throbbing pain—I'm* not *taking a Vicodin today.*

While absently brushing chocolate donut crumbs off a page, my focus narrowed to a few words in an email to Danny Thompsen: *I don't understand why you took a job. I told you I needed you to recruit in WD.* I looked at the date: June tenth—around the time Thompsen was hired at the Walmart in northern Illinois, and eight days before he'd visited AJ Corbell and the girls at the motel in Janesville. The message Danny sent in return read: *Got to make a living. 40% or no deal.*

"Look at these messages, Matt, and tell me what you think." I handed him the pages with the messages highlighted in yellow.

I followed his eyes as he read them through twice, then flashed me his gap-toothed grin. "They appear to suggest Danny worked as a recruiter for somebody, and he and that somebody'd had a difference of opinion on his monetary worth. I'm guessing that somebody was AJ Corbell, who wanted him to recruit business in Wisconsin Dells. Too bad we can't get an IP address off these messages—remember I told you he used an anonymizer?"

"Not to worry. We'll have AJ's cell phone and laptop in hand soon and be able to prove he sent 'em. And if Danny was drumming up Johns for AJ's business rather than just frequenting the business, he'll face a heftier sentence when we convict him."

"Maybe that'd be enough to get him to roll over on AJ."

"Y'know, you're right. Maybe his lawyer hasn't been completely candid with him about the sentencing guidelines—especially if the lawyer's being paid by AJ or his buddy."

44

I RETURNED to work at my office part time on the following Monday. Dad planned to stay through the week and had urged me to try "getting back in the saddle"—as he put it—at least for a few hours a day. I'd been able to function without Vicodin for a couple mornings in a row, so I opted for an eight-to-noon schedule. Dad would run the kids to school for the first few days, until I could test my stamina.

I'd asked George Cooper not to tell my co-workers about the plan "in case I can't get it together to make it on Monday," so I thought I could sneak in without fanfare. I should've made the same request of Matt.

He met me in the parking lot at seven forty-five—thankfully sans donuts. "Hey! Fancy meeting you here."

"I told you I was coming back today. Why are you here and why do you look so suspicious?"

"No reason. Anything you want me to carry up to your office?"

If Dominic had pulled something like this, I would've had his head. Why does it seem so innocuous 'cause it's Matt?

"Thanks," I said with a laugh, "but unless you want to be my round-the-clock errand boy, I'm gonna need to handle it myself." I deftly exited the car, put my messenger bag over my shoulder, and donned my crutches. "I decided to go one-legged today—just in case anyone missed the memo!"

He shook his head. "You're a piece of work, Caroline," he said as he followed me into the elevator.

"Seriously, why *are* you here? I thought you had a conference or something."

"I do, but it's only a few blocks from here and doesn't start until nine. Thought we could review a few more of Danny's emails before I go. Jimmy said he'd deliver the stuff to your office first thing this a.m."

Sure enough, Jimmy stood in the hallway outside my door with a dolly full of boxes. "Welcome back," he said.

"Thanks." I unlocked the door with my key and reached around to turn on the lights.

I jumped when five of my fellow prosecutors and four support staffers yelled, "Surprise!" A welcome back cake and a balloon bouquet sat prominently displayed on my desk.

"Oh. My. God. You scared me half to death! And no one was supposed to know I'd be here today."

"You can thank Matt for letting the cat out of the bag," Lauren said with a grin, "and George for letting us into your office."

"And he's too ashamed to show his face?" I asked.

"Not true," George said, rounding the corner and putting his arm around my shoulder. "By the way, your story about 'maybe not being able to get it together' simply wasn't believable. We all knew you'd make it. And we're too proud of you to let this day go without ceremony."

I felt my eyes tear up. "Thanks, guys. You're the best. And what a great way to start a day—cake for breakfast!"

AFTER THE CELEBRATION, I dove into the paper in my physical mailbox, pleased to find nothing earth-shattering. But Oliver Pooley, Danny Thompsen's lawyer, had sent me a letter requesting a meeting. I called his secretary and scheduled it for Wednesday morning, then began calculating Danny's tentative sentencing guidelines. I fully intended to scare him into cooperating with us against AJ.

While I worked at my desk, Jimmy set up shop in the conference room. He texted me around ten o'clock with good news: *A guy at Verizon agreed to begin the search today.* He signed off with a smiling emoji—so uncharacteristic that I rechecked the sender's ID.

Great! I replied. If AJ Corbell hadn't abandoned his cell phone, there was a good chance we'd know his location before the day was out.

After a trip to the restroom a half an hour later, I stopped by the conference room and found Jimmy intently studying a paper on the table in front of him. "How goes it?"

He looked up absently. "Oh. Didn't hear you come in. I'm reading a text thread between AJ and his friend Zach Prescott that I think you'll find interesting."

I sat in the chair beside him and he handed me the page:

June 19
　　AJC: Trouble. Had to leave J/J. B#1 only for now.

June 26
　　AJC: DT in custody-he will call u re atty.
　　ZTP: ok.

"June nineteenth—the day Josie died and the cops came," I said, "and AJ tells Zach he had to leave the girls and to contact him only via his first burner phone?"

"Yep," Jimmy said. "And the following week, AJ tells Zach to arrange an attorney for Danny Thompsen."

"So Zach's in it up to his ears. Let's hope we can find more evidence. I'd love to indict him for conspiracy—and to induce his cooperation against AJ. I'm glad you talked me into holding off on interviewing him. The first time we approach him we'd better come out with guns blazing 'cause he might not give us another chance."

"I hear ya."

By noon, I'd managed to calculate Danny Thompsen's criminal history category—one of the two components that would be used to determine his presumptive sentence of incarceration. He scored out as a Category V offender, the second-worst possible classification. *Interesting. And AJ Corbell—who has no countable criminal history—will score out as Category I. Danny might find himself looking at more prison time than the despicable person who sold his own daughters.* I put a fluorescent-green Post-it on the page with my calculations so I'd be sure to find it before Wednesday's meeting with Oliver Pooley.

Jimmy startled when I knocked on the doorframe to the conference room. "I'm heading out now," I said, "but thought I'd check to see how it's coming."

"Only a few less-obvious-but-probably-incriminating text messages between AJ and Zach," he said. "I'll let you know if I find a smoking gun."

"Good. And you'll call me the minute Verizon gives us AJ's location?"

Jimmy grinned. "My first call will be to the marshals' fugitive task force so they can go arrest his ass, but I'll pencil you in as C#2."

It took me a moment to get his joke but I couldn't help LOLing.

"How'd it go, kiddo?" my dad called from the living room the moment I opened the front door.

I hung up my messenger bag, threw the car keys on the foyer table, and went to say hi. "It went pretty well—after the cake-and-balloons surprise greeting, that is."

"I know you hate being the center of attention, but you *do* deserve their good wishes." He got out of my chair and motioned for me to sit. "Relax a bit and I'll go make you some lunch."

"Uh, Dad?"

"What?"

"You packed me a lunch before I left this morning, remember? Tuna salad on rye, yogurt, carrot sticks?"

"Oh, yeah. I guess I'm just feeling a little useless sitting around here. Grace came today to clean and do laundry, and I already made dinner."

"Why don't you go to a movie? Or over to Vitense to

hit a bucket of golf balls? Remember, Grace and Amanda are resuming the after-school pickup rotation today, so you've got plenty of time."

I couldn't miss his crestfallen look. "Okay. What's on your agenda?"

"Gonna put on my prosthesis and get in a little practice. Then take a nap."

"How's the pain?"

"Only about a three or a four. I guess it helps to be busy using my brain."

JIMMY CALLED JUST as we'd gotten the littles to bed. "Just talked with Verizon," he said breathlessly. "They tell me AJ's holed up in a cabin about ten miles from Arkadelphia, Arkansas, a little over an hour from Little Rock. Problem is, the marshal there won't have the manpower to go pick him up until sometime tomorrow night and we want to arrest him before he disappears on us. I've asked our SAC in Little Rock to send an agent or two with local sheriff's deputies, but he's gotta get back to me. If not, I guess the locals will have to handle it."

I felt an inexplicable pang of anxiety, then reproached myself for it. *Arkansas's made it to the twenty-first century. I'm sure they have perfectly competent rural sheriff's departments. And, while AJ's a complete creep, we have no evidence he's armed. What can possibly go wrong?*

"You're right," I said. "We *don't* want to wait till tomorrow night for the marshals. If you want, I can call the US Attorney's duty officer down there and ask them to put some pressure on the FBI to get involved."

"I don't think that's necessary. The guy sounded like

he really wanted to help, but there's an AMBER alert in Little Rock and they're assisting."

"You don't think—"

"That AJ's got something to do with a missing kid? Nah. That'd be way too much of a coincidence."

"I'm sure you're right. Thanks for the call, Jimmy. Call me when they've got him—no matter what time."

As IT HAPPENED, AJ *hadn't* had anything to do with the missing Little Rock child. But he did have a runaway sixteen-year-old girl from Chicago with him when the fresh-out-of-the-academy sheriff's deputy went to try to arrest him.

"Sorry to wake you," Jimmy said when he called shortly after midnight. "But news of the fiasco in Arkansas's probably going to go viral and I didn't want you kept in the dark."

"Tell me."

The knot in my stomach grew as I listened. "So the deputy goes around to the back window of the cabin and sees AJ sitting alone watching an old black-and-white TV. He doesn't see a gun—or any other obvious weapon—so he knocks on the front door and waits. By the time AJ answers, he's got the runaway standing in front of him and he's holding a Glock nonchalantly at his side. AJ asks what he wants, and the deputy says there'd been a report of some break-ins and he's just checking that everything's okay. Son of a bitch probably stuttered the whole time he was talking. AJ says, 'Everything's fine, but you're trespassing and I suggest you leave right now.' The deputy drives back out to the main road before he calls for backup, and by that time AJ and the girl are in his car fleeing the scene."

"Lemme guess: the deputy gives chase."

"Yep. At pretty high speeds on narrow country roads. AJ spins out on some pea gravel, runs head-on into a tree, and is knocked unconscious. The runaway girl is pinned in the car and they gotta use the Jaws of Life to extricate her."

"Is she okay?"

"Yeah. Non-life-threatening injuries. AJ's concussed and has some broken ribs, but he'll survive, too."

"Had he kidnapped the girl?"

"She says she met him in Kansas City and was traveling with him willingly—that he was 'super-nice' to her. The ER said she had a bunch of track marks on her arms and a high concentration of oxycodone in her system, so I'm guessing she and AJ had arrived at a mutually satisfying arrangement. She swore he hadn't pimped her out."

"How long had she been a runaway?"

"Most recently six months. Her parents are on their way to get her and re-enroll her in rehab."

"Can one of the Little Rock agents take a formal statement from her before she leaves?"

"Already on it."

"And AJ's officially in custody?"

"Yep. Under marshals' guard at a hospital in Arkadelphia. They'll move him to Little Rock once he's medically cleared, probably by noon, and have him in front of the federal magistrate before close of business."

"Thanks, Jimmy."

45

I CALLED the clerk of court first thing Tuesday morning to unseal—or make public—our arrest warrant for Ambrose Josiah Corbell. I'd already had three voice messages from reporters in Little Rock who'd gotten my contact info from the local sheriff. The car chase and ensuing accident were big news in Arkadelphia, and the scuttlebutt about the driver being a sex trafficker had started a feeding frenzy.

My second call was to Glenda. "Jen's father was arrested last night. And since he had a sixteen-year-old, drug-addicted runaway with him when he crashed his car trying to avoid apprehension, it's gonna make the news. Can you get over to school and let her know?"

"Yeah. I'm s'posed to chaperone Jake's field trip at nine thirty anyway, so I'll tell her before we go. Was her dad hurt?"

"Concussion. He'll live."

"Sorry to hear that. I'll text and let you know how she takes it."

"Good, thanks. By the way, he got popped near Little Rock, in case you want to Google whatever details might already be out there."

The text from Glen came half an hour later: *She handled it ok. No tears. No smiles. Didn't see any need to take her out of school.*

AFTER STOPPING in the break room to refill my coffee mug, I wandered over to George Cooper's office. "Got a minute?" I asked him.

"I've got an hour." He motioned me to his couch. "Thanks for the heads-up on Corbell."

"Did my text wake you?"

He shook his head. "I learned a long time ago to leave my cell phone in the kitchen at night. I'll hear the ring tone if I get a call but not the silly text message notifications. Sounds like the arrest was a full-fledged cluster. Too bad Corbell didn't die when he hit the tree—the world'd be a lot better place without him in it."

"Funny. You're the second person who's said that to me today."

"What's on your mind?"

I took a sip of coffee, stalling for time to phrase my question. "When you brought the records to my house last week, you said we'd *talk* about my handling the Thompsen trial. Where, exactly, do you stand on it? Is it gonna be yours or mine?"

"Caroline—"

I gave him a *stop* gesture. "I got a letter from his lawyer asking for a meeting to discuss a possible plea, and I set it up for tomorrow morning."

He tore his glasses off the bridge of his nose and sat forward in his chair. "Did you plan to tell me about it?"

His zero-to-sixty escalation took my breath away. "Of *course* I planned to tell you," I said in the calmest tone I could muster. "It just slipped my mind yesterday, what with Verizon agreeing to initiate the ping and all."

George leaned back and sighed. "Sorry I blew a gasket. That trial's been nagging in the back of my head for a while. I'm not as up-to-speed on the evidence as I need to be to go to trial, but I'm afraid it would be too physically taxing for you to handle at this point. You know how emotionally and physically exhausting even a two-day trial can be…"

"I know." *Boy, do I know. And the thought of it both excites me and scares me witless.*

"I made it clear to Oliver Pooley that I'd reassigned the case to myself," George went on. "Why would he write to *you* asking to meet? Unless he's trying to play us off against each other. Maybe he thinks you'll be more of a pushover."

"If that's the case, he'd have another think coming. The guys turned up some emails and text messages suggesting his client *worked* for AJ Corbell, recruiting Johns."

George scratched his head with the bow of his glasses, which he still held in his hand. Then his face broke into a wide grin. "In that case, we could seek a superseding indictment, charging Thompsen with conspiracy to run a sex trafficking operation…"

"Which would start the Speedy Trial clock running again and let us try Thompsen at the same time as AJ…"

"Which is now workable since AJ's in custody."

I returned the grin. "Which would allow me time to regain my strength and handle the trial myself!"

We sat in silence for a few moments, savoring the possible resolution of both our concerns.

"Y'know," I finally said, "it'd still be better if Thompsen agreed to plead guilty and testify against Corbell. We'd be less likely to need Jennifer's testimony that way, and she's still kinda hinky."

"True."

"Are you free to meet with Pooley tomorrow at ten?" I asked.

George got up and flipped a page in his paper calendar. "Yep, but I want us both to be there. And let's use the small conference room—it's much more intimidating."

"Maybe because of that stuffed black bear standing menacingly in the corner." I referred to the illegal taxidermal specimen that had been confiscated by US Fish and Wildlife agents decades ago and had graced the office ever since. "That thing almost made me rescind my application to work here."

"Glad you didn't, though, aren't you?"

I nodded and started to rise.

"Before you go, let's draft a press release about Corbell, and I'll see if Andrew"—the US Attorney—"has time for us to brief him on the facts. I'm sure he'll want to handle the TV folks himself."

I'D JUST POWERED down my computer and closed my briefcase to go home when my desk phone rang. "It's Cal here in Little Rock again," my caller said. "The hearing's over. Took less than ten minutes to get Mr. Corbell officially locked up tight and ordered back to your district. The judge's exact words were, 'The defendant poses the clearest danger to the community and risk of flight that this court has ever had the displeasure to witness.' Guess he frowns upon crashing into a tree with a loaded gun and a teenaged runaway in your car!"

I laughed. "Thanks, Cal. We'll look forward to seeing him here."

"Sounds like it'll be a while. The marshals say he just missed the last bus and will have a good three weeks of jail and diesel therapy before he arrives at your doorstep."

I usually abhorred the long, circuitous trips inmates had to endure to get across the country from one courthouse or prison to another. But the awful images of Josielynn Corbell—alive and dead—had killed any compassion I might have had for her father. *He deserves a long, slow bus ride.*

"Seems like you worked a little more than *half* time today," my dad said when I arrived home at two o'clock.

"I know, I know. But one of my fugitives was arrested last night and we had to deal with it. If you watch the evening news—both local and national—you'll hear about it."

"*National* news?"

"Uh-huh. 'Sex trafficker arrested after car crash with teenage runaway.' This guy's gonna have his fifteen minutes of fame—or infamy."

"Did the teenager live?"

"Thankfully."

Dad nodded. "Looks like you could use a nap."

"And several ibuprofen."

"Sleep as long as you want. Abby and Bert are bringing dinner, but they'll understand if you skip it for some extra z's."

I kissed his cheek and headed for the stairs. "Thanks."

It's been a trying day and you need sleep, I told myself. *One Vicodin won't hurt.*

46

LOOKING DISHEVELED AND FLUMMOXED, Oliver Pooley arrived half an hour late for his ten o'clock appointment and—as we'd hoped—startled at the sight of the bear in the corner. "What in God's name—"

George rose from his chair to shake the lawyer's hand. "That magnificent animal was shot illegally by a nefarious criminal game hunter many years ago. You might call him our office mascot."

As he approached the table, I extended my hand to Pooley. "We only set aside an hour for this meeting, so we'd better get down to business." No offers of coffee or exchanges of pleasantries, George and I'd decided as the clock had ticked further past the appointed hour.

"Fine," Pooley replied, sinking into a chair and pulling a legal pad and fountain pen from his Montblanc leather briefcase. He paused for a moment before continuing, "I've suggested to my client that the most prudent course of action is for him to plead guilty—"

"Prudent because?" I interrupted.

"May I be frank?"

"Of course," George replied.

"I'm afraid he can't afford the expense of a trial."

My boss and I exchanged knowing looks. *His retainer's run out and AJ won't pony up any more money.*

"You're aware that the court will inquire at the plea hearing whether Thompsen's pleading guilty voluntarily —and will offer the services of appointed counsel?" I asked.

"Of course, but he's not anxious to go that route. I've advised him of the likelihood of conviction, in light of the weight of the evidence against him."

"Another big consideration should be the potentially lower sentence he'll receive for pleading guilty," George added.

Pooley nodded.

"As has always been our position," I said, "Thompsen's plea agreement will require him to testify against AJ Corbell—who, by the way, was arrested Monday night."

"So we heard."

"You also need to know that we've uncovered new information showing Thompsen was *significantly* more involved in Corbell's sex trafficking business than we'd previously thought. He'll be expected to tell us about that, too." I passed several pages of printed email messages— the negotiations between AJ and Danny regarding his role as a recruiter of Johns—and a handwritten summary of my sentencing guideline calculations across the table to him.

I watched Pooley's face fall as he read. By the time he turned to the final page, a vein throbbed prominently on his temple.

- *Criminal history category: V*
- *Offense level (as a recruiter): 38*
- *Guidelines without plea: 30 years - life*
- *Guidelines with guilty plea: 21.8 - 27.25 years*
- *Probable sentence with cooperation: lower.*

"How much lower?" Pooley asked.

George shrugged. "Depends how cooperative he can be. No guarantees. But if he doesn't plead guilty and cooperate, we'll be seeking a superseding indictment for conspiracy to engage in sex trafficking and recommending life imprisonment."

Pooley grabbed the papers and his belongings, pushed away from the table, and stood to leave. "I'll be in touch."

IT DIDN'T TAKE Pooley long to confer with his client. He called me shortly before lunch. "Considering you've granted him immunity for his testimony," he said, "he'll agree to cooperate against Corbell—though that's not the name he knew him by."

"Let me make sure you both understand: Thompsen'll have immunity from prosecution for anything he tells us about that we *didn't* already know. Information he simply corroborates is fair game for us."

"Yes. I understood that and made it clear to my client. He agrees."

"Fine. Do you want to be present when my agents interview him?"

"That won't be necessary." *No surprise, since the money supply ran dry and you won't get paid for it.*

"After the interview's done," I said, "I'll schedule the plea hearing."

"Fine."

I buzzed George. "Thompsen agreed to cooperate!"

"Hallelujah! And with that, I'm officially handing the case back to you."

I texted Matt and Jimmy: *Great news! Danny took the plea agreement. When can you debrief him?*

Matt called me two minutes later. "I'm really happy to hear it. Jimmy and I are heading over to see him right now."

"Wow! I didn't expect you to drop everything to do it."

"We're getting bleary-eyed wading through all these records. If Thompsen can tell us what to look for, it'll be well worth it."

"Let's hope he's not just trying to play both ends against the middle."

"Yeah. Wouldn't be the first time someone tried that."

"I'm heading home soon, but feel free to call. I've been taking shorter and shorter naps lately."

Dad found me halfheartedly lifting weights in the family room before he headed out to pick up the kids. "The sky's finally clear," he said, "so I think I'll take 'em to the park to burn off some energy. Luke's teacher called while you were napping and said he seems agitated and angry today. He was picking on Amy and almost got into a fight with another boy."

"Oh, shit. What d'ya think that's about?"

"Probably two rainy days in a row when he hasn't been able to be outside."

"Hope you're right. Thanks, Dad."

But an hour of running, swinging, sliding, and climbing didn't improve my son's mood. He ran into the house, wailing about a bloody, skinned knee but refused to let me clean or bandage it. "No!" he yelled when I stooped down to hug him and examine the injury. "I want Grandpa."

My dad shrugged at my questioning look and took Luke by the hand to the bathroom to find the first-aid kit.

"How'd your brother hurt his leg?" I asked Amy.

"I dunno. On the jungle gym, maybe. Can I have a Popsicle?"

"Me, too?" asked Red.

"Sure," I said, followed them to the kitchen to get the treats, and got them settled on the screened porch. "Yell when you're done and I'll come wipe your hands."

"We will, Mommy," Amy said in her goodie-two-shoes voice. I rolled my eyes.

"Luke, there's a Popsicle waiting for you when you're done in there," I called toward the bathroom.

"I don't want one," came his forceful reply.

He doesn't want a Popsicle? Has he been possessed by some look-alike alien being?

The cell phone in my back pocket vibrated and I fished it out and glanced at the screen. A text from Matt read, *Interview went well. Call if you want or talk tomorrow.*

Though curious to hear more details, I knew Luke needed my attention. I sent back a canned *ok* and went to figure out what had gotten into my son.

I could still hear sniffling when I knocked gently on the bathroom door. "Can I come in?"

"Uh…we'll be out in just a minute," my dad said. "Meet you in the living room."

"Okay."

My chest tightened as I settled into my overstuffed chair and put my leg up onto the ottoman, and even Sparky—trying to nuzzle my elbow—failed to pull me from my rumination about Luke.

After what felt like an eternity, my father and son appeared at the living room doorway. Luke's freshly scrubbed knee and brand-new bandage stood in stark contrast to his filthy, torn gym shorts. I opened my mouth to comment but my dad signaled me to shush.

"Luke and another kid had a kerfuffle on the climbing bars, which ended in fisticuffs on the softball diamond. The other kid's mom and I broke it up. We decided they were both equally responsible and deserving of some kind of punishment—maybe a night or two without screen time."

"Was the other boy hurt, too?"

"Both of 'em got a little scratched up, but nothing a little Neosporin and some Band-Aids won't cure."

"Luke, what were you two fighting about?"

He stared down at the floor and kicked at the edge of the area rug, his lips firmly pressed together.

I gave my dad a *what on earth is going on?* look. He shrugged.

"Fine. If you won't answer me, you can go to your room till dinner. I'll be up in a minute to get your Leap-Pad, which is off-limits to you for two days. No TV either. Understand?"

Luke didn't respond but turned on his heel and stomped upstairs.

"Sorry, I couldn't get him to open up, either," my dad said. "But I think it'd be best if I were the one to go get his electronic thingy. I don't want him to throw it and compound his problems."

"Thanks, Dad." *I don't know how we're gonna cope after you leave.*

AT MIDNIGHT, after two hours of tossing and turning with physical discomfort and worry, I finally gave in and took a pain pill.

I awoke in a cold sweat from a nightmare, seconds before my six o'clock alarm.

47

I GLANCED out my bedroom window to see pregnant dark clouds and felt sadness for my son. *Another day cooped up in a classroom with only "inside recess"—an oxymoron, in my opinion —isn't gonna be good for his soul.* My soul didn't feel so swell, either, what with the guilt of having succumbed to Vicodin yet again last night.

After a long, steamy shower—with the luxuriously fragrant Thymes eucalyptus body wash I typically saved for special occasions—I emerged from the bathroom determined to make it a good day.

"Happy Thursday, my peeps," I said, walking into the kitchen with crutches and two legs. "How is everyone?"

"Good," Amy and Red replied simultaneously.

"Great, Mom," Lily said, as she gave her brother a surreptitious kick under the table. "Say g'morning."

Luke glanced up absently and deposited a spoonful of Cap'n Crunch into his mouth before mumbling, "Morning."

You gotta pick your battles and this one ain't worth it.

I poured myself a cup of coffee and sat next to Lily. "You've got a volleyball game after school today, don't you?"

She nodded. "Four o'clock."

"Dad, would you mind gathering Red and the twins and meeting me there? I've got a midafternoon court appearance and will be working a bit longer today."

My dad nodded. "No prob."

Lily looked up in surprise. "You're coming, Mom?"

Oh, shit. I never thought to ask whether she'd want me there— or if the presence of her now "differently abled" mother would be a distraction. "I planned on it, but if you'd rather I not come, I'd certainly understand."

She shook her head and smiled. "Why *wouldn't* I want you to come?"

"Well, you know, the gimpy mom thing."

"Mom! That's, like, crazy. It's just that you haven't been able to come to any games this fall 'cause it hurt too much."

I felt my cheeks flush with embarrassment. "Oh. The pain's getting less and less all the time. Much of the time I hardly notice it."

From the corner of my eye, I saw Luke staring at me, but he averted his gaze when I turned toward him. *Let it go.*

MATT AND JIMMY wandered into my office around ten to find me hyperalert, having just finished my second cup of tea. "Rough night?" Jimmy asked, glancing down at my trembling hand. *I must really look like shit if Jimmy notices and comments.*

"I've had better, but the jitters are from the espresso shots in my tea."

"Whoa, Nelly," Matt said, "and slow the truck down. You're supposed to be taking it easy till you re-acclimate to this crazy-assed office."

"Yeah. Well…" I folded my hands together. "Sit down and tell me what Danny had to say."

They settled into my visitors' chairs and Jimmy opened his leather portfolio to look at his notes. "I haven't finished the 302s yet, but we can give you the highlights." He glanced at Matt, who gave him a *go ahead* wave of the hand.

"Oliver Pooley musta scared the bejesus out of Danny 'cause he sang like a little birdie. He confirmed that AJ's buddy Zach paid his legal expenses—he said that was their agreement before he began working for AJ a year and a half ago. An implicit part of the agreement was that Danny not testify against AJ."

"Yet now he's agreed to do just that," I said.

"Right," Jimmy said. "But the retainer's already gone and AJ's in jail, so Danny figured he didn't have much to lose. Plus, he's pissed that he's facing about the same amount of time as AJ, who he describes as 'scary and batshit crazy.'"

"Believe it or not," Matt added, "Danny asked us, 'What kind of man pimps out his own *daughters*?' I wanted to remind him that *he* literally raped one of those daughters, but I held my tongue."

"You were being 'good cop,' I assume?"

Matt laughed. "Nah. Wasn't really necessary to role-play yesterday."

Jimmy continued. "Danny first met AJ at a bar in

Chicago when he responded to one of AJ's online ads. AJ's practice was to eyeball the Johns before he let 'em up to the room to meet Josie. Danny told him that was fine, but it seemed like he was wasting a lot of time and profit doing the vetting himself—though he didn't use that word —and he'd be willing to do it for him. After a couple more meetings, they reached an agreement: Danny would hang out in bars and recruit and vet the customers in exchange for fifteen percent of the proceeds. Later, Danny negotiated for twenty-five and the occasional free access to Josie—when they happened to be in the same place."

"Didn't they travel together?" I asked.

Jimmy shook his head. "Not often. Most of the time, Danny went to a city ahead of AJ and the girls, kinda like an advance man. AJ thought it'd be safer that way. And AJ didn't want the girls to get to know Danny."

"Those emails we found suggested Danny quit working for AJ and took that job at Walmart. Did he say why?" I asked.

"He quit a few times," Matt replied, "mostly 'cause of disputes over money—Danny believed AJ was underreporting their income, which he probably was. Plus, Danny had to hold down a 'real job' to satisfy his parole officer, so he'd do the recruiting trips either between jobs or on his days off. Said the PO didn't have any way to monitor his travel outside the state, but he was a stickler on employment."

"Did Danny say how many Johns he sent AJ's way?"

Jimmy flipped through his notes before answering. "It depended on the location, but in cities like Chicago, Kansas City, or St. Louis, he scheduled as many as ten a day. He said there was always at least one a day, so probably on average six or seven."

My stomach lurched into my throat and I turned toward my wastebasket in case I couldn't calm it. Jimmy must've noticed, because he quit reciting the numbers.

"It's a wonder those poor girls survived," I finally said.

"Uh-huh," Matt said. "He gave us a basic list of the services AJ offered and the prices he charged, but you can read about that later if you want. We're heading over to see Danny now to have him help us decipher some of the coded texts and give us more details about how their communications went. Figured we'd need that for the trial."

"Yeah, we will. Good work, guys. By the way, did you advise Danny not to tell anyone he's snitching?"

"Multiple times," Jimmy replied. "And he assures us he's smart enough not to do that."

"Let's hope he is. We want to keep this quiet for as long as we can."

AFTER THEY LEFT, I texted George to say I was taking an hour or two off. The worn but comfortable couch the building manager had found for me and installed against the far wall of my office looked too inviting to be ignored. I locked my door, closed the blinds, and swallowed two extra-strength Tylenols with a stale glass of water. I went to the couch and removed my prosthesis, then lay down with my Packers fleece blanket up over my face, breathing so deeply I felt the air tingle my toes. *Yeah, you're not gonna be able to sleep after the espresso, but you still need rest in order to make it to Lily's game.*

My coworker Lauren's call to my iPhone startled me awake at two twenty-five. "I'm in Judge Coburn's courtroom," she said, "and your office line goes straight to voice mail. Did you forget you had a plea hearing in a few minutes?"

"Oh, shit—I slept for three hours! I gotta call the clerk's office and see if they'll continue it till I get there."

"Don't bother, I can cover it for you. I've got my laptop. Just email the plea agreement and your notes. The judge took a ten-minute recess, I suspect to take a dump," she whispered, "so there's time."

With phone in hand, I hopped to the desk—where I'd inadvertently left my crutches—and frantically searched through my computer to find the documents Lauren needed. "Okay, they're on the way…"

"Got 'em, with seven minutes to spare. I'll text when it's over."

"Thanks. You're a lifesaver."

"No biggie."

How could you have been so careless? It would've taken five seconds to set an alarm. You gotta tell George before he hears it from someone else. Now!

"Hey, what up?" my boss asked, after answering on the first ring. "I thought you were in court."

"About that. Lauren's covering for me 'cause I lay down to rest and fell asleep. I. Am. So. Sorry. It'll never happen again, believe me."

"Geez, Caroline, chill. It's not the first time one of our attorneys has missed a court appearance."

"It's the first time *I* have," I moaned. "Should I send Judge Coburn an apology?"

"Why? Did it cause him any delay?"

"No."

"Then there's no need for *mea culpas*. Go home and rest."

Yeah, sure. Home ain't so restful with my pissed-off five-year-old son to contend with. Besides, Lily's expecting me at her volleyball game.

48

Sunday—the day I'd been dreading all week—arrived way too soon and rolled in with an ominous slate-gray sky. *Damnit! I sure could've used some sunshine to make today at least* appear *cheerful.*

The three littles had acted out and whined at bedtime the night before, I suspect because they'd sensed both my dad's trepidation and my own. None of us wanted him to go, but it was time.

Today he conjured up a more elaborate breakfast feast than usual: cream-cheese-stuffed French toast with strawberries, sausage patties, and freshly squeezed OJ. The twins were already seated at the table when I walked in with Red in tow, and Dad buzzed Lily on the intercom. "Do I hafta?" she moaned.

I like to believe that if she'd seen his crestfallen look, she'd have apologized immediately and come running upstairs. Since she clearly hadn't, I stepped over to the intercom and spoke into it, trying for a tactful tone. "Lily, your grandfather made an incredible breakfast for us to share before he leaves. I expect you to join us now." Then I said a silent prayer, *Please, God, help my children behave like the kindhearted people I know they can be. My dad deserves a happy send-off.*

Everyone managed except Luke, who acted kind-heartedly toward everyone but me. "I can do it myself," he snarled when I reached over to help cut his French toast, and he then proceeded to start ripping it with his knife and fingers. My dad lowered his eyes.

Lily, sitting on Luke's left, spoke up, "Hey, buddy, that's really kinda gross. Let me, please." I cringed, expecting a huge scene. But Luke watched her cut the hunks he'd created into bite-sized pieces and returned to eating as though nothing had happened.

WTF?

"Shall we show your mom the chore board we made?" Dad asked after everyone'd finished eating.

"Yes, I'll go get it!" Amy said, bounded from her chair, and headed for the dining room. She returned a moment later, carrying an eighteen-by-twenty-four-inch whiteboard that Abby'd found at a garage sale a few years ago. The twins had gotten a kick out of drawing on it for about a week, and it had sat in Amy's closet collecting dust ever since.

"Look, Mommy," Red said when Amy set the board on the floor. "Our names and our chores."

Lily had drawn a calendar grid on the board and written a list of "assignments" beneath it. Lily's chores were the more difficult, such as *put away clean laundry* and *bathe Red*. Amy had *carry dirty laundry downstairs* and *help clear table*. Luke had *take out trash* and *water flower beds*. Red had *pick up toys*. The list went on, of course, in a similar vein.

My dad held up a ziplock bag full of reusable stickers, with which the chore-doers would signify completion of their assigned tasks. "The kiddos all agreed Lily could be the enforcer," he said, "and they'll FaceTime me a couple times a week to show me how it's going. If they do their assignments for a whole month, I'll send them a special allowance to spend any way they want."

"Impressive," I said as the kids went to tackle the day's tasks. *And I'm super glad Lily'll ride herd on the rest of 'em, because that sounds like a chore in itself.*

My dad must've read my mind, because he said to me under his breath, "If it gets to be more trouble than it's worth, you can hide the damn thing."

I laughed and blew him a kiss.

Dad and I stood at the counter together while I washed the frying pan and he loaded the dishwasher. "I can't thank you enough for everything you've done here the past month and a half..." I said.

"Please stop. I know you're grateful, but this has been a labor of love, and aside from watching you in pain, I've enjoyed every minute of it. With Grace and Amanda working the extra hours and Abby and Bert stepping up their help, things are gonna go smoothly. Your mom and I'll come back anytime you need us—like when you have a trial or when Abby and Bert go on vacay."

"I'm pretty confident I can handle everything, with the possible exception of Luke."

Dad gave me a quizzical look.

"You have to have noticed how angry he's been lately."

"He's been a little testy, yeah, but I haven't seen anything alarming."

"What about the fight on the playground the other day?"

"He's a boy."

"When we were growing up, did Buddy act like Luke's acting now? More temperamental, I mean?"

Dad paused. "I don't know if more temperamental is accurate, exactly. But definitely more vocal than you. Boys are *different* than girls."

"I hope it's just that."

AN HOUR LATER, the kids and I stood on the front curb waving good-bye as Dad drove away in his shiny silver Cadillac CTS, the car he'd so proudly driven up in six weeks earlier. We all cried unabashedly, but Luke grieved, his skinny shoulders heaving with sobs between each intake of breath. He didn't notice when I placed my hand on his shoulder as a small gesture of comfort.

BEFORE BED THAT NIGHT, I flushed the remaining five Vicodin tablets in my prescription bottle down the toilet. *Forgive me for contributing to contaminated wastewater, but I gotta get these out of the house. And God help me refrain from ordering a refill.*

49

I'D GOTTEN a call from the marshal's office after close of business on Wednesday saying that AJ Corbell had arrived in Madison and they were holding him at the Dane County Jail.

First thing Thursday morning, I called to schedule his initial appearance in our court. "Will three fifteen this afternoon work for you?" the deputy clerk asked me.

I checked my calendar. "Fine with me."

"Do you know whether he's got an attorney yet?"

"Sorry, I don't."

It didn't much matter to me whether he did or not. The hearing wouldn't take long either way, and I'd have plenty of time to get to Lily's parent-teacher conferences at four thirty.

I PARKED the G-car in the lot adjacent to the courthouse at three o'clock, finger-combed my hair, and swiped on some lip gloss. As I checked my look in the rearview mirror, I saw a Harley Davidson pull into the lot. The driver pulled up next to another motorcycle on the sidewalk and dismounted just as I used my key card to enter the locked side door. He raised a hand to hale me to hold the door.

I mouthed, "Sorry, not allowed," and proceeded inside to chat with a couple of my colleagues in the lobby.

Ten minutes later, when the elevator dropped me on the fourth floor, Harley guy was seated on a bench outside the courtroom, in his stocking feet, pulling tasseled loafers from a duffel bag. He glanced up at me. "Might you be Caroline Spencer?"

I nodded. "Yes. And you are?"

"Vince Waterford, attorney for Ambrose Josiah Corbell. And pardon me for not standing to greet you— I'm running a few minutes behind." When he lifted his right foot and placed it on his other knee, I could clearly see its outline through the sock. Prosthetic.

"No worries," I mumbled. "See you in the courtroom."

I'd taken off my own prosthesis after lunch and hadn't bothered to put it back on. Now, feeling somehow naked in front of this man with my left pant leg pinned up, I walked quickly on my crutches and pulled open the door to the courtroom. Matt Witte waited at the prosecution table.

"You look a little flushed," he said when I sat down beside him. "Something wrong?"

"Not really. But AJ Corbell's attorney was changing from his motorcycle boots to loafers in the lobby and I noticed he's got a fake foot. I guess it just surprised me."

"So he hired a lawyer, who probably won't let us

interview him. Anybody we know?"

Hmm. I guess the "fake foot" didn't seem interesting to you? I thought but didn't say. "Says his name's Vince Waterford. Never saw or even heard of him. Looks like an expensive bike and expensive shoes, though."

"Chicago?"

"Probably."

A moment later, Waterford walked down the aisle, set his duffel bag on the floor next to the defense table, and came over to extend his hand. "Hello again."

"Hello," I said with a smile. "Vince, this is my case agent, Matt Witte. Matt, Vince Waterford."

Matt stood and shook his hand, wincing slightly when they disengaged.

"Would it be possible to meet with you for half an hour after the hearing?" Vince asked me.

"Sure," I said, then looked toward Elizabeth, the deputy court clerk seated next to the judge's bench. "Is the third-floor conference room available for us to use after the hearing?"

She checked the calendar on her computer then nodded.

Matt leaned over and whispered to me, "Good idea: keep him out of your office."

I wanted to ask what he meant but a nanosecond later, two deputy marshals—their faces reflecting clear disdain—came through the side door escorting AJ Corbell.

"At long last," Matt said under his breath.

One deputy unlocked Corbell's handcuffs while the other pulled back the chair beside Waterford's and muttered, "Have a seat."

"Thanks for getting here on short notice, Vince," AJ said to his lawyer.

"No problem. I was at my house in Lake Geneva and just zipped over on my bike."

Matt and I exchanged *Well, la de da!* looks. The two deputies, now seated behind AJ, simultaneously rolled their eyes.

While we waited in silence for the judge to appear, I stole a few glances at the defense table. I didn't relish the idea of opposing Waterford *or* Corbell in front of a jury—both were ruggedly handsome in an *Aw, shucks!* kind of way. Thick, dark hair, deep-set eyes—Waterford's green and Corbell's brown—framed by lush lashes. I noticed the attorney edging away from his client, and three-days-without-a-shower odor periodically wafted our way. But there was no question that Corbell would clean up nicely for trial, cleft chin and all.

"All rise," the clerk intoned as Magistrate Stanley Brillstein walked through the door behind his bench. A short, moon-faced man with a recessed chin, his looks belied his tough-as-nails reputation, exactly the kind of jurist I wanted for the likes of AJ Corbell.

We entered our appearances and, as Matt and I had predicted, Vince Waterford announced he was from Chicago. "I've been admitted to the bar in the Northern District of Illinois," he told the judge, "and request permission to represent the defendant in this district."

Judge Brillstein scrutinized him over his reading glasses. "Very well. Please provide the clerk with your contact information before you leave the building." I knew the judge would do some checking on his reputation, as would I.

"Mr. Waterford, has your client been provided a copy of the indictment in this case, and do you wish to have it read aloud?" the judge asked.

"We have received it, Your Honor, and waive the reading."

"Ms. Spencer, would you state the penalties the defendant would be subject to if convicted?"

"Yes, Your Honor. The defendant has been charged with two counts in violation of 18 US Code, Section 1591, sex trafficking of children by force, fraud, or coercion. As to count one, he faces a mandatory minimum term of fifteen years to a maximum term of life imprisonment, and as to count two, the mandatory minimum term is ten years to a maximum term of life…" *I intend to argue for the latter. And am I imagining it or did AJ flinch when I said life imprisonment?*

"How does the defendant plead to the charges, guilty or not guilty?" Judge Brillstein asked, without looking up from his desk.

"Not guilty, Your Honor," Corbell replied. Those were the only words we'd hear from him today—and quite possibly ever.

"And for the record, Your Honor," Waterford added, "we do not intend to contest the entry of an order of detention pending trial."

"Well," the judge said, "thank you for allowing us to skip that perfunctory step. We'll move on to scheduling. Ms. Spencer, will you be able to provide counsel with discovery by next Wednesday?"

"Yes, Your Honor."

Judge Brillstein nodded and began reciting dates for pretrial motions, conferences, and finally the trial—

which Vince Waterford requested be postponed until mid-January because he had non-refundable tickets to Bali for the holidays. Matt and I exchanged a surreptitious fist-bump beneath the table—we'd be happy to have the holidays free for our less-than-exotic holiday celebrations.

And for healing, I thought, *for both Jen and me.*

The trial would be held in front of the district's newest judge, Marguerite Neumann, who'd taken the bench only six short months ago and had gotten her feet wet with civil cases. I'd appeared before her twice for plea hearings and had been impressed with her courtroom demeanor. Still, we had no clue how she'd handle a criminal trial or sentencing.

"WE'LL MEET you in the conference room. Elizabeth'll show you the way," I said to Vince after the hearing adjourned—I wanted to be situated at the table, as if it were *my* turf, when he walked in.

"Second home in Lake Geneva, alligator loafers, holidays in Bali, yada yada yada. Are you impressed?" Matt asked with a grin when the courtroom door closed behind us.

We had to wait for an elevator, I presumed because the marshals had secured one of them to move Corbell down to the sally port. And that, of course, gave Elizabeth and Vince time to catch up and ride with us. We rode down in silence. When we got to the conference room door, Vince held it open—making a sweeping gesture for Matt and me to enter first. *So much for my home turf advantage.*

"Do you ride the Harley in and around Chicago?" Matt asked Vince as we took our seats.

Vince laughed and shook his head. "Only a fool would do that. No, I keep it at my summer home in Wisconsin, where I can ride relatively safely on the weekends."

I made a show of looking at my watch. "As I said before, I *do* have half an hour, but that's all I can spare today. What did you want to see me about?"

Not at all chastened by my "keep it to business" admonishment, Vince smiled. "Certainly. I wanted to introduce myself personally since we'll be involved in the same case for a few months. I've heard very good things about you specifically and the court in general, though I suppose the new judge will be a bit of an enigma." He reached into his breast pocket, pulled out a leather fold, extracted a card, and wrote on it with flourishing strokes of a gold pen. "Here's my business card with my direct line—my cell number's on the back."

I kept an envelope full of *my* business cards tucked between the pages of my battered paperback US Code book—which I carried with me to every court appearance. I took one out of the envelope and handed it to him. "Sorry, but I don't give out my cell number."

Another smile. "I understand. I also wanted to talk about how you handle discovery here. First of all, could you give me a rough estimate of how much material you've gathered so far?"

I looked at Matt. "What do you think? About three Bankers Boxes so far?"

Matt nodded.

"Should I have our courier come to pick them up on

Wednesday?" Vince asked.

"I'd recommend it. We'll send you any additional discovery as it becomes available."

"Thanks—"

"Will your client consent to be interviewed by my agents?" I asked before he could move on to his next agenda item, making every effort to keep my face expressionless.

Vince's cheeks dimpled as he gave a rueful smile. "Now why on earth would we want to do that?"

"Gee, maybe for a three-level downward adjustment in the sentencing guidelines?" I replied without masking my sarcasm.

He chuckled. "Unless your case is a whole lot stronger than I think it is, we won't be pleading guilty."

"Fair enough." I wheeled my chair back from the table, grabbed my crutches, and stood up.

"Are you a recent amputee?" he asked.

I felt my cheeks grow hot. "That's a personal matter I don't intend to discuss."

Vince stood up and put out his hands, palms facing me. "I apologize if you took offense. That absolutely wasn't my intent. You see, I lost my lower right leg— during the first Gulf War—and I feel an affinity for others who've had similar experiences."

I didn't reply.

He bowed his head in contrition. "Again, I'm sorry."

Geez, you don't have to be a bitch about it. He's a wounded warrior, for God's sake. "Apology accepted," I said and extended my hand.

Vince covered my hand in both of his. "Thanks. And I'll look forward to working with you."

"Caroline, don't believe a word that guy says," Matt said when the door closed behind the defense attorney.

I sank back into my chair. "Why? Because he's rich? And good-looking?"

"Because he's a manipulative, misogynistic creep."

"Manipulative I can see. But how do you know he's a misogynist?"

"Men can spot these guys a mile away. He comes in here all GI Joe with the cycle and all. Politely shakes your hand, then uses a vise grip on me like he's the alpha dog marking his territory. Asks a rude personal question to get under your skin, and then comes off all contrite when he 'apologizes.' I saw him take your hand in both of his—that's textbook patronizing. He was all flirty with Elizabeth, too, and I *saw* him staring you both up and down from behind. I'm warning you: he views women as second-class citizens who he can wrap around his little fingers."

Wow. And I thought I overreacted. "You may be right, Matt. And I can already picture him trying to woo a jury."

"Especially the women on a jury. And let's hope Judge Neumann doesn't fall for him."

Vince ran into us again at the elevator, just after exiting the third-floor men's room, attired once again in his biker boots and leather jacket, with his duffel bag slung over one shoulder. *Shit! I thought surely he'd be gone by now.*

"One more thing," he said to me. "How would I go

about making arrangements to interview Jennifer Corbell?"

"That's not something I'm gonna help you with," I said as the elevator opened to let us on. I waved my hand toward the door. "You go ahead. We'll wait for the next one."

"Effing snake," Matt muttered when we stood before the closed door.

BACK IN THE PARKING LOT, I climbed into the G-car and noticed a missed call on the cell phone I'd left on the console. Dr. Jim Morgenthau, a prominent child psychologist who'd been recommended to me by Glenda and my own shrink, had left a detailed message forty-five minutes ago. I pushed *play* and listened. "I know this is short notice, but I've had a cancellation for tomorrow morning at eleven and I know you've been anxious for me to see your son. If you want the appointment, please let me know by four o'clock today. Thanks."

I glanced at my watch. It was already five past the hour. I dialed his number but the call went straight to voicemail. "I just got your message," I said after my breathless introduction. "If it's not already too late, we'll take tomorrow's appointment. Thanks."

Twenty minutes later, while walking down the school hallway to meet Lily's homeroom teacher, I received Dr. Morgenthau's text: *Appointment's yours. See you at 11.*

Thank you, God! I prayed. *I don't know if I could've gone on very much longer, dreading every encounter with my son. And please, please, may this doc have some answers.*

50

My HANDS FELT clammy on the steering wheel when I pulled up in front of Edgewood School the next morning to pick up Luke. I stared at the front doors, willing them to open and for him to appear. I glanced at my watch—ten forty, only twenty minutes until our appointment on the west side. *C'mon, c'mon. Don't make me come in there and get you.*

Just as I reached for my phone to text the school office, Luke walked out the door and waved off the teacher's aide who'd accompanied him. "Thanks," I mouthed to the aide. I hated to play the disabled card, but it took a lot of energy for me to walk from the parking lot to go in and pick up the kids when they could much more easily come out to the curb.

"Why do I hafta go to the doctor?" Luke asked for the tenth time, while he struggled to buckle his seat belt.

I looked in the rearview mirror and waited until he made eye contact. "As I told you, this doctor is a psychologist and he's going to help you figure out why you've been so angry lately."

"It's stupid," he said, kicking the back of the seat in front of him. "And I'm not angry."

Disengage, I told myself. *No sense arguing with him.* "All I ask is that you talk with the doctor. I hear he's really nice."

He crossed his arms in front of his chest. "Fine."

The handicapped spots in the clinic parking lot were all occupied when we arrived. *Shit, shit, shit. Why today? When we're already running late.*

I'd broken a sweat and my stump had begun throbbing inside my prosthesis by the time we got to Dr. Morgenthau's unstaffed waiting area. *Just like Dr. Melfi's office in* The Sopranos, *except with toys and kids' books,* I thought with a spontaneous and unexpected smile.

"There's nobody here," Luke said in bewilderment.

"The doctor will be out to get us when it's our turn," I said. Then, nodding to the play area, "You can check out those trucks while we wait. Looks like some pretty good ones."

The interior door opened five minutes later. "Mrs. Spencer, Luke. I'm Jim Morgenthau," said the bearded man who stooped to shake our hands. "Sorry to keep you waiting. C'mon back."

Luke's eyes widened as we walked down the brightly painted red hallway, decorated with framed children's artwork, toward a large glass-enclosed playroom.

"Luke," Dr. Morgenthau said, "do you want to go in and play while your mom and I sit and talk for a few minutes? We'll be right here where you can see us." He gestured toward a sitting area with three upholstered chairs and a coffee table, in full view of the playroom.

Luke nodded and went in.

"I read your intake questionnaire," the psychologist said, motioning for me to sit. "Tell me a bit more about what's been happening with Luke."

As I settled onto the chair, one of my crutches clattered to the hardwood floor, the harsh noise shattering my fragile composure. I burst into tears. "He's been hateful to me lately," I mumbled. "So angry. Won't let me hug or kiss him. Refuses things I offer him—even his favorite treats. He doesn't act that way toward other family members. Just me."

Dr. Morgenthau pushed a box of tissues toward me and waited while I took one and blew my nose.

"Sorry. I didn't mean to be histrionic."

He laughed. "I'd hardly call you histrionic. More like frustrated and anxious—for valid reasons. How long's this been going on?"

I shrugged. "I can't pinpoint when it began. So much has happened in the past few months. He seemed fine when he visited me in the hospital and at rehab. So probably shortly after I got home—about a month ago."

"Do you recall anything specific that might have set him off? Changes in school or daycare? Anything like that?"

"Well… my dad left on the ninth."

"Is Luke pretty attached to your dad?"

"Yeah. We all are. But I don't think that's what's bothering him—in fact, I remember a specific incident before Dad left. And it seems like he was pulling away prior to that blowup."

"Not to worry. Sometimes we can identify the problem pretty readily. I'm going to play with Luke for a while. You'll be able to watch and listen, but I'll have Luke sit with his back to you so he's not distracted by your presence. I'll be recording the session in case we want to watch it later for more clues."

Luke craned his neck to see Dr. Morgenthau's face when he went into the playroom, but the psychologist quickly maneuvered himself into a giraffe-like, pretzel-legged position on the floor. "Do you like to be called Luke?" he asked my son.

"Uh-huh."

"Great. Call me Jim, okay?"

Luke nodded.

"Do you like to paint? Or draw?"

"No—not unless I hafta. I'm not very good at it."

"That's fine. I see you like cars. Show me how you play with cars."

I watched in fascination as Luke selected several favorite cars, crafted a roadway and a bridge out of wooden blocks from a nearby bin, and drove the cars off the bridge—making sound effects as they crashed. *Is this about his father dying in a car accident? If so, why is he struggling with it now?*

Jim made a few innocuous comments along the way, but didn't ask any questions. Perhaps twenty minutes into the session, he said to Luke, "Do you mind if we play with some other things for a while?"

"Okay."

"I've got a playhouse and a bunch of different dolls over here, kinda like action figures. I was hoping you could pick out some to make a family and show me what they might do together."

Luke looked skeptical. "Uh, I guess I could."

Jim scooted over on the floor while Luke approached the doll shelf. He selected a boy doll and a similarly sized girl doll, both with dark hair. "These are twins. They're five."

Jim nodded. "Great."

Luke grinned when he found a gray-haired man doll. "This is the grandpa." He frowned as he shuffled through a plastic box containing more dolls, finally selecting a curly-haired baby and an older girl with long dark hair. "I guess this one'll be Red, whose real name is Lucy. And this one is Lily—she's thirteen."

Guess he's taking this seriously. His hypothetical family has two sisters who just happen to have the same names as his *youngest and oldest sisters!* I held my breath, waiting to see which doll he would choose to represent me. But Luke simply turned to Jim and said, "What should I do with them?"

"Pretend they're doing stuff a family would do together."

Luke nodded. His eyes landed on a ball near the doll-house. "Yeah. They could play kickball." He proceeded to have the dolls kick the ball and run around imaginary bases, cheering them along.

"Great," Jim said. "Maybe they would eat dinner together?"

"Yeah," Luke replied. He deftly constructed a table with more of the building blocks and set the dolls around it. "This is where we sit. And the twin sister says stuff like, 'You eat like a pig,' and Lily tells her to be nice."

Luke took the doll family to the zoo, using several

stuffed animals as props. "Grandpa always buys ice cream after the zoo," he said with a smile.

"Well, Luke," Jim said a while later, "our time's up for today. But I really enjoyed playing with you. Would you come again next week?"

"Sure," Luke said, popping up from the floor and bouncing on the balls of his feet. "It's cool to be out of school."

"Great. I'll take a quick picture of the dolls you chose for the family so we can find them next time." He waited for Luke to line them up, then snapped a pic with his phone. "Would you mind putting the dolls away while I go talk to your mom?"

I had difficulty holding back more tears when Jim approached. "He didn't pick a mother doll," I said, shaking my head.

"He didn't pick a father doll, either."

"But his father's dead. I'm not."

Jim nodded. "We'll explore that with him next week. In the meantime, don't overreact. It's uncomfortable for both of you, I know. But in my opinion, Luke's a normal kid who's working through your illness in his head."

51

WHEN WE'D LEARNED from Jen in late August that her dad's friend Zach Prescott had given her and Josie presents from a trip to "some island," I'd asked Jimmy to look into his overseas travel history. I'd also gotten subpoenas for Prescott's bank records, both here and abroad—though the latter was likely as useless as the paper it was printed on.

Later, armed with Prescott's phone and at least some bank records, we'd decided it was time for the FBI to talk with him.

On Friday afternoon, Jimmy brought over the report of the interview, which had been conducted by field agents in Little Rock.

"He hedged at the end," Jimmy said when he gave me the copy, "which makes me think he may be an accessory to AJ's crimes. Maybe it's time to grant him immunity to roll over on Corbell."

"Lemme read this and then we'll decide."

"Okay, call me later," he said on his way out the door.

The Little Rock agents had approached Prescott for the first time at his office. He expressed his willingness to talk with them but said that "out of an abundance of caution," he wanted his attorney present at the time.

The actual interview had taken place on October eighteenth. I donned the leopard-print glasses I'd been using lately and settled back to read Special Agent Otto Reingold's report.

> *Zachary Thomas Prescott III was interviewed at the office of his attorney, James Willoughby. Prescott was advised of potential penalties for making a false statement.*
>
> *Prescott stated he first met Ambrose Josiah Corbell in 1993, when they were both confined at a juvenile detention facility in Escambia County, Florida. Prescott stated they kept in touch, and when Corbell's parents kicked him out of their home in 1996, he resided for about a year with the Prescott family.*
>
> *Prescott stated he and Corbell became as close as brothers and remained so over the years. After Corbell, his wife, Casssandralynn, and their two daughters moved to Arkansas, Prescott relocated there as well. His own career in the banking industry "took off," though Corbell was less successful in his sales positions.*
>
> *Prescott stated he and Corbell were both devastated at Cassandralynn's death. Prescott admitted he established an investment account for Corbell in the Cayman Islands in which he could place the payout from Cassandralynn's life insurance policy. He said he did so not to avoid tax liability, because no tax was owed, but rather to yield the highest return on the investment. When asked to provide the name and number of the account, Prescott declined.*
>
> *Prescott reported that, at AJ Corbell's request, he sent a*

retainer for the attorney to represent Danny Thompsen. He stated he did not know the specific charges against Thompsen, nor had he ever met him.

Prescott stated Corbell asked him to find a criminal defense attorney for him after his arrest in late September. He knew the charge involved sex trafficking and emanated from the Western District of Wisconsin. Prescott stated he made several calls to locate the best attorney in the vicinity whom Corbell could afford, and he then arranged to retain Vincent Waterford of Chicago. The retainer, like the one for Thompsen's lawyer, was paid from Corbell's Cayman Islands account.

Upon advice of counsel, Prescott elected not to discuss whether he had knowledge of the sex trafficking with which Corbell was allegedly involved.

I found the folder containing information that had been compiled about Zach Prescott. His rap sheet reflected no convictions, and he'd successfully completed deferred prosecution programs for the drunk driving and possession of marijuana arrests over fifteen years ago.

He'd inherited a cool million dollars when his dad died five years ago and another two million from his mother last year. He'd purchased a new Mercedes within the past six months, but the remaining monies were safely stashed in brokerage accounts. His bank records didn't show any suspicious transactions or influxes of cash. He had a near perfect credit score.

Zach served on the board of directors of a Little Rock hospital, belonged to a couple of civic organizations, and had joined his new wife as a member of a suburban megachurch. *What's a guy who seems too good to be true doing with a friend like AJ Corbell?*

I closed the folder and rang Matt and Jimmy in on a conference call. "Talk to your bosses and find out what they need from me or George Cooper to okay your travel. I want one of you in Pensacola and one in Little Rock, and the sooner the better. Reach out to anyone you can think of to see if there's *anything* on Zach Prescott that would make me regret it if I give him immunity. Contact drug and kiddie porn task forces and see if they've even *heard* his name. We need cops to ask their snitches. Talk to local newspaper columnists and neighbors."

"My captain has already authorized me to travel if you need it," Matt said. "He's got a real bug up his ass about getting justice for those girls."

"My SAC will agree, too," Jimmy said. "He won't want the FBI to be upstaged by Janesville PD. I'd prefer to go to Pensacola than Little Rock, though, 'cause a buddy of mine's there."

"Sounds good. Thanks, guys. I know I can count on you."

I left the office feeling optimistic: two great investigators would be in the trenches working to lock AJ Corbell away for a long time, a respected psychologist was working with me to get Luke back on track, and Abby and Bert were hosting my three littles for a sleepover tonight. *Hallelujah!*

52

GLENDA CALLED around six thirty that evening. "I hear via the grapevine that you're kid-less tonight. What're you doing?"

"Right now I'm eating a slice of leftover pizza and watching an episode of *Justified*."

"Is that the show with the hot guy, what's his name?"

"Timothy Olyphant. Yes, it is. And yes, he's hot."

"Can I come over?"

"If you bring a bottle of wine—I'm all out."

I'd locked the front door after Lily left for her babysitting job, but Glenda knew the entry code. She sauntered in a few minutes later carrying two bottles of wine. "Couldn't decide between Pinot Noir or Pinot Gris. What's your preference?"

"Noir, please."

"Back in a flash."

She returned from my kitchen with two glasses and a corkscrew and proceeded to leave bits of cork, pieces of metal from the bottle's seal, and dribbles of red wine on the coffee table as she opened and poured the wine. "Honestly," I teased, "I'm not sure how your family puts up with your messes."

She handed me my glass. "You know I'll clean it up before I leave. How'd Luke do at the shrink's today?"

"Huh? Oh, yeah. I forgot I texted you last night to tell you there'd been a cancellation."

She raised an eyebrow. "Your text had more than a few typos. Had you been drinking?"

I nodded—a tad sheepishly. "Just a couple glasses of wine after I put the kids to bed. My stump was throbbing from a long day and then walking from the far reaches of the parking lot into school for Lily's conferences. I rarely drink anymore, so wipe that judgmental look off your face."

"All right, already. So fill me in on the appointment. Did you like Jim Morgenthau?"

I told her, omitting the part about my tears when Luke didn't select a mommy doll for his family.

"We've got another appointment next Friday," I concluded, "and Jim seems pretty confident he'll be able to get Luke to open up."

I paused and took another sip of wine. "What's new with your fam? Seems like it's been a while since we've had a chance to catch up."

Glenda crossed her legs pretzel-style and leaned back against the couch cushions. "Let's see. Talked to Trey last night and he's doing well in all his classes. Says he's making some good friends. Nothing new with Sarah other than our wars over her makeup. Jake got sent to the principal's office yesterday for mouthing off in gym class. And

Jen's been trying to convince Dr. Peters and me to let her see her dad when he gets here."

"What?"

"You heard me."

"What I meant was, how on earth could she stand to see the man who sold her into prostitution and, for all practical purposes, caused the deaths of her mother and sister? Especially now that she knows she has a family who *does* love her."

Glenda pulled out her hair tie, finger-combed her hair, and put it back up into its messy knot. "I asked her that. She mumbled something about needing to tell him in her own words how much he hurt her. Dr. Peters and I reached a compromise with her: she'll put what she has to say in writing and we'll see to it that her dad gets the letter. She's gonna start working on it and show it to Dr. Peters at our upcoming session."

"Well, her dad arrived in Madison Wednesday night, so at least we'll know where she should send it. As a matter of fact, I saw him personally yesterday in court."

"Really? What'd he look like?"

"He looked—and smelled—like he hadn't had a shower in a few days. But he's classically handsome: clear brown eyes, dark hair, cleft chin. His lawyer's eye candy, too, though Matt Witte says he can tell he's a chauvinist sleaze."

"Hmm? Jealousy?"

I knew she was baiting me and purposely ignored the comment. "Anyway... the lawyer asked me how he could arrange to interview Jen but I refused to answer him. Just to be on the safe side, you should probably notify the school not to let anyone talk with her without your permission."

"How would he find out where she is?"

"He shouldn't be able to, but it wasn't that long ago that Jen made surreptitious calls to her dad and now she says she wants to see him. Who's to say she doesn't have some way to get a message to him—maybe through a friend of his?"

"This just gives me the creeps. I mean, her dad's in jail, but all those other men who abused her and her sister are walking around free. And ever since she heard about his arrest in Arkansas, Jen's been acting a little wonky. Not doing as well in school, losing her concentration, having a few nightmares."

"All the more reason to alert the school."

"I'll do it first thing Monday."

53

By the following week, Luke was barely speaking to me. He often pretended he didn't hear me and answered any questions he couldn't avoid with gestures or one-syllable responses. He'd asked me no less than six times when my dad was coming to visit again.

I picked him up for the appointment with Jim Morgenthau in the middle of a rainstorm and groaned to myself when he ran from the school to my car without his rain slicker.

Luke pulled at the door handle, which I'd forgotten to unlock, and yelled, "Lemme in, damnit!"

You little shit! Right now you're lucky I don't pull away from the curb and leave you there to get wetter and wetter.

Inhaling and exhaling deeply to clear my head, I pushed the *unlock* button and waited while he climbed into his booster seat and slammed the car door.

"I'm sorry I forgot to unlock the door, Luke. But I expect an apology for swearing at me."

I watched in the rearview mirror as he feigned difficulty buckling the seat belt. When it finally clicked, he muttered, "Sorry."

The thwacking windshield wipers sounded discordant in the absence of conversation, but I stubbornly refused to turn on the radio. *If he's gonna give me the silent treatment, I'll hand it right back.*

Finding the most distant handicapped parking spot vacant, I breathed a small sigh of relief. *It's not too far—I can use one crutch to steady myself and have a free hand for the umbrella.*

Luke dashed from the car to the clinic entrance, eschewing the shelter of my umbrella, and looked pathetic when I joined him in the lobby. "Come with me," I said, holding the door to the family restroom open. "Now."

He moaned as I grabbed a handful of paper towels and blotted his wet hair and shoulders. There was nothing else to be done and I felt a tinge of pity for him as he shivered on our walk to the psychologist's office.

Jim Morgenthau greeted us with a smile. "I'm guessing you forgot your jacket, huh, Luke?"

Luke nodded, a bit sheepishly, I thought.

"There's a sweatshirt in the playroom that'll probably fit you. We'll pull off your wet shirt and let it dry on the air vent." I waited in the seating area while Jim took my son in to get him situated, dressing him in a two-sizes-too-large Wisconsin Badgers sweatshirt. "You can play with the cars till I come back from talking with your mother."

When he sat down, he asked me, "Any new developments this week?"

"More of the same, only worse," I replied.

"But I notice you're not tearful today."

"Yeah, but I'm not sure that's progress. I think I'm replacing sadness and worry with anger. He's really pissing me off."

Jim laughed. "Let's see what his little family does today. I may call you in to talk with us in a bit."

I observed through the window as he rejoined my son. "Okay, Luke. Last week you picked out four kid dolls and a grandfather doll for the family. Let's find them."

Without referring to the photograph Jim had taken, Luke went to the shelf and collected the dolls he'd picked out before. "What d'ya want me to have 'em do?"

"You decide."

"I think they'll go back to the zoo." He proceeded to place stuffed animals around the area, and the dolls went to visit them. "Look at the elephant!" he had the boy doll say. "He's running away from the giraffe." And the doll family stayed in one place—apparently just watching—while the animals galloped around the zoo.

After about five minutes, Luke sat down and asked Jim, "What next?"

"Hmm. Can I ask you a few questions about the family?"

Luke nodded.

"I notice there's no mother or father doll. Where are the children's parents?"

"They're dead."

"Oh, that's sad. How did they die?"

Luke looked down at his lap. "The dad was in a car crash. The mom had cancer. She was okay for a while but it came back and she died."

"Huh. Luke, do you know anyone who died when their cancer came back?"

"Well… a kid in Jake's class—his mom did. And Jake told me. And he knows 'cause he, like, went to the funeral."

"When did this happen?"

Luke shrugged. "I dunno."

"Was it during this school year?"

"Yeah."

Oh, shit! I should've known all the Edgewood kids would be talking about the death of a second- and an eighth-grader's parent. Why did I assume kindergarteners would be oblivious to the news?

"Are you worried that *your* mom's cancer might come back?"

Luke didn't speak for a moment. I couldn't see his face, but his shoulders began heaving and I heard him answer between sobs, "Uh-huh…Amy says it won't…but I don't believe her."

"Why not?"

"She was wrong about Mommy having her leg cut off. She's pro'bly wrong about this too."

"I'd like your mom to come in and talk with us now, okay?"

Luke sniffled and nodded. I walked into the playroom and sat on the edge of the low-slung couch. He ran into my open arms, and I hugged him till his crying ceased. "Oh, Luke. I wish you would've told me why you were scared. My cancer was very different than the kind Mrs. Jorgensen had. I had a kind that grows very slowly. And even if it did come back—which it almost never does— they would have plenty of time to give me medicine to get rid of it."

"Really?"

"Really. And I really, really need you to tell me when you're worried about something like that. Okay?"

"Okay," Luke snuffled and wiped his nose with the cuff of the loaner sweatshirt. "Can I play some more?"

Jim nodded. "You can play with whatever toys you want while your mom and I talk again."

It took me a couple tries to rise from the couch, but thankfully neither the psychologist nor Luke—preoccupied with putting dolls away and searching for more intriguing toys—noticed. I felt a strong need to demonstrate my physical capabilities. To show Luke I could take care of him as well as myself.

"Looks like your son's recent hateful behavior was him pushing you away preemptively," Jim said when we sat in the observation area. "It's not uncommon in kids."

"I'm not sure I understand."

"Luke distanced himself from you emotionally before you could up and die on him."

"Oh, my God," I said with a hitch in my voice. "That poor kid."

Jim nodded toward the playroom. "It looks like he fully accepted your reassurances. He's driving those cars and trucks with a grin on his face."

"Do you think that's the end of this rough patch?"

He laughed. "I do, though I'd have another talk with all your kids and reinforce the fact that you're healthy. And don't hesitate to call me if you're flummoxed by the next rough patch, because with four kids, most assuredly there'll be one!"

I HAD a one o'clock meeting that afternoon with Matt and

Jimmy to discuss what they'd learned about Zach Prescott. Matt had been in Little Rock since Tuesday and would be flying back into Madison around noon, so I'd texted him when I dropped Luke off at school and asked if he needed a ride from the airport. *Yes. Just landed. Gotta get my bag, though, so maybe twenty minutes.*

He stood waiting under the awning when I pulled up to the door near baggage claim, jogged over to the car, and threw a small, wheeled suitcase into the back seat.

"Why didn't you just carry it on?" I asked as he buckled his seat belt.

"I haven't jumped through TSA's hoops for permission to carry my firearm on board."

"Oh, I guess I didn't view this as the kind of mission where you'd need to be armed."

"Caroline, you asked me to meet with snitches and other lowlifes who might know AJ's pal Zach and I wasn't gonna go do that unarmed. AJ was carrying when he got arrested. For all we know, Zach might've gotten him the gun."

He'd said this all matter-of-factly, but I still found it sobering: the work our case agents did could and did put them in harm's way on a regular basis.

"Geez, how oblivious could I be? And I'm glad you made it back safely." *And how corny are you being now?*

Matt's face colored slightly. "I'm lucky I did. On the flight from Little Rock to O'Hare, we hit a pocket of turbulence and the plane must've dropped ten thousand feet. People were screaming and crying, and an ambulance met us on the tarmac 'cause one passenger got a huge gash on her forehead when she flew out of her seat."

"Oh, my God. I'm sorry," I said, checking my mirrors to merge onto West Washington Avenue.

"Was the trip worth it?" I finally asked.

Matt shook his head. "Not in my opinion. Only one semi-promising lead to check out in Chicago. I'll fill you in when we're with Jimmy. I presume he's back from Pensacola?"

"Yep, he texted me to say he got in around midnight."

"WOULD you guys mind pulling the chairs over near the couch so I can elevate my stump?" I asked when Jimmy joined us. "I sound like an old geezer, but this damp weather sure makes me achy."

I situated myself crossways on the couch, a study pillow wedged behind me to support my back, two bed pillows under my residual limb, and a Bankers Box alongside to serve as a coffee table. Matt dragged the chairs over to face me. "Is this good?"

I laughed nervously. "Yeah, but I feel a little high-maintenance."

"For chrissakes, you had your leg amputated less than two months ago and you're already back to working full time," Jimmy said impatiently. "Give yourself a frickin' break."

"Couldn't've said it better myself," Matt added.

I had to swallow the lump in my throat before replying. "Thanks, guys. So, are we ready to offer Zach Prescott immunity?"

Neither responded. I gave them both a quizzical look, then nodded toward Matt. "You said you still have a halfway promising lead?"

He drew in a breath. "Yeah, but lemme start with what I *didn't* find. I met with Otto Reingold, Jimmy's counterpart in Little Rock, first thing Monday to let him know I was in town and would be asking off-the-record questions. He was cool about it and gave me the names of some undercover and task force cops to talk with. None of them had ever heard of Prescott but they agreed to ask their snitches. All but one got back to me by the time I left, and the snitches had nothing on him, either."

He tilted his chair onto its back two legs, ignored my *you're making me nervous!* look, and went on, "I followed Prescott all day on Wednesday and didn't come up with anything remotely suspicious. Last evening I tailed a couple of tellers from his bank to the bar across the street and eavesdropped on their conversation. Seems Zach cheated on his first wife with the woman he's married to now, and now he's cheating on *her* with one of the tellers —a very attractive blonde who's in her mid-twenties."

"Were you able to get her name?" Jimmy asked.

"Yeah. Got her plate number when she left and ran it through DMV. Suzanne Childress. Anyway, Suzanne told her friend she was excited to be going to Chicago this weekend with Zach. She said they 'always' stay at the Peninsula Hotel near Michigan Avenue and she gets to order room service while he 'goes and does his business.' The friend asked what kind of business but Suzanne didn't seem to know. I figure it's a long shot, but it might be worth making some inquiries at the hotel."

"I'm free this afternoon and tomorrow," Jimmy said. "Want me to go down and nose around?"

"Yeah, please do," I said. "What'd you find out in Pensacola?"

He shrugged. "Nothing concrete, and nothing at all via any cops or informants. One of the family's former neighbors told me Zach's mother was housebound for about three years before her eventual death last year. She had bone cancer, with debilitating pain"—at this, Jimmy glanced away from me, perhaps concerned the bone cancer reference might be upsetting to me?—"and according to the neighbor, there was always a slew of doctors coming and going. She said Zach visited frequently, and it made me wonder if he might've made a connection to get the oxy AJ was feeding the girls. The neighbor didn't have any names, but lord knows there's no shortage of doctors who'll write scripts in Florida."

"Any way to follow it up?" I asked.

"I've been racking my brain trying to think of how, but haven't come up with anything. I just have a gut feeling Zach was more than a financial advisor who hired lawyers for AJ and his cohort Danny Thompsen."

"If I'm hearing you guys correctly, you think we should see what more develops before offering Zach Prescott immunity?"

Matt and Jimmy nodded.

"I'm still reading AJ's emails," Jimmy said. "Maybe something of evidentiary value will turn up."

"Let's hope."

54

"THAT SOCIOPATHIC SON OF A BITCH!" Glenda said, storming into my kitchen and flopping into a chair at the table one evening the following week. "I feel awful that Dr. Peters and I agreed Jen could visit her father. It was complete and utter negligence on our parts."

I put the tater tot casserole that Grace had made into the oven, poured two glasses of Cabernet, and handed one to Glenda. "Take a sip and calm down." I sat beside her and covered her free hand with mine. "Now tell me what happened—skipping the self-flagellation."

"The *only* thing I'm glad about is that the jail staff wouldn't let us have a contact visit. Otherwise I would've strangled that godless bastard."

"Glenda—"

"Okay, okay." She sighed and took another sip of wine. "First of all, Jen was nervous as hell. Brad Tollefson and I told her several times that she didn't need to go through with the visit—we'd already made sure her dad got the letter she wrote. But she insisted it was something she had to do."

"She took the letter with her?"

"Uh-huh—though, as you suggested, I kept a copy. Brad asked the jailers to give it to Corbell when we checked in. By the time Jen, Brad, and I got to the visitation booth, he was reading it, and he'd already conjured up blotchy cheeks and big tears. And the eerie lighting in the visitation booth made him look like he was terribly sick, possibly dying."

"I'd like to see the letter when you get a chance."

"It's right here on my phone. You can look at it now while I go smoke a cigarette." She stood up and headed for my screened porch.

I zoomed in on the scanned copy and began to read.

Dear Daddy,

I know you have been arrested for what you did to me and Josie and that you are in jail. My psychologist said I should write you a letter and tell you how I feel instead of coming to see you and tell you in person.

I am very mixed up. It was so hard for me when Josie died and you were gone. I couldn't even talk because I was too upset. It was awful coming off of the pills you gave me, and I got super mad when I found out they were not to help me with depression but to get me addicted. My whole life after Mom died was blurry, and like a terrible nightmare.

I think you gave Mommy anorexia by saying all those mean things to her about being fat. You know she wasn't fat and she didn't deserve to be treated like that. She was such a good mother and teacher. She was a good person.

Josie killed herself because of what you did to her. I know you made her have sex with you and that is just wrong. It was wrong for you to let all those other men have sex with me and Josie. It hurt, and I cry whenever I think about it too much. I have a hard time even talking to boys at my school because of what you made me do. I don't know how to act like a fourteen-year-old girl. And I miss my sister, who was my best and only friend.

The police and prosecutor say you will go to jail for a long time. Maybe even for the rest of your life. You deserve it, but it still makes me sad. You were the only dad I ever knew till I moved to this foster home. The dad here would never do anything like what you did.

I hope you are sorry,
Jennifer

By the time Glenda returned, I was in tears. I blotted the end of my nose with a paper napkin and looked up at her. "So how'd Jen react when she walked in and saw him crying?"

She poured us each another glass of wine and resumed her seat. "For a few moments, she just cowered behind me, staring at him. Then he put his hand up flat against the glass partition and beckoned her to do the same. I wanted to scream, 'Don't fall for it!' but she approached the window and did as he hoped she would. And, of course, she started sobbing." Glenda shook her head, as if that might erase the scene from her memory.

"Did they talk?"

"AJ did. He took his hand away from the glass, picked up the phone, and motioned for Brad to give Jen the handset on our side. I leaned in to listen with her. AJ said something like, 'I'm so sorry you feel this way, baby.

Please believe me: I would never intentionally hurt you.' Jen didn't reply, so he repeated it. And then he had the frickin' audacity to tell her he didn't realize the meds he'd given her were something other than antidepressants, and that she must've imagined all the bad things that she said happened to her because of an adverse reaction to the pills."

"You've gotta be kidding me!"

"I wish I were. And the worst of it is, I think part of her wanted to believe him."

"Did Jen say anything back to him?" I asked.

"Uh-uh. It was like she couldn't get any words out. I just hung up the phone and turned her away from the window. And Brad knocked on the door to let the guard know we were done. I didn't see it, but Brad said Jen looked over her shoulder at her dad on the way out and gave him a shy wave."

"Shit, shit, shit!"

She'll never be able to testify against him. He'll undermine her confidence and make her say things that aren't true. And she'll be scarred for life whatever she does. I've gotta make a rock-solid case against AJ without putting Jen on the stand.

WHEN GLENDA LEFT, I sent an email to George Cooper with copies to Matt and Jimmy. "I need to meet with you ASAP tomorrow morning for the okay to grant immunity to Zach Prescott." Jimmy hadn't learned anything about Prescott in Chicago—other than that he was a philanderer, which wasn't something we could prosecute. He still wanted to hold off a while longer before giving Prescott a pass, but I needed to move off square one.

55

A WEEK AND A HALF LATER, bright and early on Monday morning, Matt and I flew to Little Rock to interview Zachary Thomas Prescott III. With our grant of immunity from prosecution, Prescott—according to his lawyer —would be willing to talk freely about his knowledge of AJ Corbell's sex trafficking business. We were still suspicious that Prescott might be more involved than we knew but had to take our chances.

This would be my first air travel since my amputation and I found myself more than a little nervous. *Will going through security be an embarrassing nightmare? Do I have the stamina to walk the long corridors to reach our gates? What if I have to rely on a motorized cart—with everyone annoyed at us as we beep-beep by them?*

Abby and Bert had spent Sunday night at our house so they could get the kids up and to school, and my household was still fast asleep when Matt picked me up at five thirty. Even in the predawn light, I could see he, too, was jittery.

"Rough night?" I asked when we pulled away from the curb.

"Huh?"

"You look kind of edgy—like maybe you didn't sleep too well."

He gripped the steering wheel tightly and stared straight ahead. "I hate to admit it, but ever since that last trip, the mere thought of flying scares me shitless. I didn't tell you this when you picked me up that day, but I seriously thought of taking the bus back from O'Hare after my brush with death on the plane from Little Rock."

"Geez, I'm sorry."

"Hannah wrote me a prescription for Xanax, but I didn't want to take one till I got to the airport. She said it'd wear off before our one-thirty interview."

"Sounds like a good plan. And you'll be too loopy to notice my mortification if I hafta use one of those godawful carts."

"Hell, I might need one more than you." He glanced at me with a forced smile. "And thanks for not giving me a hard time about my newfound fear."

Matt parked the car while I entered the terminal to check on our flight. As I'd feared, it would depart from the most remote gate. He found me staring at the electronic information board debating what to do. "It's a no-brainer," he said. "We ask for a wheelchair."

I lowered my head. "That feels like defeat."

"In the words of a very wise man," Matt said in a deadpan voice, "for chrissakes, give yourself a frickin' break!"

I grinned. "I never thought I'd hear you quoting Jimmy McGee."

"And if you ever tell him I did, I'll deny it."

The kind but far from patronizing gray-haired woman who pushed my wheelchair blazed an easy trail through security and to the gate. I managed to walk aboard the aircraft without incident. Matt stowed our carry-on bags, sat down, and promptly fell asleep, his head lolling against my shoulder.

As an added measure of intimidation, I'd made arrangements to conduct our interview at the Little Rock US Attorney's Office. Zach Prescott and his lawyer, James Willoughby, arrived precisely on time, a good sign, I thought.

Prescott's clammy handshake belied the confident look on his face, and I noticed large circles of perspiration under the arms of his freshly starched button-down shirt. *Good, he's sweating already.*

Matt started the tape recorder and set the stage for the interview, introducing the participants, the date, time, and location.

"Mr. Prescott," I began, "we have reason to believe you could be prosecuted as an accessory in relation to Ambrose Josiah Corbell's sex trafficking offenses, facing a maximum penalty of up to fifteen years in prison—obviously no small matter." I went on to explain that he would be immune from such a prosecution if he gave a complete and truthful statement and, later, testimony about his involvement with Corbell. "Do you understand?"

"Yes, ma'am, I do."

I took an immediate dislike to him and gave Matt our signal—scratching my chin—to take over his questioning.

"I'd like you to read this copy of Special Agent Rein-gold's report of his interview with you," he said, passing the paper across the desk to Zach and his attorney. We watched in silence until they finished. "Is this an accurate account of that interview?"

"It is," Willoughby replied.

"The answers need to come from Mr. Prescott," Matt said and nodded toward Zach.

"It's accurate," the latter replied.

"When did you find out that AJ Corbell was running a sex trafficking operation?" Matt asked.

"I don't recall exactly, but probably about two years ago. Shortly after Cassandralynn's death, he told me that Josie had run away. When he found her—in Kansas City —he learned that she'd been supporting herself through prostitution and was making quite a bit of money. He said they reached an agreement: she'd return to live with him and Jennifer, and he'd assume the role of keeping her safe while she conducted her business. AJ had been unable to secure lucrative employment, and he said this was a good arrangement for everyone. Plus Jen had been really depressed while Josie was gone and she was happy to have her sister back."

Matt didn't ask a follow-up question; he simply waited for Zach to continue.

"I was appalled and tried to talk him out of it, but he said Josie was adamant that she wanted to help support the family."

"When did AJ start prostituting Jennifer?" Matt asked.

"He'd never do that to his daughter," Zach replied without skipping a beat, then paused as if puzzling over our expressions. "Oh, I know, I know—Josie *was* his daughter through adoption, but you gotta admit that's different than having your *own* kid. AJ never really viewed her as his. And Cassie's family never let him forget that he wasn't as good as Josie's real father. Sure, they bought AJ and Cassie a house and let him run their little charity, but really, they treated him like a second-class citizen. That's why AJ, Cassie, and the girls moved away from Birmingham—to get away from all of Cassie's dad's micromanaging."

I felt my blood pressure rising and had to speak before I exploded. "Mr. Prescott," I said, "there's evidence that Jennifer was sexually abused. Her *real* father *did*, in fact, prostitute her. And he used opiates to drug both girls into submission. Do you know anything about how he might have acquired those drugs?"

The blood drained from Prescott's face and he gave his lawyer a questioning look. Willoughby leaned over to whisper to him and then said aloud, "I've told him the grant of immunity applies to his response."

Prescott exhaled loudly before answering, "My mother suffered from excruciatingly painful bone cancer for several years before her death. I got prescription pain medications from one of her doctors in Pensacola and sent them to AJ to give to Cassie. She had fibromyalgia, but her doctors said it was all in her head and wouldn't give her meds for the pain. Later AJ started taking them, too—when he hurt his back lifting her—and pretty soon they were both addicted. I just kept getting the pills for him after Cassie died. Honestly—I had no idea he was giving them to the girls."

"Both Josielynn and Jennifer had high levels of oxycodone in their systems when they were found in the

Janesville motel," I muttered. "Josie was dead from an overdose, which—as it turns out—you enabled. And you're going to testify to having provided those drugs at AJ's trial."

Willoughby cleared his throat. "Might we take a short break?"

"Sure," I said. "Five minutes. The restroom's down the hall to the left."

When the door closed behind the two men, I stood up to pace, my crutches thumping into the low pile of the conference room carpeting. "That son of a bitch has the audacity to tell us it was *Josie's* idea to sell herself..."

"And that he had no idea AJ was selling Jennifer," Matt added, "or that the drugs were going to the girls."

I stopped in front of the window and stared out over downtown Little Rock, trying—without success—to find something to distract me from my anger. "What next, Matt?" I asked.

He sighed. "I'd like to take another Xanax, get on the plane, and forget this whole interview. But I think we should nail down details about the doc, the mechanics of how Zach got the drugs to AJ, and specifically how he handled his money."

"Okay, sounds like a plan," I said, resuming my seat just as Zach and his lawyer returned.

While taking copious notes, Matt and I peppered Zach with questions until we could think of no more.

"We'll have this interview transcribed and send a copy to you for your signature," I told them.

"Will AJ get a copy?" Zach asked.

"His attorney can file a motion with the court to get a copy, but only after you've testified at the trial," I replied.

"Your name'll be on our witness list, so I suspect the attorney may try to talk with you before the trial. You can decline."

WE FINISHED at shortly after five and summoned an Uber to take us to the Marriott near the Arkansas Riverfront. We'd dropped our bags off with the bellman there before the interview, but the rooms hadn't been ready to check in. Now, we registered, got the keys to our adjacent rooms, and took the elevator to the fifth floor—Matt wheeling our overnight bags and me plodding along behind him.

"Hopefully I'll be able to walk on this fake leg without crutches soon, so I won't need somebody else schlepping around my stuff," I said when we reached my room.

"Happy to schlepp," he said, then looked down at the floor with embarrassment. "That didn't sound right."

I laughed and punched his arm lightly before unlocking the door. "I think we're way beyond worrying what things sound like."

He left his bag as a doorstop and hoisted my suitcase onto the dresser. "What d'ya wanna do about dinner?"

"What I want to do is take this damn leg off and hit the bar. I'm sure dinner ideas will materialize at some point, but all I can think of right now is an ice-cold beer. Ten minutes?"

"Yep. C'mon over when you're ready."

FIFTEEN MINUTES LATER, I knocked on Matt's door. "Right there," he called, then came to let me in while toweling off his wet hair. Shirtless, he wore faded jeans and one sock. "Sorry. I had the heebie-jeebies from talking to that guy and needed a shower before I could relax. I'll just be a minute."

He disappeared into the bathroom and called through the closed door, "The beers in the minibar are good and cold. Grab one if you want."

I glanced around and noticed—next to the pile of clothes he'd worn all day—an open can of Coors sitting on the dresser. *Might as well join him. Maybe it'll make this feel a little less awkward.*

I settled back into the easy chair, put my foot on the footstool, and popped the top of my can. The beer bubbled up through the opening and I sipped quickly to stop it from spilling over. *Almost-frozen-cold and heavenly!*

"See what I mean?" Matt emerged from the bathroom, fully dressed, and grabbed his own beer.

"Yeah. By the way, you were smart to take a shower. I probably would've been better off to do that than to call my kids. They manipulate my mother-in-law and her husband into all kinds of forbidden foods, and I could see them all on my FaceTime screen buzzing around maniacally."

"Well, at least you don't have to put 'em to bed."

"True that."

He opened the minibar again and took out another beer and a jar of mixed nuts. "Hors d'oeuvres?"

"Sure."

He sat on the bed, leaning against the headboard, and we shared the nightstand as a resting place for our nuts and beers.

"Seriously, Caroline, your kids are great. Each one has

a distinct personality but they fit together perfectly, kinda like a jigsaw puzzle. I know you didn't give birth to three of them, but it's so clear that they're all yours. I guess that's why it really pissed me off today when Zach Prescott talked about adopted and real kids—and that it was understandable for AJ to sell his adopted daughter."

"I know. I didn't like Prescott from the get-go, and my dislike grew to animosity quicker than with anyone I've ever met. I may need to have George Cooper second-chair the trial so he can be the one to question him."

"Do you think it'll even be worth it to call him as a witness?"

"I dunno. I don't trust or believe him and the jury probably won't, either. He's got some pretty damning testimony, though—about sending AJ the drugs that presumably ended up in the girls' systems, and about hiring a defense lawyer for Danny Thompsen. I think it should be enough to keep Jen from having to take the stand."

When I finished my beer, Matt crushed the can and tossed it into a trash can next to the desk. "Want another one here or should we go to the bar?"

"You decide."

He got up, headed for the minibar, and pulled out two more beers. "Let's stay here and order room service. You look way too comfortable to move, and I can't bear the thought of making small talk with a bartender or waiter or other customers."

He handed me my beer and the room service menu and settled back on the bed with the remote control, flipping through channels on the TV.

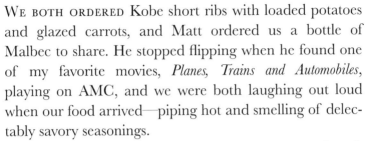

WE BOTH ORDERED Kobe short ribs with loaded potatoes and glazed carrots, and Matt ordered us a bottle of Malbec to share. He stopped flipping when he found one of my favorite movies, *Planes, Trains and Automobiles*, playing on AMC, and we were both laughing out loud when our food arrived—piping hot and smelling of delectably savory seasonings.

I took one bite of meat and potatoes and grinned. "This is amazing. And that room service guy was perfect —not one syllable of chitchat."

The movie, starring John Candy as a traveling shower curtain ring salesman and Steve Martin as a businessman trying to get home to Chicago for Thanksgiving, had always touched me. In the end, Martin realizes that Candy—who speaks endlessly of his wife and happy home—is really a widower with no permanent home, and invites him to his join his family for the holiday. Matt and I both teared up at the final scene.

"What are you doing for Thanksgiving?" I asked him.

He laughed. "You're not feeling sorry for me—the weird guy with no wife or kids—are you?"

Shit—I shouldn't've had that wine. The filters between my brain and my mouth are clearly not working. "No. Just wondering if you'd like to join us. My folks aren't coming, and the Fosters will be busy entertaining Magnolia Barr and her husband and kids. It'll just be Abby, Bert, my kids, and me. You know, the jigsaw puzzle kids?"

"Now I know you're making fun of me."

"Maybe so, but that was a really cute analogy and I intend to use it as often as I can."

"I'd be happy to spend Thanksgiving with you."

"Good."

We sat in silence for a while, staring at commercials for the next featured movies. Long enough for me to doze off.

Matt shook my shoulder. "C'mon," he said, extending his hand to pull me from the chair. "Let's get you to your room. We've got a ten o'clock airport shuttle."

56

My semi-sedate Thanksgiving plans had morphed into something far more chaotic: My late husband's sister, Julia, invited herself, her two teenaged kids, her new significant other, Thomas, and his six-month-old puppy named Rex, who—with separation anxiety—was unable to be left alone. I hadn't seen enough of Julia, Carlos, and Maria lately, so I welcomed their company, and Thomas's sense of humor brightened a room. Rex, however, tipped the balance. Sparky took offense to his presence and had to be banished downstairs, where he wailed plaintively for much of the day.

Despite his dog's distress, Luke loved every minute of the get-together. In addition to his standby ally Bert, he had Matt, Thomas, and Carlos, with whom to talk cars and football and play Legos and shoot Nerf guns.

The house smelled heavenly with Matt's cornbread and sausage stuffing, Abby's freshly baked pumpkin pie, and Julia's signature sweet potato casserole. I'd brined the turkey for two days, and everyone commented on how juicy and flavorful it turned out.

Still embarrassed by my overindulgence in Little Rock, I limited my wine consumption to one glass. Julia noticed me shaking off a refill and, never one to mince words, had to comment at the dinner table. "You look like you've got a stick up your ass," she said. "Relax and have another glass."

Matt, who'd just taken a bite, sputtered and covered his mouth with his napkin to prevent mashed potatoes from spewing out willy-nilly. He took a sip of water and said, "What she said!" Even I had to laugh. And I accepted the proffered wine.

AFTER DINNER, the male contingent left—in two separate vehicles—to take Rex and Sparky to the dog park. Lily and my niece were downstairs giving manicures to their grandmother, Amy, and Red.

"So, Dominic really is old news?" Julia said as she and I stood in the kitchen cleaning up.

"Yes, he really is," I said, depositing the last handful of silverware into the dishwasher.

Julia finished drying a serving platter, threw the damp towel onto the counter, and plopped into a chair at the table. "I coulda sworn he'd be the one, but I like Matt just as well."

"Matt and I are colleagues and friends, not an item. We went out a few times when Dominic and I were on the outs, but it didn't go anywhere."

"Thomas and I started out as friends," she replied,

"and we've grown to be soul mates and lovers. It could happen to you."

"Julia, look at him. He's the whole package—handsome, smart, kind. He's also five years younger than me. He needs someone his age who can give him kids."

"Listen to yourself," my sister-in-law said sharply. "You and I both adopted kids and we love 'em with all our hearts. Matt'd be a great dad to yours."

I didn't reply.

"Is it the one-leg thing?" she asked.

Hot tears stung the backs of my eyelids, but I refused to cry. I'd done enough of that in the rehab center. "Didn't anyone ever tell you to mind your own business?" I muttered, settling into the chair beside her.

She laughed and gave my shoulder a quick squeeze. "Plenty of times. And I'll butt out if you want, but something tells me you need to talk about this."

"You're probably right," I said with a sigh. "So...I get a strong sense that Matt would like our relationship to move beyond friendship, and I *think* I would, too. But what if his fondness for me is based—at least in part—on pity? I broke up with Dominic because he was patronizing to me, and now I'm hypervigilant about how people view me."

"Oh, honey," Julia said, "I've watched Matt. I don't think he pities you."

"Even if he doesn't, me being *afraid* that he does could be just as bad. I have to get over my own insecurities about myself as an amputee—a woman amputee—before I get into another relationship."

She nodded. "What if he falls in love with someone else before you're ready?"

"Believe me, I've considered the possibility," I said with a hitch in my voice. "But I have to take that chance.

57

I'D TAKEN the day after Thanksgiving off, but I anxiously awaited a work-related call from Matt. When we learned that Jen's godmother would be in Madison for the long weekend, he'd arranged to talk with her about her memories of AJ Corbell and his friend Zach Prescott. They'd made plans to meet for coffee at ZuZu Cafe at eleven.

He texted me shortly after noon, *Can I come over?*

Yes. Door unlocked. Come in when you get here, I replied.

He found me in the kitchen, conjuring up turkey sandwiches for the kids' lunch. "Want one?" I asked.

"Nah," he said, sitting at the kitchen table. "I had a piece of ZuZu's to-die-for carrot cake, which almost did me in."

I called Lily to come get the sandwiches so the kids could eat while watching a movie in the family room. She made two trips, carrying a pitcher of lemonade, a stack of paper cups, and a bag of chips down the second time.

"Thanks, kiddo," I said to her, then turned to Matt. "So…did Magnolia have anything interesting to say?"

"Oh, yeah. She remembered Zach Prescott pretty clearly. Said that when the Corbells still lived in Birmingham, he'd come visit them every couple months. Cassie told Magnolia she thought Zach was a bad influence on AJ—that he had a drinking problem and liked to 'cat around.' But AJ convinced Cassie she was just imagining things."

"Just like he tried to convince Jen that she imagined being a sex slave."

"Uh-huh. Anyway, Magnolia kept in close contact with Cassie's father, Dr. Whitaker, after AJ moved her and the kids away. She says he knew full well that Magnolia'd never had an affair with AJ and that story was all a manipulative ruse to separate Cassie from her family and friends. Remember Dr. Whitaker hired a private investigator to try to locate the Corbells, without success?"

I nodded.

"Well, the PI *did* find Zach Prescott," Matt continued, "and Whitaker sent a message to AJ through Zach—namely that he wouldn't press charges over the embezzlement from the charity and would give AJ and Cassie a hundred grand a year if they'd just move back to Birmingham. Zach got back to him about a week later and told him AJ said he'd never compromise his principles like that. AJ said if Dr. Whitaker ever tried contacting them again, he'd press charges for harassment."

"Surely the doctor realized that was an idle threat?"

"Maybe. Magnolia said he was so heartbroken over the whole thing, it was as though his daughter and granddaughters had died."

"And two of them eventually did, thanks to AJ."

Matt glanced through his notebook again. "I guess

that's the most important stuff," he said, just as his phone started to vibrate on the kitchen table. He glanced at it and accepted the incoming call. "Yes, this is Matt Witte."

I couldn't make out what the caller was saying, but Matt listened intently. "Can I put you on speakerphone?" he finally said. "I'm here with the prosecuting attorney and she needs to hear this, too. Caroline, this is Jonathan Miller, an undercover detective I met with in Little Rock several weeks ago. One of his snitches just got back to him about Zach Prescott. Jonathan, Caroline Spencer."

"Hey, Caroline," came the raspy voice with a Southern twang. "My snitch tells me he was in a strip club last year, sitting at the bar next to a guy named Zach. I showed him the pic Matt had given me, and he ID'd him as Prescott. Anyway, they were slamming down shots of whiskey and the snitch started complaining to Zach about the caliber of the strippers. Said they were old hags and he wouldn't take a free lap dance from any one of 'em."

Jonathan paused, and we heard him take a drag on a cigarette and exhale it before continuing. "So Zach asks if the snitch likes 'em young and he replies, 'Who doesn't?' Then Zach pulls out his phone, cues up a picture of two teenage girls, both naked with their legs spread, and says something like 'what d'ya think of these girls?' He tells the snitch they're sisters who'll be in town in a couple days and he can set up a date with 'em if he wants. The snitch asks if they'll do a three-way, and Zach says sure."

My stomach lurched and I swallowed the bile in my throat, desperately wanting to plug my ears. *This is your* job. *You've got no choice but to listen.*

"Zach takes the snitch's number and says he'll call

when the girls are available. And three days later, he did. He mentioned the girls' names—which the snitch said both started with the same letter—and the price. I asked him if the names were Jenny and Josie. He said 'something like that' but couldn't be sure. Anyway, the snitch says the price was too steep so he turned Zach down. Claims he's never seen him again."

"Do you believe that he didn't go meet the girls?" Matt asked the detective.

"Dunno. He's usually straight up with me, but he's no dummy. He knows these girls are legally too young to give consent, so this'd be first- or second-degree sexual assault. He'd be wise not to admit it if he did."

"Could you press him on it?" I asked.

"I *could*, but I won't. He's feeding me solid intel on a group of dealers who're responsible for two deaths from fentanyl ODs in the past six months—and one of the vics is not much older than your girls. Sorry, but I'm not gonna burn him."

"We get it. Thanks for getting back to me, man." Matt rang off, shaking his head in frustration. "Son of a bitch. What do we do now?"

"I can tell you what we *don't* do, and that's put this scumbag on the stand. And maybe ask George to figure out a way for us to charge Prescott with conspiracy or aiding and abetting sex trafficking."

"And Jen? D'ya think you'll have to call her as a witness?"

"At the very least we'll need to have her waiting in the wings."

58

DANNY THOMPSEN'S plea hearing on the following Monday made me somewhat more confident about our case against AJ Corbell. Jimmy and Matt had debriefed him several times now, and his accounts remained consistent with the facts we knew. They believed he'd make a credible, though unlovable, witness.

In return for Danny's guilty plea and truthful testimony against AJ, we'd agreed to recommend a significantly reduced sentence.

Judge Neumann accepted Danny's plea and scheduled his sentencing hearing for the day after AJ Corbell's trial —when everyone would have a better idea of the extent of his assistance.

EVEN AFTER COMBING through all the texts, emails, and photographs found on Danny Thompsen's and AJ Corbell's devices, I didn't believe we had enough slam-dunk evidence against Corbell. Especially if, for some reason, Danny "went south" on us, or if the jury didn't believe him.

So I reluctantly added "Jennifer Corbell, in care of GAL Bradley Tollefson" to our witness list. And, of course, Vince Waterford contacted Brad with a request to interview her. "I told him not no, but hell no!" Brad told me proudly in December, at our first meeting to prep Jen for trial.

Jen heard his comment and beamed. "It's so cool that people are, like, looking out for me."

"That's what adults are supposed to do," I replied, determined to help her understand she'd been abused in countless ways. "But Vince Waterford isn't gonna be looking out for anyone but your dad at trial, even while he pretends he's being nice to you."

Jen nodded. "Yeah. I get it."

"We have a decision to make: whether to have you testify in the actual courtroom where your dad, his lawyer, and the judge and jury will be present, or to have you testify from a different room on two-way, closed-circuit TV. Everyone would still be able to see you and vice versa, but you wouldn't have to be in the same room while you're answering tough questions. Either way, Brad or Glenda can be by your side—even holding your hand if you want. Do you have a preference?"

"I don't wanna be in the same room with him. He tried to…I dunno, like, con me into believing him when I went to visit him at the jail. And that was hard enough, seeing him through glass and all."

Good girl!

"That'd be my recommendation, too. We'll have to get the judge's permission to do it by TV, but I can't see any reason why she wouldn't grant our request. I'm sure Dr. Peters will be willing to write the judge and say you'd be fearful of testifying in open court or that doing so would cause you emotional trauma."

Jen gave me a skeptical look. "I dunno. She's all about empowerment and facing fears, but I can ask her."

"You don't need to ask. I'll call her after we're done here."

Two hours later, after the conversation with Dr. Peters, I sat dumbfounded at my desk. As Jen had predicted, the psychologist told me she believed our fourteen-year-old victim was fully capable of testifying in open court. "Rather than being traumatized by it," she'd said, "Jen will gain strength from confronting her victimizer. She's resilient and much tougher than we sometimes give her credit for."

I called Glenda to get her opinion. "I can see both sides," she said. "If it turns out testifying face-to-face is too tough, can we have the TV setup as a fallback?"

"Yeah. The law clearly allows for that."

"Then that's what I'd recommend. Dr. P and I can explain to Jen why we think this is the best way to approach it."

I felt as though I'd fallen through the rabbit hole. *WTF? But they're the experts, not me.*

59

I LEFT work early on this Tuesday with mixed emotions about the coming ritual—the kids' school Christmas concert and our pre-concert family dinner. I loved the dinner part and relished the kids' enthusiasm for music, but I dreaded sitting in the cacophonous, crowded auditorium for far longer than my body felt comfortable.

During our Thanksgiving dinner, Luke had invited Matt to come along. He'd remembered that Matt had gone with us to Ella's Deli before Lily's band concert a couple years earlier and was anxious to have him see the kindergarten choir perform. I'd been surprised that Luke enjoyed singing, though I'd often had to stifle grins at his loose interpretation of the lyrics and melodies. Bless his heart, Matt had agreed.

Tonight we'd be dining at the Copper Top—the restaurant Amy had chosen when we drew her name out of a hat.

"He's here!" Luke yelled when he saw Matt pull up in front of our house.

Pressed for time, we met Matt in the driveway and piled into the minivan. I drove, Lily rode shotgun, and Matt climbed into the way-way back to commune with the twins.

All of the handicapped parking spots at the restaurant were filled—thanks to the many elderly patrons who'd come for the early-bird special. I found a semi-close spot and congratulated myself on having the sense to leave my prosthesis at home.

We ate with a minimum of drama, though a few other diners gave us the stink eye at Luke's loud and exuberant "Holy cow! Look at this waffle!" when his meal was delivered. And thanks to speedy service, we arrived at the school twenty minutes early—in time to chat with the Fosters before the kids took their spots.

Jen, who'd sing with the eighth-grade chorus, wore a red velvet dress, wedged heels, and understated makeup. "You look wonderful," I said, giving her a quick hug.

The smile she gave in return lit up her face. "Thanks! It's so amazing that I can be doing this."

I felt my eyes tear up. Glenda sniffled and looked down at the floor.

"When do you leave for Birmingham?" Matt asked Jen.

"Day after tomorrow. Hank's taking me to Chicago so I can get a direct flight and don't have to change planes. I'm not too nervous about flying, but if I'd hadda change, that would've been really scary. Magnolia and the kids are gonna meet me at the gate."

How far you've come, honey, I thought. *Stringing multiple sentences together—and speaking to a man with confidence. I think Dr. Peters is right: you can handle in-person testimony.*

Matt nodded at me, as though he'd read my mind.

Two weeks later, the night after Jen returned from her Christmas trip, Glenda came over to chat. "Where is everyone?" she asked when we'd gotten settled in the living room with hot chocolate and a bag of microwave popcorn.

"The littles were exhausted from swimming all day, so I put 'em down early. Lily's in her room glued to her phone, but I didn't have the energy to argue about it. How was Jen's trip?"

She blinked back a couple of tears and took a tentative sip from her mug. "When I asked her, she said she loved every minute of it. Of course, I didn't think to hide the disappointment on my face. And then she added that she really missed us, though. I felt terrible making her feel guilty about having a good time…"

"Y'know it's possible to like being in more than one place. I mean, I enjoy it when I go back to St. Cloud and visit my relatives there, but that doesn't diminish my feelings for everyone here."

"Yeah. But Jen'll be going back to Birmingham for good before long—maybe as soon as right after the trial."

I ached for my friend. And for Lily, who'd grown close to Jen. "Is that what Jen wants?"

"She's torn, and so are Dr. Peters and Brad Tollefson. I'm praying she'll agree to wait until school's out."

I nodded. *Will that make it any easier?* I thought but didn't ask.

We munched and sipped in silence for a while. "When

you're ready, you can always take in another foster child," I finally said.

"I don't know if my heart can handle it—it's way tougher than I ever imagined to let her go. I'm not sure I could face doing it again."

Sparky plodded over to the couch, climbed up beside her, and rested his head on her lap. He didn't move the whole time she cried.

60

MY PARENTS WERE SCHEDULED to arrive midafternoon on the Sunday before AJ's trial. I knew I needed every ounce of mental and physical energy to make it through the three-day ordeal and couldn't spare any to handle the day-to-day details of parenting. But my guilt still dogged me.

That is until I saw the pure unadulterated glee on my kids' faces when Mom and Dad plodded through the snow on the sidewalk and came through my front door to greet them.

Red bounded into my dad's arms and cried, "Gammmpa!"

My mom knelt to hug the twins and grinned when Amy said, "You don't smell like smoke anymore—you smell *good!*"

Even Lily, who'd been in a sullen mood for a couple days, laughed when my dad engulfed her in a bear hug. "Lemme help you with your bags," she said, without my prompting.

So when Jimmy McGee picked me up at seven o'clock Tuesday morning, I had confidence my household would survive the trial.

MATT MET us at the door to the courthouse, carrying one box full of reports, photos, notes, and the criminal code-book we'd need to present our case. "Nervous?" he asked me.

"Not so much about the trial as I am about falling on this snow," I replied, carefully placing my crutches before each step.

"Not to worry," Jimmy said. "I'll catch you if you start to slip."

Matt and I exchanged surprised glances. Jimmy'd never seemed chivalrous, much less observant enough to realize someone might need his help. "Thanks, Jimmy," I said with a hitch in my voice.

WE'D BEEN ASSIGNED A SMALL ATTORNEYS' room next to Judge Neumann's courtroom on the third floor, and it's there where we shed our coats, boots, and gloves—and where I would leave my crutches. I'd been practicing walking on my prosthetic leg without them and, though I knew I limped a bit, was fairly confident about my newfound abilities.

We checked and double-checked the exhibits we planned to present and reviewed my notes. As the primary case agent, Matt would sit with me at the prose-cution table. Jimmy had to wait outside the courtroom until he was called as a witness, but could stay inside afterward.

At five minutes before nine, Matt and I took our places at the table. Vince Waterford, wearing a cashmere overcoat and scarf that probably cost more than my car, strode in a moment later. "Glad I came in last night," he said. "This godforsaken city's pretty slow with their snow removal." He folded his overcoat and put it on the chair behind him and took one file from his briefcase, placing it on the table in front of him. His hands and face were deeply tanned. "Ready to rock and roll?"

We ignored him.

The marshals brought AJ in a few minutes later. He wore a well-fitting but inexpensive gray wool suit, a bright white shirt, and an understated burgundy tie. His thick hair had been recently cut, and I noticed his nails were impeccably manicured though unpolished. Grinning, he went through a convoluted handshake-fist-bump routine with his attorney, then nodded in our direction.

We ignored that, too.

Judge Neumann emerged from her chambers and took the bench precisely at nine. In her mid-fifties, about five eleven and a hundred seventy-five pounds, she wore her graying, shoulder-length hair pulled back into a no-nonsense French twist, exposing small gold hoop earrings. The rhinestones on her reading glasses were the only hint of frivolity, though her smile suggested she had a sense of humor.

Two hours later, we'd picked a jury—six women and six men with two women as alternates—predominantly middle-aged white folks. The exceptions were an Asian-American male in his twenties, a thirty-something Latina, and a strawberry-blond woman just out of high school.

"What d'ya think?" I whispered to Matt once they were seated.

He shrugged and jotted a note on my legal pad: *Keep eye on #4. He might be hinky about women in authority.*

I STRODE with confidence to the podium, which, angled slightly to face the jury, stood in front of the counsel tables. Without notes, I gave the opening statement I'd practiced at least ten times—not verbatim but with extemporaneous comments to fit the looks I received from the jury. Several times, I spoke directly to juror number four, making it a point to use more passive words. "After hearing the evidence," I concluded, "I have no doubt you'll find the defendant guilty beyond any doubt."

Vince Waterford deferred making his opening argument until beginning the defendant's case. *A double-edged sword,* I thought. *He's keeping me guessing about how he plans to attack the evidence.*

My first witness was Matt Witte. He was clean-shaven today and sporting a quarter-inch crew cut, and Jimmy and I'd teased him about trying to look like Jordy Nelson —a well-loved Green Bay Packers receiver. Matt smiled shyly at the jury while stating his name and occupation.

With confidence and intentionally limited words, he laid the groundwork for our case: the 911 call, arriving at the motel to find two victims—one deceased and one traumatized, and who took over from there. Vince Waterford asked him only two innocuous questions on cross-examination, I suspected simply to let the jury hear his voice.

The medical examiner came next, testifying about the physical evidence and his conclusions as to the cause of Josielynn's death—though she was referred to as victim number one. Vince asked him no questions.

I called Harold Burnside, the motel owner, to the stand. He wore a rumpled brown sport coat and khaki pants—pulled up over the middle of his ample belly—along with black shoes and white socks. His answers stretched a tad longer than I would have liked, but the jurors clearly found him interesting. He proudly identified the photographs he had taken of AJ and the girls and described the nighttime visitor's car.

"Thank you, Mr. Burnside," I said when I'd finished.

Harold stood up to leave the stand. Vince Waterford jumped to his feet before the judge had time to respond. "Please be seated, sir. I still have questions."

Judge Neumann smiled at Harold and motioned him back to his seat, then glared at Vince. "Cross-examination."

The attorney asked too many questions, calculated, I thought, to trip Harold up. But Harold kept his cool.

"Back to this photograph, which you claim to be of Mr. Corbell dropping a cigarette butt on the ground," Vince said, jabbing his finger at the eight-by-ten-inch print. "How do you know that cigarette butt wasn't already there before my client drove up?"

"Because I pick up litter in the parking lot every morning at six, when I start my shift. And I always pay special attention to the area just in front of the rooms.

Furthermore, the cops told me his DNA was found on the butt—"

"Objection," Vince barked, "outside the scope of the question."

"Sustained," the judge said. "The jury is instructed to disregard the last portion of Mr. Burnside's response."

Vince gave the jury a hangdog look and wisely excused the witness from further questions.

Danny Thompsen, wearing a set of blue scrubs from the Jefferson County Jail, was my next witness. AJ and he exchanged hateful glances as he took the stand and swore to tell the truth. No doubt embarrassed by his brown and broken teeth, Danny'd tended to mumble during our trial prep sessions. Today, he spoke softly but clearly and answered my questions with no apparent bashfulness.

We made it clear to the jury that he'd pleaded guilty in hopes of receiving a reduced sentence for his cooperation, but that no promises or assurances had been given to him.

Thompsen testified for more than an hour, fully recounting how he'd met AJ Corbell, how he recruited Johns for the business, and how they communicated through burner and regular cell phones and Corbell's anonymizing email account. With downcast eyes, he described tying up a struggling Josie and forcibly raping her in the Janesville motel on the night before her death.

Matt took notes during Danny's testimony and showed them to me when I finished my questioning. *Jury glazing over about cell phone numbers. Jurors seem appalled about sex, esp. #6 & #10. They don't like DT but give AJ hateful looks.*

"Thanks," I mouthed back.

The judge ordered a fifteen-minute recess before

Danny's cross-examination. Vince Waterford was loaded for bear when the trial resumed.

"Isn't it true," he railed at Danny, "that it was *your* idea to become the recruiter of customers for my client?"

Danny nodded. "Yes, I already said that."

Good work, Danny. You saved me from having to object and sound like I want this trial to last an eternity!

Vince persisted, "And weren't *you* the one who suggested what prices to charge for various services?"

"Yes."

"And that was because you had experience running a prostitution business, wasn't it?"

"No. It was because lots of the guys, uh…the customers, told me what they'd be willing or what they wouldn't be willing to pay."

"So you never ran a prostitution business before?"

Danny leaned forward toward the microphone. "No, sir, I didn't."

After another half hour of similar questions, Vince finally muttered, "Nothing further," and Danny left the stand.

The judge didn't disguise her relief. "Ms. Spencer, how long do you estimate your next witness's testimony will take?"

My next witness would be Jimmy McGee, and we needed him to introduce lots of evidence, much of it technical. "At least an hour, Your Honor."

She gazed down at her desk and massaged her forehead for a moment. "In that case, we'll recess until nine o'clock tomorrow."

~

MATT and I joined Jimmy in our conference room. "Sorry I didn't get you on today," I told him. "Vince Waterford badgered Danny Thompsen mercilessly. Good news is, Danny handled him well and I think Vince pissed off the jury. What d'you think, Matt?"

He nodded. "Yeah, I agree. I don't get it, though. Vince must be way dumber than he looks."

I sank into a chair and stretched my arms over my head. "He obviously inherited his wealth along with his good looks—he sure didn't get rich off his smarts."

"Or maybe," Jimmy said, "he realizes he's got a loser of a case but took it to trial so he could hit AJ up for the big bucks. And AJ's narcissistic enough to want his 'day in court' whether it's in his best interest or not."

"Could be," I said.

I texted Glenda to confirm Jen wouldn't be called to testify today—she'd kept her home from school, and my plan was to have them come to the courthouse about an hour before we anticipated needing her. *Maybe mid-morning tomorrow,* I typed. *How's she holding up?*

OK. Talk to you later.

I glanced over at Jimmy and saw he'd pulled out the reports he'd be testifying about tomorrow.

"You've had all day to study that stuff," Matt said to him. "Why don't you give it a rest?"

"I read a book all day," he replied. "But now that I hear Vince Waterford's a prick on cross-examination, I want to figure out what he's gonna badger me about and prepare a few pointed comebacks."

"You know the evidence like the back of your hand and can think up your comebacks later," I said.

"Just fifteen more minutes," he said.

"I'll give you a lift home, Caroline," Matt said. "My car's in the ramp—meet you at the side door in ten."

"Thanks," I said. "You'll lock up, right, Jimmy?"

He nodded absently.

"How'd it go?" my dad yelled from the living room when Matt and I stood in the foyer stomping snow off our boots.

"Good," I called back. "Meet us in the kitchen for a beer if you want."

A few minutes later, sitting around the table with open bottles of Spotted Cow and a bag of pretzels in front of us, we recounted the day's highlights to my dad's delight —leaving out any mention of our victim's identity. Glenda and I had counseled Jen, too, to avoid talking about the court case, even though it was clearly on her mind.

"What would you think about me coming to watch tomorrow?" Dad said. "I've only seen you in action once, and that was a pretty boring hearing."

I shook my head. "This trial's gonna be closed to the public during much of the testimony. How 'bout next time?"

"Promise?"

"Yep."

Matt declined Dad's offer of a second beer. "Want a ride tomorrow morning, Caroline?" he asked as he stood to go.

"No, thanks. I'll drive myself since there's nothing to carry."

"Okay. See you around eight thirty."

61

I'D FALLEN asleep only hours before my alarm rang Wednesday morning, but my usual trial-day jitters precluded hitting the *snooze* button.

I stepped out of my hot shower to find a steaming cup of coffee sitting on my dresser and the aroma of bacon drifting up from downstairs.

"Eggs over easy?" my dad asked when I walked into the kitchen, dressed and ready to go.

"Too nervous to eat," I said, with a quick peck to his cheek, "but the coffee was a godsend."

"You need to keep up your strength. At least have some toast and yogurt."

"Okay," I said, taking my place at the table. My mom and the kids wandered in while I ate, and I was glad I'd stuck around to see them. "This trial'll be over tomorrow," I said when I kissed them good-bye. "We'll go out for dinner to celebrate, okay?"

JUDGE NEUMANN quickly dispensed with the morning's preliminaries and summoned the jury to the courtroom.

At nine fifteen, I called Jimmy McGee to the stand. Through him, I introduced the DNA evidence found on the cigarette butt and under Josie's fingernails, along with the DNA evidence showing the two victims were half sisters. Next came the initial medical, toxicological, and psychological reports on Jen, compiled during her hospitalization. Finally, he introduced the girls' birth certificates and fingerprints confirming their identities, along with Cassandralynn's marriage and death certificates and Josielynn's adoption papers. Vince Waterford could've stipulated to the girls' ages and relationship to his client and saved the jury about fifteen minutes' worth of boring testimony, but he'd stubbornly refused.

Though tedious, my direct examination went smoothly. Jimmy made good eye contact with the jurors and even smiled a time or two. And, miraculously, Vince Waterford made no objections.

"Thank you, Agent McGee," I said. With legal pad in hand, I turned away from the podium to return to counsel table and the toe of my left shoe—covering my prosthetic foot—caught on the carpet. That minute glitch somehow upset my precarious balance and, before I could correct it, I fell to the floor.

My cheeks burned with shame as I struggled into a position from which I could rise. Matt and Jimmy rushed to my sides and, though I shook them off, they grabbed my elbows and ushered me to my feet. "Are you okay?" Matt asked, walking me to the table.

I nodded.

"I'd like to be heard at sidebar, Your Honor," Vince said when I was seated.

"Very well," Judge Neumann replied curtly. "Detective Witte may assist you to the bench if you wish, Ms. Spencer."

"That won't be necessary, but thank you," I said with more certainty than I felt.

Vince and AJ strode up beside the bench, away from the jury, and I waited until they were situated before joining them—walking slowly and deliberately—gaining confidence with each step.

"I move for a mistrial, Your Honor," Vince said. "The prosecuting attorney's 'fall'"—and here he used his fingers to make quotation marks in the air—"was a clear attempt to win sympathy from the jury."

The judge gave him an incredulous look but didn't respond. I suspected she couldn't find words.

"You've gotta be kidding," I sputtered, then regained my composure and spoke as calmly as I could. "May I be heard, Your Honor?" She nodded, and I continued. "The Court may be aware that my left leg was amputated above the knee about four months ago. Though it would have been much more comfortable for me to try this case without my temporary prosthetic limb, that would have necessitated using crutches, thereby calling attention to my disability. I chose instead to wear the prosthesis—on which I am sometimes less steady—in an effort to *avoid* any appearance that I was seeking the jury's sympathy vote. I resent defense counsel's accusation, which is not only unfair but untrue."

The judge shook her head and glared at Vince.

"*Mister* Waterford, your complaint is outrageous and completely unwarranted. I find you in contempt of court and order you to pay a fine of two hundred dollars. Your motion for a mistrial is denied. Ms. Spencer, I'm truly sorry this happened to you in my courtroom."

"Thank you, Your Honor," I said, again waiting for Vince and AJ to clear out, and returned to my seat.

"What was that about?" Matt whispered to me.

"He moved for a mistrial—accusing me of flopping to try to win over the jury," I replied under my breath. "She found him in contempt."

He shook his head. "Dumber than dirt *and* an asshole," he muttered quietly. "You'd think he'd behave better, being an amputee himself."

Similarly hushed conversations could be heard throughout the courtroom. Judge Neumann reached under a stack of papers to find her gavel and banged it on the desk. "Let's come to order and proceed, please. Ladies and gentlemen of the jury, I apologize for the delay."

I wondered if Jimmy, who'd resumed his seat on the witness stand, had caught the drift of Vince's motion—and if so, how he'd react. *Keep your cool,* I tried to tell him telepathically.

Defense counsel's cross-examination proved pointless, the questions so ineffectual that Jimmy didn't even bother with his planned retorts. Most of the jurors fidgeted in their seats, probably out of boredom.

They wouldn't fidget long, though, because my next witness was Jen.

Judge Neumann cleared the courtroom, having previously granted my motion to do so. Only the jury, AJ, his attorney, the court clerk and reporter, the marshals, Matt, and I remained—still a lot of people for Jen to face while describing the abuse she'd suffered. Fortunately, the law allowed "an adult attendant" to sit by her side throughout her appearance, and Glenda would fill that role.

My breath caught in my throat when Glenda and Jen, hand-in-hand, walked down the center aisle and through the bar, up to the witness stand. Jen wore a pastel blue turtleneck sweater, black wool pants, black flat shoes, and only a touch of lipstick. She looked impossibly young and terrified, her eyes darting around but seemingly registering nothing. Her hand shook as she raised it to take the oath, and her voice was barely audible. *Why didn't I pursue my argument for closed-circuit testimony?*

I'd gotten the judge's permission to stand near Jen while questioning her rather than at the podium—risky, now, because of my fear of falling. But I felt compelled to signal to Jen that I represented *her.*

We started slowly: name, age, where she'd lived, how she'd been homeschooled and was now in eighth grade. Jen answered the questions confidently, faltering only when I asked her to identify the defendant. She raised her head and looked at him for the first time, pointed for an instant, and croaked, "The man in the gray suit at that table is Ambrose Josiah Corbell—my father." Tears welled in her eyes and I could see her clutching Glenda's hand more tightly.

I walked Jen through the death of her mother and the nomadic months afterward, how AJ had begun prostituting her sister, the first time he'd required her to have intercourse with a John, and the later acts in which he'd made her engage. She testified about AJ giving them drugs, how they made her feel physically, and the withdrawal symptoms she felt when he withheld or delayed the doses. Many of the jurors listened with their eyes downcast, some took notes, one stifled a sob.

"Jen," I said, "now I need to ask you about your sister's death. You were the one who found her unconscious on the bed at the motel in Janesville, isn't that correct?"

"Yes, when I came out of the bathroom after a long bath," she replied, with tears streaming down her face. "She wasn't breathing and there was a note on the bed."

"What did the note say?"

Glenda handed Jen a tissue, and she blew her nose before answering, though the tears continued. "Just 'sorry,' and it was signed with x's and o's. I freaked out, tore it in little pieces, and flushed it down the toilet. Then I just sat on the other bed screaming."

"Do you know why you flushed it?"

She shook head. "I dunno," she said between gut-wrenching sobs, her voice so low we had to strain to hear. "I guess I thought our dad would be mad 'cause she killed herself."

Everyone startled when Vince Waterford jumped from his seat and barked, "Objection—"

"Overruled," Judge Neumann barked back. Her eyes glistened as she held up her hand to signal for silence. "Let's take a fifteen-minute recess."

"You're doing great, Jen," I told her back in our conference room. "But there're still some hard questions ahead. Do you want me to ask the judge to allow you to testify by TV?"

"No!" she practically shrieked. "I can do this."

"We know you can, honey," Glenda said. "But you might not *have* to. Wouldn't it be easier without everyone watching?"

"It doesn't matter who's watching," Jen said more calmly. "It's picturing the scenes in my head that's hard. And it'd be just as hard in front of a TV camera."

Yeah, we're all picturing those scenes. And it's gonna be hard to erase those pictures.

WHEN WE CONTINUED, I asked Jen about AJ leaving them in hotel rooms. "Did he give instructions as to what you could or couldn't do while he was gone?"

"Yes. He said we couldn't use the telephone, leave the room, or answer the door, and we hadda keep the chain or bolt on the door."

"Did he say what would happen if you disobeyed?"

Jen bit her lip. "Not at first. But one time, Josie left the room to get ice from the ice machine. He saw the filled bucket when he came back and wouldn't give her any food for a whole day. And then he said if either of us ever left the room again, he'd kill her."

"Did he ever threaten to kill you?"

"No, just Josie, 'cause she wasn't his real daughter."

Jen had been on the stand for almost two hours by the time I finished my list of questions. Judge Neumann leaned over and asked her, "Would you like another break before the other lawyer asks you his questions?"

"No, thank you. I'd rather get it over with."

The judge smiled. "I hear you. Your witness, Mr. Waterford."

Vince wisely stood at the podium to conduct his cross-examination and started with some innocuous questions. He turned frequently to smile at both Jen and the jury. *His head looks like it's gonna swivel off,* Matt wrote on my legal pad. I nodded with half a smile, almost lulled into believing Vince would play nice.

Wrong.

"You said that my client threatened to kill your sister if you left the room. How long would he typically leave you alone?"

Jen shrugged. "Sometimes only a half an hour or so. The longest was pro'bly two days."

"Two days?" Vince bellowed. "Did he leave you anything to eat or drink? Any of the medicines you said he gave you?"

"Uh-huh. He said not to eat, drink, or take them all at once because they'd have to last till he got back, but it might be more than a day."

"So, based on the provisions he left, you knew he'd be gone for a significant amount of time. Why didn't you leave?"

"Where would we go? We didn't have any other family or friends."

"How 'bout to the police?"

At this, the tears Jen had been blinking back spilled over and ran down her cheeks. She brushed off Glenda's proffer of a tissue. "He said no one would ever believe us. That the police could arrest us for prostitution and put us in separate foster homes. That we'd never see each other again."

"Do you like the foster home where you currently reside?"

"Yes."

"But isn't it true that on two occasions after you began living with the foster family, you called your father?"

"Yes."

"Isn't it also true that he gave you and your sister two numbers at which he could be reached—any time of the day or night?"

"Uh-huh."

"During the two phone calls you made, did you tell your father you loved and missed him?"

Jen nodded.

"You'll have to answer out loud."

"Yes."

"And during the second call, did you ask your father to come get you?"

"Yes."

"Why would you do that if he was selling you as a prostitute?"

"My counselor says it's because—"

"Pardon me, but we don't want to know what your counselor thinks. We want to know what *you* think."

Glenda leaned over and whispered something in Jen's ear.

"Objection," Vince yelled. "The adult attendant is coaching the witness."

The judge turned to Glenda and Jen. "Please, Jen has to formulate her own answer."

"Your Honor," I said, "I object to counsel's whole line of questioning—because it's irrelevant—and I apologize to the court and this witness for not doing so earlier."

"Sustained," the judge replied. "Move on Mr. Waterford."

"Do you know what an orgasm is?"

"Objection," I said. "Relevance."

Judge Neumann gave me a doleful look. "I'll allow her to answer."

"Yes," Jen replied almost inaudibly, her face beet red and blotchy.

"Isn't it true," Vince went on, "that you and your sister sometimes had contests to see which one of you could bring a customer to orgasm the quickest?"

"Objection," I yelled. "Relevance. How these two victims coped with being sexually abused has nothing to do with the defendant's guilt or innocence."

"Sustained. Watch yourself, Mr. Waterford," the judge said wearily.

The attorney flipped through the pages of his legal pad and opened his mouth to continue, but AJ Corbell knocked forcefully on the table to get his attention. Vince turned around in annoyance but reluctantly went to his client's side and leaned in to listen to him.

"That's enough," AJ hissed, loudly enough for Matt and me to hear. "No more questions."

Vince didn't return to the podium. "Nothing further of this witness, Your Honor."

Judge Neumann couldn't hide her surprise. "Redirect, Ms. Spencer?"

"May I have a moment to confer with my case agent?"

"Briefly, please."

I turned to Matt. "What d'ya think?" I whispered.

"I think that's the first remotely fatherly thing he's done in years."

"Way too little and way too frickin' late," I said. "But what I meant was, should I have Jen clarify some of her answers?"

"Nah," he replied. "Let Dr. Peters do the 'xplaining."

I nodded and looked toward the judge. "No further questions of the witness, Your Honor."

It took a while for Glenda and Jennifer to rise and leave the stand, supporting one another as they walked. Jen glanced over at the defense table and I watched in horror as her dad raised his hand and gave her an almost imperceptible wave. *Ignore him!* I wanted to shout. Jen glared at him and walked past.

AROUND THREE O'CLOCK, I called my last witness, Dr. Judith Peters. A short, stocky woman with spiky gray hair and kindly eyes, she wore a tent-type beige linen dress and oversized African jewelry, which clunked when she took her seat.

Dr. Peters recounted her credentials and, despite defense counsel's objections, the judge certified her as an expert witness in the field of psychotherapy. She described Jen's condition when she first began seeing her, as well as the progress she'd made in treatment. Most important, she quickly put the kibosh on Vince's earlier suggestion that Jen might've liked her life of prostitution. Finally, she explained why abuse victims are often reluctant to leave their abusers and, moreover, might have mixed emotions toward them.

"It's understandable that on some level, Jennifer loves her father, regardless of the horrors she suffered through his actions," she said. "He was, after all, the only father she'd ever known. He fed her, clothed her, and gave her the drugs that her body came to crave. He cuddled her and told her he loved her. She had no frame of reference to cause her to doubt him."

Vince chose not to cross-examine her.

"The prosecution rests, Your Honor," I said when Dr. Peters left the stand.

"I, for one, have had enough for today," the judge said to the jury. Several jurors nodded in return. "Let's recess until nine tomorrow."

"GOOD WORK TODAY, EVERYONE," I said to Matt, Jimmy, and Nancy Drummond back in the conference room. Nancy had driven Glenda and Jen home, returning in time to hear the end of Dr. Peters' testimony.

"We make a good team," she said. "It was rough on Jen, but she was so proud—and almost elated—after it was over. I'm glad she chose to face that jerk of a father in person."

"Let's just hope the jury convicts him," Jimmy said.

The rest of us turned to him incredulously. "Why wouldn't they?" Matt asked.

"Juror number four—the one you asked me to keep an eye on—never looked at Jen the whole time she testified. He seemed a little miffed when the judge kept admonishing Waterford this afternoon, and he rolled his eyes a couple times when Doc P was talking."

"He's just one of twelve," Nancy said. "No way is he gonna convince the others to vote not guilty."

"Maybe not, but he could hang the thing," Jimmy said. "I'd hate to have to do this all again."

JIMMY'S WORDS echoed in my ears around midnight, as I tossed and turned and ruminated.

62

I PULLED into the parking lot at the courthouse at seven o'clock the following morning, intent on having an hour to myself to practice my closing argument.

"I heard your trial's going well," the lone security guard on duty said to me when I walked into the darkened building.

"Yeah, I think so. Trouble is, you never know with juries."

In the conference room, I poured water into the Keurig machine that Jimmy'd loaned us and waited for my tea to steep. I adjusted my prosthesis and tested it out with a few laps around the table, still debating whether to trust myself today without crutches.

I stood at the edge of the table, pretending it was the courtroom podium, and began to speak, "Ladies and gentlemen—" And I almost screamed when Matt opened the door behind me.

"For God's sake, what are you doing here so early?" I said, holding my chest in an effort to slow my heart rate.

"Weather report called for snow and I didn't want to get stuck on the interstate if they were right."

I laughed. "You're as compulsive as I am."

"Is that a bad thing?"

I shook my head.

"Want me to go sit in the hallway while you practice?" he asked.

"Uh-uh. You'll be there when I give it for real; might as well hear it ahead of time."

He gave me a thumbs-up when I finished, but I couldn't be sure he was objective.

VINCE WATERFORD HAD TOLD the judge his opening statement and the presentation of his case would take about two hours. When court convened at nine, though, he surprised us all by waiving both. "I do, however, move for dismissal of the indictment against my client. The government has failed to present sufficient evidence to support a guilty verdict—"

"Denied," the judge said. "Anything else before we bring in the jury?"

And so it was that, before I had time to work up much anxiety about it, I stood at the podium to make my closing argument. Knowing I needed to win over our potentially troublesome juror, I'd purposely chosen my navy gabardine pants suit—less severely tailored than the ones I'd worn the first two days of trial—a light blue blouse, and small pearl earrings.

"Ladies and gentlemen of the jury," I began, making quick but friendly eye contact with number four, "thank you for the close attention you've paid to the evidence presented in this case. I know it's been tough…"

I went on to describe the elements of the offense and how we'd proven them—with physical evidence in the form of medical examinations and DNA, sworn admissions from a codefendant, and testimony from the remaining live victim. With each point I made, my tension rose. *You* have *to find him guilty,* I wanted to scream with anger. *We shouldn't have had to put anyone through this—not you the jury, not me or my witnesses or the judge, and especially not Jen.*

I took a deep breath and tried to speak calmly. "In summary, there is *no* reasonable doubt that Ambrose Josiah Corbell provided his two daughters to customers for commercial sex acts. Both were under the age of eighteen, but the victimization began when the younger was *under fourteen years of age.* He did so by threats and coercion, which included providing the girls with addicting drugs. Those drugs directly caused the death of the older victim —when she was but *sixteen years old.* Please see that justice is done for these two children. Thank you."

I sank into my chair but couldn't stop trembling. Matt reached under the table and squeezed my hand. "You nailed it," he whispered.

VINCE WATERFORD APPROACHED the podium with a single sheet of paper. He smiled at the jury, then looked down at the paper shaking his head. "The Fifth and Fourteenth Amendments to the United States Constitution guarantee an individual's right to due process. Since at least 1895, the Supreme Court has held that due process means a defendant is *innocent until proven guilty beyond a reasonable doubt.* In other words, Ambrose Josiah Corbell doesn't need to put on a lick of evidence for you to find him not guilty. It is the government's burden to *prove* him guilty. They have *not* done so."

Judge Neumann covered her mouth with her hand, I was sure to stifle a laugh or at least a sigh.

Vince went on, arguing first that Danny Thompsen was an unreliable witness who had fabricated the story of AJ's involvement in order to avoid punishment for raping Josielynn.

Next he argued that Jennifer was equally unreliable. He characterized her as a mentally ill liar who'd claimed to have been abused to get attention. Vince alleged that, against AJ's wishes, both his daughters had engaged in sexual activity with men they'd met on the streets when he was at work. Finally, he said, AJ had never given them drugs of any kind and had, in fact, been at his wits' end trying to find them help.

"We submit, ladies and gentlemen, that the facts I have just outlined are equally as plausible as the incredible evidence the government provided you. You can and must find my client not guilty."

Dear God, please don't make me regret not calling Zachary Prescott as a witness! Please, please, don't let the jury buy this cockamamie story.

I GAVE A FIVE-MINUTE REBUTTAL, emphasizing the holes in Vince Waterford's sketchy argument, but couldn't get a sense of whether I was preaching to the choir or a bunch of doubting Thomases. I scrutinized the jurors as they left the courtroom, desperately trying to read their faces and body language. They began their deliberations at ten thirty.

"I'm going back to the office," I told Matt, Jimmy, and Nancy. "If they haven't returned a verdict by noon, how 'bout we order a pizza and eat it over there?"

"Good idea," Matt said, "but mind if I hang out in your conference room while we wait? This little room is giving me claustrophobia."

"Me, too," Jimmy said.

"Sure, I'll even give you a ride so you don't need to move your cars."

AT TWELVE THIRTY, Matt, Jimmy, Nancy, George, and I sat around the conference room table staring at three open pizza boxes, bunches of paper plates and napkins, and several cans of vending machine soda.

"I thought surely they'd have reached a verdict by now," Nancy moaned. "This pepperoni and mushroom pizza is divine, but I'm too nervous to eat another slice."

"You managed to scarf down two," George said sardonically, "I don't see why you can't manage another. Clearly you'll have to eat Caroline's share."

A perfect triangle of pizza, but for one missing bite, sat on the plate in front of me. I picked it up and brought it to my lips, but a whiff of garlic hit me and set my stomach spinning. "Sorry, guys," I said, returning it to the plate. "I thought I could handle lunch, but I was wrong."

"Get a grip," Jimmy said. "The jurors are probably dawdling because they want a free lunch."

"I doubt it," Matt replied. "The food they usually get just isn't that good."

"How do you know?" Jimmy replied.

"Guys, guys," I said. "I've already got a headache and you're making it worse with your quibbling."

"Why don't you go back to your office, take off the fake leg that's making you grimace, and lie down?" George offered.

I took him up on it, never imagining I might actually drift off. My phone woke me at quarter till three—the clerk's office telling me to come back to court.

"It's show time," I said when I called Nancy, who agreed to round up George, Jimmy, and Matt.

Ten minutes later, we'd resumed our usual seats in the courtroom, Vince Waterford sitting alone at his table waiting for the marshals to bring in the accused. He seemed not at all nervous—which ratcheted up my own anxiety tenfold.

AJ Corbell looked both nervous and angry when escorted to his spot. He grumbled as the deputy struggled to unlock his handcuffs and shifted his shoulders away when the other deputy signaled for him to sit.

We all rose when the judge appeared and continued standing as the jurors filed in and took their seats. None of them so much as glanced at Corbell. *Good sign? Who the hell knows?*

Judge Neumann looked at the jury. "Mr. Foreperson, have you reached a verdict?"

Juror number four rose and replied, "Yes, Your Honor." Matt and I exchanged surprised glances. *Yikes, they elected* him *as foreman?*

As instructed by the judge, AJ and Vince stood for the

reading. Matt and I gripped the arms of our chairs. I held my breath.

"As to count one of the indictment," the clerk intoned, "we, the jury, find the defendant, Ambrose Josiah Corbell, guilty." AJ slumped into his seat and remained there while the clerk read the verdict for count two—also guilty.

I breathed deeply, relishing the sweet sense of accomplishment. We'd found some measure of justice for Josie and Jen.

63

NANCY and I parked our cars in front of the Fosters' house. I slipped the snow-grip tips onto my crutches and made my way slowly up the sidewalk and steps. Glenda held the door open when we got there and gave me a questioning look.

"Jen needs to be the first to know," I said.

My friend ushered us into the living room. Jen lay curled up in front of the fireplace, resting her head on one throw pillow and clutching another. I stopped in my tracks—her position was almost identical to Josie's in the death-scene photographs.

She startled when Glenda said, "Jen, honey. Caroline and Nancy are here," and sat up immediately to face us.

"Did they find him guilty?"

"Yes. Guilty on both counts," Nancy replied quietly. She'd warned me that Jen might have mixed emotions about the news.

Jen stood up and hugged Nancy, then me. "Thank you," she said, her face impassive.

"Join us for a minute," Nancy said, sitting on one end of the couch and patting the middle cushion.

I took the spot on the other end.

"The judge scheduled the sentencing hearing for two months from now," Nancy said. "You'll be allowed to speak at it if you'd like, though you don't need to decide that any time soon. I do plan to schedule a meeting with you and your team—Brad, your social worker, Glenda and Hank, Dr. Peters, and me—early next week to discuss the victim impact statement we'll give to the judge. And plans for the weeks and months ahead."

Jen inched down into a slouch and looked up at Nancy with a lone tear wandering down her cheek. "You mean if I'll stay here or go to Alabama?"

"Uh-huh."

"Do I get to choose?"

"You'll have input—certainly—but legally it'll be up to Judge Baker in Janesville. And he'll get recommendations from the rest of us."

Glenda—sitting cross-legged on the floor across from us—hugged her own knees and bit her lip.

"Okay, I understand," Jen replied.

"Do you have any other questions?" Nancy asked.

She shook her head.

"You were very brave, Jen," I said, giving her a quick hug. "I'm really confident you won't let what was done to you define you. You've got a great future ahead of you."

"Thanks," she said, doubt written all over her face.

AROUND NINE O'CLOCK THAT EVENING, I returned a call to Matt. "Sorry it took me a while," I said. "We took the kids out for dinner tonight, service was slow, and then they didn't wanna go to sleep."

"No biggie. I just wondered how Jen reacted when she heard the verdict. Y'know, I overheard Nancy saying she might not be elated."

"Yeah. She wasn't elated, but I did sense a bit of relief that the trial's over. I think the big thing on her mind is what'll happen to her now. Like, does she have to stay here until her dad's sentencing, or till school's out, or what?"

"I saw Judge Baker at the courthouse in Janesville a week or so ago and he asked how she was doing. He didn't say it outright, but I got the impression he'd let her go to Birmingham after the trial if that's what she wants."

"That's what Glenda's afraid of. And, selfishly, that's what I'm afraid of, too. Nancy's gonna get everybody together with Jen next week to talk about it."

"Glad I don't have to sit in on that meeting."

"Yeah, me, too."

"See you tomorrow. Danny's sentencing's still on for ten o'clock, isn't it?

"Yep."

MY STOMACH CHURNED as I watched the deputies bring Danny Thompsen into the courtroom the next morning. He'd done everything we'd asked him to do: he'd given multiple statements to Jimmy and Matt—often helping them to decipher coded communications between himself and AJ Corbell; he'd testified truthfully and in an even-tempered manner that hadn't alienated the jury; and he hadn't tried to sugarcoat his own involvement in this heinous crime.

But that was the rub—he'd been actively involved in recruiting Johns to rape, sodomize, and humiliate two teenage girls, one of whom I'd come to know and love.

I was bound by my agreement to recommend that Judge Neumann sentence Danny to *less* than what the guidelines called for. She didn't have to accept my recommendation, but she couldn't sentence him below the mandatory minimum sentence of fifteen years.

"The parties have stipulated," Judge Neumann began, "that the advisory guideline range in this case is 262 to 327 months in prison. The government has moved for a downward adjustment. Ms. Spencer, do you wish to be heard?"

"Your Honor, as I outlined in my motion and sentencing memorandum, we recommend a three-level downward departure to the range of 188 to 235 months, with a life term of supervision to follow the incarceration." Though we'd agreed not to argue for a sentence at the high end of the imprisonment range, I secretly hoped the judge would go there.

She nodded toward defense counsel. "Mr. Pooley, your comments?"

Pooley stood and buttoned his suit coat. "Thank you, Judge. You heard Mr. Thompsen's testimony at his codefendant's trial. It was extensive, credible, and damning to both himself and Corbell. I submit it is the Court's responsibility to set aside his self-incriminating testimony. Instead you should consider only the *assistance* he provided in the prosecution of an evil man, who used and abused the children he had a moral duty to protect. Not an easy task, I understand."

Pooley paused and flipped a page on his legal pad before continuing. "I sat through the Corbell trial. Without my client's testimony, I do not believe the jury would have had sufficient evidence to return guilty verdicts, and those poor children would have been denied justice. I respectfully recommend you sentence Mr. Thompsen to no more than the mandatory minimum sentence of fifteen years."

Fifteen years, I thought. *To win a conviction for the baddest guy, we have to live with another bad guy getting out of prison while he's still young enough to wreak more havoc on society.*

"Mr. Thompsen," the judge stated, "I've read your written statement. Do you have anything further you wish to add before I sentence you?"

Danny Thompsen stood up awkwardly and leaned down toward the table microphone. "Only that I'm so, so sorry for my part in all this. Those girls didn't deserve to be treated like that, and I'm ashamed that I not only let it happen but helped make it happen."

Judge Neumann imposed a fifteen-year sentence with a boatload of conditions for treatment and monitoring during his imprisonment and his life term of supervision.

Let's hope it works.

ON SUNDAY AFTERNOON, Lily found me on the living room sofa dozing with the newspaper across my face. "You awake, Mom?"

"I am now," I said, scooting to a sitting position to look at her. "What's wrong, kiddo? What are you crying about?"

She plopped down beside me and burrowed under my arm. "Jen just told me why she's in foster care. About what her dad did to her and her sister. About how you prosecuted him…"

I sighed. "Oh, honey, I hope you don't feel betrayed because I couldn't tell you."

"No, it's not *that*. I just feel so bad for her. How could her father do something so awful? And how can Jen, like, get up and go to school every day? I mean, it's bad enough that her sister killed herself and that her mom was dead. But she was *raped*, Mom. Like all the time…"

I hugged her to me. "I wish she hadn't told you."

She wiped her nose on the sleeve of her hoodie. "Why?"

"'Cause now you'll have a hard time looking at her without thinking about the awful things that she went through."

Lily nodded. "She says that's why she wants to go live in Birmingham. Because you and Glenda and Hank—and now me—we all know and can't help pitying her. And she says even some kids at school are asking questions, like they've put two and two together, and she feels like they're staring at her or something."

Shit, shit, shit. She's right. Being pitied is a pretty awful feeling, and being stared at is right up there. How well I know.

"Jen's godmother knows what happened," I said.

"Yeah, but not all the details. Her kids don't know anything other than that Jen's father took the family away, and Magnolia has told her they never have to. Jen said she had so much fun hanging out with Sam and Nicole Barr and talking about the little things that she's remembering from when she was a kid. And it sounds like more and more memories are coming back to her—good memories."

"I see."

AT MIDNIGHT, awakened by a bad dream, I struggled to untangle myself from a mass of sweaty sheets. I'd had a difficult time falling asleep in the first place, and I knew my insomnia and my nightmare stemmed from the decision I needed to make.

I got up and changed the bed, then took a long

shower—steaming hot at first and later turned down to warm.

Climbing back into bed, I felt more clarity—I'd spoken for Jen in court and she deserved to have me speak for her again.

MONDAY MORNING I TEXTED GLENDA, *What are your plans for lunch today?*

She called me back. "My plans are to do the same thing I do every Monday at lunch time: sit at my desk with the lights out so everyone leaves me alone, eat an egg salad sandwich, drink a Diet Coke, and try not to succumb to the temptation to get a candy bar from the vending machine. Why on earth do you ask?"

I laughed. "There's something I want to talk with you about and it'd be easier for me in person. Would you have time to meet me at the Java Cat coffee shop? I can get there first and place our order. And it's my treat."

"Since you've piqued my curiosity, how can I say no? How's eleven forty-five?"

"Great. Look at the menu online and text me what you want. See you there."

I ARRIVED at Java Cat fifteen minutes early, ordered two bowls of beef stew and a grilled cheese sandwich on herbed focaccia for Glenda and me to split, and found a table in the rear of the shop where we could speak in privacy. My friend barged through the front door, a wave of cold fresh air following in her wake, narrowly missing the barista who'd just delivered our food.

"What's this about?" Glenda asked, stomping her feet and rubbing her hands to warm them up.

"Take off your coat and sit down, then I'll tell you."

"You're perverse," she replied, but did as I asked.

Steam rose steadily from the stew, so I didn't feel compelled to eat it immediately. I stirred my coffee, though, while stalling to choose my words. "I think it's time for Jen to go home, and I think she'd appreciate your blessing to do so."

Glenda's jaw dropped. "I thought you agreed that her staying till the end of the school year made sense?" she asked, unable to mask her anger.

"I did, but I changed my mind."

"Why?"

"The quicker she leaves Madison, the better chance she'll have of not defining herself as a victim. You and Hank and I—and now Lily—can't look at her without thinking of the awful things that were done to her."

Glenda raised an eyebrow.

"Yeah. Jen told Lily about it yesterday. And she said some kids at school have been asking questions."

"Well, it's Jen's own fault for telling Lily. And she can just tell those other kids it's none of their frickin' business."

I took a sip of coffee, hoping she'd calm down. "For God's sake, listen to yourself, Glen. Kids talk, and nothing's gonna stop 'em. Jen deserves a fresh start—away from people who pity her and treat her differently. People who are constantly assessing how she's doing, however well meaning they might be."

"How can you be sure she's ready?"

"I can't, and neither can you. But don't you think she deserves the chance to try things out in Alabama?"

Glenda pointedly avoided eye contact with me and nibbled distractedly at the sandwich. I blew on a spoonful of stew and put it into my mouth, though I can't say I really tasted it. We sat like two robots, eating in silence and without pleasure until our meals were gone.

"I hate it when you're right and I'm wrong," Glenda said, wiping her mouth with a crumpled napkin.

"I don't think it's a question of right or wrong—"

"Oh, please!" she interrupted. "I've seen for myself how much Jen enjoys hanging out with Magnolia and her kids. I just didn't want to admit it."

"And if things don't go well for her in Birmingham—"

"They will. But I'll make sure Jen knows she always has a home with us if she wants it."

I nodded. "You can recommend that Judge Baker not set anything in stone until she's had a chance to check things out down there. Seems like he might agree to that."

Glenda stood abruptly and grabbed her coat and scarf. "I gotta get back. Thanks for lunch."

"I'm proud of you—" I started to say, but she was gone before I could finish.

65

ON THE LAST Saturday of January, a caravan of cars drove to the Dane County Airport in a kind of farewell parade for Jen Corbell. She rode with the Fosters in the first car, my kids and me in the second, Dr. Peters in the third, and Nancy Drummond bringing up the rear—no doubt grumbling at the snail's pace with which we traveled.

Judge Baker had approved the plan several days earlier: Glenda would fly to Birmingham with Jen and meet personally with the local judge who would appoint Magnolia Barr as Jen's temporary legal guardian, delivering school and treatment records to those who'd need them. Magnolia had arranged for Jen to be homeschooled for the remainder of the year, with plans to enroll her in a small private high school in the fall. Lily had already wheedled a promise from me to let her visit Jen during spring break. And, most important to Glenda, Jen would come to Madison to spend three weeks with the Fosters in

June. If all went well, the Barrs would become Jen's adoptive parents the following year.

It was corny, we all knew, to say our good-byes at the airport rather than in the privacy of the Hank and Glenda's home. But Jen's heroism and kindness had touched us all and we wanted to give her a little pomp and circumstance.

After hugs, kisses, and tears, Glenda and Jen ascended the escalator to the security checkpoint. At the top, Jen turned around and called to me, "Hank's got something for you."

Hank looked at me with puffy eyes, reached into the pocket of his down parka, and handed me a long white envelope. "She asked me to give you the statement she wrote for court."

I placed the envelope carefully in my purse. "She's quite a kid, isn't she?"

Hank sniffled. "Oh, yeah."

66

Much to the littles' chagrin, it was a relatively mild winter—including several weird sixty-degree days in February and March—with not enough snow for sledding. It was a godsend for me, though, as I became more adept with my prosthetic leg. I set a goal of being able to run on the one-year anniversary of my amputation, and my physical therapists conceded it was a lofty but attainable ambition.

Glenda and Lily, who felt Jen's absence most acutely, managed to distract themselves with new endeavors. Glenda began working full time to fill in for a colleague on maternity leave, and Lily became a mentor and tutor for a sixth-grade girl who'd moved to Madison from Somalia. They both kept in close contact with Jen, though, and seemed truly glad of her quick and happy transition to life in Birmingham.

Before I knew it, April had arrived—and with it, AJ

Corbell's long-awaited sentencing hearing.

"All rise," the court clerk intoned as Judge Marguerite Neumann took the bench.

Nancy Drummond and I sat at the prosecution table, with Matt and Jimmy directly behind us in the spectator seats.

AJ had fired Vince Waterman immediately following the verdict, and Judge Neumann had allowed substitute counsel, a young woman from Milwaukee named Rebecca Watson, to handle the sentencing phase. If she was uncomfortable sitting beside a convicted sex slaver, she didn't show it.

Rebecca and I had conducted our arguments about application of the sentencing guidelines in writing, and we simply awaited the judge's ruling on them.

"Ms. Watson, Ms. Spencer," the judge began, "I commend you both on your written submissions, which were thoughtful and to the point. I agree with the prosecutor that the appropriate guideline sentence is life imprisonment, but the sentencing guidelines are only advisory. I am, of course, bound by statute to impose a sentence of at least fifteen years.

"Ms. Spencer, how do you wish to proceed?"

"Your Honor, I have nothing further to add to my written sentencing recommendation and to the victim impact statements provided by the treatment team members. However, Ms. Drummond, our victim/witness coordinator, would like to read a personal statement from the victim in count one."

"Very well."

Nancy strode forward, Jen's written statement clutched in her hand. She placed it on the podium, smoothed out the wrinkled page, then gripped the edges of the podium tightly. "These are the victim's words verbatim," Nancy began, "'Dear Judge Neumann, Thank you for holding a fair trial, for treating me so kindly, and for letting me give my opinion about how long my father should be in prison.'"

Nancy paused to clear her throat. "The statement continues, 'I really believe he caused my mother's death by keeping her from her family and friends, by calling her names, and by giving her drugs. My sister killed herself because of him. And because of him, I became a prostitute and a drug addict when I was just a kid. He should never have done what he did. He should have acted like a father, not a pimp. He should have pleaded guilty, but instead he hired a lawyer to lie for him at trial. And to ask me embarrassing, awful questions about things I never wanted to think or speak about, much less in front of other people.

"'I really, really hope you will send him to prison for the rest of his life without any chance of getting out, so I never have to worry about seeing him again. Thank you.'" Nancy returned to the table, sank into her chair, and rested her head in her hands.

"Thank you, Ms. Drummond," the judge said. "Ms. Watson, you may proceed."

Rebecca stood. "Your Honor, I stand by my written sentencing memorandum." She'd argued for a twenty-five-year term of imprisonment to be followed by a lifetime term of supervision.

"Does the defendant wish to be heard before I impose sentence?"

"No, Your Honor," AJ replied in a near monotone.

The judge looked him directly in the eye. "Mr. Corbell," she said, making no effort to conceal her contempt, "the evidence of your criminal conduct presented at trial was the most reprehensible I've ever heard. I can only hope and pray that no future trial will be as difficult for the jurors, witnesses, attorneys, court staff, and me personally.

"As their father, you had not only a moral but a legal obligation to protect these victims. You not only failed them, you purposefully *caused* them to be used and abused by countless strangers. You drugged and intimidated them. You drove one to suicide. It's a miracle the other victim survived, and I intend to follow her recommendation and that of the attorney for the government. I find the appropriate sentence is life imprisonment—without the possibility of early release. Anything short of the maximum term would depreciate the seriousness of the offenses and the horrific harms they caused."

I breathed a deep sigh of relief.

JEN HAD GOTTEN her first cell phone a few weeks earlier as a reward for working hard with her homeschool teacher and had proudly called Lily to try it out. I'd promised to text Jen the minute the sentencing hearing concluded, and now I couldn't wait to do so.

With Matt, Jimmy, and Nancy standing over my shoulder, I typed, *Great job on your statement. The judge gave AJ life in prison!*

The response came immediately—a smiley-faced emoji blowing a kiss. A second later, my phone pinged with another message, *PS thx 4 everything. Luv u, Jenny Lou.*

ACKNOWLEDGMENTS

Many thanks to my dear friend, Corinne Hollar, who read every draft of this novel and provided excellent suggestions and expert advice on the law. Thanks once again to Martin Altstadt, retired Janesville Police Detective, for his help with plotting and police procedures. Any factual errors are mine, not theirs.

My cadre of beta readers contributed in so many ways, each of them offering valuable professional or personal experiences: Kathryn Benes Baker, Jane Erickson, Kent Miller, Luann Schuhler, Nick Spinelli, and Lauren Truman. I'm very grateful to all of you for sharing your time and talents with me and for your honest opinions.

Thanks to Amy Knupp, my editor at Blue Otter Editing, whose professionalism, common sense, and eye for detail were invaluable. You were a joy to work with.

Thanks to Julie Barr Altstadt for entering my "name the villain" contest: Ambrose Josiah Corbell fit him perfectly.

And, as always, I owe a huge debt of gratitude to my husband, Nick Spinelli, for his constant love and encouragement.

ABOUT THE AUTHOR

Leslyn Amthor Spinelli has written three previous novels in the Caroline Spencer series: *Taken for Granted*, *Taken by Surprise*, and *Taken for a Fool*. All are drawn on her employment experiences in the federal criminal justice system. Leslyn lives with her husband, a retired private investigator, in the Minneapolis area. They enjoy spending winter months in San Diego, California.

Contact her via her website:
   www.LeslynAmthorSpinelli.com

Made in the
USA
Columbia, SC